C1

Chaotic Ocean
╪

Bekim Perolli

CHAOTIC OCEAN

Copyright © 2006 by Bekim Perolli
ISBN: 978-1-4116-8993-0
All rights reserved.

Note to the reader,

If you have happened upon this book, know that it has been independently printed, and does not exist in large quantities.

If you would like to help the author become published, write to whichever publishing company you see fit, and tell them of your pleasant experience.

Additionally, it is the intention of the author to make this independent printing available on the major commercial websites, so do not refrain. It can also be purchased directly at www.lulu.com/content/231337.

It is of primary concern to have the writing reach as many readers as possible. If you enjoy the work, open your mouth. Tell friends, family, and co-workers. It is not easy to establish oneself in this industry, so any help would be immensely appreciated.

For additional feedback, comments, or general discussion, feel free to contact the author directly at bekimperolli@yahoo.com.

Enjoy!

Chaotic Ocean

"Even the strongest current of water cannot add a drop to a cup which is already full." -Tolstoy

Chaotic Ocean

All that follows is unreasonable twaddle.

Chaotic Ocean

*"And when out of plasma
Men perceived light and dark,
Nature fully understood the folly
Of having bore human beings..."*

Text abridged.

CHAPTER ONE
☦

THE DAEDALIAN INANITY

*

The garden was filled with fresh lilacs. Pink and over-washed, the flowers emitted an aroma like that released on sun-filled days in Spring, which invariably follow the torrent of revitalising rain. The scent that ascends into the air when a fresh storm begins is that unlike any other. It is as if all the hidden, beautiful ambrosias are working in unison, not as a machine, but as a tender emotion, too pure to smell or taste in mere words or syllables. The humbling and breathtaking flowers were meticulously well kept and lined the garden's exterior. There was a slight breeze in the air, which silently calmed the senses on some faint and indiscernible plain of sensation. Freshly trimmed green grass left nothing to the imagination for perfection, though to have perfectly imagined would have been far too crude an act. An aged stonewall surrounded the quaint garden and stood nearly six feet tall, just high enough to separate the enclosure from the distractions of the outside civilisation. A wooden-arched bridge was the centrepiece to the garden, which overlooked a rather small, but beautiful man-made pond. Its beauty was not in its creation, but rather in the reflections it gave off to its onlookers. It was somewhat well renowned as having been a miracle pond of sorts, perhaps an eighth worldly wonder. While it contained no perceptible power, no gift of infinite youth through mere touch, no hidden secret shrouded from the eye of man, it was all the same, undeniably captivating.

Throughout the garden were cobblestone footpath trails in the shapes of overgrown roses. These were Zigmund Sardoce's most treasured of carvings. He was a man of thirty years, but the wrinkles beside his lips and atop his brow gave him the appearance of fifty. He had auburn unkempt hair, which was matched only by the un-cleanliness of his unkempt beard. It had taken Zigmund almost two full years to finish his intricate decor. Each night when the sun crept down, he retired to his workshop and recovered hammer and chisel. The man often laboured through the long hours of the night so not to raise any suspicions about his diligent task. Zigmund wished for these to be his ambitious gifts to the world, his gift to modern art. It is somewhat ironic and cruel that when the name Zigmund Sardoce is spoken, one does not think of his magnificent carvings, but rather, of his pond, which had been part of the property far before he had ever purchased it.

It was oddly overcast outside, though still, Zigmund had invited his friend of many years to join him for a walk in the garden. Kyla Demark was a middle-aged woman, mysterious in demeanor, and oft reveled at the chance to debate. She had a broad body structure, while still upholding a gracious air of femininity about her person. Kyla's golden hair fell halfway down her back, and was, in all senses of the word, mystifying when in contact with the garden breeze. She arrived around three, and the two immediately retired to the garden. Zigmund generally took pleasure in formulating the first thought, and more importantly, the first word.

"I adhere to no philosophy, because no one philosophy in its entirety is agreeable. I am not bound to the chain of any man, but rather, willingly tied to that of my compatriots. I do not wish or will the world to be different, but I do see its flaws, as well as my own. My eyes serve only as tainted, faded peepholes in exchanging ocular perception synapse to the vessels in my brain. I am a man. I am a God. I am a mistake, and I am a blessing. I am a hypocrite. I am close-minded. I am open-minded, and I see everything and nothing under the sun. I ramble and rant and rationalise and oblivify (I am pompous enough to create new word tenses as well), and I see it all. I am not below, and I am not above. I am I and she and her and he and you and we. But most of all, I am not excluded from my own questioning, thinking, or scrutiny. To each word a new contradiction, and to each day a new realisation."

"You really do enjoy the haunting sounds of your own delusion, don't you, Zigmund?" remarked Kyla.

"Ah now, Kyla, what you confine as delusion is merely a societal view, outdated and overused by lofty scholars who feel the need to restitute their own minds by any means necessary, likely in order to placate their own biased thinking."

"You have no right to criticise. You are merely a scholar in disguise, who, over time, has learned to shroud his own insecurity just a slight bit better than the next. You simply mask life's glaring truths with semantics and obligatory questioning, all in the divine hope of never speaking a single word of hypocrisy, and in the process, learn little."

"I was not criticising, Kyla; I was merely commenting. As I said, I do not proclaim to be different. I am as clear a thinker as I can see soft snow on a gelid Winter's day. Delusional is one thing I am not."

"You might deem it a confine, Zigmund, but without truly defining the term, you can gain nothing from it. You do not even understand the empty words that you speak. Being delusional is not a black or white brand, but rather an intricate and complex mentality, choosing only to see the particular aspect one wishes; or even, exaggerating or under exaggerating one's perception of what one does happen to see. In general, Zigmund – truly allowing one's mind to distort reality. You may call it what you will, but for a man who claims to see clearly, you are very quick to judge that which you do not know about others, including their methods of thought, though perhaps I too am guilty."

As the two bickered on, the sky became increasingly ominous. Clouds formed in moments, as if undetected by the observations of either Zigmund or Kyla. The various colourful flowers swayed lightly, then more heavily as the breeze quickened. The two decided to retire to the safety of the cobalt-blue canopy, which served as an entrance to the Sardoce mansion. The rain seemed angry, as if it had been wronged by the hands of thankless savages. Indeed, perhaps it had been. Humans do not seem quite capable of appreciating such simplicity as precipitation, of appreciating that which we have always known, but have never been able to fully grasp. The pattering was growing, feeding, seething, and fell like glass marbles unto a solid surface. Suddenly, as if horrific lions doing battle, thunder crackled through the dense London skies, and so also through the veins of Zigmund Sardoce. The hum seemed to last for miles and miles, as it was later spoken of and referred to as: the night the "Gods clashed."

"You really are quite a ferocious woman, Kyla," smirked Zigmund with a look of half resentment upon his face.

"Ferocious?" replied Kyla. "No, I am merely a traveler with an unnamed journey on an unknown path in an unknown direction. It is quite easy to create armour these days, as safety has purely become a long forgotten desire. I seek no shelter, nor would I need the hospitality of a kindred kindness. It has been said: 'Master thy self, then others shall be bare.'"

"This is quite possibly true. The weather is Hell tonight, you know, but then, what can one expect from our mother London. I've actually grown quite fond and accustomed to it all. I rather enjoy the occasional downpour."

"It is a symptom, Zigmund, a symptom of the people who live to waste."

"That is quite a cynical view," unthinkingly blurted out Zigmund. "I presume you've lived some, or rather, endured some hardship which has brought you to your grand cynical outlook?"

"I," hesitating, but poised, "do not favor the mentality behind your accusation," snapped Kyla. "Do not group me with the selfishness of humanity's so-called 'selfless' who speak only on behalf of familiarity, only on behalf of related prevention in hope of alleviating some nonexistent, but all too surreal fear of ever being associated with the ever suffocating actuality of life's imperfections. Show me someone who truly does not know the definition of the horror called Consumption, or any other fatal illness for that matter, who has never had a family member fall to the disease, who has never known a friend to have been so unfortunate to come in contact with it, who has never even seen its face or known its supremacy, but has the humility and the intangible desire to give and help the ill, all the while doing so out of goodness, out of kindness for fellow man, and not out of some self-serving, whether hidden or surfaced, desire to free himself, or his own, of such vileness and inconvenience, AND, and then I will show you a truly selfless person. So to answer your question, no, Zigmund, nothing has happened to me which brings me to my conclusion, no great tragedy suffered."

"Hmph," sighed Zigmund, sitting back, taken back for a minute or two by the conviction displayed in Kyla's throbbing words, by the emotion conveyed for the sake of mere emotion and, for a while, he had not an idea how to reply. Then it came, like the striking fist of a champion.

"We do not know what we are not affected by. It is quite impossible to understand without having experienced; and compassion, as you've touched on, is nonexistent without understanding. And I'm not of the opinion that most people even care to help, so when that rare occurrence takes place, I do not feel sublime enough, or that much above, Kyla, where I can pass judgment."

"You really don't have a clue, Zigmund, like a lamb to the slaughter, pardon the cliché, and perhaps once you've actually rid yourself of your current seclusion, which by the way, besides promoting pure abnormality, is actually just unhealthy."

"You... you are the one who does not understand, Kyla."

Kyla had seemingly brought out something long suppressed within Zigmund, something lurking, brooding, something perhaps unstable even. His eyes were set aflame, as if Prometheus himself had been revived, an entity summoned from Zigmund's blood to set wrath and havoc upon humanity's weak.

"You do not know a Hellish thing about me. I'm sure by now you've classified me into every kind of generic archetype known to man, but you do not know my complexity, my thoughts, my feelings, my urges, my desire. You're very bold to think so. Very bold, indeed."

"You should know by now," whispered Kyla, "that I am not an apologetic person. I've no regret. Take your useless angst elsewhere if you need."

"I see quite clearly, my dear Kyla," speaking with a more mild-mannered tone now. "Not many people have found what you often find within me. For that I applaud you. But not for much else."

"Heh, you've not changed a damn in all your so-called enlightenment since moving onto this monstrous estate," replied Kyla. "But that is okay."

"I grow tired of this," sighed Zigmund, pulling quickly away from the harsh attack.

"You've grown tired of yourself."

"Possibly. Still, leave me to the silent refuge of solitude. We will speak again, I am sure, in the near future. Good-bye now, Kyla."

"Stay well, Zigmund. Good-bye."

*

Kyla walked slowly, confidently, out from the canopy's helpful shelter, not once turning back to wave, or smile, or leave sendoff, or to see Zigmund walking half slouched, somewhat beaten, and somewhat cut down. It was still heavily storming, now perhaps with even more conviction. As she walked past the garden, the rain inched down her face, but did not change her expressionless, and even partially cold, demeanor. Everything was too right to quiver, too warm to cringe, too perfect to change, to move, to modify the moment which engulfed her. Kyla knew what Zigmund had been speaking of when he mentioned that he enjoyed

Chaotic Ocean

"the occasional downpour." She had known very well the idea which he so blatantly, so plainly, and so easily expressed without a drop of thought. She knew it like a mother knows the sound of her first-born's cries. She knew it like a scholar knows the teachings of wondrous philosophers. She knew it like lovers know it when they peer into each other's eyes, taken away and drawn completely within, completely surrounded by and swelled inside a second in time. Kyla Demark knew it, because she felt precisely the same as Zigmund, but was perhaps too modest, or too embarrassed, or even too ashamed to admit this to such a man, whom she so longed to overpower. The woman could simply not comprehend how someone like Zigmund Sardoce could have come to the same conclusion as a woman such as she. It seemed almost unthinkable. As she kept on, she tried not to let the thought disturb her anymore, and tried more to focus on their conversation, of which she had obviously been the victor.

"Obviously," she thought, "right?"

Then a feeling of unease struck deep inside of her, a thought so cruel and inhumane that it almost paralysed her, as if stiffened by a chloroform so pungent that Thor himself could not break its chain.

To herself, Kyla thought, "If I have so, indeed and in fact, won the argument, then why do I linger? Why is the thought embedded into my brain? Why am I the one still over-analysing every tedious, audible, and yet inaudible word? Why has this struck me, and yet, Zigmund, who I know has not contemplated a single thought of what's taken place, is most likely in deep slumber, with no care to awaken him, no fear playoff playing the same role another day, and performing the same act one hundred times over? Have I really, truly, prevailed in this instance, or in any? Perhaps he has overcome my method, perhaps he is.... No, this cannot be! Has this always been so? Have I fought one thousand useless battles only to take second seat? This cannot be, I will not let it."

Kyla's over-thinking was entirely too distracting for her to even enjoy the simple ideas to which she first began. While passing the drooping pink and yellow flowers of Zigmund's design, she almost stumbled over one of his magnificent rose carvings. This only infuriated her further, altering her look of stone to one of anger. Kyla's straight and pressed lips curved downwardly, and her eyes turned from having exuding good-hearted cockiness, to that of slanted hatred. She finally arrived at the main gate of the Sardoce Estate. It was a large wooden door with one of the old-fashioned metal facets attached, which really seemed to serve no purpose save for mere decoration. The structure stood about fifteen feet tall. One might say that it loomed. Kyla sought nothing more than escape. With the rain now streaming down at an intolerable pace, she pressed both hands upon the gargantuan gate, and with all her force, jarred it open. Upon exiting, Kyla did not bother to shut it.

For some unknown reason, the sky seemed brighter ahead with the thought of Zigmund behind. It was no longer a darkening grey out, but rather, almost a lightly coloured shade of blue. The rain was still falling like relentless monologues of politicians, which drag, and at the same time, vampirically drain on to no avail, with no idea of mercy or compassion. Kyla started slowly up the quaint cobblestone walk. In the daylight, the walks reflect the beauty and architecture of London's finest cathedrals, yet, there seem to be rare instances when one can appreciate the ingenuity of such intricacy. More times than not are the cobblestones drenched, showing colourless transparency, and most of all, showing no feeling. As Kyla continued on, she focused more on the street. The Sardoce Estate was directly off of Westminster Avenue, and had it been up to Zigmund completely, his mansion probably would have been built on a dirt road away from everyone and everything. However, Westminster is more of a main road of sorts, which attracts many passersby, and is extremely well known for its good-hearted pubs, cunning cathedrals, and classical theatres, not to mention its breath-taking museums filled with some of the most well-renowned pieces to date. She looked up and noticed a few cabs passing through, followed by one or two rust-coloured old bangers.

To herself, she thought, "Hmph, Zigmund would never be caught dead in an old banger like that."

As she continued to walk on, the cat's eyes embedded within the street seemed to be staring at her. Kyla resented them so. They truly seemed vile to her, as if only depraved pieces of art set in to merely appease society's high and mighty. Kyla could not stand the high and mighty, who seemed so above and so refined. They dared not associate with the lower classes, which to them seemed uncivilised.

"The nerve of us, with so little culture," she thought.

*

Kyla decided to stop in at one of the older Victorian cathedrals. It had no more than four or five sand coloured stone steps leading up to its grand double doors. They were an offset mahogany and were polished tri-daily. She put her hand on the impressive golden handle, which was not plated or coated, but rather, was very pure. Nothing but the best for the Protestant faith. Kyla pulled it wide open, slowly creeping inside, allowing it to shut behind her.

She was not surprised at all with what she discovered. Rather than people with hanged heads, in quiet manner with pressed hands, Kyla found more adoration than use of the cathedral. People were snapping photos of sacred religious icons, admiring the tributary candle lightings, and most of all, were commenting in regard to the "genius of it all," to the "geniuses that built this castle." The architecture, all aside, was very beautiful, however, it seemed to Kyla that this was no place of piety. It was all such a joke. She decided to vacate its unholy mockery and proceeded to the door, when suddenly a man stepped in front of her.

"Hey dovey, ain't this church rather ace? Ya' quite au fait with London's finest?" said the odd fellow.

He was a man of about sixty years with grease stains on his raggedy clothes. He wore half-ripped, faded brown pants and an untucked, worn-looking off-white t-shirt. His stomach hung down over his waist, most likely due to a drinking addiction. The man had a very

Chaotic Ocean

offensive odour about him, likely a mixture of sour smelling food, and produced a complete want of overall cleanliness. He was unpleasant at best to look at. Kyla began to speak.

"Actually, sir, I'm not that fond of these cathedrals; they seem much more for decoration, and to me, that seems curious in such a place of worship. It is one thing to appreciate, but it is another to totally overexploit."

"Ah, ya're barmy woman! I'd bite my arm off ta serve down and kiss the ground ta the man with the plan who created such a bute as this. Gawd blimey if I've overlooked its genius. Gawd blimey!" he exclaimed.

"Sir, if I may ask, why did you stop me in mid step from leaving the cathedral?" asked Kyla.

"Well, truth be told, ya' just seemed ta be standing all alone, looking all brassed off, and ya' just seemed really cheeky-looking, as if something were wrong. Blokes don't come ta these here cathedrals ta scrutinise, letlone, philosophise 'em; they just come for reasons like me, ta sit on me bum, kick back, snap a few stills, and all the while get a few prayers in for the man upstairs, and bobs your uncle. I know yer type."

"Excuse me?" snapped Kyla.

"Yer type. Never ever just relax and get bladdered to have a good time. Spend yer whole bloomin' life with a blinkered eye never once knowin' that not knowin' is what ya' do best. And all the while, love, ya' think ya're doin' some good, or helpin' some cause, when really, ya' ain't much different from the blokes ya're probably trying ta stay away from. And ya're probably thinkin' right now that ya' can't be fagged with the likes of me. But if ya' wanna talk philos'phy, lovey, ya' probably hate people when they do what ya' do. It's all degree. That's all."

"How have you any idea of any of this sir?" she angrily replied.

"How? The how's easy. Ya' can read people with one line o' the face, lets lone their whole look. Ya're easy doll. Don't think ya' ain't. But I gotta get on my way and make on back ta my feeble decorations as ya' call 'em. If ya' ever fancy ta happen this way again, I'd be glad ta chatter away about nothing. The name's Horris, dovey."

The strange man stumbled back to his friends and immediately, carelessly, began pointing all about, hinting at the way the ceiling swept in almost like a gull's wings. Kyla again started for the door. As quickly as possible, she yanked it open, moved down the steps, and was once again off down the cobblestone streets.

As Kyla paced along, she thought to herself, "Gawd blimey? Have I befallen once again and let the weak over-will me? Was Horris not one hundred times more cunning than I and one million times more intelligent? Oh, if Zigmund could have only... Are these thoughts to be the end of me, and if so, have I truly lived, fueled on mere wit and will alone? Or are all of these merely cruel manifestations of my consciousness brought forth by chemical induction, environment, societal hierarchy, or whatever and ever? I cannot bear to think my life commands so little. So very little."

Chaotic Ocean

Unlike before, the woman now sought comfort. She decided to continue en route to her quaint little house along St. Jung Street. Now, not only was the unforgiving rain falling at an incorrigible speed, but the all too infamous "London fog" had slowly begun to slither in.

"Ah, precisely what I need to brighten my day," thought Kyla.

The fog was a dark-purplish colour and seemed as thick as dense clots of cotton. It swept through the city, as if undetectable to the masses of desensitised, familiarised Londonians. Kyla, however, felt as if she were being strangled by her own umbilical cord, suffocating her, wrapping its clutches around her neck with a grasp as deadly as a cobra's.

She thought, "What is toleration? Is it purely accepting that which we cannot change, or is it more? Perhaps, changing the very ideas, those which we cannot accept, curbing our own mentality to merely appease our own tolerance? Or perhaps every thought I think is, in actuality, a pseudo-intellectual rant, conjured up in some divine hope of proving to myself the usefulness of my own pathetic being. In any scenario, I cannot stand myself, nor this damned fog one second longer."

Kyla began running, increasing her speed to that of a sprinter. With her arms flailing, her hair blown back, and beaded sweat running down at the temples, she began to feel slightly different. The tire of thought faded from her eyes as the adrenaline took its unwanted place. She did not bother to stop and analyse footprints. She did not bother to examine how the common man fulfilled his life. She did not bother to think about the hypocrisy that dictated and swelled around the city. She simply focused on running, running far and fast away from it all, away from herself, possibly. And for a while, it worked. For a while. Freeing oneself from the self is truly liberating. However, in all the joy, in all the release of this, consequence had been left astray. Maybe that is alright, but Kyla could not let go that easily. Suddenly, she stopped, as if air-breaking to avoid collision with mother and child. She had no longer cared for direction, and realising the fright of her action, had not a clue as to her current location. This depressed her greatly. It was not being lost that got to her, but the actuality of what had taken place.

She thought, "If only for a second. I cannot let go for even ephemeral seconds in time. I am trapped. My only release, ultimately, will be my death. There is no letting go for me. Though, perhaps as much is melodramatic!"

*

It was around 6:15 now, and the sun slowly began to fall over the horizon. The dense fog prevented much, if not all of the visibility. Kyla felt fortunate to have been subjected to something so stunning and so undeniably striking, because had she been witnessing the birth in another continent, or in another country, or possibly even in another city, she might not have been able to appreciate it for even one half its worth. By now, large puddles had formed in gelatinous creations all over the streets. Kyla made no effort to avoid them.

Chaotic Ocean

To herself, she thought, "Oh, what is the difference if I return home clean, proud, and confident, or mud-soaked, dejected, and full of torpor? There is none. I've no one which to even return, no warm greeting, no familiar voice to which I can plead and cry, and nothing even half resembling a normal piece of sanity."

Upon thinking of misfortune, Kyla realised that she ought return in any case, for she needed the shelter. She had been out walking for quite some time, and her once shining clothes were now drenched in sweat and rain.

Kyla remembered her mother often saying, "You'll catch your death, child, if you don't pay attention to the weather. It'll change more times than you realise. And when you think it's done for good, that's when it will snatch you up!"

Her mother would then swoop the little girl off of the floor, cradle her in her strong arms, and whisper, "Just be sure to check the tele before leaving the house, Kyla sweetheart."

Something then occurred to her.

"I've been caught in a storm. Why didn't I check the weather before parading on my way? Why have I gone through doubt after doubt, all the while not realising the obvious? There is nothing abnormal about what I've been churning over, nothing abnormal with self uncertainty, nothing odd at all. I am human. I've the right as much as Zigmund or Horris. I did not ask to be cognisant, but I am not ungrateful that I am. Certain facts of life may disturb me more than others, certain silly idiocies might cut through me more than others who have become more accustomed, but there's no sense in destroying oneself because of said annoyances. Oh, if Zigmund could have only seen me, could only see me, struggling over trivial arguments within myself, in my own mind, surely he'd mock me. Thank Heaven he is at home, innocent as a field mouse. It's all rather ironic and humorous to think of myself in such ridiculous ways. It is behind."

Kyla then searched out the nearest street sign with half a feeling of ease now in her chest. Having reassured herself, she was confident enough to make her way onward. The thought was only half true, though. One pat on the back was not enough to wash away Kyla's fear and insecurity. The thoughts still lingered on, if not up front, then at least growing within her subconscious. However, sometimes letting go, at least for minutes or days on end, can be therapeutic, so we will not chastise her. She was on Locke Street, which she knew to be only a few away from her destination, St. Jung. A cab passed through and Kyla immediately signaled it to stop. The rain began to feel a bit much for even her. Or so this was the idea that she passed off to herself, nevertheless. The cab pulled quickly over to the walk, which she had been impatiently waiting upon. It pulled in so suddenly that it splattered Kyla with droplets of rain and soot. She, however, did not notice this. It was a fairly older cab with faded, corrugated writing on its passenger door. The tires looked somewhat deflated, and the cab seemed to be emitting an extremely foul, brownish fume from its exhaust. Its engine was louder than most, like an angry, senile old man calling for his walker.

Suddenly, "Hey lady, stop admiring the cab and get in, you ain't writing a book!" said the driver.

"Sorry," said Kyla, as she reached out for the oily, silver handle, grasped it, pulled it open, and got in.

The seats were black and smelled like cheap leather. A pine air freshener hung from below the rear view mirror. The side windows were filthy, covered with dirt and hardened bird feces. Up front, the window was slightly cleaner, with at least some visibility where the windshield wipers had been raging back-and-forth, doing a less than adequate job. Below her feet were dark grey floor mats, stomped with mud from the frequent rain-soaked travelers. The cab's mile tracker looked old and outdated, and did not seem fastened particularly well. The buttons were crooked, and a few were even smushed in.

The cabby pressed the re-clock button with his dirty finger, turned around, and let out, "Where to, lady?"

His countenance was crude and aged, not like Zigmund's, due to over consumption and inactivity, but rather from the scars of life, day-to-day living with no guarantee or assurance of the next, filled with hardships and an inherent ability to forge on. He had dark blonde hair that was long in the back and on the sides, and hung down haphazardly over his ears and eyes. The man wore a half-grown, gruffy-looking mustache that was reminiscent of pre-pubescence. He had a crooked nose, as if having been in one too many brawls in a pub, and his eyes were as black as the silky skin of a panther. The cabby appeared about forty-five years of age.

"Just drive around for a while," said Kyla. She had now a sense of calm and did not appear in a great rush to return home, dissimilar to prior demeanor.

"You, uh, just want me to drive? That it lady?" said the cabby with a look of confusion on his face.

"Yes sir, if it's all the same, that is what I'd like," said Kyla.

"Okay lady, it's your money. The meter is running," said the cabby with an almost anxious look of deceit in his eyes.

He proceeded to drive around for quite some time, passing by Westminster Street, Holland Avenue, Delaney Park, and even St. Jung Street. Kyla sat uncomfortably in the back seat with her head pressed upon the dirty window, trying to make out people and places. She remained silent, allowing the hum of the tires treading on the road to lull her even more. She knew there was nothing stupendously interesting upon returning home. Kyla, at first, thought it the better to sit in silence, allowing for the meter miles to pile on and consequently, allowing for the cabby's contentedness in his joyride. She then thought to make a conversation, if nothing else, for sheer curiosity.

"The name is Kyla Demark," said Kyla leaning forward. "What's your name?"

"My name? Nobody usually care to ask me my name lady. What's it to you?" said the cabby.

Chaotic Ocean

"Sir, forgive me if you thought my remark was motive driven. The only motive behind my action was to make a conversation, to make our time together enjoyable."

"You're sure an odd one, makin' talks with cabbies. What an odd thing to do. I wouldn't talk to no cabbies if they was givin' me a ride or not. It's Sean, though."

"What do you think of me, Sean?" questioned Kyla.

"Think of you? I don't think nothin'. You're a customer. I'm a driver. I ain't paid to think about you people. People do too much of that already. I leave that work up to people who got nothin' else to do and the like."

"What do you mean, people do too much of that already?"

"Well I'm no professor lady, I'm just talkin'. But if you must know, I got a wife and two kids at home. Think I really care 'bout the likes of the universe or symbols or Dickens? Some people think they can learn life with some of that stuff. Maybe you do too. Who knows? But I got my darling family every single day of the year to come home to, and when I walk into the door of our two-room flat, I got one kid on each leg, and a long kiss from my wife. And I couldn't be happier."

"You might not believe this, Sean, but I envy you."

"You, envy me? Ha, that's a joke. Come on lady, you got your expensive clothes, probably a well kept home, and everything I could never even think to be thought of havin'."

"That's exactly what I think of you." Kyla calmly replied.

"Hmm, nothing you can't learn in a children's book I guess. Who would have thought the City Mouse and the Country Mouse would be teachin' me lessons in my age. That's what I'd do if I could talk sophisticated like."

"What is it that you'd do?"

"You know, children's books. They're so simple and so, umm..." The cabby thought for a minute as the words escaped him. "So, real, you know? There's no questions or lies or politics in those stories. Just lessons to be learned. I think maybe if everyone in today's world had been read to more as kiddies, then they wouldn't be so damned backwards. But I guess you can't blame 'em, right?"

"Heh, you know more than you think, Sean, of the so-called unimportant things in life. Bring me to 29 St. Jung Street please."

"Whatever you like, lady. What is it that you do?" asked Sean to prolong the conversation.

"I work as a psychologist at the hospital."

"Nice," replied Sean, as if truly impressed, despite his earlier dig on a related profession. "Helping people is a good thing."

The cab arrived onto St. Jung Street in just under seven minutes. It of course took the expected roundabout route, but Kyla did not seem to mind. She could see that it was still heavily raining outside and wondered when it would end. Finally, she could see her house through the centre of the front windshield on the lower right hand side. Sean pulled the cab over to the side of the road, turned around, and began to speak.

Chaotic Ocean

"This was definitely one o' my most interesting rides, lady... Kyla, maybe I'll see ya' again sometime. It's £15.54 for the ride."

Kyla handed Sean the money, said good-bye, and got out of the cab and onto the walk. She watched it clanker off down on its way back to a main road with rain spattering all over, as if having been caught under a Summertime sprinkler.

*

Kyla turned toward the drive of her house and began to make her way near it. There was only one quaint chestnut tree, situated about ten feet from the front door, standing outside, as if acting as a reliable night sentinel. It was in half bloom with tiny, yellow-brown lumps extending from each limb. Its branches struck left and right and sprawled out like an intricate spider's web. Red dear were often seen grazing on its prickly fruit, and prancing around the area in general. The walk had not been refinished in quite some time and was starting to deteriorate, mostly due to the exorbitant amount of yearly rainfall. Small pieces of the cobblestone were falling awayat the edges and sides. Kyla made her way past the chestnut tree, and then soon after, to the front of her house. There were only three small, worn, dark brown steps leading up to an old-fashioned-looking front porch, which seemed to make the home more cozy in appearance. The house was situated upon a small, inclined hill, but was much so at level with the rest of the dwellings on the street. Most were similar-looking with slightly different styles and conventions. The structure itself was a pale light blue colour with speckles of faded time embedded within its walls. It had a flimsy-looking, black and brown cheap roof with a poor drainage system which generally resulted in large amounts of rain pouring over the front porch in spasmodic fashion. Behind its inviting exterior, past the house, were endless miles of cultivated farmland. The well-secured, medium brown fences began about fifteen feet from the rear, leaving little to no property, and were strewn about in such a way whereas to have looked upon them, one might not have understood their usefulness. Brown and white spotted cows were the most common of residents upon the land's somewhat comforting grass floor. In Winter time, the view from the back of the home was mystifying, as snow-covered hills enveloped every single bit of civilisation, leaving only the purity of the soft, unimaginably perfect, joy-soaked snow.

She made her way up the three steps and paused before entering. Turning around, switching to the polar direction of the entrance, she looked out upon the world, took in a breath of air, and let out a sigh of relief. Kyla gazed up with difficulty into the storming sky as she attempted to search for constellations. She could never find constellations. The moon was magnificently breaking through the clouds, with its usual crucifix hung about its face, impressing upon the eyes of millions. Kyla thought, "God help me." She turned back around. The door was ghostly white with little decoration or accolade. Its handle was an ugly brass colour and had not been cleaned in some time. Pressing upon on it, Kyla stepped into the house.

Chaotic Ocean

It was a compact, one-floor place of dwelling, which, at first glance, appeared well kept, orderly, and friendly. The first room was a cold, tiny area without furniture, based with a hardwood floor that had not been shellacked over in all places. The walls were bare with nothing but a few Davinci reproductions hanging from them, and were an eggshell white colour. She quickly made her way about through the unfeeling room. There was a connecting corridor from the first room that was rather narrow, possibly only three feet wide. It was carpeted with one long, ugly multicolored throw mat. A pull cord attached to the attic door hung daintily about, almost taunting passersby, however, mostly this taunted Kyla. She had not been up there in years, and had also long forgotten the items that she had stored. Her reasoning for having not gone up in some time was mysterious. She had been noted as having called the attic everything from a "sewer of raised deceit" to a "Hellish thing of ill-beauty and cruelty." The attic, for some reason, disgusted Kyla. As she passed the pull cord, she threw her hand out in a raging attempt to brush it away from her face.

At the end of the corridor were two wooden doors on adjacent walls. Making her way to the doors, she opened the one off to the left. Kyla reached into the dark, as the room was unlit, and searched her hand along the wall like a blind man pressing his fingertips along brail, and flicked the light on. The whole back wall was filled with a daunting bookshelf, which stretched from the base of the floor to just below the ceiling. All the classics were present. Gogol and Wilde held staff positions in the far left of the top shelf, while various others were situated in the middle of the second shelf. The collection was an eclectic gathering of authors and poets from around the world. Psychology books were also in large abundance.

On the left wall of the room, there was a light wood-coloured desk that had papers scattered about. It was directly facing a large, two pane, clear-glass window. A black telephone stood atop a nightstand with a shaded orange lamp beside it. The carpet was dark red and had long lost its aura of newness. Kyla walked over to the desk and pulled out the black leathered, uncomfortable chair. She sat down and pulled herself closer to the desk to further examine what she had hitherto been working on. There laid the scribblings for the first handful of pages or so of a novel that Kyla had started. The main protagonist was a homeless man, a genius who was open in every sense of the word, and figured himself ten times over, each time finding trueness and peace. The other central figure was a rich woman, stupefied with over-information, cultural degeneration, and under-satisfactory, equivocal emancipation, not to mention parasailing. The book was entitled *Superfluous Description and Over Ambitious Vocabulary*.

Her intent was to share all her acquired knowledge about the world, with the world. She thought that the greatest gift would be in leaving a lasting staple on literature, on thought. What Kyla did not realise, however, was that she knew very little of any of the aforementioned subjects, and had such an entirely narrow approach to the whole concept that the only goal nearing accomplishment was the possible placation of her own ego. Her main character was also creating a book. In that book, the main character was writing a book about how a man writes a book about a woman writing a book... Kaleidoscope. Kyla had come to a halt in her writing. At first, it was something huge, and actually, still was, but she rather enjoyed it, each and every personally tendered word. She used to sit effortlessly, when she first began, typing away as the words flowed onto the blank paper like propaganda from an activist. Each page was a new adventure, a new cunning and delicate twist. However, her desire of current was lessening. She had come to stops and jerks in the un-thought plot, and it had further become increasingly tiresome in attempting to work them through. Kyla had thought, "If only I could complete the first chapter... then it would all fall into place."

The woman enjoyed creating new approaches to life, and also enjoyed figuring new ways to analyse it. She had tried taking her current stumbling stone and relating it toward her own criticisms, ultimately realising something: if one does not enjoy writing, for whatever reason, the art will not be enjoyable, for the most part, to others. Kyla thought that, since in the beginning it was very easy, perhaps too easy, the fact that she was now struggling indicated that the art ceased to be good and was no longer enjoyable. After long periods of thought and doubt, she also realised something else: making use of the seemingly useless and inadequate, morphing weakness into strength, and clearing blockage into pathway would be her ultimate challenge. However, it was one that Kyla welcomed, and tried as best she could to stay open to the concept. Words move on just as people do.

*

Kyla no longer felt like staring into the ineptness of her own creation, so she slid the chair back, neatened the papers, and got up from the desk. She was just about to vacate the room, with right hand in mid air swiping for the light switch, when the phone began to ring. Walking back over to the humble little table, she picked up the receiver.

"Hello?"

"Ah, I see you're relaxing just fine, dear Kyla, no less in the quaint surroundings of your study."

It was the voice of Zigmund Sardoce. Kyla harbored conflicting emotions for Zigmund at that moment, and it took her a second or two to reply. She was somewhat relieved to hear a familiar voice, one she could identify and laugh with, but she also resented it somewhat for having caused her such a miserable day, or rather, having been the indirect root of her current state of confusion. Kyla ultimately understood that the responsibility rested upon her own shoulders for what had mentally taken place since her departure from Zigmund's, but it still felt good to pass blame for at least an unquestioning, thoughtless second. She regained composure and began to reply.

"Yes, Zigmund, I was just looking over some papers of something I'd been working on."

Chaotic Ocean

"Oh? But what is work anyway, Kyla? It all seems so undesirable, so pointless. I'm sure it's not brought you much, if any, pleasure, knowing the person that you are."

"I'm able to find so much more in writing than you've ever even considered the possibility of, Zigmund. But I'm not much for discussing it at the moment, I've had a tiresome day."

"That's fair enough. Kyla, something has been on my mind. I've looked through my library, time and time again, overlooking nothing, no author left astray, shelf upon shelf, sieved like a detective, and one thought has been swelling around my brain. The great pieces of literature have come from all around the world, from various countries and various minds. Our thoughts have been provoked by some of the greatest Russian minds since time immemorial, by some of the most eloquently spoken French tongues of this and past centuries, by some of the wondrous Eastern philosophers, and by, of course, our own ambitious maid, England. And who knows, maybe even the United States will produce a great mind one day, not likely though. But you see where I am headed with this."

"Not really," interrupted Kyla with a tone of torpor in her voice.

"As I was saying, it simply seems that all the proof in the world, such as is strived for within mathematics, leaves little room for any pondering, whereas in theory, in poetry, and in writing, there is much. *I've always looked at math as a man's struggle for inner security in an insecure world."

"Do you think that a man of mathematics is any different from a man of literature or a man of God?"

"I do not think the men to be different, Kyla, but I do understand their views of the world to be different. This is not to say that one's profession dictates one's view of life, but in most cases, one's field of study, one's specialisation, is from where one's ideas are drawn. You would never base one of your own theories in something you weren't accustomed with, therefore bias is your brother from the start of every thought, whether you realise this or not."

"So, what you're implying is that your thoughts are not totally valid due to the imposing and influential world around you, whether due to voluntary or involuntary circumstances that have made you to be or think one way or the other. That might be valid, Zigmund; I don't proclaim to be unattached to the confine of society, nor do I totally relate my own thoughts to the seclusion and space of my own brain. However, unfortunately, while all of this is agreeable, it also means that your opinion on the matter is totally worthless due to your own logic. Having no logic is a much higher freedom, Zigmund. It really doesn't seem just or profound to create logic, or rather, sensible, not to pun the point of logic, due to its own backbreaking inevitability. Your view of one's own thinking seems very acute anyway. It's been theorised that we, humans and the like of living creatures, cannot be held to the single confining spaces of our own minds, because the very thought behind consciousness is not a singular idea, not something to be thought on the individual level. I'm not saying I buy into the idea, but under different lights, it knocks you back sometimes. We, humans, thinking mammals, form an environment in which we live, breed, and die. However, the environment is merely part of a larger system of space and matter that is all connected, and while we can only see ourselves as the highest beings alive, in the tangible realm, we merely blend in well and gel with the rest of our surroundings. Yes, we have brains which function and allow for this thought, but that is what they are, functions, not profound consciousnesses of their own liking. I don't know, Zigmund, it just seems difficult to pass bias off that quickly without first examining the whole scheme of things."

"There you go again, my dear Kyla, taking a simple sentence of mine and twisting and warping it into my grand philosophy on life. Oh, I hope God is merciful on your soul, because you've purged through all the goodness of man with your cynicism."

"So now you're open to the idea of God, Zigmund?"

"That's your tragic flaw, Kyla, you won't let people become anything else than what you've already set down for them. I admit the fact that I've been skeptical on the entire outlook of God and any sort of holy afterlife, but I've thought about this to endless limits. How can so many people be one hundred percent wrong? In every country of the world, in every region and continent, religion exists, thrives, and is a major part of people's lives. God is simply a term that has been integrated into our society to explain something for which we have no other word. The name of the deity is generally unimportant."

"You know, Zigmund, religion is one of those issues which creates enemies. I do not wish to make enemies with the world. I'm also not arrogant enough to proclaim right, wrong, yes, no, or God or no God. It's an issue that has been emblazoned about my brain to an all too countless number. It's also an issue that upsets me, makes me uncomfortable, makes me weak, vulnerable, and feeble-minded. The issue itself seems fabricated, but the idea, or ideal behind it seems almost too possible."

"Do you know what I find odd, Kyla?" replied Zigmund in a cool manner.

"What's that?" answered she.

"The fact that we are completely content in giving away the underlying meaning of life, without having even discussed the lines. It makes me chuckle every now and again. I have unique experiences, as do you, each apart from each other's. We both bring our lives back to the poker table, set the rules up for a game of five card draw, and each take the maximum number of cards. I know no other person whom I've been able to do that with, Kyla. Most passersby, or even other friends, seem to be caught up on all the detail, on all the cosmic plasma of the solar system that makes up and creates the very pathway for analysis and understanding. With us, the maze and mouse trap is not needed; you and I both sniff and smell the cheese before gorging in of course, but what is the point of going through the twisting hallways if you can only step over them to the truer finish anyway? We see the waterfall..."

Chaotic Ocean

"Okay!" interrupted Kyla "enough obscure metaphors. I get the idea without you breaking your own back once again. Stop making glorified excuses for our literary inadequacies."

"Heh, fair enough," laughed Zigmund in a hearty manner.

"Anyway, Zigmund, without delving into the lurks of my own morality and opinion on such matters as religion, I'd like to express a simple idea to you that I was handed in a conversation much more Daedalian than this one. I do not necessarily subscribe to this idea, nor am I bound to its reasoning, however, it is a most provoking thought to me, and now I am sharing it with you. People all around the world, as you've mentioned, have religion, yes, but what you've failed to include is that, while millions have religion, there are plenty of nay sayers and skeptics around as well. Admittedly, I am one of them. Every now and again you'll meet someone who knocks you back on your knees, or hear a song that makes you weep and crumble, or read a passage that simply turns you in and out, reversing every idea you thought you understood. I've often questioned God, the man, the entity, the reality, and more times than not I've come up shorthanded on answers and reasoning, thus bringing me to my doubtful position. Not being able to understand God has led me to my skepticism. However, a friend of mine, a dear friend of many years, told me this. *Not being able to understand God, or comprehend the existence of such a being, is no reason to have doubt. When analysing the whole concept, an analogy can be drawn. The ameba is to the human, as the human is to God. It knows nothing of us, who we are, what we are, or even that we exist and coexist with it. It simply does not have the intelligence, awareness, or cognisance to do so. God, supposedly being the most powerful source of enlightenment in the world, cannot possibly be within the human's miniscule understanding. The reason that we cannot comprehend the concept, or accept it fully, is because we, humans, do not have the capacity. Therefore, God, being something beyond our present understanding, is of course impossible to reason the existence of. It would almost be disappointing if we could understand such an entity, such a force so far and beyond our own, as God."

*

It is at this point that the author had originally inserted a preventable and confusing digression, that only pages later was assumed inconsequential, and asked of the reader to be forgotten. The author has hung his head in ignominy many a night over this inelegance. Though, perhaps it is only conjecture that the reader would have taken poorly to the disruption. However, if the reader pleases, assume the most fantastic of disturbances. Let the mind wander and concoct like never before. And finally, imagine a conclusion that really would have left the jaw open, urging the reader onward into the next chapter. Cheers.

CHAPTER TWO
☨

ALL THAT WE SEE OR SEEM

*

"I must admit, Kyla, the theory is mildly interesting. However, I must go now," said he.

"So soon?" replied Kyla, feeling utterly alone, hoping to at least keep Zigmund a few more minutes, if for nothing more than to pass the time left in the day.

"I am sorry, but it's getting a bit late. It is one thing to discuss life in person, where I may at least feel some form of dignity, knowing that, or feeling that I am at least somewhat important enough to be a part of, but it is quite another to be berated over a telephone, point by point, axe by axe, all the while knowing that the only vice keeping me from ending any misery is my own will to simply hang up. That, to me, is an unfair emotion that I do not wish to think about, let alone ever render or project onto you, dear Kyla. So for both our sake, I will go now."

"Fine, Zigmund!" snapped Kyla, "just let it all fall away without an ounce of self responsibility to show for the whole thing."

"Kyla, you're tired; perhaps you should go to sleep. Don't be angry," calmly replied Zigmund.

Kyla hung up the phone in an annoyed manner, not caring to say good-bye to her friend. She stood there for a minute in the dimly lit area of the room, looked around, and eventually let out a sigh. She slowly began to vacate the room's lifeless premises, swaggering slouchedly to the door. Kyla was somewhat beaten and cut down. She felt torn in every direction known to man, as if having been stretched to the absolute maximum by fabric workers who had misjudged some minimal measurement, who then in turn had to try and compensate for the mistake with sheer force and brute mentality. Kyla felt never more alone in her own home, never more alone in her own body. She began to question her actions and thoughts, not knowing truly if they were results of self-control, will, desire, or rather, random acts, which were ultimately uncontrollable to her and to her own forms of reaction and reason. She, for the very first time in her life, was utterly confused, without a guiding light to lead her through the tunnel of silence and blinding darkness. Though Kyla could see, hear, and speak, touch and smell, she felt as if the most horrid form of sense deprivation had been struck upon her, weakening her every movement, her every thought, to the point of pointlessness, a pointless existence in which no point served as any sort of revelation, and to her, this was death, a cold, chilling, numbing death.

Chaotic Ocean

*

In the hours to come, sleeplessly writhing about in a half aware state of being, she began to let go. Under her freshly bleached, white cotton sheets, staring blankly out of her small sidewall window, Kyla began to un-think. One thought came protruding in and out of her mind: "Sleep cures all." Her room was fairly cozy with a quaint feeling of wholesomeness about it. The navy blue curtains were neatly tied back. The rug seemed always freshly vacuumed, as the carpet stress marks were clearly visible where the machine had been pushed back-and-forth. The television was a modest thirteen-incher with poor reception, that sat atop a shellacked, small, brown cabinet. Suddenly, like a surprise guest having left no form of warning or notice prior to visit, Kyla was asleep. For the first time in what seemed like a decade-long day, her mind was at ease.

During the few hours of the night when she was set free to dream, set free to escape her own reality, thousands of images came to her, most of which nonsensical. However, one dream in particular was especially impacting.

It was set in an unusual black and white dreariness that seemed to contain a sense of eerie timelessness. Kyla found herself in a thickly wooded forest with no direct sign of civilisation. She seemed to have been shielding herself or hiding from some unexplainable force, which, while drawing her in, also seemed to push her violently back, as if having been excommunicated from the church for sins of lust and wrath. Horrid shadows seemed to envelop the very consciousness of the state, intruding thought like murderous dictators breeding purely wicked commands. The dark and saddening landscape underwent drastic changes for short one-second intervals, occurring no more than every five minutes, whereas the brightest light imaginable would appear or flash into existence, ever more showing the bleakness of the atmosphere. Kyla stood naked by a tree with not a defense with which to take comfort. Her body was dirtied with barbarous tattoos of macabre images of rape and vulgarity. She violently struggled to wipe them off, to brush them away, but her efforts yielded no result. She felt almost unholy. The sensation was new and fresh, however, was in no way refreshing. The hair on her arms began reacting in electromagnetic fashions, standing up stiff as a sergeant on alert. Her spine no longer felt like part of her body, but rather like a separate being attempting to emancipate itself from the confine of human existence. It seemed to squirm and stretch inside of her, making every moment an uncomfortable point in time in which she wished for escape. Kyla was too ashamed to move though, too embarrassed to show weakness, and too unwilling to search for help, thus, she crouched there like a frightened, stubborn child. It was cold out, not cold enough for snow, but just bitter enough for ground frost, a cold so chillingly cruel whereas it showed the glimpse of beauty, but did not give into the fully completed desire, save for the negative effects that would ultimately partner with that beauty. She moved not, and often glanced out into the open dim lit field across the way. Now and again, Kyla thought she saw speedy images or creatures within the surroundings. This plane was of no pleasure, nor did it please the eye or psyche.

With blood-tainted vision, she peered out into the distance, somewhat transfixed on a being with which she knowingly had no connection. He, it, was consumed by some type of unGodly passion only noticeable to the Lords and Demons. The creature's (or man's) hands flailed about in spasmodic and uncontrolled mannerisms. The lower half of his body appeared savage and nomadic, with scruffy, blackish hair sprawling out in haphazard directions. The creature was one with the darkness. It seemed almost canine in a way, under a certain viewing light, but possessed qualities similar to those only native to humans.

While Kyla was disgusted with the Hellish creature, she could not look away. Whether it was due to fright or merely to some compelling force, she found herself inching closer, slithering about, attempting to capture a better glance. No longer did she notice her want of clothing and security. She paced forward still, trying to see to what this Devil was clinging. It seemed like he was gorging into something, like a ravenous predator gnawing out the innards of a freshly brutalised meal. To herself, she thought, "What on Earth..."

The creature suddenly turned toward her. With numbing fear, she stood stone-like, too overwhelmed to have been rational. It looked at her, but more so, through her. The eyes were like pale moons showing no feeling whatsoever. It had blood running down the sides of its mouth and dripping onto the ground. She spotted two horrific fangs, as if he were some vampiric creature come to drain existence. Its skin was greyish, unlike any human form Kyla had seen prior. The look upon its countenance was sinister and menacing, as if it had no discernable soul. To herself, she thought, "This is no man." Kyla looked down in utter disbelief to see what it had been thriving on. It was a man, a human. The man had been literally torn in two halves with his jugular ripped right out. Blood consumed the ground and made the dirt around it soggy. The creature began to make his way toward her. Still, she could not move. Kyla did not know to reason or to run. It walked with an almost self-centred pride about, yet, it was also less a person than she could figure, and so it came off as plainly stunning to Kyla, in a way. As it came closer, she began to see it more clearly. It wore torn black shorts and nothing more. To herself, she thought, "My God, why? Why does this beast Devil have on a man's shorts when clearly it is no man!" Still, it inched further and further, till it was face to face with the woman. She did not know if this was to be her end. It leaned closely in. Its breath was foul and cold. The beast started to open its mouth. Kyla began to scream, but before she could place perspective on the situation, it whispered to her.

"Your fear is your shortcoming, Kyla."

And then, like passing sand blown about in the wind, it was gone. She found herself nude in the middle of an open field, with hardly a recollection for what she had just experienced.

Kyla suddenly awoke, shivering with sweat, feeling insecure and abandoned. Inner isolation was her dictator. She thought to call Zigmund

Chaotic Ocean

to tell him of the dream, but then decided not to bother him. Lying slowly back down, as her eyelids rested, she began to fall back into sleep.

*

In the morning, with the memory of her awful nightmare in the distance, Kyla sat up slowly, drenched in her own torrential sweat. Though, as not to dwell (as such she believed was the proper and dignified way to behave in order to live a fulfilling life), she attempted to be objective and clear-minded about the day ahead. When she walked outside to retrieve the morning paper, the sky was dumping its surplus of snow unto the land, perfectly, beautifully, in a sense so systematic that to have glanced away, to have turned from the complete opacity of the whiteness, would have been to miss the phenomenon, to have been deprived of all the light and knowledge of all existence. She began to descend along the snow-trodden steps, making semi-shallow impressions. The paper was encased in a plastic baggy of sorts. Kyla reached down and suddenly lost all sense of balance. Before she could make sense of her fumbling, she was on her backside, out from under the protective ledge of the flat, staring up into the heavily falling precipitation. The sun was breaking through the dense snow, shining, looming almost, creating an image of comfort, so warm (and in actuality, so cold) that she was almost engulfed in its essence. She lay on her back for some time, allowing the soft, cotton-like imperfections to nest and melt in her skin. Within seconds, her hair had turned in color, taking on the form of a hundred-year old woman. Kyla began to ponder reasons why it would have been more beneficial to jump to her feet and spring inside the flat, though, could not dismiss the importance of breathing in her contemporary life, of absorbing the moment. She lay there for some twenty minutes, coldly, shivering, but enraptured in bliss. Finally, to stave off the possibility of frostbite (and this is perhaps the only reason at all that Kyla moved from the spot), she picked herself up, reached for the plastic baggy, and ascended her stoop, moving quickly into the flat.

She eagerly thrust open the paper, anxious to learn, to inhale the human element. Mostly, the stories were bland, obtuse little trivialities. Though, on the back page, there was an article called "Thunder Blunder on Me Bum." The quirky and perverse title grabbed her attention, though she would more likely have attributed as having been enticing based on the interest of word structure, rather than on anything having to do with sexual connotation. Upon reading the first paragraph, Kyla was even greater engulfed.

> *Last night, in the cheeky city of London, a great noise rang throughout the countryside. This voluptuous, quadruple D thunder seems to be the talk of the commoners, all wondering where this beast-Satan demonstration had come from. Of course the Londoners have known thunder in their lives, but for a peculiar reason, this, said one native, "is not the bloody norm." It seems to be the current lore of town gossip. The people here are referring to it as 'The Night The Gods Clashed.'*

Chaotic Ocean

Next week, perhaps the Londoners will express their opinions on the Lockness Monster and the Abominable Snowman. The gossip and uselessness of this city never ceases to amaze me. The people here will find anything to take away from the habitual boredom of their transitory lives. God have mercy on their insignificant souls.

-William Blormy, Odds and Sods

  To herself, she thought, "I do recall that, that unholy hum when I was at Zigmund's yesterday. How odd, how very odd." And with mild derision and much pity, she dismissed the article.
  The phone suddenly screamed. She quickly shuffled over to it and picked up. It was Zigmund on the other end, hysterically and almost maniacally yapping for her to meet him at once, for her to immediately come to the mansion. He was making no sense, and she had never heard him like this before. After all, Zigmund was one of the calmest and most collected people she had known, for this was probably the side effect of extreme self-centredness and inability to look beyond himself. Some children fail to recognise individuality of person in others, and this is a growing developmental despair among parents worldwide. Zigmund clearly had no medical disorder, though was quite childlike in a slew of undiagnosed ways. Kyla then decided to adhere to the spontaneous request, threw on a quick outfit, and headed out. She took the old banger parked stolidly in the drive. Obviously, it was rarely used, mostly on occasion, or when she felt too lazy to walk to Zigmund's or to her place of work at the nearby hospital. In truth, Kyla was probably insouciant to both methods, but preferred one or the other out of sheer mood or convenience. So is rationale.
  She, as it now may seem integral and of use to know, had worked at the Hutchinson Mental Hospital for thirteen-odd years, as a psychologist by title, helping various delinquents, miscreants, and mentally disturbed patients. She had never been accused of false altruism, and quite enjoyed the work. We will get back to this in a bit.

*

  Kyla motored about in the clunker for a few short minutes till she approached the familiar Sardoce Estate. She parked on the cobblestone-laden rode and walked cautiously up to the gate. It had been opened prior to her arrival, as if Zigmund had been childishly waiting for her, too anxious to contain himself. Judging from his intonation minutes earlier, she had not a clue of what to expect from him, possibly for the first time in the relationship. Zigmund had been waiting under the canopy where they had last conversed. As she approached, he made motion to come inside the mansion this time. It was roughly one hundred feet from the end of the canopy to the entrance of the mansion, though to note, the canopy *was* in actuality, an extension of the entrance. When the two had gotten to the door, Zigmund fidgeted about his pockets, searching for the key. The door was strangely locked, as if he were paranoid that from the time

Chaotic Ocean

he was to be greeting Kyla to the time they would be walking back, that somehow, somewhere, someone might have been able to invade his grand abode.

The estate had been passed down within the Sardoce family. His great, great, great grandfather made the riches at the turn of the century through loitering, blackmail, and any other monetary subjugation that was a possible fit for one's personal gains. His grandfather, Byron Sardoce, had created a family document that he called The Capitalist Manifesto. In it, he detailed various theories, furthering the concepts and perversions of Adam Smith, John Locke, and Charles Darwin. Simply stated, the manifesto preached:

Your money is who you are; it makes you divine, holy, and blessed by God. This money was worked for, was slaved for, therefore, you do indeed deserve it. To give it to those less fortunate, to those in need, to those struggling due to varied circumstance, would be a mar on Heaven's soul. This act would be unnatural and one can only assume that if carried out, one is likely under Satan's evil influence. If one works, one can gain all the money in the world. This should in fact be the goal of every man, the central theme in becoming a complete individual. Thus is our irrefutable economic system. To those who would offer a hand to a beggar-man on the street, let them burn with Stalin. Cherish your money, Sardoce's, because, there are many who will be cynical and critical of your very own free will, and will label you immoral, cheap, cold, and heartless for not aiding the worthless poor, for not destroying the perfect system of capitalism. These men are fools, socialists, communists, fascists, and deserve not the same air as you and I, my sons, my children. Competition is both necessary and natural for our very survival, as is palpable. We evolve over time, and interfering with evolution is the work of the atheist and of the wretched papist. Capitalism, I reiterate, is perfect, and is law, and one need not feel guilty in taking what one works for and deserves.

Kyla had never really discussed politics or economics with Zigmund. She figured it to have been too much trouble and too little worth to semantically argue over. This could be said of religion too, though, that far more interested her, so was more fulfilling when it did arise in conversation. She figured to have had the extreme opposite view on issues such as welfare and aid, because, after all, Zigmund, having been spoiled by the fruits of his family, likely would have seen no problem in the manifesto, since it was he who directly benefited. As hitherto mentioned, he was very much self-centred and lacked the ability to look beyond the walls of his estate. In this, he could have never truly understood what it might have been like to find oneself poor, or to have constant worry about feeding oneself and one's children. He could have never understood that the only difference betwixt him and say, a street beggar, was the simple, insignificant, unimportant, disgusting concept of coincidental circumstance. As such, Zigmund was atop the game, and had never a worry about the morality of it, about the ethics of ignorantly standing by in a powerful position while doing nothing to aid the powerless. To him, this was probably proper, who knows, noble even. Such is the perversion of life and equity.

*

The Sardoce Mansion was an edifice of grand scale. To stand nigh the front wall, one's view could have never been satisfied, for the old, maroon-coloured bricks stretched on until the eye could see no further. The structure was well maintained, but appeared quite out of place, as if stolen from a time past, lifted, as it were, from some fairytale only dreamed of in books. Large pillars characterised the make, and various unique arches were present over the many platforms and bi-levels.

Giant darkly shaded gables shaped the architecture of the roof, numbering in total, five. The three foremost gables loomed over the mansion like a spirit of burden, adding to the dreary feeling of deadness. The two rear pillars were smaller, and more lavishly coloured with various shades of cyan, and were often glimpsed shimmering in the sun when the master had turned his back.

It is nigh impossible to imagine, even as the weaver, the happenings on one solitary individual across this vast land of mortar and brick. Compared with the common abode, the estate stood approximately three to four times as high. To say it was anything but glamourous would be a certain understatement. The one curious modification was that the structure had few windows. A handful could be glanced upon the higher levels, though, the majority had been boarded shut, and eventually, had been transformed into extended sections of the wall. Though maintained, water damage persisted in certain areas of the brick, as perhaps cannot be avoided in London. Zigmund had never much taken notice, nor did he care to pay the price of repair.

The door to the mansion was solid black. It had a musty scent to it which made it strangely appealing and yet at the same time, much so very awkward. The further details are relatively unimportant. After unlocking the door, Zigmund pulled Kyla harshly in, as if trying to evade a dire threat, and slammed the door. It was dark, but the sun managed to creep in through the cracks and underneath the entrance, providing semi-ample lighting. By this point, Kyla had begun to wonder about Zigmund's sanity.

"Do you not ever ponder how many innocents abroad do not know the difference betwixt realise and *realise*?" spoke Zigmund rapidly.

Shocked, Kyla remarked, "You are truly mad aren't you? What on Earth are you speaking of, Zigmund?"

"Nothing much, I don't know, I've just been doing a fair amount of contemplation this morn. I can't seem to get around my own mind. Realise and Realise are so different, one so often used, the other used more rarely but in excellent tact."

"They've not started repeating words in the dictionary, have they, dear Zigmund?"

"No, you're not understanding. In one sense of realise, it refers to an acknowledgment, a revelation, you might say; it is comprehensive and offers understanding. As in, 'Do you *realise* what has just happened?' You see? It is like noticing, paying conscious attention to something that has happened in actuality. However, there is also the word Realise. This means to create, to bring to life, to make something real, to bring about. Break it down, you'll see, REAL-ISE, ISE meaning to make occur. As such, in realising our ambitions, willing them to certainty. Oh my, it boggles me."

"Zigmund, now I am certain you have gone mad. But thank you for the lesson in word misconceptions and ignorance. Is this all the fuss? Is this why you've called me out, to explain the subtle, infantile, and utterly simplistic difference in 'realise?' Could you have not done this over the ringer?"

"I am sorry, 't was on my mind; simply needed to alleviate that notion and get it off my chest. I've called you here for a grander reason. Did you happen upon the paper this morn?"

Suddenly, a quirky feeling ran through her blood. With hesitation, "Yyyess, why?" she responded.

"There was this odd little article regarding, of all things, thunder or something or other. And it at first struck me, much unlike anything else, in an insouciant manner, till I began to recall our conversation from under the canopy the other day. I much so believe that the thunder that may have gone unnoticed betwixt us that day is indeed the thunder to which the young chap is referring. Do you recall that Hellish bang upon our conversing?"

"Of course," Kyla thought to herself. "No, Zigmund. Cannot say I do."

"I'm simply, I don't know, having perhaps a middle life crisis, and I can't say that I can pin point why. Sure as day it is not a middle life crisis, but as of now, I suppose, I just do not wish to be alone. Do you understand?"

Kyla mostly did not understand at what he was getting. "Every individual has these moments of uncertainty, Zigmund; it is nothing to fret over and feel the need to dissect greatly." And without hesitation, Kyla proceeded to alleviate herself the awkward ramblings of her friend.

"Have you anything else on mind, dear Zigmund?"

"Frankly and honestly, a great amount, more than I had ever dreamed possible of one man, more than I knew existed in the universe. Do you know that feeling? It is said that Mozart composed entire symphonies in his head, many at once. He could not possibly write them all down since it took lengthy periods of human time to merely record one. In that, ninety five percent of his true genius was never realised or praised. Imagine that."

"You're a man of culture now, are you, Zigmund?"

"I am what I make me. I was reading a book of science last night before I descended off into slumber, the topic of creation and evolution. Have you any idea of the squabbles, my dear Kyla! Any idea at all?"

Chaotic Ocean

Pompously, to herself she gloated. "Yes, I do believe I have perhaps heard of the debate here and there. Did you happen across anything of importance or contemplation?"

"I can understand how it is that science cannot refute religion, in that they are routed in vastly different scales and methodology, science utilizing hypothesis, evaluation, and evidence, and religion working in faith and acceptance of grand ideologies passed down with time, though I cannot comprehend how it is that religion can in fact, refute science. How is it that aged fossils from all over the world, Africa, Europe, tangible proof of the past existence of a brand of humanism, can simply be overlooked, blind-sighted? Is it so that these two-legged creatures that have been clearly shown to walk upright, to hunt, to mate, are some other species wholly unrelated to man's development? How can this evidence be dismissed? How can it be looked over? Is this is an act of utter ignorance in further catering to one's own personal belief system, or is it another brand of tomfoolery that I have misjudged? I do not proclaim to be an advocate of either theory, either thought process, though I do enjoy watching the two butt heads, so to speak. Furthermore, I find that with human history comes great misunderstanding. It seems almost impossible to believe in something, God, theory, or matter of science, that is so completely antiquated and universally accepted as truth. In most cases, we find that the large of humanity, the 'consensus,' is what or who has been flawed in thinking. The individuals of our time, the Galileo's, the men who have pushed modern thought to its very limit to discover other planets and solar systems, these individualists are, to me, much more likely to be correct. I merely cannot put my heart into something that so many others so easily can. Though, I find it best not to enwrap oneself in the entanglement of age old banter."

"You are correct in some ways, Zigmund; indeed, with human history comes great misunderstanding. What you cannot fathom of dismissal, I cannot fathom of your inability to view the larger picture, to be inclusive of collective mentality, to circumstance, to upbringing, Hell, to archaic residue, even. What is most disheartening about science vs. religion, or whatever it is being called these days, is misunderstanding of course, but even more so, a discourteous disrespect of and to one another. No man of science will ever convince a man of religion, and vice versa, without some form of mutual regard. The two systems vary immensely, so much so that one puts no value to the conclusions of the other. This is why the dispute is 'age old,' why it will continue to baffle philosophers for hundreds of years. It is my feeling that to formulate a healthy and all encompassing version of existence, it will take an interlocking relationship betwixt contrasting views. It is quite possible that somewhere in the slew of arguments and stumbling blocks, there will be at least one agreement, one possibility, or one connection betwixt groups. Perhaps the architects will be two men, or two women, and in that, from that, will spawn a circular spiraling effect of new and exciting theory which just may, possibly, teach us all something about ourselves, and ultimately, about each other.

Chaotic Ocean

Though, perhaps we sometimes speak similarities and pray they are at loggerheads."

"Kyla dear, walk with me. Walk with me to my pond."

"As you wish."

*

The two strode lightly to where Zigmund's beautiful pond lay. The water was unusually full of life.

"What is moral in life, Kyla? What is proper? Can such a conclusion even be drawn from such a question rooted in such subjectivity? Is morality no more than fanaticism of popular choice in adherence of an inanely bland system? Or is morality something more. Does it perhaps transcend human bickering; does it transcend one's perception of self? Is it perhaps much more finite than we have given it credit for? In every society of life there have been established or implied laws, be it in the range from physical brutality to mental entrapment. Does this not say something about the nature of man, the very essence of our existence? Does this not perhaps bring forth the prior spoken finite idea that morality exists in and of itself, and that man is merely the vessel and not the originator?"

"Zigmund, morality perhaps transcends every thought that has ever been attributed unto it, though to say it transcends the human soul or spirit is to deceive oneself. There is nothing of morality that is not relatable to inner choice and thought. Right and wrong are words, Zigmund. They do not convey specifics, though. The very fact that laws exist gives one a false sense of universal morality, of a universal inherent life-form of sorts that lives of itself. Laws define for us what is right, wrong, and accepted. Though, by no means do they affect what we feel to be moral. Every man must make his own decision on such a matter as morality. In this he must take into account the law, punishment, and consequence, though while the law can influence our behaviors on matters of morality, it cannot control our inner thoughts and urges. Though, one must not live a moral life simply to be seen as moral to the law; one must live morally or immorally as dedication to one's own inner balance. However, perhaps moral and immoral is a false dichotomy. Was it not Hamlet who said that there is no right or wrong, yet, thinking makes it so? We are thinking mammals, Zigmund, perhaps the only of our kind with such a powerful cognition, and in this, choices have greater attachments than pure animal instinct. This is our gift. This is our blight. We must embrace our human ability, though, we must not misuse it."

"If such is the case," quipped Zigmund, "than who is to say if a man exudes morality or if he lacks it? And the greater question is, if man's inner contemplation leads to his morality, and it is not an external force, then is man responsible for his morality? If not, what is the point of being mindful that it is a subjective inner choice? One can argue if man is not responsible, then morality indeed is external and transcendental."

"Man aids in the enforcement of his own morality, though he himself is not fully or even largely responsible for its creation, however, this idea goes against the principle itself, which without hesitation, is rather quite immoral. You see, Zigmund, morality, like much else in life, comes with influence. We are driven by our parents, our peers, our elders, our neighborhoods, our families, our situations, and a slew of other x-factors that sway us. We gain knowledge and bias from all things. As such, all things are knowledgeable and biased. So, yes of course, morality is no different. Though, at a certain point, man must accept the fact that he lives on past energies and on current energies. The past he cannot control, but the current he can. Man must continually integrate new information into his past schemas, our ever-changing ideas and perceptions of the world. No one is to say who is moral or immoral, however, man can deem himself such a label if he so chooses. This is choice in purest form. However, I have never been one for labels. Kierkagaard said, 'once you label me you negate me.' Putting too much stress on morality may cause one to miss too much of the current while bewailing on too much of the past or future."

The two began to gaze into the pond together, each slightly tired of the endless banter that marked the central importance of their friendship. Kyla began to sink into a feeling of stagnancy and boredom of the evening. The water was beautifully reflective. Each could see his countenance clear as utopia.

Kyla thought silently, "I have never put forth the effort to realise how beautiful this pond is, among other creations on this estate. Perhaps I have let Zigmund's spoils sour my view of the natural goodness that co-exists in this place."

"I... I suddenly feel ill, I believe," uttered Zigmund.

His body began to quiver all over with emotion. Sweat rolled off Zigmund's forehead like a Goddess of blue, falling rain. His eyes danced uncontrollably in a daze-like manner, and he seemed unable to speak. As if bewildered on ancient soma, Zigmund's hands trembled and flailed haphazardly. Delirium was his homeostatic medium.

He seemed in an unconscious conflict with a mighty lion, the keeper of some sacred, holy tomb not to be disturbed till proper time of awakening. Though, the lion were not like any lion of normalcy. This creature were to have been jaded, scarred, with some self-evident stake or punishment in the entrapment of the slumbering being. As such, with so great a personal claim to the situation, the lion were to have been savage and cannibalistic, not to mention having a desire of pure malcontent due to such servitude and solitude. Combined with the beast's obvious frightful qualities, would lie something more, something quite brooding and seething and furtive, perhaps an inherent sadistic outlook on life and death. And though this beast an animal, a man he more so acted. Though his eyes reared instinct, cognition dost they gleamed. And, as if enraged by Zigmund, enraged to bring about all the forces from the darkness, the creature, this Hellish mistake, were to have been in physical opposition and turmoil with Zigmund. I digress.

Zigmund's body exuded an aura of instability, as if emotionally broken in half by an abusive father. He shook and shivered. He cried an ocean without one look of heart wrench upon his countenance. The man battled armies with a look of humor. What can one conclude from rationality when one's thoughts are purely irrational for no sensed reason? He had been struck dumb with in-articulation and blessed Heavenly with a sense of uncertainty.

"Dear Zigmund, what is happening to you; do you need a medical professional? Please, Zigmund, tell me of your plight, and allow me to help you!"

Just as it seemed that he had fallen into a comatose state of inner battle, as if his body's immune system were fighting off some deadly virus, a calm broke over him. Slowly, Zigmund returned to normalcy. As he peered back into the pond to see himself once more, he began to speak.

"Kyla, I am alright now. I am not sure what sickness momentarily befell me. I assure you, I am in great debt to you, merely for your concern. I am sure it is of the most sincere form. Though, as such is the case, I sense you've grown tired of speaking for the evening, and perhaps you'd like to be dismissed. You may be, if such is your desire."

Zigmund's clarity of perception shocked Kyla.

CHAPTER THREE
✢

AVANT GARDE

*

Zigmund proceeded to walk about his property after having escorted Kyla to the gate. He pondered if he had gone daft 'apeth, not quite having been able to sort out the day's happenings, and thought to himself.

"I am like any other man. I do not see time as anti-clockwise. I do not write in blood. I wake in the light and slumber in the dark. I am not entirely gormless; I am thoughtful after all. And yet, my problem lies not in having too little thought, but rather, in having an overriding stimulation of senses and ideas. I cannot make sense of myself. I feel as though I am one with someone other than myself. Is this a message from God? Surely, it is not a message from Hades of the underworld. No, no, this is not divine. It cannot be. Why did I call Kyla to my mansion? Why was I elated with conversation and emblazoned with provocation? Why am I overly entranced on this day and not on days prior? What is different; what has changed? I find nothing has, and yet, everything looks and feels new, as if I have discovered life for the first time. Yet, I am no more enlightened now than say four days or years ago. What had I done prior to ringing Kyla this morn...? Beyond reading the morning paper, I cannot recall. Perhaps a stroll outside to take in what others find beautiful, but surely nature's breeze had no hand in my altered state, no hand in my sickness earlier. There is surely a simple explanation. I would dismiss the entire concept though, if my mind would allow it, though, for some unyielding reason, it surges on, urges me to regurgitate my very thoughts and questions. Surely, further contemplation will bring forth no results, though my brain falters. Perhaps if I concentrate on some Mevillian dribble, I will be alleviated of my mental duties for the evening."

Zigmund began to focus on <u>Billy Bud</u> and its thinly veiled and unnecessary allegorical context. Not even for two moments did he find joy in the playfulness before he was struck with a notion.

"*Depression and unhappiness breed humor, for in a truly content state of being, there is no ability to further an already widened smile, thus humor is a product of the environment around it and would not exist within euphoric consciousness.*"

This thought angered him and he lamented, "Why do you force yourself upon me! Why must you invade my most private space and lure my body to succumb to your vicious mental quandaries? I am not Kyla. I do not seek to figure out the universe in one day. Leave me be to my old

Chaotic Ocean

self. This is all I wish. If nothing else, show me why I can see rather than making me blind with light."

Zigmund scurried about the shrubbery on the edges of his property, madly peering out into the streets of London, as if seeking an external mental entity that was the cause of his plight. He ran wildly across the lawn, many times about in circles, hoping to overload on rapid sensation thus forcing long-term rebel thoughts to be pushed from his accessible memory. Though, while this trick may have fooled his mind momentarily, his body was in no mood to take the constant upheaval of motion.

"Why! Where! Tell me!" Zigmund began to shout.

In his panic, he had not realised what he had accomplished. Through the muddied lawn, he had unknowingly walked about not in a haphazard manner as he desired, but in a systematic, mathematical, pattern-like formation of lettres and words engraved into the dirt. Zigmund had written: M Y   R E F L E C T I O N.

"Damn the high Heavens and sink the gates of wisdom into the sea. Even in my sporadica, I am unsafe. Even in my randomness lies thought and cognition. What subconscious Devil has befallen my actions? Has my free will fallen out to randomness? Is there even a difference betwixt the two in life? Oh stop it! My reflection, I see no mirrors about. What am I trying to tell me? What indeed!"

He began to visually scan his property, as if searching for an answer to present itself to him. Zigmund walked about, once again in an undetermined manner, with his head up to the Heavens, looking to the skies, to the clouds, and to the birds. He looked, to above all questionable things, God. Staring blankly out into space, Zigmund was perhaps hoping that he would be blessed with understanding. Vicious thoughts intruded his mind even as he searched. He began to increase his walking pace. The pace of his heart also increased. Zigmund could feel it beating and trembling inside his chest, as if calling for freedom from his pathetic body. No longer was his heart a silent internal muscle, but rather, now a creature with a life and an external feeling about it, inflicting terror along his upper torso. Zigmund's mind raced with the pulse of his blood, as did his feet to his body. Had a passerby stopped in at this very moment, the situation may have seemed rather peculiar. He was energised with fright and vigour. In Zigmund's excitement, he had managed to lose sight of where he had been trampling along the yard. Suddenly, he tripped harshly over his beautiful pond, and crashed fast into the water headfirst.

When Zigmund awoke, he was lying on his back, staring up at the sky, soaking wet in the pond. He lifted himself up to a sitting position, realising he had taken quite a harsh blow to the head. His neck ached as he stretched his arms out widely. Zigmund crawled feebly over the side of the cobblestone-bordered pond, then, bent over to bathe his face in the crystal water. He engulfed handful upon handful of refreshing moisture unto his skin. This was the most exhilarating moment in his life, so it seemed. Like a starved prisoner, he became one with the nourishment, feeding his insatiable desire. Zigmund began to breathe heavily.

Chaotic Ocean

"This is like no water I have fed upon before," he spoke aloud. He continued about, repeatedly cupping the water with his two hands pressed together. Abruptly, he ceased, staring down into the water. It was no longer clear and blue, but rather, was grey and murky. Zigmund had not a clue of what to think of this sudden alteration.

"Has the weather taken side with my psyche to increase my paranoia?" he ranted. "Have my eyes gone grey with stupidity? Surely, I have never observed such a transformation before. Surely, this is some profound absurdity. Surely, this is a trick. Who is the deceiver, though? Who would care to do such a thing? Has Kyla perhaps set this scenario to bewilder me?"

As he questioned on and on, he became shocked once again, much so to the point of mortification. Images began to glare at him from the murky water. Some seemed familiar; some did not.

"Am I hallucinating? Have I spent too much time in isolation to tell myth from fact?"

And before he could continue on, Zigmund noticed an image appear in the form of the alphabet, twenty-six lettres three dimensionally sprawled out in space like soldiers awaiting their commander. Underneath this set of lettres existed a number. 1415 flashed brightly unto the image and unto his mind. Without an ounce of contemplation, he came to know that the fourteenth lettre of the alphabet was N and the fifteenth was O, thus forming the word NO, as if answering his open ended questions, as if guiding him out of amorphous inner banter and into a queer tangibility. The pond had answered his questions, so it seemed. This was no hallucination, so it seemed. This was no effect of isolation, we must believe. Zigmund began to cry, simply due to want of a better emotion. He was confused; he was excited. He was scared beyond belief and could not fathom who or what had created this wondrous entity.

"Dare I ring for Kyla," he thought. "No, certainly not. This is mine. I own the land and the pond. She would chastise me for certain if I told her of this divine gift. She would question my sanity and my character. Who is she to be so bold, to be so righteous? I need examine every inch of this newfound mystery. Though, the sunlight wanes, and perhaps it is time to be off, to call it a day. My curiosity drives me mad with passion, though. Never the less, I must exercise control in this instance, as is proper of high social class. The morning shall perhaps bring about my purpose on this place. Perhaps all shall be well from this moment on. Perhaps."

*

Zigmund scurried quickly about, again entering into his luxurious mansion. The walls were cold with feeling. about a soulless aura marked the mansion, as the walls were mostly an amalgamation of colourless brick and grey cement filling. The ceilings were of olden creation, reaching upwards of thirty or forty feet. Dark, heavy, suede curtains protected every glass window in the house, not even allowing for proper lighting in the daytime. The windows too, like the ceiling, loomed, and were created

Chaotic Ocean

in life-enlarging fashion, spanning many feet wide and seemed ten to fifteen feet tall. Cobwebs nested toward the higher portions of the windows where Zigmund had been far too apathetic to dream of cleaning.

Giant purple pillars trademarked the design, leaving an archaic impression upon the house. There were many rooms with closed doors, and the structure carried a spacious and open feel about it, which at the same time made it quite unfeeling and wanting of life. Papers had been scattered about on porcelain end-tables, as if Zigmund had been working on something of the utmost importance, though, had neither the will nor desire to complete. Or perhaps this was purely for effect, if a passerby had ever happened to have the misfortune of having been soured by Zigmund's friendship.

His sleeping quarters lay at the base of the long stairwell, off and to the secluded side. It was actually situated directly under the staircase, as if a tunnel had been dug to shield it from something. The stairwell itself was quite winding, and protruded ostentatiously in a useless way, save for decorative aesthetics. Though, waste had never been an issue for Zigmund or for his family of prior generations, thus, they cared not for their gleaming over-consumption, over-indulgence, and over-emphasis on thing of lesser importance.

Zigmund walked quietly to his room of slumber and unlocked the door. It seemed as though he kept every door locked at all times. His bedroom gate was burgundy and wooden-looking. Upon entering, there were no electric lights. He had set up candles and oil lamps about the room, as if devolving to an earlier epoch, one of less technological burden. Perhaps this was his rationale. Perhaps he favoured the look. Shadows cast themselves frequently about the walls. The room itself was not much larger than eight feet by eight, and he enjoyed the comfort and the coziness. Zigmund felt entirely secure when in his secluded, tiny, hidden, locked, little bedroom. It was as if all worries could not force through, could not bother him. Quite contrary to the simplicity of the lighting, the sheets on his bed were red satin. Soft as silk, each night he plunged into his nightly grave and felt nothing but comfort. This night was no different. He lay down timidly upon the silk, flailed his feet up, propped his pillow, and submitted. His body welcomed the rest for the day. Zigmund thought, *modestly*, "'T is life, a God." He rested his eyes, dismissing the earlier excitement for the night, and was off into a deep, calming slumber, where in which he began to vividly dream.

*

It was set along the windy streets of New York City. The air was brisk out, as the Winter freeze had set in. With each breeze came a chilling, permeable feeling, as if clothing and skin were transparent. With each wind came the sensation of shivering tremor shiver in the chest, almost shocking the entire body into bitter submission. The disregarded newspapers howled wildly in the wind, floating homelessly from corner to corner. The cold did not affect the mentality of the working people, save for putting a scarf on, or gloves to prevent frostbite. Some, in fact,

Chaotic Ocean

increased their normal walking speed, not to escape the cold, but rather perhaps, to increase time and profitability, as was oddly motivated by the weather.

Zigmund found himself living on the streets, a commonplace beggar, wearing nothing more than a long, worn, corduroy trench coat and black sneakers that were three sizes too large. He felt his leathered unshaven countenance and looked about in bewilderment.

He thought to himself "Where am I? The States? Where is my mansion, my property, my pond, my security? I am no beggar."

He rose to his feet to notice his back and spine were agonizing him. Apparently, the rock-hard surface of the street is not as comfortable as it looks. He began to pace about, up and down the walk, to view the other beggars in his situation. He thought *empathetically*, "The poor fools, why do they choose to live like this?"

His first instinct was to search for work. Zigmund had never known the feeling of needing to, though, this is what had been burnt into his skull. He walked up to a stoplight and waited eagerly to cross while the automotive congestion was forthcoming. Unexpected cries came from the suits around him.

"Oh my! What is that stench?"

"Get off my cawner, bum!"

"Go procreate and have some more poor crack babies or something you dirty, disgusting peasant!"

The rude comments shocked Zigmund. After all, who were these commoners to speak to a man of such dignity as Zigmund?

"Brothers, fear not. Do not buy this cowl, this façade. I am like you, and you, and her. This stench is but a mere mystery. I am fortunate and rich beyond your most superfluous dreams!"

"Hah, yea sure you is; sure you is pal."

"And I'm the king of the Gawds, right? Call me Zeus."

"Go sell your lies around another cawner, Mac. Just get out of my sight. I think I'm gonna be sick."

The light turned, and the people scurried off to cross the street. Zigmund stayed behind with a confounded look upon his face. He could not figure why he was treated so poorly for no reason at all beyond public perception and decided that the cruelty of a few was most likely an exception. Zigmund then crossed the street at the next light, and began eyeing the buildings for large company names at which to potentially locate work.

"Surely, I will be named President of one of these large conglomerates. If nothing else, some other lofty position. Do I not deserve it so? I think I do."

He stumbled into the revolving glass doors of a large industrial firm. It was his picture of bliss – organised workers, diligent in duty, running all about in hopes of gaining lateral corporate movement. He walked rapidly to the front desk where a receptionist congregated, typically fashioned, with eyeglasses, a white blouse, and a grey, knee-length skirt.

Chaotic Ocean

"Madam, I seek work. I am Zigmund Sardoce, of the London Sardoce family. Can you please tell me where I might find an office or some such?"

"Sir, for one, I cannot tell if you're joking or not, but we don't accept homeless, delusional, beggars as workers. You're going to have to leave now, or security will be called."

"Madam, I am Zigmund Sardoce!" said he with an anxious tone of dejectedness in his voice. "I am fine for President or perhaps the position under that. Do you not know of my family's lineage? Have you never heard the Sardoce name before?"

"Sir, I don't care who you say you are. You're obviously poor. We don't take poor applicants. Do something good for yourself and find yourself a shelter. Maybe they can help get you on your feet. Good-bye."

Zigmund walked off, now more confused than ever. He could not fathom why she would have rejected him. All he could figure was that she was uncultured and unlearned, and had not heard of his name prior. Our character likely placed much pity on the woman's soul for this grand omission. Zigmund next decided to walk to a restaurant and order a meal. He imagined it might be 'on the house', as is said in the States.

It was still as bitter out, and he clenched his trench coat tighter. Though, this did not yield much more warmth. He had oft heard of a lofty restaurant called The Four Seasons. Zigmund figured this to have been the proper place for high dining. After some searching, he happened upon it. It was a work of art, beautifully crafted like a masterpiece. The smell of polished shoe leather and fresh designer three-piece suits emanated from the very entrance. It was a palace to him. There lay a red, velvet carpet upon the entrance floor. He walked smugly in and came to a podium. Zigmund waited anxiously to be seated among the wealthy aristocrats.

"Sir, can I help you?" condescendingly posed the host.

"Yes, my good man, I would like a table for one, to be seated among the finest of your customers."

"I am afraid to inform you," spoke the host, "that I cannot do anything of the kind. Even if I had wished to, out of sympathy, I would not. It is frankly against the law."

"Against the law to dine? Absurd! Whatever are you speaking of?"

"Sir, have you not heard of the Neo-Decretum? It was recently passed nation wide with a landslide majority."

"Neo-Decretum?" questioned Zigmund.

"Yes, that's correct. It states that no man of poor background, past or present, shall be able to dine in established restaurants. To allow such a vulgar injustice is purely immoral. The wealthy can only eat with fellow wealthy, the poor with fellow poor. Such is the way of life."

"This is mad. What of those who begin life with nothing and climb the ladder to become the wealthy?"

"Sir, you must have read too much Ayn Rand. No such thing exists except in minority cases. Rich remain rich from their past. That is how it always has and always will be. You poor, thinking you're so divine, just cannot grasp this hierarchy, can you? Please take your uselessness elsewhere."

And with that, Zigmund was escorted once again back out to the street. The wind began to blow colder, leaving him no place to go. He was hungry and bare. For the first time in his life, he was in need. However, no hand was there to give or feed. Even the invisible hand had turned its invisible back on him.

Zigmund awoke suddenly in a frightful sweat, disturbed greatly by the dream.

"Oh my, the thoughts my mind wraps me around in slumber. I become irrational in sleep. To think I had pity for myself in my pathetic station of life. Having conscious sight, I truly cannot blame that wretched host. He actually made quite a bit of sense. We might be able to use a Neo-Decretum."

And with that, he fell back to sleep without another thought for the night.

*

As the sun crept up, a new day was upon the world. Zigmund woke around half past nine, yawned grandly, and tossed his legs over the side of the bed. He slowly stood and walked over to the candles, which had remained lit through the course of the night. Bending over, Zigmund leaned in, and blew each out in a tactful manner.

Deciding to waste no further time, he eagerly strode through his mansion in the direction of the entrance, thinking, "Ah, today I shall find out what mystical power this creation harbors. I will bathe in the enlightenment."

Zigmund burst through the entrance and into the sun-lit yard. It was a beautifully harmonious day outside, unusually so, as he headed toward the pond with eager anticipation. As it came into view, it once again seemed murky and grey, as it had the day prior. Zigmund was a bit awe struck, with not a clue as what he need do to harness its command.

He said aloud, "God, if ever you are present, if ever your tool, religion, is fact, give me the strength and knowledge to lure the mystical light from this grand prognostication."

Abruptly, the pond roared, as if overcome with emotion and life, and began to ripple heavily. Zigmund could not believe what was before his eyes. Without warning, images rapidly formed in the water, as if mirages to delirious desert walkers deprived of water. He saw pictures of death, destruction, religious symbols, the crucifix, war, and mass graves. His mind also began to flicker, as if symbiotically connected with the pond, though, free enough to think upon its own will. The following came to mind, as if extracted from the depths of a conversation betwixt two battlers:

"Surely, as ever I am certain, religion is not divine, but rather, is wicked, created by the deceitful hand of the Devil. God has absolutely no stake in its name, for God's will is of purity, of holiness, of peace and oneness. Religion, assuredly, represents none of these qualities. Religion creates pain, fear, and war. We kill one another in its name and torture our fellow man for its cause. Religion creates separatism and division. It pits us against one another, ultimately testing our beliefs and faithfulness. We are at odds within ourselves and with others. This is a constant pull, a constant holy juxtaposition in which we are all unified with an inherent hatred and judgment for our brothers. We occupy countries, claim holy heritage to land, back sly political decisions, send off suicide bombers, praise murder and destruction, and fight to the death for our individualistic, selfish leaders, our Gods. Can one actually attribute a creation such as this to a God, to a greater cause? Would it not be so that if religion were nonexistent that over half of our problems would cease to be, would cease to manifest into murderous hatred? Could one not say that if religion were never realised or practiced that the world would not be more unified, more whole, and more understanding and peaceful? If not, assuredly, then we have all fallen unto this great façade, unto this benevolent tool of Lucifer. The Devil surely thrives on hate, on dying, on power and position. We have all dutifully carried out his wishes, his desires, unknowingly, and unquestioningly, all in the hope of doing what is right, taught, moral, and ethical. Is any of what we've done to each other really moral or ethical at all? Has this grand scale mentality to do the Lord's work made us any better as humans or as brothers? No, surely the answer is no. We are all slaves to our own dogma, slaves to Satan, to the underworld. There is no chance in Heaven that we will be spared or relieved of our unholy contract with the darkness which we delude mindlessly as 'good,' as being good religious followers. I beg each night for mercy. Heaven help us."

Zigmund stood back for a moment. "Where has this thought come from? Why has it struck my mind? Am I to speak this to Kyla? Is this a thought being conveyed to me through the very stones of the mysterious pond?"

It then befell him, or so he figured, that this was no accident, no mistake, but rather, divinity and foresight, true enlightenment from every meager common thought he had ever hitherto taken ownership.

"I am no normal man. I have kindled a great entity. Life from this moment on will be of the purest clarity. For I now will know all there is to know. And yet I ponder, how is it all connected, how is it that this has come to be? What event has occurred to shape this? Ah yes, I need no pond to figure this. 'T was surely the Night the God's Clashed, as is known. That treacherous thunder which was even documented in the morning paper must be at cause. Though, cause seems to have such a negative connotation tied to it. Rather, it was at praise for such a deed. And that I am the chosen puts me in forever gratitude to such the Gods, to such the weather. Yes, it all makes perfect, logical sense now that I reflect. I remember. I had a daze of thought and provocation and called Kyla over, as I was eager to speak and converse. But it was unlike any other creative mental burst. It was different. A force drove it unbeknownst to me – at the time, as it were. Though, I now know differently. I now know truth."

Chaotic Ocean

*

By this time in the morning, Kyla was off to her place of business, far across the town. She worked in a hospital on Shire Street. Her specialty was in treating mentally ill patients. Her work was as a clinical psychologist, though, the title was more honourary than anything else, each day working with various troubled souls, or more specifically, minds. Kyla was more a counselor than anything else. The hospital was situated in a fairly scenic area, with various trees and greenery lining the exterior. In Winter, of course, the trees were bare and represented but a skeletal diagram of the natural life. Some say the Winterly trees gave the hospital a sense of fright and horror. Though, to those who appreciated them, they spoke of their beautiful reach and how they were the stalwart guardians of the hospital walls.

The parking lot was rather quaint. It was large enough for its collective of usual 'customers,' though, if there were ever to have been a city wide emergency, for instance, this place of medicine would not have had the ability to save many extra lives at all. The exterior was mostly red brick, offset with the modern fashion of combining building mediums, as such with aluminum siding and various other materials.

The entrance had a modernised, revolving glass door. It was quite large and was two-ply instead of the usual quadrant dividend style. This made for easier access and easier transport of patients, if having to leave for any reason. The hospital itself was fairly new, constructed perhaps in the last ten years. The floors were off-white and squeaked when walked on due to their omnipresent lustre. Brown double doors separated the hospital into wings from A to H.

H wing was the mental ward. This is to where Kyla dutifully reported each day of her service. She was required to clock in with a receptionist in order to proceed to the office, which was located at the far end of the wing. Sometimes the overhead lights in the long, narrow hallways flickered due to insufficient wiring. The hospital had good intent of fixing the problem, though, how long one can truly ride intent is questionable. Dealing with the line of work she was in, this sometimes made the situation seem cliché, as if stolen from a low budget horror scene or some such. The door of her office was uncharacteristically yellow, unlike much of the other brown doors. She had requested this specifically, as she felt that sometimes monotony was not the best exercise for a mental patient. Though, mostly, she found kicks in the granting of such an obviously inane request. Kyla found it amazing what respect was given without an ounce of thought to a man or woman on mere merit of occupation.

She worked with various patients on and off, though, had a core handful of patients, which she diligently laboured with and knew well in personal totality. The work of the mind brought great insight to Kyla and provided her a positive outlet with which to help others.

*

Chaotic Ocean

The first of her three main patients was a younger aged woman of about twenty years named Laurna Tangly. She was about 1.68m with a slender waistline. Her hair was curled and her eyes were green. Laurna was an attractive woman with much grace but with also much insecurity. She was quite excitable and had severe neurosis of needing to succeed in life. Laurna was the paranoid type with a constant fear of being judged by others. She was quite good in her years of schooling, always attaining grades of the elite. In part, this was driven by family pressure and as well, a self-ambition to succeed and acquire monetary status in society. Laurna placed an unhealthy emphasis on working and assumed as most modern capitalists do, that if one has no job, one is quite worthless. The young woman also had a love of inanimate objects and could get much closer, emotionally, to such things rather than 'things of life,' such as children. She had been pained in the past and thus had a ubiquitous affliction to true closeness. In this, she kept her distance from any kind of real feeling. Laurna also exhibited a cynical outlook on life and to others. She was quite jaded, and her sessions with Kyla seemed characterised by venting of anger than of anything else. Though, the young woman was rather intelligent, and, while distrustful, still had a clear perception of the world.

Laurna generally scheduled tri-weekly sessions, coming in near the beginning and end of the week, with one meeting dead in the centre. This session was unlike any of her others. Kyla had been sitting in her office and peering out a window, waiting for Laurna to arrive. Laurna came in precisely two minutes early of her set time, as per usual, with a healthy amount of this-and-that of which to alleviate herself.

"Hello Laurna, how are you this eve?" said Kyla.

"I'm pretty well. I mean, you know, as well as well can be when the world acts like it does."

The sessions were always rather informal. Kyla attempted to maintain a comfortable environment so that the patient felt safe and secure enough to speak their problems and woes. She refrained from integrating too much obvious formal practice, as she felt it was cliché and antiquated, not to mention, may have made the patients feel inferior.

"How so do you mean, the way the world acts?"

"Kyla, people are sick. They do such vulgar, twisted things. And the thing that hurts most is when such practices are in our own homes. I've always thought that the ones who love you the most are also the ones who have the greatest capacity to do the most damage and inflict the most personal hurt. Strangers are purely impersonal people whose remarks might be crass and mean, though, they tend to bounce right off. You have no personal connection to these people, these strangers. Though your brother, your father, your sister, these people are the most dangerous. You have an unintentional connection with them your whole bloomin' life. When they set out to harm you, and aim for your heart, it is not often that they do not succeed in breaking your spirit for long periods of time. These people are those to shy from the most."

"Laurna, why do you feel so strongly afflicted to those around you? Is there no love from close ones to offset the occasional pain?"

Chaotic Ocean

Laurna paused for a moment and thought silently, "Sometimes, in certain situations, people do things which they simply cannot be forgiven for." She then spoke aloud.

"There are rare moments in life which I call deal breakers, doc. These moments either make a man, or destroy him. In some instances, the moments can be foreseen, and the exact happening holds a set of pre-existing expectations to either fail by or succeed through. Though, most times, the deal breakers occur out of randomness, out of unwilled, anti-fate induced sporadica. These are the moments that which we must judge ourselves by, that which by we define our character and ability to act out of our own humanness. We can look upon our past choices and recollect the various instances, however, these times are not most widely used in personal reflection. No, they are used as the noose of lucidity, as the scale of hatred and judgment by every man and woman who surrounds us. Hate is not a mutually exclusive gap from love. And the reaction time of one flashing synapse to bridge said gap is quite miniscule. Choice is free will in pure form of course, so one need not consider the actions or thoughts of others which outflow from any choice, however, it is truly advisable in life that you try not to break too many of those deals for people, in terms of how others look upon you, as you will be greatly more content having not done so. However, in the end it is all rather trivial to think of such matters in such blatantly black and white manners. Defining moments or not, I find it quite useless to waste effort in changing people's minds or actions. In the end, we all reap the harvest that we've sown, so to speak, and to me, that is the most comforting and frightening idea in the world."

"Laurna, of course there is truth in what you say, and I am not seeing you to make false your observations. However, not as a guide, or as a professional, or as a counselor, but let me say to you, that thinking how you do may keep you secure from deadly arguments, from false friendships, from ill advised relationships, and from all the viruses of the world. Though, to do so in your way is a very cold, bitter, and lifeless existence. Protection from and avoidance of all things is not security; it is death."

Laurna began to squirm in her seat. She often changed the topic when there was something said to which she did not have a response. So was her defensiveness.

"Well, you're damned if you don't grant the religious ecstasy of battling one hundred and two buffalo," said Laurna.

"Excuse me?" questioned Kyla.

"If you're happy enough to lie in a pair of shoes then sign me up to the Summer classes on Yoga. That wouldn't not be a great thing, no, yes?"

"Laurna, I fail to make any kind of rational sense as to what you are saying or getting at."

"Subjectaphors, Kyla, subjectaphors. Come on, you're the counselor here, not me."

"What is a subjectaphor, if I may ask?" spoke Kyla.

Chaotic Ocean

"A subjectaphor is a manner of speaking, derivative of subjectivity plus metaphor. If one speaks in subjectaphors, there is no rational way of ever counteracting or arguing what they say because it is all subjective, and wonderfully, also all metaphorical."

"Where on this bloody Earth did you come to find something as perversely inane as that?"

"Oh, I think I got a flyer about it on my stoop this eve before I came down for my session. Was written by a chap of the name Sardoce I think, Ziggy, yeah that's it. I guess they are being given out to all the locals. It said it was the first of many 'enlightenments' to come or some such speak. I figure hey, if some chap wants to learn me some new knowledge, then I'm all for it if all I have to do is open my door each morn."

Kyla was baffled, but attempted to rest her confusion by the wayside. The new information was somewhat unsettling, but Kyla figured to move on to additional topics of conversation. The two then spoke of relationships in general for nearly twenty additional minutes, back-and-forth like a sports match. The girl then checked her chronometer.

Oops, I think my time is up here. See you next session."

And with that Laurna was gone. Kyla, left to herself, thought, "Why in Heaven has Zigmund taken to poisoning the minds of the young with his silly gobbledygook and nonsense?" She desired to leave her place of work and speak with Zigmund, though could not abandon her patients. Kyla patiently worked on some folders and profiles as she awaited her second case.

*

Dorian Knots was a man of Russian and Asian descent, the son of a social philosopher and a political writer. He had long, silky, black hair that fell down his back in a very straight manner. He also displayed a full goatee or sorts, though, his mustache hair was not as competent as he would have liked, which gave off a scraggily, visual impression. Dorian wore a long, dark, looming trench coat and often showcased a black bandana. For this reason, many shied from him, though this was laughable, as to know him was to know a very easy going and joyous individual. He was a college student bound for medical school. In this, Dorian was extremely well read and learned, but beyond such, was a natural intellect blessed with insight and quick wittedness. Well, insight or curse is a debate for the field of philosophy to decipher. He had a history of depression, but what great thinker has never been depressed at some time in his life? Additionally, a tendency of speaking over his friends marked the man's character, and thus, he often became frustrated with humanity's want of coherent comprehension. Though, this presented much a problem to the compassionate-hearted Dorian. He was torn much of the time betwixt being kindhearted and accepting, and being sarcastic and judgmental of his fellow brethren.

Chaotic Ocean

Dorian had much love in his heart and was therefore able to maintain much bliss in and about his life, as his outlook enabled him to rise to heightened plateaus of pleasure.

He arrived three minutes late, opened the door, and in his quirky sense of humor boasted out, "How 'm I smellin'?"

"Dorian, you're a few minutes late, but it is no large deal. Please sit down so we can speak."

"Whateva you say. I was wondering something, though."

"What's that?" questioned Kyla.

"Can you do me a flavor?"

"What might that be?"

"Let me know where Subrosa is. Allow me to see how she touches your very own personal life? Is Subrosa your pitcher or catcher, hehe? Jest aside though, Kyla, why do you do what you do? Why take the time here, tedium considered, to converse with patients? Arguably, altruism is a nonexistent idea, so you're probably no different, save perhaps for reification of the concept, though, that depends on how bold and righteous you are."

Dorian was a patient who had no trouble in starting and carrying out conversations without much pre-formality.

"Dorian, you've always interested me with your delightfully hounest remarks. It is difficult today to find brutal truth in the words humans speak. But, you somehow bring it about each and every time you open your mouth. For that I thank you. But to ask of my subrosa in regard to my occupation is truly an unfair question. How does one gauge such a thing in oneself? Easy we find this task in assessing other's actions, but in our own, our subrosas remain silent, shrouded, and hidden. One would have to be quite enlightened and utterly honest with oneself to be able to see such in oneself. Though, the argument then is if this is healthy to one's sanity. Perhaps some form of unknowing is best, as a mechanism not for delusion, but for reality viewed one bit by bit at a time. If such mechanisms were not in place, there is grand possibility that we would all be in shock and direct opposition to our truest selves."

"Maybe so, but you fail to answer the question. For what latent purpose are you of this profession? Come on, it can't be that difficult to decipher. Maybe your mother left at an early age and you are looking for compensation, in helping others with their problems. Something like that, you know."

"I am sorry, Dorian, but if I could consciously pull the answer, I would. But at this moment, I cannot. I am not so bold to assume I am free of the concept and criticism, though, as stated, I simply do not know."

Dorian had long been a follower and disapprover of politics of the world. Everywhere he looked, he noticed inequality and stubbornness and disgustingly distinguished classes of people, treating each other accordingly for no good reason at all, treating others by class instead of humanness. He often enjoyed speaking of such to Kyla.

Dorian spoke, "It is so difficult these days to take heart in anything true and purposeful when so much is concentrated on money, class, and an inanely artificial lifestyle. Countries all over are perverse and conceited. The way we treat one another is purely incorrigible and inexcusable. Why!"

"Dorian, please do go on."

"Kyla, many countries are either capitalist-based or communist-based, though I suppose one can argue no true communist society has ever existed, true to original doctrine. Regardless, this I am sure you are fully aware of. Though, it upsets me that both terms have such preconceived notions about them. Is communism not simply a monetary plan like capitalism? Is it not simply a system of ownership and distribution? Confound it if it is not. However, when we hear its name we think Red Scare, we think evil, we fear for our wallets. This has been burnt into us for generations and in turn, no one has a valid, unbiased opinion of anything anymore. And can you blame them? Not to mention that the history of the term has taken on many faces, shaped by reformers and philosophers alike over the years. Can you actually blame them for being innocent and malleable? I don't think so. "

"Go on," sympathetically listened Kyla.

"Who's to say what the truest definition is for something like communism, when it may be so the that common person speaks of a broader social agenda, or of Marxism, or of Stalinism, or of Trotskyism, or of a variety of other manifestations with varying degrees of meaning? Often, many confuse practices of Party with ideas of Economy, which are certainly different. And yet it seems clear that the Term is quite certainly negative, somehow.

I do know this, though. Capitalism, on the other hand, is a false ideology. Driven by an unreal sense of everyone having equal stake and equal chance. Though, we know better. That is not how it is. Just look at the States. The top few percent own the vast majority of resources and money, while the bottom struggle to stay alive. One cannot attribute this to merely work ethic or the like, can one? If it were completely sound, perhaps it would be better, but it's not, plus the added fact that man is of the greediest animals, always urging for more and more with an insatiable need, never once thinking of necessity and equality... and yet, yet the human doctrine is rooted in equality of man, born equal, you know the speech and rants. Clearly, this is not so.

And the counterpart, communism, one can scarcely mention its name without falling prey to the trap of a false label. We hear the consonants and vowels come together, and instantly we associate the name with some kind of constant pull for power and for position. We call it communism as a generalisation when we see a suffering, controlled society. Though, is this not merely totalitarianism using communism as its preference or tool? We have specific words in our human language to mean specific things, yet people bastardise the language and come to grand misunderstandings.

One cannot say that any capitalist-based society is lacking in the pull for position and power, yet never once has the system been dogged by the totalitarian tag. If one is corrupt, why is the other a godsend? If one promotes health, why does the other necessarily promote sickness? Why is it that both are not recognised in the same?

I suppose those who have been oppressed under totalitarian dictatorships – governments using the name but not the nature of communism, have a natural aversion, and man has not been inculcated into the idea of an oppressive capitalism, so he assumes all communism is oppressive, is totalitarian. Perhaps all versions of communism have been this way, though as I mentioned, there has never been a true instance of the system of economy, unhindered by dictatorial rule, and the generalisation of the word as malicious is wholly incorrect.

Still, it makes me sob sometimes. What's most disheartening is that hardly anyone can make sense of this due to the lies and dishounesty of it all. All other things being equal, if corruption were not the norm, a communistic government free of dictatorship might be quite a desirable system. Imagine a world of everyone sharing possession and money and equality. Imagine such a place where everyone thrived of content and never once had to worry of a monetary matter. This would be bliss."

"If economic euphoria could reasonably come into being..."

"If any euphoria could come into being, but that's a philosophical debate. And likely the answer is no, as in, is unrealistic, and such a discussion as ours is mere conjecture, as communism may well continue to remain the weapon of tyranny and totalitarianism. It matters little. I am not a communist. But I am not a capitalist either. The only point I wish to make is that people who truly believe in a different social system, who do not veil a rapacious desire to beat, seize, and control under the name of an ideologically pleasant system, are not malevolent or marked of sin. A social idea such as communism may never work, may even fail if it did not suffer misnaming and misuse. But I do not wish to be branded as traitorous for merely discussing the word."

The two conversed for some time, upwards of an hour about various topics that Dorian wished to expound upon.

"Jesus."

"Pardon?" questioned Kyla.

"Now that's one bugger who's rubbed me the wrong way, and I don't mean wrong as in naughty, which would definitely be right."

Without notice, Kyla rolled her eyes, but continued the veil of interest.

"My, Dorian, how is it that you've been wronged by Jesus Christ?"

"Well," began Dorian, "I know for damn sure I didn't ask him to go and die for me. He did that all on his own, thinking I'd appreciate it after the fact. Dying for my sins... what garbage. Do you think this fine specimen before you has sinned?"

"I..."

"Yeah, yeah, course I have, but I didn't ask for the burden of his death being on my conscience. It's like, he died for humanity's collective sin, and now there's this huge collective debt for that. So, no matter what anyone does, it is all ungrateful, because, after all, how could anyone possibly live up to repay martyrdom?"

Chaotic Ocean

Kyla thought for a moment.

"I'm not quite sure a tangible debt is to be paid, Dorian. The story would more indicate a personal decision, befitting a character such as his, with consequence to him alone. No?"

Dorian fondled his stringy mustache.

"All I'm saying is that the whole thing was very *presumptuous*, to say the least. He might have, had he the common courtesy, asked a few opinions here-and-there. That's all. Sure, I'm a goddamn sinner like all the rest. But what good does dying for that do? People are no different now than they were, 'cept now they got the ability to deify someone of that status."

"If it makes you feel any better, if I'm ever feeling like a martyr, I'll surely contact you first," joked Kyla with levity.

"Heh. Okay, Kyla, I guess that is all for this time. I will go lament some more on my own, hehe. Lates."

"Good day, Dorian," remarked Kyla.

*

The third of her three patients was perhaps the most difficult to deal with and speak with on a tri-weekly basis. She was a young girl of about only fifteen years who went by Cecelia Greene. The teen was an innocent and susceptible young girl who had very angst-driven tendencies. Cecelia was generally reluctant to visit with Kyla, but was forced to do so by her parents (who had instated her on a long-term basis in the mental ward). Often, she threw tantrums and fits, and was frequently dragged off to the office. Cecelia was an exceptionally depressed person, too much so for a fifteen-year-old. Her self-image was low and was driven mostly by societal pressures. In turn, she was often bulimic, unhealthily shaping her body to regress toward nothingness. In addition, she partook in self-mutilation, perhaps never feeling quite worthy, cutting her arms and wrists from time to time in a violent manner.

Cecelia meandered into the office, seeming somewhat dejected and down. However, she was unpredictable, because as often as she was dejected, she was also quite manic. The young girl had short, boyish, died hair and a rough exterior. Her clothes were drab and unattended, which provided an interesting contrast, since in one sense, she cared for what the world viewed her as, and in the other, directly opposed everything with a keen sense of defiance. Her frame was 1.57m and very gaunt, most likely from the eating disorder. On most days, Cecelia was not in the mood to converse, though, when one could get her speaking, the girl opened up and boasted loudly like the ocean, conveying personal thoughts and secrets that she would have otherwise kept inside.

"How have you been, Cecelia?" questioned Kyla.

"What do you care? What does anyone?"

"I do care. If I didn't, I wouldn't have sessions with you twice a week, and with other patients."

Chaotic Ocean

"Whatever, Kyla; whatever gets you through. So what are you here to profess to me about today, huh? If my parents' preaching didn't work, why in the Hell do you think yours will? I don't even know you."

"Cecelia, you know better than that. I do not like to think of my profession as some kind of evangelical preaching. Such is not my purpose in speaking with you. I *am* an outlet, here to listen, to give a sympathetic ear, and hopefully to help you through some trying times."

"Sure, that's what they all say."

"I know how difficult it is to be fifteen. I too was once fifteen. I'm sure I too faced the same fears and challenges that you do now. So please, allow me help you."

Kyla's patience and understanding only seemed to infuriate the young girl more.

"Leave me alone!" she shouted angrily. "You're just like all the rest of the people who wanted to help me. Just another arsehole! So don't even try. Just belt up you bugger."

"I don't think you're being fair, Cecelia. In all honesty, I am here for you. It would bring me no greater joy than to see you happy and well-adapted."

"Well adapted? Why don't you just go the full monty and put the bullet in my head for me? I already tried to do that, love. *I got scratches all over my arms, one for each day since I fell apart. I'll show you the marks if you need proof."

"I don't need proof. I realise your troubles, dear. But let me inside your world. You needn't this front to protect you. I am not going to harm you, Cecelia. I want what's best."

"Kyla, I've been gutted my whole bloomin' life by helpful femmes and buggers like yourself, and where has it got me, all this so called help? Nowhere. Here. A mental ward. So why should I try to even help myself anymore?"

"Because, Cecelia, you owe it to yourself. If to no one else, if all exterior concern for your well-being is dismissible, you have the sole right, as an individual, to be happy, to be content. In which way you achieve such is ultimately up to you, though."

Cecelia was taken back for a moment. For perhaps an instant, Kyla's words made sense. She did not feel like fighting it anymore, but rather, submitting into an open state of innocence, and fright, and vulnerability. Cecelia began to sob.

"Oh, Kyla, I try so hard to block everyone and everything out of my life. I try so hard to be good and do what society has set forth for me. But time and again I fail miserably, I fail, and I fail, and I fail. I puke and slit and fail; that's the story of my bloomin' life."

"Dear, you are not a failure. You are a fine young lady with a good heart and good character. You've not failed in life. Why, you are only fifteen years old. A lifetime awaits you, a lifetime of happiness. You only need to learn how to kindle that, to allow yourself a good time."

"Kyla, how do I do that though?" questioned Cecelia.

Chaotic Ocean

"No question that unspecific can be answered in an easy way. I will not lie. These matters of the heart take time to mend. They take time to be reflected upon. It takes time to accept and to move on. But, thankfully, Cecelia, time is what we do have. We have plenty of it."

"Well, what do we do with it? The time, I mean?"

"Just what we are," answered Kyla. "We speak, we reflect, and we talk about the choices you've made in your life, and the actions you've taken. We talk about how you've felt and how you'd like to feel. Change is not impossible. But it takes the effort of both your mind and your body. Please, just tell me what's on your mind, what you've been lamenting lately, anything that has been upsetting you. Trust in me. We will discover happiness one day and one hour at a time. It will come. I promise you."

"Well," Cecelia said hesitantly, "I've just been thinking lately, and this may sound cliché or whatever, but, maybe if I ain't looking like them models in the States and Europe and Africa and what have you, then maybe I won't find this happiness as you've spoken of, because, what man will ever desire me if I don't look like the typical image?"

"Cecelia, I think you'll be happy to know that there have been many related studies done on this subject. And the average woman overestimates how thin she should be by a great amount, and in addition, overestimates her perception of what a male looks for. But if we're being hounest, of course everyone is self-conscious in some aspect of his or her physical form. Even the models you speak of have hang ups, just like you or I. They are no different. So, I wouldn't compare myself if I were you. I suppose what I am saying is that, for the grand portion of life, we are dealt parts, that which most times we cannot alter a great deal, for instance, our bodies, and for our prolonged happiness, it is imperative to be accepting of others for this reason, and even more so, of ourselves."

"Maybe you're right, Kyla," said Cecelia softly.

The two talked casually for the remainder of the session. Cecelia's negative image of herself concerned Kyla to a great degree, and she knew that the girl had to be handled with a vast amount of care and caution. The girl seemed obsessed with images portrayed in the media, and devoted an unhealthy amount of her time to knowing the trends. Kyla always thought to balance serious issues, such as the girl's insecurities with lighter material, so to provide for a comfortable atmosphere. It was direly important that the girl trust Kyla, but each session proved unique, providing for various degrees of success and failure.

"It appears, though, that our session's time has expired, dear. Be positive and think about what I've told you. I will look forward tremendously to our next visit. Take care."

Cecelia got up, and with a feeling of tiny hope, perhaps held her head slightly higher as she walked out. She was a fragile creature, but this session had surely raised her esteem at least one level or so.

*

Chaotic Ocean

For the remainder of the evening, Kyla worked on various forms and the like. She revisited old profiles and updated them, and reevaluated her methods as she enjoyed doing to stay vital and up to date in helping her patients. For a portion of the evening, Kyla also studied modernism in relation to mental disorders and problems. She thought it important to be encompassing of older ideas and theories with the newest methods to be learned in totality of the subject at hand.

Kyla began to think of Zigmund, as she often did while at work with not a great deal to do.

"I wonder how Zigmund is. Perhaps I should have read more into his enthusiasm the other day. Perhaps I should have stayed longer to tend to his sudden illness. I hope he is okay. Though, Zigmund has never been a sickly person, so he must have revitalised by now."

Though, her rationalisations did not placate her mind enough to entirely dismiss the idea of Zigmund falling ill, or alleviate her guilt of perhaps not doing enough for him while she was able. Nevertheless, Kyla did indeed brush the idea from her mind, denying responsibility.

What interested her even greater was a memory from a few days past, of Horris, the man at the church whom she had conversed with. Kyla thought to revisit him, as he had welcomed her to do so, as she had not quite been the same since her conversation with him. Before their encounter, she had been a confident and secure woman, with a set routine about her life that she enjoyed and felt good in. However, Kyla had been feeling different since Horris. She felt frail and insecure, as if all she had known prior was for not and useless, and now saw the hypocrisy in her own work. "How am I to counsel my patients on feelings of insecurity and worthlessness, when on another level, that is entirely how I feel?" she thought. Kyla realised that she had quite some time left till her workday was to expire, and began to read the daily paper. This London publication was odd in the fact that it had a mid-day printing, unlike the other papers that printed at night and arrived first thing in the morning. She came to a section that caught her attention.

Eugene, My Forgotten Ideological Brother
By Timothy Sleiney

The Eugenics Movement of some time ago, Paris, has long since been forgotten and ground into the sands of time with a dismissible spirit and apathy. The movement was originally created to measure human traits in order to encourage or discourage reproduction. Imagine a world in which we could eliminate childish insults, by not reprimanding the individuals for being cruel-hearted or wrongly raised, but rather, eliminating the very flaws that which these children single out and scrutinise. We would not have the trouble of our young ones being cruel to a child of low intelligence, simply because there would exist no child of low intelligence. We would not have nations and continents of obesity (scoff scoff Etas Unis) to chapper at, because we would diagnose ahead of time the likelihood of a child being predisposed to such a trouble and eliminate that possibility by not allowing certain parents to procreate. It was suggested to me sometime ago that parents should be forced to take intelligence exams prior to reproducing, in order to determine competence of child rearing, which would rid us of miscreants and juveniles alike. If you have never contemplated such a plan I implore you to smack your face, because I do not believe you. Why then if such makes so much sense has the Eugenics movement been banished to the old thinking, to archaic, silly, thought? Why have we repressed such a plan? Was it to further our ethics and do what is right for the choice of man? Was it to be moral? Tell me then, how are we moral in all that we do now, in how we treat the unequal, the lesser, the unfortunate? We might as well go the whole shebang here and not pretend to be holy and proper. I for one am of the vote to bring back this wondrous movement, in order to at least, alleviate us of this half-bottomed hypocrisy.

To herself she thought, "Tim Sleiney, why does the name ring so familiar? It seems as though I have heard it before. Odd." And with this, she let the idea fly from her mind, as she could not figure why it rung so close to her. She then turned to an obscure section of the paper, located toward the back, and happened upon another article of interest.

Chromosapien Man
By Berg Daye

In our age of information and knowledge, we often happen upon incredible discovery and wonder. However, various items remain and continue to confound our intellects. We may, of course, hypothesise our best scientific explanations, though, science is hardly encompassing of all attitudes. We still search doggedly for a link to the definitive creation of Earth. We still fathom the improbability of the Ancient Egyptians' ability to carry and load huge, immovable stones to form Pyramids. We still long for proof of the existence of a divine entity. And yet, through all of our searches, we mostly come up empty, in information and in feeling. At best, we can guess at such bewildering questions. Though, a breakthrough has occurred, that is currently under development, which is perhaps more important than any of the mysteries aforementioned above. But of even greater interest, while this discovery may be more important on a singular scale, it may also lead to the answering of such open ended questions such as the pyramids, the universe, and God. This discovery has been modestly titled, Project Chromosome 6. Through various tests and experiments and hours, our biologists and psychologists alike, through complementary tedium, have located the chromosome in the human body that has been linked to intelligence. Chromosome 6 has a vast possibility about it. In terms of gene research, it presents the opportunity to cure habitual illness. It presents the possibility, furthermore, to prevent mental illnesses and various child-born diseases. Perhaps in the far future, much like corrective eye surgery, there will be offered corrective intelligence procedures. Will this present other issues and implications? This remains to be seen. Though, the bettering of man through surgery has been a long practiced tradition. We put a deity-like quality unto doctors that is unparalleled. To say that to better one's brain is any different than a corrective spinal problem, or a hearing loss disorder, is simply absurd. Chromosome 6 will hopefully prove to bring us into a new era of mental awareness. Perhaps we can reach a new plane of existence. Perhaps we will reach a grand illuminatio, basking in our profound understanding of our very being. This project is possibly the most important research that has occurred to date. Allow me to be the first volunteer to become a Chromosapien Man.

She did not recognise the name of the author on this article, but just the same, contracted a bizarre feeling about her body, as if the article were shrouded in something more than it let on.

*

Kyla looked at the clock, only to realise a decent amount of time had passed and it was therefore time to retire for the day. She walked out of her yellow office door and back through the narrow hallway. The doc stopped in briefly with the receptionist to clock out and was off.

As Kyla proceeded through the Hospital's main entrance, the weather once again looked beautifully bleak out. She could feel her body turning numb with the cold. The clouds were thin and shapely. As she looked up into the sky, peering symbiotically at the sun breaking through the clouds, as if a child waking up for the first time with not the strength to open its eyes, she felt a flake fall onto her nose and melt into her skin, as if a reminiscent memory from but the other day. The vision of the falling flakes against the fading sun's breaking backdrop was a sight of art. The force of the snow began to increase as the flakes fell more speedily onto her clothes. The ground had a fresh salting of precipitation on it, as if a silk blanket covering an infant. Each step she took created an impressive depression in the snow. Kyla felt pure walking within nature. It felt almost like a cleansing. She thought back to a disparaging conversation she had once with Zigmund.

Zigmund: It has come to my attention that I do not enjoy the company of certain individuals. This is driven by the fact that these individuals have done things in their lives and other relationships that I do not deem proper.
Kyla: Living your life and existence through the lens of others' experiences will probably just about isolate you from every living person in the world, because, in some way, we are all connected to one another.
Zigmund: Maybe so, but one cannot be expected to be kind to a rapist, or kind to a habitual schemist, can one?
Kyla: Judging others upon past actions is unhealthy, Zigmund. It is okay to acknowledge the actions, and keep a wary eye as a causal result of the actions, but to judge on past proceedings will likely get you

Chaotic Ocean

no where. Forgiveness is essential to the life of a human, and it is necessary to do so in order to live a happy existence.
Zigmund: We shall see.

Kyla thought to herself, "My, the cynicism is amazing. It is truly a mystery how a man can live a life so full of distrust and fear."

Perhaps the thought struck as result of having been of the moment. Perhaps the snow inspired her, as beautiful weather often tends to do to folks. Perhaps she was purely being mindful of the past. Or perhaps, rather than any other explanation, Kyla was simply internalising a connection to Zigmund that she could not reason. Perhaps the connection frightened her and made her question her own actions and sanity, as to why she would have ever had the desire to continually think of and speak with a man so cold and bitter.

"This surely cannot be love, can it?" she thought with confusion. "Perhaps I have never felt true love, but I would not imagine it to come of a man so incapable of ever loving anything in the same capacity which he has for himself. Confound the thought. Zigmund is a mean, sarcastic, ungrateful bastard who will live a life of inner grief and pain. I do not wish to attain those qualities in a lover, or a love, nor would I wish those qualities on a foe of the worst nature."

She walked speedily to her old clunker in the parking lot. The windows had a slight freeze and frost upon them. Kyla took her hand and swiped it across the dirty windshield. It made her feel cold and alone. She did the same to the back window. Though, only a few minutes had passed since she had walked out the main entrance, the snow was dropping hard *like tin angels falling down. Just before entering the vehicle, Kyla heard a voice call to her.

"Lamentation's a smeg, ey?"

It was an old, homely man of nearly seventy years of age. The gentleman was of tall and slender build. He had a short, pointed beard, and was dressed in black slacks and a black, long sleeved shirt. He seemed to have been without home or destination, walking with a gimp and utilising a cane to aid in his balance.

"What was that, old timer, how did you know that I was...?"

"You just seemed deep in thought. That's all, dear. Are you troubled or in a heap of trouble?" questioned the man.

"No sir," remarked Kyla with a look of confusion. She had not even known this man and yet he was asking questions of her well-being.

"Excuse my lack of formality," exclaimed the man. "My name is Otsih Pem. I am a Russian immigrant to this country. I am looking for work, as my previous employer has little use for me of current. Are you of a managerial position in the hospital?"

"I am afraid not, Mr. Pem. I just work there. Though, I could speak with some people tomorrow if you'd like to see if there are any openings. Surely, there has to be some line of work that would suit you. What line of work did you say it was that you were in?"

"Again I must apologise, for I did not speak that to you. I was a personal assistant of sorts, though, you might say I did the Lord's work."

"Oh, well then I am sure your heart is kind, sir. And kindness is what helping others, such as in a hospital, is all about. I will do my best. Good day."

As Kyla started to once again proceed to the car, the man interrupted a second time.

"I can help you with your problems and confusion. It is more shapely and physical than you might think. All one needs is a little help from the right source."

"What?" Kyla was bewildered as to why this man was postulating about her personal existence, as to why he assumed she had a problem, and as to why he thought he could somehow help. "What problems do I have sir, and how on this Earth would you bloody know?" Kyla found herself becoming defensive. She tended to slip into common street slang when such occurred in her.

"Pardon my assumptions, Kyla, but I tend to be a good read of people. This is all. If you'd like help in whatever it is you're bewailing, then I am here to speak or aid you."

She found this somewhat ironic since her career was based on counseling people and being there for them to speak to, in the hopes of alleviating their problems.

"How did you know my name, Mr. Pem?"

"I... let us just say that I am good with names."

This somewhat frightened Kyla, though, not as much as the man's upfront demeanor. However, as was her way, she thought not to discriminate of things that she did not comprehend from the onset.

"Well sir, I have been thinking of late of my friend, Zigmund, whom I left fallen ill the other evening."

She could not understand why she was now allowing herself to divulge personal information to a stranger that she knew not but from this initial encounter.

"Ah, Zigmund, of the Sardoce estate, do you refer?"

"Yes," she exclaimed. "That is he. He has become quite infamous in these parts, I suppose."

"Zigmund is quite the model of idealism, I must say. He has well lived a life of perfection."

"Mr. Pem, you cannot be serious can you? Zigmund Sardoce is a truly questionable creature, truly troubled," said Kyla.

"Then why, Kyla, do you dwell upon the thought of him? Why do you waste your mind on such a person of such malfeasant character?"

This question did strike Kyla as one of important nature. If this stranger could so easily ascertain a flaw in her thinking, then why was it still so troublesome to her?

"That my friend," admitted Kyla, "is a wonderfully magnificent and yet simplistic question that confuses even I. I truly do not know the answer to it."

"Perhaps you do. Perhaps you've known it all along but have not allowed yourself to notice it, or bring it about to consciousness," quipped the odd man.

Chaotic Ocean

This took Kyla back. Not only was this man a complete unknown to her whom she had been conversing with, but also now, he was bold enough to suggest ideas about the dark nature of her unconscious mind. And yet, this intrigued her further, to surge on and speak more.

"What do you mean sir?"

"Oh, nothing much," answered the man.

"No, I am not offended, Mr. Pem. Please tell me to what you were referring. What do I not see of myself that relates to Zigmund?"

"Kyla, so eager... one man cannot give all the secrets of the world in a mere single speaking, can he? I am purely an old man, with perhaps just a little too much acquired cynicism in me."

"I must admit, Mr. Pem, I am entranced in your knowledge and perception. You are unlike any other I have come across before," remarked Kyla with anxious intonation.

"Perhaps I am, as you say, unlike any other," said the man in an odd tone of voice.

"It is snowing quite heavily now, Mr. Pem."

"Yes. I suppose we should retire," said he.

"About that hospital position, I will see what I can find for you tomorrow."

"Do as thou will'st; don't break your back for me. However, I will appreciate any help you can offer." "Then I will meet you here, tomorrow, at the same time, to tell you of any news or work," said Kyla.

"Sounds like a deal to me," said the man. "Tell me, what do you know of the *lapis*?"

"The lapis? I am not sure I have integrated such a term to my vocabulary, sir. What of it?"

"It is perhaps the most precious artifact in existence, which by now has become mystical lore, like a story of time forgotten by the main of society, but passed on secretly by close followers of alchemy and the like of ancient literature."

"Why do you bring such lore to conversation?" asked Kyla.

"Does it not intrigue you? Does it not burn at you, in your mind, as if you must know more because you simply do not know much at all?" remarked the strange man.

Were the man already not an odd character, this remark may have in itself sparked some interest and question. Kyla continued on with him as the snow fell angrily, as if aiming to destroy rather than to beautify. It fell hard, creating poor vision, and it became difficult to keep conversation as it engulfed the two speakers.

"Does not the cold deter you, Mr. Pem, as it makes your lip quiver?" questioned Kyla into the heavily falling snow.

"Would it not be foolish to trade valuable conversation for transitory comfort and warmth, Kyla? Cold and warm, what a divine dichotomy, wouldn't you agree?"

"Excuse me, I didn't hear what you said, the snow is blowing about too harshly," exclaimed Kyla as she maintained her balance.

"Oh, it was not important," exclaimed Mr. Pem.

Chaotic Ocean

The snow continually stampeded down from the sky. It was quite miraculous in the fashion in which it was occurring. Snow, the traditionally docile of weatherly serpents, now had transformed into a torrent of force and will.

"Whyyy did you bring up the lapis, Mr. Pem?" shouted Kyla into the air, as it became less audible out.

"I wished for you to know of it in all its glory. I have utter faith in you that you will do favour to me tomorrow when you plead for a job for a man whom you've absolutely no known connection with. And I wished to reward you for such an act."

The man reached into a knapsack he had been carrying under his arm. He pulled out slowly what seemed to have been some sort of rocklike formation. Through the snow, it seemed to exude a transparent and bright orange color. The thing was beautiful and magnificent. It was about the size of two clenched fists, but in a unified round creation. Kyla had no words to speak, for she did not know what to think. The man, however, began to speak once more.

"This is my only valuable worldly possession Kyla. It has been passed down to me through the centuries of time. My family received ownership of it somewhere in France in the 1100's, I believe," remarked Mr. Pem.

"What is it?" Kyla said hesitantly with some fright.

"My dear," said the man, "it is the greatest force to be handled. It is separate of man and his vice. It is unknown and clandestine. It is tradition. It is honour. It is purity. It is none other than the lapis! Please, take this and go; take it and keep it safe."

Kyla was bewildered. Before this conversation, she had not known of the artifact's (either mythical or factual) existence. And now an old, homeless man was claiming to have the stone in his possession, and was furthermore giving it to her as a gift for future aid. She questioned to herself if she had gone mad, and furthermore, if perhaps this man was mad.

"I am not sure I can accept your gift," she spoke sympathetically, as if addressing a child with a foolish idea.

"You do not have a choice!" said the man angrily. "Take the stone; take it now!"

He walked over to her with determination, thrust her hand open, and forcefully put the lapis inside her palm.

"Treasure it. Do not lose it. It is more important than any human force or life form."

"Mr. Pem, surely you cannot expect me..."

Before she could finish her sentence, the odd man began to fade off into the distance, into the white, crisp, snowy air. She could no longer see to where he had vanished. His voice called to her.

"I beget the light, but the darkness too is my nature; I beget the light, but the darkness TOO is my nature."

The man's voice trailed off within seconds of having repeated the odd phrase. Kyla was dumbstruck. She was frightened, and yet at the

Chaotic Ocean

same time, dually interested in her new possession. Making her way back to the vehicle, Kyla hopped in quickly, and began to drive away with the haunting line still ringing in her head. She said aloud, with almost no thought or cognition in so doing, "the darkness too is my nature."

CHAPTER FOUR
☦

A TACTILE EXISTENCE IN QUESTION

*

Within minutes, the snow began to recede into the Heavens, as if having been offended by some insincere act of unholy barbarism. It was a curious sight to see, the dead of Winter one moment, then as if a spark gone dim, the cool, brisk sight of aftermath.

Kyla had fore-planned proceeding home as a measure of safety, though, since the weather permitted, changed her mind and decided to go visit with Horris, hoping that he would remain residing in the church, as was with the previous run in. Much like her encounter with Mr. Pem, she could not truly decipher why it was that she was going to see such a man. Kyla felt her heart drawing her places that her mind would never dare.

She recounted upon her first meeting with Horris, that he was in appearance, simply a layman, even less than lay. Kyla remembered having acted judgmental, as if condemning the reasons why simpletons go to church in the first place. Horris had spoken to her in a somewhat abrasive tone, and with one quick whisk of his wit, crumbled Kyla to the grounds of her mental aptitude and made her feel like a child in limbo, in question, in doubt, rethinking every and any idea which she hitherto had thought to have understood in totality.

This bothered Kyla. The fact that she was overtaken was not bothersome, but rather, was the idea of Horris plunging into her mind and splitting it wide open, such as with craniotomies, without an once of effort, further causing her much inner grief. She longed to see him again, not to redeem herself and not to triumph in some infantilism, but more just to see him, perhaps to diminish him even in some subconsciously selfish manner. Perhaps Kyla was merely impressed. Perhaps she desired to gain knowledge from the simple man, though, this she would never admit to others or even to herself, if such were the case. Perhaps the impending visit was driven by nothing more than a curiousity of mind. Sometimes in life, events occur that of which one cannot make immediate sense. Though, as long as one follows one's curiosity and one's heart, so to speak, there will not be a great amount of damage done in terms of depriving oneself of too much life. However, such a definition could be quite manifest and obvious, without looking enough into the latent function of the event. Horses for courses.

She parked along the sidewalk, in a seemingly cleared area, as it was possibly salted within the last few minutes. Kyla opened the door of her old banger, stepped out, and stood coldly in the amounted snow. Though, only did the storm exist for a handful of minutes, it fell so wildly that it gathered nearly three or four inches on the ground. Kyla could feel it seeping in through her shoes. She proceeded toward the church. Her feet crunched in the freshly fallen snow.

She thought to herself if she had locked the doors upon exiting the car. Even though Kyla would not have admitted it, she was feeling very protective of the lapis of which she was now in possession. She thought that she would get back to that later, perhaps when she arrived home, to fully examine the artifact. "I wonder if it is mentioned in any of the history books that I own in my abode," she pondered. "Alas; one happening at a time. I hope Horris is in."

She walked up the brick steps of the church, just as she had done prior. It felt almost eerie, as if a feeling of de-ja-vu had struck. Kyla placed her hands once again on the giant, mahogany double doors and pulled them open. The church had recently let out from a mass of sorts. A foreign choir had traveled to perform a few ditties, thus, the Londonians gathered to hear the music, as it created a stir of popularity about the town. This was true of London. News spread rapidly as the townspeople were always informed of the daily rumors and poppycock talk.

As such, on this occasion, the church was quite full. It was almost as if some popular musician had come to perform upbeat versions of Protestant hymns and prayers. The aisles were full with faith and eagerness. Dedicated citisens even sacrificed the use of seats and settled humbly for the "standing room only" sections.

As Kyla walked around solemnly, she searched for the man known as Horris. It was difficult to make out faces in the heaps of praying persons. After only a few short moments, she was prepared to give in and admit defeat, though, she then experienced surprise. A man, as if out of nowhere, appeared behind her and put his hand upon Kyla's shoulder.

"Didn't think I'd fancy ya' here again, love," abruptly spoke Horris.

"Didn't think so myself," replied Kyla.

Horris was in similar drab as the last occasion when the two had first met. He looked slightly cleaner, though.

"I don't suppose ya're in for the choir festivities. 'em red, whitey blues can really sing a note though. I'm impressed with 'em. Can't fight for dogs' bollocks, but singing they can pull."

"No, Horris, I am afraid not," remarked Kyla.

"Ah then, maybe ya've come to tell me what a useless ol' bugger I am then, behavin' like I act, mouth watering over some fleeting hype or some such of the like," said Horris.

"No, actually I am not here for that reason either, Horris."

"Well com'on lady, don't say nothing. In nothing there says a lot more than in something. Least in something it sounds like effort or care, even though it's likely just bloomin' codswallop."

"I suppose you are correct, Horris. I will try to be blatantly hounest with you. It is only fair," remarked Kyla.

"Now we're making some tracks!" said Horris.

Kyla did not know how to express her feelings of uncertainty. She did not know how to convey the idea that she was unsure even to herself as to why she had desired to visit Horris for a second time.

"I suppose I will be direct. My reasons for coming here again are completely self-serving, it would seem. Perchance this is nothing more than selfishness. I feel as though am wrong to visit you, in your dwellings, expecting to speak hounestly in an open conversation when I was rather condescending on last occasion."

"Hey dovey, don't be so hard on ya'self. I ain't been rubbed anyway but everyway by everyone. Don't think ya're so special and memorable, heh," jested Horris in a light-hearted tone.

"Thank you, Horris. On that account, I will admit that I do not, for once in my life, have explanation as to why I have been drawn back here. Ever since our last encounter, I have been wrestling about my mind on the inside, rethinking all to think."

"Well a little contemplation ain't never killed no one, love."

"It's just that, you dismiss me with nothing, with no effort. And yet, I have lived my whole life creating a harsh exterior to guard against people like you. Though, it seems as though for one, my exterior is not valuable enough to blow my ego on, and possibly more disturbing, is perhaps I have been guarding all these years for nothing, with no cause. Perhaps there is nothing worth guarding in me if it can all be so easily dissected in a moment."

"Now ya' just wait right there, ya' just hold up one bloomin' minute, Kyla. I know people my whole life. Some of 'em folks are cruel; some are caring. Some be more wise than me, and some even give me an ego complex. This is the world. This is why it goes round. Surprise and revelation are good things, long as ya' can deal with 'em on an emotional level. Life ain't worth livin' if ya' can predict every part of it."

"Maybe so. Maybe you're right," said Kyla.

"Everyone's got their shite, their vices, ya' know. Don't exclude myself from 'hat list."

"Everything lately just seems so off centre. It seems as if my inner balance has been disturbed, like my compass for living a happy life has been broken and needs mending. Everyone I speak to seems to leave vague impressions on me, as if I am missing something."

"What do ya' mean by 'hat, dovey?" said Horris.

"Well, for instance, just take this conversation, on merit, on base alone, of what it is. You and I are, in essence, strangers. Yet I feel as though I can speak to you as a father, as a friend, as a challenger, or all of the above in one culmination. Do I have nothing personal in my life that I can cherish, or even discuss with those that know my very aura from years of experience? Just a short while ago, I even spoke to a Mr. Pem in the same fashion that you and I are conversing here."

"Mr. Pem??" snapped Horris.

"Yes, I believe that was the man's name," replied Kyla.

"What did he look like," asked Horris with a tone of oddity.

Kyla was slightly taken back by the sudden inquisition.

Chaotic Ocean

"Why Horris, do you know of him, or perchance know Mr. Pem personally in some capacity?"

"I once knew a man, some years ago, who went by a similar name, though, it was slightly different. I believe it was longer perhaps, perhaps Russian sounding. We had once met outside, not around the Church. We were actually good mates, dovey. Though the more and more I got ta know him, the more and more he became distant and different... bollocks. He started doing things, odd things 'hat just no man of sane mind would think normal. He used to set up what he called 'moral tests' ta see how different people would react under certain circumstances. Once he became involved in such practices, I retracted my friendship, like any self-respectin' man 'ould do. He was no longer a man 'hat I would have wanted to associate myself with. I suppose he went his own way. I went mine. Though, I'd heard he'd migrated south of here. So, it is startling to think this chap would be back for any reason. Do ya' think this is the same man, dovey?"

Kyla thought the description to have been unmistakably Mr. Pem. Though, she did not admit this to Horris. She had no allegiance to either of the strangers, though, that did not permit giving one away to the other for no reason save for mere inquisitive conversation. Kyla did not want Horris to know of the lapis stone that Mr. Pem had given to her so kindly. She thought Horris would like to see it. This she could not allow.

"No, that does not sound like the man I was referring to, Horris. It must purely be a similar name," said Kyla in a tentative voice.

Horris looked at her for a few moments, staring into her eyes without speaking. He blinked slowly and sighed.

"Well, 'hat is a relief ta know, dovey. Because if ya' had said it sounded like the same chap, then I'd have told ya' to stay away from him. But no need for 'hat now, right?"

"Correct," spoke Kyla.

"Well, I ain't sure we got anything figured in this conversation, and ya're probably not happy with the lack of result. For 'hat, I apologise. But as I extended last time, come back ta see me, and I will most likely be here, as I tend ta attend services a great deal," said Horris.

"Thank you, Horris. I truly appreciate the open invitation. I will surely take you up in the near future. Good day," said Kyla.

"Be careful. Good-bye. Extra ecclesiam nulla salus."

*

Kyla walked through the masses of people, attempting to navigate her way to the exit. Before opening the double doors, she looked back to glance Horris over one last time. He was gone. "He must be back in the crowd," she thought to herself. She swiftly opened the doors and exited the church.

She thought to herself, "What was that last quip he said to me? Had I misheard, due to the volume of the collective church crowd?"

Kyla pondered whether or not to visit with her friend, Zigmund. She thought to question him about his doorstep publishings that one of her patients had brought up. "Subjectaphors!" she thought. "The audacity." Kyla thought to speak to him of the newspaper articles that she read. She thought to tell him of the old, curious man. She thought to tell him of the lapis. She thought to tell him of her church going.

Kyla then was struck back once again. "Why must I divulge all of my life to Zigmund? Why must I feel the need to share every piece of significant happening? Why am I indebted to Zigmund? I have the right to my own mental possessions. I have the right to experience and privacy. I have the right to live life, be content, and attain knowledge about and for myself without having to gain approval, support, or inquisition of another human being. Though, I would like to check on his status of illness. And perhaps that would not be too much a sin."

Though, at this point she began to realise the rampant rationalisation that had deluded the whole of her inner thoughts. She became frustrated with herself, with her psyche, and decided to dismiss Zigmund for the evening, and instead ride home, so she could further examine the odd, intriguing gift that the old Mr. Pem had handed to her.

She proceeded to head home in an anxious manner. The streets were lined with melting snow, though had not yet acquired the fine taste of filth, which inevitably always sours the beauty of freshness. She seemed to be in a surreal state of being as she rode past the alleys, looking here and there at passersby in a drawn sense. Kyla felt truly full of energy and of spirit. Her body was as a conductor, connecting her to all the positivity of mother Earth and allowing her to bathe in its circuitry.

She was utterly excited, as if a girl experiencing the early signs of maturity for the first time, filled with fright, joy, and anticipation in one complete circular motion of destruction and creation. Kyla had not a clue as to what was running through her, though, this did not strike her as all that odd, as of course, she had already pointed to the idea of an off centre inner balance that had been altering her life.

She was forced into thought by an idea circumventing itself about her brain as tightly as the wrap of a deadly serpent.

"Intelligence, what I have based the grand portion of my life upon, is perhaps one of the greatest façades known to man. It is nothing more than the greatest reification to ever rear itself to the world. There is no such true thing as intelligence. It does not exist in and of itself. It does not have an intrinsic value that exudes out of nothingness. It is nothing more than an infantile, personalised account of value, expressed in self-servility, which aims at nothing more than to impose one's own personal system of beliefs unto another. We label things to be intelligent only when such things adhere to what we personally value in another, and in ourselves. Therefore, the definition is nothing more than a bias with a false name. Hence, I need not reify such an abstract to have so much concreteness, let alone any. There is no IQ. There is no measurement. There is no number. This is disgustingly man-made. This breeds inequality, and moreover, justification for such inequality. Who is bold enough to decide such a grand scale? Why must we feel the need, the urge, the necessity to judge one another for no reason save to satisfy our own insecure egos with a feeling of edification? How do we do so in such a lighthearted manner when it is absolutely irrefutable that humans have different propensities and different talents? How do we label such a thing as intelligence when truly the exact definition, all encompassing of all skills and intelligences, is far from our reach and grasp? Perhaps though, I comment with the word 'we' as to alleviate blame of myself."

Kyla was completely dumbfounded at her innermost thoughts, which spewed out volcanically, as if blanketing entire cities and claiming the lives of many. She was not surprised by the level of introspection or the depths to which she plunged, but rather by the spontaneity of the thoughts, of the "thin air" creation about them.

*

Kyla soon arrived to her quaint home and parked the vehicle in the drive, as per her usual routine. She reached over to the next seat where she had laid the magnificent lapis, and hesitantly moved to touch her hand to the stone. Just as Kyla began to lay her fingertips upon it, she suddenly withdrew.

"Ouch!" said she aloud. It was physically heated, as if it had been deep at work, such as with the motor of an automobile after some arduous four-hundred-mile journey. She clenched it in her coat so to avoid burn or shock, and proceeded to the door of her abode.

Kyla's house never seemed to change. It was a stalwart bastion of stability, truly immutable. The outside was ever-similar, as were the innards. Perhaps this was the woman's security. She often peered into the windows prior to entering, seemingly to ensure nothing had in fact changed. Though, perhaps this was not out of fright, but rather, out of desperation, out of hope that something would be different one day, as if she had been searching for some glorious and significant change, as may have been said of the main protagonist in Wells' Time Machine, to make blatant use of a literary simile.

This occasion was no different than ones past, and in her own little, habitual way, Kyla gazed into the window, as if a stranger searching for signs of alien life. Alas, all was the same. Though, this did not discourage her, for on this day, she felt somehow different, with a new sense of being, with a new gift, with the lapis.

Kyla once more considered ringing for Zigmund to at least inform him of her gift, or to at least create jealousy in his person. Though, she decided the better of the idea.

She felt oddly foreign even in her own dwelling. The last night she had spent there was when she dreamt of the creature, of the beastly being that seemed greatly ravaged and angry, but in some light, also some vessel of knowledge. Kyla was not in the farthest sense of the word a superstitious person, nor did she fear dreams or ghosts or any of the like dealing with the unknown. Though, it can perhaps be said that while she did not fear the unknown, she had a profound fear of its polar, conscious, converse – the inanity and ignorance of everyday waking life.

Chaotic Ocean

She decided to take the lapis into her dining room, to provide ample light in order to have an adequate view of it. Kyla also, in preparation, retired to the study for a brief moment in order to pull forth some aged historical texts to see if she could locate any kind of actual merit for which this "lapis" existed. She of course could not have put all her faith into the old Mr. Pem.

Kyla found three or four books that she thought might be of assistance in her quest for knowledge and brought the bindings back into the dining room, flicking on the light.

It glowed a magnificent orange sapphire colour. The lapis gave off a mystical sense of being, which in turn, created a symbiosis, a sharing of domination and submission. It was a sheer image of beauty. The stone was perfectly round, as if crafted by a tedious perfectionist, though, this appeared to have been no man-made creation.

Kyla ventured once again to touch the lapis, as if unaffected by the earlier near-burn that it gave off. She held no fear though, and was as confident as a dictator. Reaching slowly in, Kyla once again attempted to stroke the odd gift. It was not hot, nor did it burn her. It was cool as a northerly wind thrashing about, far from the equator. It made her feel good. It made her feel whole, as though some imperative completion had occurred. It entranced her and made her lose focus from all other worldly things.

An energy surged through her excited body. She felt as if she had detached from the realm of ordinary existence and had been thrust into a place or pure thought and oneness. Kyla could not think because to think was an action reserved to will and force of mind. The state she existed in was not body and mind, or even humanity, but rather, a surreal, charged state of energetic conceptualism unlike anything she had known before.

It was as if the space of her untapped mind had taken over the whole of her living awareness of and about herself. It was an existence of blackness, but in the blackness lay the brightest light ever seen or unseen by man. Thoughts whirled about. Kyla was full of information and knowledge. She existed in a euphoric intelligence and did not know how to handle the inflow of data without combusting like an overloaded relationship.

She quickly removed her hand from the lapis. It was as if she had been on a hallucinogenic trip, far removed from any known reality. She stood back, awestruck, unsure of what to make of the experience, one that seemed to go on for a thousand years, but only truly lasted a few seconds. To herself she thought, "What of this? What is this... stone? Why does it control me, break me, and assemble my mind, as if toying with a child?"

She continued to stand back, in stiffened fright of the object. The woman was surely insecure, and at the same time, almost bathed in the feeling that the stone gave her. It was the most empty and simultaneously complete feeling that she had ever experienced in her life. For one fleeting moment, she was everything and nothing. For one transitory, expository second, she understood life and also could not comprehend but the simplest aspects of it. This was enlightenment. This was torment.

Chaotic Ocean

Kyla resolved to put aside her personal questions for a moment, of and about this newness, and instead delved into the texts that she had brought with her to the table. She could not find much from what she had. Her books were simply not old enough and did not date back to the time when the lapis had existed, if in fact Mr. Pem was true to his word on the matter. All she could find was some vague definition that did not seem to do justice to the truth of the object.

In a book of precious stones, Kyla discovered a similar looking one to what she had. It was said to have been some part of a transformation process, in some capacity, that was used regularly in the practices of alchemy. She had known of the science of alchemy prior to this, but wished to assure herself of its official meaning. She proceeded to look it up in the dictionary and found it to be, as she had suspected, the medieval process concerned primarily with turning base metals into gold. This confused her though. The lapis was obviously no form of gold. It was a transparent and beautiful stone. So why then, would the lapis be related to some kind of gold shaping or altering process? Kyla had really no clue to the reason and hence, also delved through the other various texts at her disposal. However, not much was discovered. Beyond a purely historical context of the lapis stone, she had not an idea of its actual trace existence or purpose.

Regardless, aside from her ignorance of the object, she had discovered the truth in its existence. This was, in fact, a truly old stone, or at least, it originally had been. The idea that the object before her eyes could have been some aged, medieval stone seemed somewhat absurd to Kyla. To herself she thought, "Could this actually be of a time past, of some long forgotten geological world?" She did not believe so. Still, Kyla began to contemplate "What was the feeling that ran through my blood when I touched the lapis? Could it possibly have been an archaic feeling of knowledge? Was it due to some power unbeknownst to me? Confound it!"

And with that, she decided it best to put away the stone, in a spot where she would not feel tempted to come near or experiment with it. This was of the most difficult tasks for Kyla and her self-control and will, for the stone was truly a metaphorical object, symbolizing for all that she lived: to learn; to attain. And as such, to have restrained oneself from such an object was to exercise a certain level of maturity. She did this not to prevent danger or to stave off some unknown risk of experimenting, but simply, as a learned precaution, as she indeed wished to know more of the stone's history, more of the old man from whom she attained it, and for some striking reason which she could not mentally account for, more of Zigmund and what he had been keeping busy with in the time that she had not been with him.

Sternly making up her mind, Kyla placed it in a wooden chest in her study area. The chest was dark brown, and of ancient-looking make. The lock was reminiscent of American colonialism and shined a bright silver colour. It was deep and lined with a black-velvet interior. She did not bother to lock it, for she had never a visitor, let alone a criminal of sorts with mal-intent.

*

Her next mode of thought led to the idea of contacting Zigmund. Again, she could not explain to another, or to herself, why she was drawn once again to this man. This time, to note, was somewhat different in feeling. Instead of ringing him, Kyla decided to simply travel to his mansion, without any formal notice. It was not so much to surprise him, or to catch him off guard, but rather, purely for spontaneity's sake, or at least was the justification.

The giant gate to the mansion looked different. It was not a different colour, or of a different corrosion, but rather, appeared more stalwart almost, more protective, and perhaps, angrier than usual. It seemed to gleam at Kyla in a menacing manner, as if to pry hidden information from the chasm of her soul. She pushed it open and proceeded to enter the property.

Unexpectedly, Zigmund was standing about in the lawn, peering directly at the gate, at Kyla, as if he had been anticipating her arrival without having any notification of the event. It shocked Kyla.

"Zigmund!" she jumped back, "Whatever are you doing out here on the lawn?" questioned Kyla.

"I am not the one, surely, to whom the question of motive should be placed upon perhaps. Why is it you did not ring, my dear Kyla? Were you perhaps just around the block?"

She thought silently for a moment.

"Yes, Zigmund, I was around, walking, and so I thought to stop in," she lied. "I wished to check on you, to make sure you were in good health from the other day's sickness," she lied. "I hope you're feeling better." She lied.

"Oh, Kyla, you haven't the slightest. I am better than I have been at any time in the past. Better than life itself. I am completely refreshed with newness," replied Zigmund in an excited and childish intonation.

"Well," said Kyla, "that is a relief to hear. You gave me quite a scare. You really ought to get some help on the estate, so at least to have access to medical attention if need be."

Zigmund happened to be standing near the pond. He looked down into the water with an innocent and imperceptible expression. He then returned his eyes to his friend in order to respond.

"Hmm, I see. Worried for my health, were you?" he questioned in a somewhat condescending voice.

"Yes, Zigmund, of course," remarked Kyla.

"I see," he replied with stolidity. "So how have you been keeping yourself of late? A mere day seems like a lifetime when I do not get to speak with you. As you know, I do not have many visitors."

Kyla thought for a moment to tell Zigmund, at this time, of the lapis stone. She thought maybe he would understand her curiosity and precaution. Though, at the same time she thought maybe it would be best to keep it shrouded from his cynical eye. Perhaps he would have made a mockery of the thing, or not believed her. Perhaps he would have done the opposite and made an exploitation out of the gift. Neither response did Kyla long for, thus, it was difficult to decide whether or not to share the statement.

"Work, sleep, eat. You know the tiresome cycle of life," she replied, uninterested.

"You're keeping something from me, Kyla," Zigmund responded confidently.

She was unsure how to receive his comment. He had not known of her adventures of late; he could not have possibly known of anything that she was thinking. This made Kyla paranoid, as if veracity had once again eluded her, and as if this had been another disturbing dream.

"W...hat?" said she in a hesitant but questioning voice.

He stared into her eyes with much purpose. Zigmund exhaled tiredly, as if dealing with the troubles of a stubborn two-year-old known to have been withholding some important piece of information, hidden out of immaturity.

"You have not gone hard of hearing, have you, Kyla? I asked what it is that you are keeping from me. What have you in your heart that you have not told me of? What have you come here to speak to me about but have not yet vocalised for whatever timid reason?"

"I do not enjoy your audacity, Zigmund. I do not enjoy your tone either. What has gotten into you? Why must this conversation be something of an inquisition?"

She grew defensive, stupid with pride and self-safety. For perhaps a moment, she had, in some sense, become Zigmund.

"Oh come now, Kyla. Why must we play this childish game? You are obviously here for some reason. It does not take a mystic to see such. When you arrive, we speak, converse of various topics. Why should this occasion be any different at all? I simply do not have the time for such a half-arsed, round about."

Again, Zigmund's sense of confidence and clarity took Kyla back. She had not known him to be this kind of a man. Conversely, she had hitherto known him to be a frightened, insecure, childish fool. She thought, "Have the roles truly reversed? Have I become the essence of what I dislike? Have I been metamorphosised into some Demon creature?"

"Alright old friend," she began to say, "you are correct for once. This I admit. Perhaps I have much agenda in seeing you today. Perhaps I have much on my mind to discuss, possibly to even alleviate and let free. Maybe for once you have taken the reigns while I have been banished to the silent world of second place."

Zigmund looked down to the pond as Kyla was speaking to him. He saw various images. The one that most obtruded his eyes was of a fountain of youth, and a woman bathing in its power and knowledge. The woman then opened a compartment in her chest and decidedly hid the knowledge from the entire world, to use selfishly for only herself.

"Perhaps you are hiding something important from me, Kyla. Perhaps there is something you do not wish to share."

Again, this confused Kyla greatly, as she had no clue as to how Zigmund would have had such insight into such matters. She once again thought silently, "How is he perceiving such in me? Am I truly this transparent?" After some moments of inner contemplation and fright, she composed herself and spoke back in a confident manner, something she had been lacking of late.

"Zigmund, I admit all and nothing to you. Maybe it is so that I have ideas to discuss. Though, maybe I do not." Her eyes exuded a certain cunningness about them. "But I do not owe my soul to you. I do not owe you the wholeness of my existence, the totality of every thought that I keep. I do not owe you explanation or fact."

Zigmund, tired of probing Kyla for what she was keeping, walked away from the pond, and sauntered with the woman to a different section of the property. He thought to himself, "Surely my power was recognised. Surely, this pond has made me great, and Kyla sees this, and there is nothing to be done. Though, for today, I shall retire to normalcy, as perhaps there is much more to learn of the pond before fully purging Kyla's essence."

"Alright, Kyla. That is fair enough, I suppose. Apologies for my digging. Perhaps I have changed some."

He used the word "changed," as if out of normal conversation, though, it was actually a conscious decision to make Kyla aware of his newness. However, rationally speaking, he was likely ill-prepared to reveal his pond's mystical power, though, on some level, longed to, just as she longed to tell him of the lapis stone.

"Changed have you?" said Kyla.

She picked up on the word just as he had wished.

"Well, man changes. This is fact, Kyla. If we do not change, what is the point of living?"

"Obligatorily, change is no better than brand name of popularity, my friend. Change is, however, the most meaningful experience, if you know why it occurs and are prepared to embrace it. It is of my opinion that it is vital for each human to change, to grow, to be, to advance in thought and heart, to mature in a special kind of way unique only to our species. We must change with time and experience. If we do not, we are simply stuck in set patterns, destined to succumb to an unhappy limbo of sorts."

"Meaningful ey? What is meaning, Kyla? Perhaps you attribute too much to the word. Could it not be that all known or conceived values are without a base? Or possibly that life itself is devoid of meaning?"

"You've taken to Nihilism now, have you?" she questioned.

"No, Kyla. I am simply putting the scenario forth. Perhaps it is even more vital to consider all the subjectivity in the world, rather than to change about one's own idea of what produces happiness. Though, such is nothing more than a delusion. What of that?"

Chaotic Ocean

"Speak only powerful words when prepared to make powerful justifications, my friend. Speak only justly when prepared to use powerful rationale. And speak only rationally when prepared to be delusional. To each his own, Zigmund."

"You always quite amaze me with your semantics," said Zigmund.

"Semantics, glaring truths, whichever."

"A scop, Kyla, as referenced in early literature," condescendingly began Zigmund, "is a man who tells stories and tales. The scop takes common events and shapes them to make them sound different and beautiful. I suppose what I am asking is this: do you think the arts, poetry, music, literature, are all merely lofty forms of delusion?"

"Zigmund, *I think everyone I have ever met is deluded in some way or another. Sometimes delusion is called for or even healthy. Perhaps part of us needs it. As per your question, I think sometimes delusions can be some of the most beautiful poems, thought and awe inspiring. Maybe inspiration in itself is delusional, but still, would I trade the delusions to no longer see the beauty? Never."

"Kyla, do you think that beauty exists, or perhaps we merely believe it to?" questioned Zigmund.

"*In my heart, I know when I view certain things, I become overwhelmed. I know there is beauty in the world that makes me fall to my knees and weep. Is it a delusion? Possibly. Is it real and true? I feel it. I perceive it to be there. Thus, as far as my reality is concerned, yes."

"This view is not of the most comfort though, Kyla," replied Zigmund in a drawn back tone.

"The view of truth is not always the most comforting. In most cases, it is quite the opposite. Such is the way."

"This is what I do not understand," exclaimed Zigmund. "You speak of the truth, yet at the same time, you speak of the inherent delusion of the world. One can surely rationalise anything one thinks. What is the point to thinking when one knows this? One cannot know anything is right, but one can rationalise anything to be. How is this better than believing in black magic? It seems we are no less delusional than psychotics, but since we think ourselves to be, courtesy rationale, we are. It is difficult to live in such a way. Surely most humans do not ever think of issues as this, perhaps because they do not have the comprehension to course into it, or admit their own flaws, but I do."

"Are you trying to convince me, or perhaps yourself, Zigmund?"

"Kyla," Zigmund said in a defensive manner.

"What will you have me say then, Zigmund? The power of the rationale is of the greatest force. Does this mean that reality does not exist or is not worth finding? Of course not. Does this mean that one needs to incorporate all the facts? Yes. However, one must note and understand that while reality is supposedly the separation of myth and fact, dream and waking cognition, such a dichotomy is false. Not all is so easily divisible. Reality too is merely a perception, just as in perception there lays delusion. So to say that reality is free of delusion, is in full, inaccurate. One must be extremely close-minded to believe so, or in the least, simple with truly crude methods of thought. Again, this is not a comforting idea. Though, perhaps no one can be, in totality genuine, as it is not human nature to be so."

"I don't know, Kyla."

"You are exactly right. If longing to be true to thyself, Zigmund, speak those four, beautiful words of uncertainty and bask in them. It is only when we say the opposite that we get our souls in trouble. Of course though, one must intend them out of hounesty, not out of the hope to escape contradiction."

"How then have you come to so many conclusions of the world and the human element of thought, Kyla? Surely, no philosopher has taken comfort in not knowing. If such were the case, we would have thousands of empty novels without any useful ideas."

"Correct. Banter of ideas, confrontation, contradiction, rethinking, again and again, proof, denial, delusion. This is the life of the philosopher, as you mention. It is not a life of simple enjoyment. It is a life of constant struggle and turmoil. Most are not prepared for such and leave the contemplation up to these men and women. However, it is perhaps in this turmoil that one can attain the truer happiness. I am no philosopher, Zigmund, but I do include myself in this method of thought."

"Perhaps for not much longer," Zigmund said in a snide tone, as if hinting that she would no longer exude thinking superiority over him.

"Excuse me?" replied Kyla.

"Oh nothing, Kyla. It was nothing at all," said Zigmund covertly. "What are your plans for the rest of the evening? Perhaps you've some work to attend of your patients?"

Zigmund seemed to have been changing the topic at hand, as if to deflect attention.

"No, Zigmund, I do not. I generally keep my work to my office. If one allows one's career to fully infest one's personal space, one will become insane with purpose."

"Well, that is good methodology, I suppose."

"Though, you would probably know little of the issue, I can imagine my friend," scoffed Kyla.

"I resent that, Kyla."

"Resent all you like, Zigmund. Object to anything that I say that is untrue or falsified. Do not resent only because the truth insults your honour."

"Always taking defense to all, just as usual. That is what I love of you, the grand predictability. And surely, such is what drives you the most mad of your own character. Quite humorous when one thinks of it."

Kyla did not feel enjoy placating Zigmund's wounded ego. She took the comment in stride and pretended as if it did not offend her in the least sense of the word. She looked about the property; it was quite nice. The images of his rose garden had faded with the advent of falling snow. It cascaded about their outlines in a way that could be described only as flawless and breathtaking. Kyla thought to ask Zigmund out for the evening, not romantically by any means, but perhaps, for if nothing more,

Chaotic Ocean

to abdicate him of isolation. She saw the beauty that surrounded him, but she pondered as to whether or not he could see one one-hundredth of it all. Kyla pondered how much of it he could actually appreciate. Perhaps when one is given everything one can appreciate nothing. One must know the depths of servitude and ugliness before one can value anything of ease and aesthetic magnificence.

To herself she thought, "What has Zigmund, truly? His life, while externally glamourous and recognised, is most likely unfulfilling and marred by utter emptiness."

"Zigmund, I reciprocate the question. What have you to do for the evening? Perhaps sleep or sit about and futz with your thumbs?"

"In questioning, I suppose that your implication is you've nothing yourself to pay duty to today. As for I, I do not have immediate plans. I have some self-discovery as always on the agenda. I have some contemplation written down to attend to. Perhaps some research on various ideas of time. You know, the usual that I have to govern myself with. Why do you ask?"

"I thought perhaps there would be something to do, around the town?" said Kyla with bounding innocence.

"The town!" replied Zigmund, as if disgusted by the menial existence of the commoners who congregated about the city.

"Yes, Zigmund, the town. The town is where people go to alter the repetitive subsistence of their dull, little lives," said Kyla in a voice heavy with sarcasm.

"Bah. I suppose. But what has one to do among people? What has this city that I do not own in my mansion. Fine art, statues, sculptures... I have all of that. What lies in the town that presents minds like you and I a challenge or a glimmer of interest?"

"You'd be surprised when you search through different eyes. I know I have been of late," remarked Kyla.

"Perhaps."

"I have not been to the Exmoor Park in some time. I know it is becoming late out, but the snow must be a sight around the park at this time. What do you say?"

"I suppose I can stomach the park. I must change first. Wait here; I will return outside in just a few."

*

He turned round about and receded back into the mansion. Kyla was excited to have gotten Zigmund to vacate his premises. She thought it would be good for him. Also, she thought it would be good for herself as well. Perhaps what Kyla had needed was a peaceful stroll, to set her mind free of all the conflicting ideas, the lapis, Zigmund's odd behavior, the doorstep publishings that were rumored of Zigmund's distribution, and so on.

She thought, "Actually, now that it is upon me, I do realise that I've not yet inquired as to why or how Zigmund has been publishing papers and putting them about on innocent people's stoops. Perhaps I should inquire when he comes out of the mansion. Or perhaps I should not create a precursor to the park. That might be detrimental to be finding any kind of peace in this visit. Game time decision."

Zigmund was inside his room, changing his outfit about to suit that of properness of occasion. He began to think to himself:

"Why am I being dragged about? What is this foul play? Is it something of a trick? Is it a trap? Am I being lured for some reason beyond my knowledge? What is it that Kyla is up to? Perhaps I should have been sterner. Perhaps I should have lain my foot about the ground and spoken in a wholesome tone to reply her with 'negative,' as surely as my mind is human. Perhaps she sees me as weak. How incorrigible! This is a travesty. I am not weak willed or minded anymore. I am Zigmund Sardoce, I cry to Heaven, owner of everything worth owning... and more! I am Zigmund Sardoce, keeper of the gate of knowledge and man, keeper of the pond. I am Zigmund Sardoce, I say again."

He finished throwing on his new dress and meandered casually out of the room, as always, locking each door that had had the ability for fastening. Zigmund carried the keys with him to all doors at all times, and the chain seemed to endlessly loom on, as if an ocean unto a horizon. He walked out to Kyla. She had remained, and now Zigmund recognised a certain exuberance in her eyes. He could not discern if it was slyness or rather, genuine excitement for reasons wholly pure.

"How do you fancy my look?" he asked.

"How do I fancy it? Why, Zigmund, you mustn't take up the London speak now, simply because we are going out into the huddled masses of slang fighting, frenzied, fast quipped fellows. But yes, you look quite fine and distinguishable."

"Why thank you," retorted he.

Kyla looked down to his arm. She noticed that he had some minor cuts and bruises upon it.

"Are you alright, Zigmund?" said Kyla, looking down and pointing to the lacerations.

Zigmund was filled with fright. He thought to himself, "Does she know of my fall over the pond? How can one explain abrasions if one does not fall or trip over something? Is she onto me? I must retort with something believable to deflect her attention from the injury. He thought, for a moment in time.

"It is one of those sleep mysteries, my dear. Perhaps I was walking in my slumber last night and fell upon something in the room. I woke up with these in the morn. But rest assured, they do not hurt all that much. I have been meaning to put an elastor plaster on them, but haven't found the time or effort as of yet."

"Well, as long as you are okay, and that is how you are feeling. I worry for you, my friend."

"I am sure you do." He wasn't sure.

"Okay then, so are we ready to hop to the park?"

"I prefer motoring, but that's just me," he joked.

Chaotic Ocean

Kyla laughed obligatorily at the ill-humoured jesting. Zigmund did not own anything of a banger such as Kyla. His automobile was of classic stature. It was freshly polished, rarely used, and ran quite beautifully, as if the hum of a sleeping child. It was dark purple, like the colour of the royals in ancient Rome. It was sleek and slender, with an expensively fabricated interior.

"Do you ever drive this old, beat up, worthless, withered junkard?" Kyla mocked.

"On occasion."

"I am surprised you even know how to drive, Zigmund. I would think that a man of your power would have house hands and hired butlers to do the so-called dirty work."

"Well, I have thought of it," replied he.

"And?"

"And I suppose in order to have help such as you have described, one needs to have an immense amount of trust for other humans. Frankly, I do not trust anyone but one man. Myself. It is a take and take world. Have to have your protection about. Do not be mistaken, Kyla. At any chance that presents itself, the average person will jump up to slice about your throat to steal even one tiny portion of your wealth and power."

"Hopefully you don't exclude yourself."

"What's that?"

"Nothing, nothing at all," said Kyla.

"You understand, don't you? I mean, if nothing else, you must have gained some perspective of man from dealing with your patients on a day-to-day routine."

"I understand everything you are saying. You make *complete* sense," she placated.

"Okay, let us leave the mansion, to the park. Hopefully we will be provided a situation of interest somewhere along the way, but somehow, my heart tells me it is doubtful."

"Why don't we let the actuality of life decide that, and leave speculation to the dead skeptics," remarked Kyla.

"So be it."

*

The two vacated the property, both somewhat unsure about the adventure to be. Kyla was befuddled about her actions, as to why she had actually probed and protested for creating an event in which Zigmund could partake. Though, confusion was of the most commonplace emotions that she had had in recent hours and days, and hence, decided to go with it, so to speak, and not over-think the situation.

As unsure as Kyla had been of her actions, Zigmund was as suspicious of her motives. It seemed as if he had developed a paranoia of sorts, as if every slice of existence was based around the exposure of his grand secret, his grand treasure. He thought to watch Kyla with a close eye. Zigmund thought to pay close attention to the conversation, to discern if any of her spoken metaphors were foreshadowing to some

Chaotic Ocean

knowledge of his pond. He too, though, decided to go of the moment. Possibly, a small part of him even welcomed a break from the isolation that was his life.

The two figured themselves entirely dissimilar, like polar opposites circumventing the globe. Yet, at the same time, unknown to one another, they upheld the same fears, insecurities, and questions of life. They had also similar *secrets*.

CHAPTER FIVE
✠

NOESIS NOESEOS

*

Aₛ the two motored along, the remnants of the falling sun faded away into nothingness. The streets were snow covered, and the wind was moderately brisk. Glaring streetlights gleamed down upon the commoners in a wholesome, orange tint. Blackness had befallen the city skyline, as the moon slowly came into existence, as if a forgotten serpent rising up triumphantly from the depths of the bluest sea. The stars were ever-present, like the actualisation of unrealised love. They blanketed the skies and Heavens, enveloping all the Earthly plasma of the cosmos. The London night scenery was a thing of utter beauty to those who took the time to appreciate it.

The two did not speak along the way. They allowed for silence and informal expression to convey whatever they had wished to divulge to one another. It was a form of release and almost, submission. Perhaps the submission was to each other, or rather, to each themself. It is possible, though, that this form of non-vocalised expression was merely the safest mode of thought for the time being, without giving away too much to entire transparency of character.

Often did the two look upon one another, hinting at the fact that there were indeed greater thoughts looming about, rather than the typical back-and-forth semantical banter. Kyla, of course, wished to tell Zigmund of the lapis stone. She desired dearly to share her secret with another, to allow someone else to bask in the curiosity of the thing. Conversely, Zigmund had also desired to speak of the pond, but rather than to share, he had wished to destroy Kyla, of sorts, verbally, to go beyond the usual causal dissection of discussion that he tended to fall on the shallow end of, and surge far ahead in an utter thoughtful explosion, knocking Kyla unto her knees to beg for mercy and knowledge. This was his dream. Though, perhaps he was unaware of the latency that it dually harvested.

Finally, after some minutes, Zigmund and Kyla arrived at Exmoor Park. They parked on a side street that neared the place, and walked the remaining distance, which was only a far stone's throw away. The park looked empty to them. Not many Londoners happened about it after nightfall. Though, a few brave souls, perhaps in search of Winterly beauty, could be seen here and there, flashing photos and dancing in the twilight. The two stepped into the main entrance, slowly, and began to walk about.

"It is rather nice, Kyla," spoke Zigmund.

"I must concur. To me, snow is the purest of all natural beauties. It engulfs me, makes me one with it, draws me to be more than I could have ever been on my own."

"Ah, yes."

"It is okay, Zigmund, I would not expect you to understand any kind of emotion of that nature," replied Kyla.

"Again, Kyla, as I have perpetually attempted to inform you of, perhaps you do not know people as well as you proclaim to. Perhaps they can be, and are, more than you ever aim to give them credit for."

"Do you think I enjoy being of this mind, of this opinion, Zigmund? Frankly, I do not. I wish your words were true."

"So allow them to be," spoke Zigmund.

"I am awaiting the proof. I would love to be proved wrong on most of my opinions of the world, because I realise perhaps they are far too cynical, maybe far too hounest. I would like to bask in disbelief of what I have always felt and thought. Though, thus far, such an event has not taken place. Or if it has, it has not come around to my corner of town yet."

"Perhaps your day of reckoning is sooner than you think," said Zigmund.

A few passersby could be seen with oil lit lamps, leading their ways with a dimmer of northerly hope, searching for direction in their lives, in a place, at a time, where direction, sight, was the thing of greatest uncertainty. The park began to fall darker and darker. The snow on the moistened ground could no longer be discerned as untarnished white. It had taken on a look of ambiguity, overcome by a force that it exuded no will over, that it was slave to, the ever-fading sun and the ever-circling moon.

"What do you suppose the external passersby think of this, of walking in Exmoor Park, at a time when the gen-pop would not dare think of such an act, Hell, even such the contemplation of the thought of such an act?" asked Zigmund.

"Why do you suppose I care?"

"Well, one must have some opinion on the matter. It does not need to be implicitly important for one to at least have an idea on a trivial matter."

"That is correct, Zigmund; it is trivial. I do not take part in wasting my time here on this Earth with the trivial thoughts of external perception."

"Oh, you do not?" asked Zigmund in a snide voice.

Kyla paused for a moment.

"I don't think anything of what they think. I feel they are unfortunate to miss out on something such as this, of this nature and beauty, all due to some sheltered schema of the world, harvested perhaps, as an ever greater tragedy, by but a human unto them, as if a passed down, inherited, ignorant plague of humanity."

"So why not culture them, as it were, as to share with them the world that only you can see?" questioned Zigmund.

Chaotic Ocean

"I am not so bold to impose superiority of character or idea Zigmund. I allow others to live how they have to. In this, the best I can offer is compassion, so to not judge others on how they differ from myself, understanding that even I harbor the same ill-fated qualities that I speak of in others, in that the sight of such qualities is merely skewed in each of us. Thinking, as you say, to 'culture' them, is the type of thought that leads to such horrors as ethnic cleansing and extreme oppression of difference of opinion. Such is purely unhealthy and wicked."

The two began to walk once again, drifting toward a different section of the park, and continued to bantered on. Kyla felt failure growing in her blood, as she realised that arguing in the park about the same nonsense was no different or better than arguing upon Zigmund's property. She was the same person, as was he. The ideas were identical. Place was the only altered notion. She was no more secure in herself. She had no further easing thoughts about her unexplainable desire or need to converse with this man. Kyla felt at a loss for words, even though her words were 'de la mer,' or of plentiful resource. A feeling of hopelessness overwhelmed her body. A few days prior, to know Kyla was to know warmth of confidence and direction. Though, in the past hours and days, she had become one with the unknown, as if having been sewn into the black space of the universe, creating a link to everything, but dually, existing too tiny to realise one's own part in the mastery.

She began to think to herself, "Is this perhaps the transformation that which my life is taking? Am I destined to be of this mind, of these questions, of this lamenting for eons of time till I no longer am breathing?"

Even more harrowing to her was her next thought.

"Are these feelings of healthy nature? Perhaps they are normal! Perhaps they are of natural progression and I should not fear them, but instead, embrace them! Am I doomed to this, simply because it is what has been set for me? Is it actually possible that this is not an error of thought, not some power to overcome, not some obstacle to mentally tackle, but rather, it is just life?"

She thought this could not possibly be the natural progression that life had been ordered to dictate. Kyla would not allow her mind to think such horrid thoughts. A statement of Zigmund's then interrupted her introspection.

"What do you take of the unknown, Kyla?" asked Zigmund. It was to Kyla, as if he had been inside her mind, probing for the correct terminology to break her very spirit. Though, she quickly collected herself to wily form a calm façade.

"Take it for what it is, my friend, unknown. One can leave it at that, or one can change it, to make it different, to make it actually known, as if to uncover a mystery."

"How does one do such a thing?"

Kyla thought for a moment and replied in a character of half-truth, half-lie. She meant what she said; it was genuine, but at the same time, she was unsure of herself and even her ideas.

"Fear, my friend. For instance," she began to point about,

"have you ever walked through the forest in daylight to explore all the wonders of nature? I know I have. Yet, at the same time, asked the same question, how many would answer that they have undertaken such an exploration in pitch darkness? I would gather not many. People fear what they cannot see, feel, and touch. They fear darkness for a slew of unwarranted reasons. This is what their lives consist of – the inability to ever explore life in an hounest way, to see it for how beautiful it truly is. Have you ever considered, that fear itself is a thing of beauty? Or the domination of it, or even the precise submission to it... Can you not call such occurrences beautiful and perfect? Has it never occurred to most humans that fear is no different than knowledge? Has it never occurred to most that it is our duty to embrace the fear, to even adhere and crumble to it, to bathe in it, so to become one with its beautiful, intrinsic essence?"

It was ambiguous as to if Kyla had been chanting to convey a point to Zigmund out of mere conversation, or if trying to doggedly convince herself of her own views.

"And you, Kyla?"

"What of me, Zigmund?"

"Is this how you live life, how you act and behave in regard to your own theories of such things?"

Kyla did not like Zigmund's condescending tone. It had seemed as if now and then he had been posing tiny questions, giving off snide remarks, behaving purposely sly and suspicious. She observed this in him very easily and transparently. Kyla wondered if the same had been subconsciously true of her too.

"It certainly is," she replied in a defensive and very *convincing* manner.

"I see."

"I should hope so, Zigmund."

Kyla had become slightly agitated with the whole of Zigmund's comments. She noticed a change in him. It was as if he had been more interested in her comments, and was looking to prove her wrong in some self-serving manner, rather than to give hounest remarks and statements. Even his initial comments and questions, which spurred the banter, had been slightly aloof. She could not ascertain if this was an actual difference in Zigmund, or perhaps, rather, merely a difference in herself.

*

It was nearly all-dark out now. Passersby no longer seemed like men, but rather, sliding shadows, as if horrid creatures had consumed the land and Kyla and Zigmund had been the last to survive the onslaught of some foul and wretched soul-stealing ritual. This however, did not faze Kyla, or at least, she would not allow it to strike fear in her, not after having given the monologue on walking in the forest upon nightfall.

"It grows black out," remarked Zigmund.

"How observant of you," snapped Kyla.

"Should we retire soon?"

Chaotic Ocean

"Does the dark send shivers down your body, my friend? Does it leave you too uncomfortable?" spoke Kyla.

"It leaves me just fine, thank you," he proudly replied, not allowing himself to have been the one first to submission.

Though, it did seem quite ominous out. Both Kyla and Zigmund felt this independently of each other. The passersby from forth the street had nearly ceased, as well as had the fellow park adventurers. London was not extremely well known for having had an infamous crime record, though, darkness has its effect on the minds of many sane and normal people. It is like archaic lore, passed forth from generation to generation, as an inherent sign of evil and clandestine behavior. One cannot help but quiver in its eerie and strangling presence, it would seem.

Suddenly, as the two were walking about, a sight of horrible, animalistic imagery materialised before them, as if a nightmare leaping into realistic fruition. A man, shrouded by the seclusion of trees and shrubs, could be seen whipping his arms about. The awful cries of a woman shrieked through the sky like a hammer unto steel. Louder and louder did she scream, as the man exuded every single bit of power over her.

"Kyla! What is happening to that woman? Should we edge closer?"

He was in utter fright as he spoke the timid words. Zigmund was truly afraid in every essence.

"We must," said Kyla confidently.

The two began to inch closer at a medium pace, in hopes of perhaps preventing whatever act of Hell was occurring. As they did so, they realised that the man had set a lantern about the ground. The incandescent shadows it projected were of the most macabre nature. As they peered in, the actuality before them was an utter, disgusting, abomination of man and his power.

He had been lashing some type of sharp, metallic object about. The woman lay on the ground half-naked, with formidable marks all over her body. The man had been plunging the object into her defenseless, frail being, repeatedly, as if not to strike mathematically, but rather, to take sadistic pleasure in the act of vulgarity. It seemed like he was striking against her innocence, ripping the very reification from her soul.

She was of auburn hair, with eyes green as the foliage of Fall, with the countenance of Heaven. It was unclear if she had been an acquaintance of the aggressor or not, a sister, a sexual interest, or even simply, a random passerby. Zigmund and Kyla were frozen in disbelief. They had not a clue of what to do. The cries of the woman rang out like a siren, forcing each into a silent prison of guilt for not running and yelling the very instant that they had witnessed the act. The two looked at one another, as if to inwardly question how this could be happening before them, with not a soul around to hear the monstrous crime.

The man raised his arm back, like the triumphant hand of a God, and slashed the object harshly into the woman's countenance, and then into her jugular. She cried loudest at this moment, as if to cry out for redemption. Kyla peered at the woman's face for a reason unexplainable. The woman seemed to catch a glance of her and stared deeply into the essence of Kyla's being. Kyla stared back attentively, as if to provide solace, human endearment, and understanding. The woman's body was beaten and ravaged. Kyla then peered at the creator, at the orchestrator of such the brutality. Perhaps this aspect of the crime appealed to her even greater. Perhaps she thought to gain insight into the man who could bring himself to brutally take the life of another, and perhaps figured this, ruefully, more interesting than the watching of a victim having her life stolen. After all, victims in life are not uncommon. People are purged every single day of their lives due to mere circumstance, life's so-called hand.

She had expected the man to be depraved, sinister, grimacing, with the body of a Hellish Demon. She expected his eyes to have been black, his soul to have been torn, and his heart to have been that of a killer. She expected his arms to have been defined with muscular will, his neck to have had protruding veins of vulgarity, his hair to have been disheveled and filled with anger and blood. She was expecting a man truly ugly in appearance, perhaps not accepted in the norms of society. Kyla was expecting clutched hands and fists of determination and frenzy. She was expecting the most Hellish creature that she had ever seen. However, none of this is what she witnessed when she peered deeper at the man.

He was gaunt, with very little definition. His countenance was plain, not unlike many of the London commoners. He seemed semi-well-dressed, in fact. His hair was neat like that of a politician. His eyes were blue, as if crystallised into purity. His hands seemed like that of a craftsman, delicate and precious. This man was no beast. He was purely normal. Perhaps though, regular men can be driven to acts of highly irregular and questionable conduct, even more so than those not confined to the monotony of every day normalcy.

Independent from her surprising conclusions of the man's physical nature, Zigmund was brooding with a fire of guilt. He could not stomach viewing the violence like a scene on the television. He could not understand why neither he nor Kyla had done a single thing to prevent the furthering of the murder, save for staring and gazing like it was all some dream. A tremendous level of regret and guilt had built up inside of him. Zigmund thought to himself that if he were not to do something soon, he would have an empty feeling inside, perhaps for all his life. He thought it was his civic duty to help the woman, to divert the man, to at least run for help and create a distraction. It is possible that he knew this from the moment of the first cry, but feared more so for his own life, rather than truly considering the saving of the helpless woman's. Whichever the case, Zigmund could not contain his feelings inside for another moment.

"Get away from her, you beastly creature! Leave your position! Do not force me to fire upon you; the police are on the way!"

Of course, Zigmund had no intention of firing, since he did not own an arm, and the police certainly were not on the way, though, just the

Chaotic Ocean

same, it was quite a brave and uncharacteristically magnanimous thing to have done and said.

The man was shocked to look up and view Zigmund and Kyla not but fifteen feet away, and quickly vacated the area as he began to run off into the black distance. Kyla followed his path as to have one last glance of the man. As he faded away out of her sight, she saw that in addition to having had blood splattered about his face, he had a dark and enchanting region of triangular facial hair

The two rushed over immediately to the fallen woman, to see if there was any hope of her survival. She was badly beaten and slashed. It looked as if she had been a slave in olden times, whipped to bits by the hand of a domineering master. The woman was bleeding profusely from the throat and could barely even whimper.

She looked entirely innocent as the two leaned in to see if there could be anything done to aid the poor woman. Incredible helplessness exuded her. She seemed a victim, completely undeserving of the crime done unto her. Here and again she tried to mutter something, though, her throat was lacerated too badly for Zigmund and Kyla to make out any of the words.

Kyla decided to quickly run to a nearby telephone to ring for an ambulance, to perhaps save the woman's very life. She told Zigmund to wait with the fallen victim.

For one brief moment, the woman was able to speak. Looking frightfully into Zigmund's eyes, and clutching his arm, she whispered, "Kyla will stop you." Zigmund was instantly aroused by the comment, and taken back, but decided to keep an even demeanor. While he could not tangibly figure what the woman had meant, he certainly attributed it to some facet of Kyla's hidden motive. He remained silent to the remark, as he heard the trotting of his friend in the near distance.

As Kyla soon arrived back, Zigmund was attempting to say comforting things to the victim, to give the impression that this was the first communication, and perhaps had yielded nothing insightful. The victim appeared as though she wished to say something of eminent importance, but could no longer muster the effort. For a moment, Kyla wondered what had gone on in her absence.

"What is she saying, Zigmund? Have you discerned a word of it?" questioned Kyla.

Zigmund shushed her words, as if she had interrupted a truly personal conversation betwixt him and the victim. The woman looked into Kyla's eyes, as if Kyla had been somehow involved with the horrid attack. She had a look of utter fright, too stiff to move or speak though. It seemed as if she perceived Kyla as the Devil herself. This made Kyla extremely uncomfortable. Why had the woman looked so menacingly onto her? She had done nothing wrong. In fact, she and Zigmund had been responsible for the ceasing of the attack. Kyla then looked back at Zigmund.

He had been kneeling down next to the woman, like a comforting mother figure. His eyes were aflame. To Kyla's dismay, they were not transfixed on the fallen women, but rather, like rising suns, staring into

Chaotic Ocean

Kyla's face with a look of disgust. He seemed to stare right through her, past her. Kyla did not know what to make of his demeanor, nor did she think this the time to argue about proper etiquette in such a situation. All she could note was that his look was not unlike the woman's, frail, heartbroken, and angry.

To herself she thought, "What occurred in the conversation when I was making the call for the ambulance? Has this woman given Zigmund some false sense of my nature, or perhaps, the converse? Why in Heaven are they staring upon me like some barbarous, unctuous beast? Has a mark of evil been embedded into my forehead without my knowledge? Is there a scarlet lettre sewn upon my breast? Has the past linked misfortune to my present? I only long to aid this woman, to ensure that she is cared for and brought to safety. Were it not so, would I have dashed to make medical arrangements? Were it not so, would I still remain standing here like a guardian? I have clearly done nothing wrong in this instance. Perhaps my perception is having the best of me on this occasion. Perhaps I see expressions that are not truly existent. Perhaps this is all a contortion of the mind, conjured up inside of me, with no ground in the truth whatsoever. Though, perhaps I do not see false visions. What if there is actuality in this strange dance of fear?"

Kyla looked once again to Zigmund. He had begun to turn his back to her, as if too embarrassed to look at her being. For this, she could simply not understand the cause for the sudden change in mood. She decided to take it in stride, for the time being, at any rate. Kyla figured it best to discuss the situation with Zigmund when all was quiet and calm, after the ambulance had come and the anxiety of the thing had dissipated.

The ringing sound of the ambulance could be heard in the distance. The siren sounded loud and furious. It could be heard throughout the town. Not a commoner around would be left astray from the gossip. It sounded as if it inched closer in a rapid manner. It was not in viewing distance, though. The screech of the churning wheels was distinct, unlike any other vehicle of safety. It was a haven for goodness, for morality, as if blessed by holiness to always do what was inherently right. As the seconds and moments fell away, a glow of red could be seen creeping its way, reflecting off of buildings and trees.

The woman's vital signs seemed to be fading quickly. Her eyes blinked here and again, as her heart rate seemed to decrease, moving toward nothingness. She looked frightened, of death, and of life. Her body became less anxious and her limbs began to slow. Her skin had turned pale and blue. The woman's eyes had glassed over, but the tears had dried, leaving behind fallen skids of emotion, like dried sand in a desert. The ambulance arrived, and the paramedics began to rush over to the three. Kyla knelt down too, as if to say good-bye to the nameless woman, to provide comfort and consolation.

The woman jetted her hand up suddenly and clutched Kyla's arm. It was the firmest grasp Kyla had ever been given by either friend or enemy. It seemed to last for one thousand years, as if the moment had been interminable. Kyla felt the woman's soul run through her body. She felt the pain, the hate, the dismay, the horror, and the frailty. Kyla looked into her eyes for one last time, almost knowing that this life was beyond the saving of any medical professional. The woman once again choked on her own blood, attempting to speak, hoping to convey something.

With one final effort, she was able to mutter, "Kyla... don't... the stone."

She fell to the ground for good, as her eyes closed for the last and final time, like a spirit drained of life.

"How do you know my name? Please do not leave me!" Kyla ranted in vain to the fallen woman.

As the paramedics rushed in with life-preserving measures, Zigmund placed his hand upon Kyla's shoulder.

"There is nothing more to be done here, Kyla. Let us leave this place. Her life is now in the hands of others. We have no further role to play," quietly stated Zigmund.

"But, but..." rambled Kyla in a delirious frenzy, "She knew me. She said my name. How, how in Heaven?"

"Kyla, there is nothing to be done here. Please, do not compound the situation. Let us flee. It is late, and it is time to return home. I shall not forget this misadventure."

*

The two got up from their knees and walked off in a dejected embrace. They sauntered slowly and sadly, each in a surreal state, not quite believing that such an event had taken place before their very eyes. They could not fathom even the truth of the matter. It seemed like a dream. They each inwardly prayed that it was one, hoping to wake instantaneously, to abdicate themselves from the horror, from the ugliness of humanity that was life. As they walked off, the ambulance's siren became less and less.

Kyla now regretted having ever begged Zigmund out of the house. Not only had she not solved any of her curiosities, but, now she had a horrid crime to imagine of on rainy days when her normal plight was not of significant amount. She was also in utter befuddlement.

To herself she thought, "Why has such a thing taken place. What meaning has this about my life? Why have I been chosen to be a part of this savagery? Why did the woman know my name? How did she know of the stone? What am I not supposed to do with it?" She lamented on. Perhaps though, the strange occurrence fueled her hunger even greater for knowledge of her lapis.

Zigmund brooded inside as well. He had seen many things in his life. He had amounted riches and acquired worldly recognition. Though, this malevolence had been of the newest sensation to him. He did not enjoy the murder, nor did he take comfort in leaving the woman with the ambulance. All he longed to do was be home and gain perspective through his pond.

"Oh, I shall ask it, and I shall see. I shall tear through uncertainty and become one with pure knowledge. Why did Kyla lead me here tonight? Why did she seem unfazed when the murder was taking place? Why would any rational person lure another out, in the bitterness of snow and night, to go for a walk in the park? Is this not madness and extreme proof of something greater, more furtive? What has Kyla done, I cry! What has she become?!"

The two were both consumed with respective inner thoughts. They entered Zigmund's vehicle almost mechanically, and without saying a word to the other, headed out of Exmoor Park. The ride home was silent, like personified human guilt having been beaten into insecurity. Kyla could not ascertain much of the woman, while Zigmund had his own uncertainties of his friend of many years. Each did not desire the other to detect the uneasiness that they were each holding within. Kyla thought to strike up a conversation, though, was unsure of timing, as to if it was appropriate to speak, none the less converse and argue over points that now might seem truly trivial and worthless. Zigmund seemed in no mood to speak, judging by his eyes and demeanor. He was transfixed upon the road, as if focusing upon a higher plane of consciousness. Perhaps though, he simply desired not to provoke Kyla and keep about his own way.

"Do you believe they took into account murder when developing the survival of the fittest theory," suddenly posed Zigmund, as if out of nothing.

The mood seemed to alter drastically upon the question's spontaneous birth and unfeeling manner. Kyla thought for a moment. She did not understand how Zigmund could look upon her quite awkwardly and offensively one moment, and then in the next, have the spontaneity to delve into Chuck's Origin of Species and, ironically enough, its origin.

The moment of silence had certainly passed, and perhaps even the moment of grieving for the nameless woman. As she often did, Kyla took Zigmund's statement in stride, and thought perhaps this was his way of continuing life, living on to not be held down by pity and sorrow. The fact that he had asked a question of murder when that was precisely what they had just witnessed was more than eerie. His tone almost indicated a sense of purpose, not unlike before in his awkward remarks.

"Murder is brutal, no matter what theory is being applied, Zigmund," asserted Kyla.

"Perhaps." He stared at her for a long moment. "But that is what this world is about, a survival, from one generation to the next. The strong and fit live on; the weak and groveling die out. That is the single most important idea of our intelligence. We quick minded ones shall exist far into future generations, while those of feeble wit will not. Intelligence prevails, Kyla."

"That is garbage. And coming from a man like you, it is even filthier. It is quite easy to say such things when one is on top and of the benefit of his own theory."

"Kyla, come now, the less intelligent are weak, inferior to us. How can you deny such a fact?" asked Zigmund.

Chaotic Ocean

He did not bother to ponder the possibility that he himself might have been inferior to Kyla, among others, nor did he take into consideration the subjectivity entangled about the topic.

"There is not but one intelligence, but rather many. The fact that a actor may amass more money than a physical labourer, lead an easier life, work less hours, and live in a better neighborhood has nothing to do with 'survival of the fittest.' It is simply circumstance and situation. The fact that men with minds for business succeed and others with minds for tools do not reflects nothing of personal ability, but rather, what society values in humans. If we were to place highest honour with workers of construction, those who build, create, and provide for the lives of so many, the workers would be rich with respect and monetary possession. With the situation reversed, those workers would be the 'fittest,' not the businessmen. Thus, how can we call this pick and choose mentality a survival, when more likely, it is a societal preference, our true choice as a whole as to who we see flourish and who we see fail.

I am even convinced that we do not deviate as much as we'd like to think in our individual talents, as well. As prior mentioned, perhaps a writer has a greater chance at success than a physical labourer. Though, if viewed at any earlier stage in life, can such a vast difference even be detected? If one were to take the writing samples of two third graders, one who eventually becomes a professional writer, the other who becomes a construction worker, would there be any obvious difference? Perhaps there is a certain point in life where a break occurs, where the two split, either due to biological predisposition or to some external encouragement. While the worker harnesses his ability to work with his hands and place together practical materials, the writer practices on poems and short stories to further his respective ability. Later in life, when we look upon the two we say: 'Oh, he has practical smarts' or 'Oh, he has school smarts.'

Is any of this ground to discriminate against others for an archaic principle that Darwin created and then had bastardised when bigots twisted it about a social context? I think not. What gives one human the right over another to judge that his individual intelligence is of worth, more than the other's? What gives you that right, Zigmund? We must realise that we are all human, all of the same race, and all of the same development and evolution. To turn one's back due to a 'survival of the fittest' is to be of the greatest arrogance and delusion. To reiterate, my friend, we are all of different intelligences in different areas. Those who succeed might very well do so because of societal bias and circumstance. Those who do not, might very well fail because of such societal prejudice and condition as well."

Zigmund was once again struck with awe at the conviction in Kyla's defense, for the mere sake of point proving, for the mere sake of furthering her ideas more than Zigmund's to make him seem inane. This filled him with anger. Though, on the exterior he kept a calm about himself. He concentrated on the road once again, as to brood over defeat.

He mumbled silently to himself. "Whatever one needs to believe. Intelligence is not the measure of how smart you are; it is the measure of how inane everyone else is. How can one be so bold to think we are all equal, all equally intelligent when there exist certain separations in this life?"

Kyla caught only a few words of his mumbling.

"What was that, Zigmund? Speak aloud if you've grand points to put forth."

"It was nothing," replied Zigmund.

"I did not claim we are all of one level. That would be absurd and mechanical. I only claim that it is not for you to judge, not for you to take pride in or offer hatred and intolerance to others for. Why consider gifts as intelligence worthy and deserved but deem curses such as inanity and dysfunction of the same relevance, also deserved? We are all innocent in this world, all naked, all one with naivety and vulnerability upon birth. We are all of the same importance then, as we are upon our deathbeds. Why when we are alive does this change? Why must we envy our brothers for their gifts and hate our sisters for their misfortunes? It is all so juvenile."

*

The two grew weary of the banter, each reflecting the other's overt look of indifference. Zigmund did not bother to retort to Kyla's most recent remark. He had begun to feel somewhat slighted in the utter waste of a fine evening. Malicious thoughts twirled passionately about his brain as he inwardly concocted nefarious explanations for why it was, exactly, that Kyla had lured him out for the night to see, of all things, a brutal murder scene. He thought as though it had been a plan, a deviant, horrid plan, with Kyla, of course, assuming the role of the ill-hearted orchestrator, as if to plot out a tragic, poorly written Shakespearian suicide. He could not fathom the malice of it all, the very wickedness in Kyla's soul. What he could not fathom, he also could not perceive to be anything but of the most cruel intent.

He thought silently to himself, "Oh how the minutes and seconds mock me, like some holy torture of the Gods! My precious, pure, prophetic pond awaits its guardian, its true proprietor. It is very truth incarnate. It is of the most ancient descent of knowledge, I am sure of it. There is to be no question too profound, no riddle too entangled, no mystery too bewildering. I shall be one with truth, one with the eternal stream of objective information, one with mother Earth herself."

Kyla glanced over to notice Zigmund deep in inner thought. This fact much disturbed her. She had not prior known Zigmund to have been a man of contemplation, a man of introspection. She had known him to have been a man of spontaneous reaction, first word to mouth. Zigmund was, to her, a naïve child whom she could contort about her will howsoever she chose. She could not perceive a tangible difference about his outward demeanor, but rather, some slight shift in the subtlety of his character. He seemed more arrogant than was his usual intellectual dance. He seemed more antagonistic in nature. She could not understand why, or at least, did not. Either way, a feeling of discomfort and insecurity ran through her body. This newness about her compatriot seemed more an intellectual bother, more an immovable, horrifying weight than that of witnessing an innocent death, that is, not to say that all deaths are not marred by innocence.

Once again, she was entangled in her own insecurity. Additionally, to timely add in, she could also not put the poisonous thought of Zigmund's publishings out of her mind. Kyla thought back to her session with Laurna to recall the absurd phrasing. "Subjectaphors," she suddenly remembered. To herself she thought, "Is there anything more illogical than the combination of two intellectual words, forms, into such an inane bastardisation of unified language?"

She continued to peer at Zigmund, as he continued to peer into himself, in addition, of course, to focusing on the road as though he had to deeply concentrate in order to operate the vehicle safely. Kyla thought to burst into conversation, to confront him on his abomination of language, as she had been wanting, for at least a great many pages, excuse, rather, at least for the summation of the day. Frankly, she had not known or remembered why it was, earlier, that she did not bring the issue to surface, why it was that she had held her remarks. She could not ascertain.

"Zigmund," she began, "why do you feel the need to corrupt others with your obviously cynical and imperfect ideas?"

He had not a clue to the reference that Kyla was speaking. This was not due to his having been purposely obtuse, but rather, was a genuine want of knowledge of such an accusation, apart from what his own mind could have interpreted the statement as meaning.

This, in turn, infuriated Zigmund with a sense of callousness. To him, this was assuredly some round about antic, some perversion, some cruel and egotistical exercise in which Kyla could implement domination in order to further the current folly that which she had planned like a tactful sneak.

He thought to himself, "How dare this enchantress, how dare this woman of obvious ill-natured character accuse me of such an act, such a general wording at that of such an act."

In the course of few conversations, to Zigmund, Kyla had leapt from having been bothersome but friendly and intellectual, to curious in possible character, to assuredly evil and loathsome at heart. He kept his calm.

"Poisonous, my dear? It is possible that I, in my travels, have not become as learned as say, *you*, however, I hardly think that to accuse me of corruption of the whole of man, simply from my lifestyle, is just or warranted," replied Zigmund.

Zigmund's reply was not fitting to Kyla. She had not desired an answer at which to banter over. This, of course, she assumed to have been true of the reply, that it was in fact, obtuse, shrouded, and purely of ill-hounest intent. Though, to say the remark was dishounest might have held many ounces of truth in it, however, dishonesty only lies in its emotion, in its façade. To name it dishounest, on the contrary, speaking in the simplest of terms of lie and truth, it was not. To Zigmund, his remark was truth incarnate, to the fullest of his ability and belief. He had *hounestly* not known of what Kyla had been speaking.

"Zigmund, why must you put forth such an amazing amount of folly in your jest. Please, mockery aside, why did you feel it proper to publish an article without even speaking of it beforehand? Could you not bear to tell me, to put your faith and trust in your oldest friend?"

"Publish an article? What in Heaven are you speaking of, dear Kyla? I am flabbergasted and thunderstruck."

"I consider myself a patient woman, Zigmund. Alright, I actually do not, but I would like to think that I have the compassion, especially with and of my friends, to put up with at least a minimal level of tomfoolery. Please though, it has lost its novelty and attractiveness through the years. Please, speak directly. Enough of this upside downside chatter."

"I implore you, Kyla, to consider my words for what they are. Do not insult me. If a man cannot defend or take credit for his very thoughts and words, what is he? Please do not diminish me so much to the point of lies. I truly do not appreciate this kind of conversation."

"One of my patients, Zigmund, Laurna, brought up some silly quip the other day while we were having our session. She spoke of a new word termed as 'subjectaphors,' and credited you as the original author and publisher of the thought. She spoke that when a statement is both subjective and metaphorical, it is quite impossible to be argued against in the whole of any capacity. Almost the anti-thesis of contradiction, one might say."

"Well, while I would love to assume complete credit for such a thought so wonderful, I am truthfully as the falsely accused convict, my dear. This is not of my doing, not of my thinking. You surely have misinformation, Kyla."

"Zigmund, do not humour me. My patients do not tell half-truths. They have no reason to be anything but purely hounest in my presence. None have been diagnosed with any sort of compulsion remotely related to lying. It purely would not make any great deal of sense."

"So I am assuming that since your trust befalls your patients, it somewhat must pass over me, as if a Lord overlooking his servants. It is no great secret that both her and I cannot be of the same hounest action."

"I am not making a grand effort to deprecate you, my friend. I am but merely attempting to put some finality to a thought that has been plaguing me of late. That is all."

"Kyla, here is the finality that you have been seeking. I did not, have not, and have no plans of ever producing such a publication. If some mischievous fool has done so in my name, then the debauchery is just that, in and of my name, though in its actuality, in accordance to tangible events, I enforce the truth that this was not of my doing. I will do my best to investigate the matter, as it now has sparked much of my interest.

However, for the time of current, I cannot offer the name of this buffoon any more than I can give solace to you to placate your desire for closure."

Kyla did not know what to think of Zigmund's bold declaration of his actions, or lack there of. To herself she thought, "I must accept his words for now, as it will do no good to deny his half-witted spirit. Though, to accept them to thyself, is an action to which I will likely never succumb."

"Alright, Zigmund," said Kyla, as if to comfort a whining child after a vicious fit of emotion.

Zigmund did not respond. The two were almost nearing his estate. This excited him greatly, as he was anxious to send Kyla on her way and to consult the pond image on the events of the evening.

The two pulled into the drive. It was dark out. The evening carried about it a surreal sense of being, as if a dreamlike state of sensation. It was late, and Kyla desired to vacate as much as Zigmund wished she would. He had grown tired of her, as perhaps she too had grown tired of him, or rather, herself in and of the situation that she had willfully placed and submitted herself into. She longed to retire for the evening.

"Well, I cannot remark that it was without adventure, my dear Kyla," lightheartedly jested Zigmund.

"Of the greatest misadventure that I have been accomplice to, surely," responded Kyla.

Zigmund thought to himself, "Accomplice is an apt phrasing, not to mention, quite sly considering the events that have shaped the evening."

"It has come to my attention that the evening has grown long, Kyla, and that perhaps it would be best for each if we retired to our respective dwellings. What do you think?"

Kyla was struck with utter agreement, surprising even herself, for this happenstance union of thought was scarce to the history of their relationship. Perhaps on some level, this greatly disturbed her. Though, on another, she was more than willing to submit.

"I agree."

"I knew you would."

CHAPTER SIX
☦

JOHN THOMAS

*

Kyla awoke earlier than usual in her usual flat to witness the prior day's fallen snow, glistening with sunshine, as if glazed over like a tear-stricken pupil. The sun was red, angrier than normal, though, was still quite beautiful as it acted like the omnipotent onlooker of the whitened city landscape.

Kyla's flat showcased a majestic-looking back porch of sorts, which was composed of two heavy glass doors, decorated with glass pressings and designs. She lived a considerable distance from the main part of the city, or rather, more so out of the way and specifically out from the watchful eye of pop culturedome and its mass hysteria and subsequent flocking, as was where Zigmund resided. Her geographical plot was more of a brink, that of betwixt the whole of the masses and of the far less industrialised section of the country where one might bask in the simple pleasure of viewing nature's vast impact and unity with the land.

As such, the hills and terrain stretched on for what seemed like a captivating eternity, as was hitherto mentioned in the initial description, but is perhaps now relevant to reinforce. Actually, upon further examination, the initial description may have been daft'apeth, or more specifically, nonexistent. Let us dismiss the digression and allow it to give way to the greater good of literature and to one's own realised inadequacy.

What the initial description would have said, or possibly still does, if it has simply been overlooked in the slew of one hundred some odd pages, was or is: the hills and land gave way to a beautiful feeling in Kyla's heart. They provided comfort, ease, solace, whatever one chooses to use as his customised adjective. When the day had treated her poorly, or injected a cruel discomfort into her soul, the simplicity of the land always seemed to cleanse Kyla's spirit, to rejuvenate her inner compass. The effect had always been greater when the freshly fallen snow existed, exuding a compounded feeling of newness and perfect submission.

This day was not unlike any other. Kyla, feeling awake and alive, quickly dashed about some clothes and proceeded through the glass doors. Sleep, as it so often had for Kyla, relaxed not only her body, but also her mind. The impossible and forceful feelings from the day prior, of her inexplicable attraction to the Sardoce Estate, gave way to freedom and comfort. The self-questioning that subsequently followed her examination of Zigmund's regard to subjectaphors fled like feeble mice from a trap and created space for only whom the Gods were holy enough to invade or alter.

Chaotic Ocean

She peered out into the lace-laden fields, which had been constructed not of man, but of nature herself.

To herself she thought, "Man in all her glory, in all her mechanisation, industrialisation, culture, civilisation, and societal norms, it is quite clear to me, will never – not even sear the surface of – come remotely close to harnessing the wind, taming the oceans, cultivating the magma, labeling the clouds and Heavens that are Earth herself. Man may claim ownership, may assume that its very destiny is manifest, may toil over exhausting every natural resource with which we have been blessed till we in fact no longer exist to toil, may build roads, highways, and railways all for the sake of economy, may tear down forests for the sake of shelter, may pollute the air for the sake of cost efficient gas masks, may force its very being and hegemony unto its very own mother and breeder, all for my sake, your sake, and God's sake, all to such a bloated extent by which we can name ourselves rulers of our exterior, but, there is no doubt that we will remain naïve to our own selves, foolish to the Gods, and mistakenly egotistical.

A thousand men's sweat and labour stands feeble when'st a typhoon renders her onslaught. A million bricks laid and secured run to shit when our skies demand flood. The entire civilisation of man, that is to assume man is civilised, not to mention civil, stands no chance against the Heavenly winds, Earthly quakes, and bitter colds of nothingness. Why is the one entirely simple fact that we are subject, we are but servants, but men paying Earthly leases to our mother, so incredibly difficult to programme in and fathom? We are not humble as men should be; we are arrogant and entirely thankless. We do not consider life a gift, be it divine or coincidental; we do quite the opposite. We make ourselves Gods. We conquer and plunder. We create for ourselves a quite illogical sense of existence, dwell inside of it, and not for once do we consider the global and large-scale consequences of our individual and unique actions. We live quite blissfully, quite blissfully indeed."

Kyla had a sizeable portion of time before having to ready herself for the new day of work that was ahead. She performed her unconscious, obligatory acts, as per usual, for instance: showering, clothing, and making her hair become silky fine. To comment, it is quite amazing how much we are able to achieve in our daily lives without an ounce of forced cognition. It is stunning how much of our existence is based upon habit and repetition. We are but the movers of the immovable stone. We are but the animals that mate and die. We wrap ourselves in the identical towel each day; we wrap ourselves in the identical manner; we reach, bend, yawn, speak, sleep, and toil in patterns that not even God herself could break. This is but our conditioning. We do not, to say for the most of us, realise it in ourselves, but perhaps this is for the better, for the far greater. We are reapers of our own sanity, that is to say on an individual basis, viewed under a large-scale collective lens, but we must digress.

There was but one thought on Kyla's mind. It was not Zigmund Sardoce; it was not Mr. Pem, though, she would be meeting with him later in all likelihood. It was not of concern for a patient, nor was it of concern for any religious or political inconsistency.

"The lapis," she echoed to herself externally, as well as internally. She obediently, in regard of obedience of her own mind, made her way about the flat to the place where she had been storing the mysterious stone. It was as it had been, innocently placed in the unsecured, wooden chest of her study. Kyla reached for it, as if reaching for the random. It was oddly cold, not freezing, as if having been stricken into a polar climate, but rather, cold as in lifeless, lacking in activity and subsequently, seemed unused and unloved.

"For when I last gripped the stone in my very hands, it exuded a warmth, a physical heat, yet now it taunts me, as if to dismiss my very actuality and memory. This is of the cruelest mockeries."

This angered her. Kyla had purposely stored the lapis away so that it would not have tempted her to figure its origin and use. She recalled her action with it of the day prior, how she seemed to surge with energy like some great, electrical wire strewn across all of an empire. She recalled how it diminished her very cognitive power, how it made her inferior not only to herself, but also to the whole of the world and existence. Kyla recalled how it made her seem one with a force entirely alive, able to share its knowledge of all things worth knowing. This was not the action currently taking place.

She touched the stone repeatedly, as if to summon it, to conjure up some unknown spell to bring about its life. This of course, was quite an infantile method to enact, considering Kyla's truer intelligence. She thought perhaps that it would react somehow by element of sun or water. Both were to no avail. Kyla laid the stone on her bed and decided to dismiss it.

"Perhaps I have received too much sun," she joked to herself. "Perhaps I am going quite crazy. I must have been looked upon as a fool to have actually attributed any kind of emotion or tangible action to this wretched, quite boring, stone."

She went on to rationalise for some minutes, and then took up where she had left off in readying herself for the day. Kyla left the lapis on her bed where she cared not if it would be safe. Actually, there was some solace to be had in the event, or lack of, or more specifically, perhaps she was able to regain some certainty about her life, some stability, in this feeble action.

Kyla was nearly ready to vacate the flat and be off for the day, but felt the extreme desire to once more look over the hills and see the comforting image of the angelic snow, delicately patted about the pasture behind her abode. She made her way to the glass doors and began to peer out.

The snow seemed different somehow. It had acquired a sordid, yellow quality about itself, mostly in three-foot, circular patches. This she had not noticed prior.

"What in Heaven?" she pondered to herself. "There must have been some wilde, grouchy animal toddling here last night. I cannot think

Chaotic Ocean

of another reason for the sudden discolouring in the snow. Surely, the ugliness of the thing will be washed away upon next snowfall. Till, I may have to deal with a less than majestic view."

And with that, she was off, somewhat disappointed in Mother Nature for bestowing a creation as such into her homely life.

*

The roads had been heavily salted over to prevent ice-related accidents in the old London streets. Sweepers seemed in abundance at the slightest weatherly inconvenience. Perhaps on snowy days, the cab drivers merely altered their daily occupations.

The day after a fresh downfall of snow was always somewhat refreshing. There seemed a rejoicing in the air. Families were more apt to show themselves, children more apt to play, and kindness more apt to have been in great quantity. Universal suffering makes for better people, not to say that snow could ever, in anyone's even dreariest of imaginations, cause any form of actual suffering; rather, one may say, it causes newness and break from habit, which for some may be seen as eternal damnation. The gossip, though, like the fine postal workers of the U.S. of A., did not quit through rain, through sleet, through snow, through the Apocalypse, etc.

The drive after such snow was always quite enjoyable one, for Kyla was enabled the ability to see all of London's family units, and all of the beauty of youth coming together. Though, the drink was not without poison, for it, in addition to making Kyla feel worthwhile and deserving of existence, made her feel like a *culture-barren train wreck, as if to say that the town was comprised of happy souls who could convey to their loved ones, while she herself had not a soul in which to confide.

Though, still the same, she uniquely identified with the feeling of paralysing snow coming forth like a random, sarcastic remark, stunning men in their gossip spewing places, having it alter their routines for the subsequent days, and then feeling all quite different, like a cyclical metaphor, to only and inevitably arrive at the point where it all begins and ends.

As she approached the Hospital, so familiar, she remembered her promise of searching out a form of work for Mr. Pem. This did not seem a great challenge, for she prided herself of being true to her word. She pondered what, if any positions, the hospital had open from a homely, immigrant man.

Kyla thought empathetically, "This man may deserve to reside in the hospital for all I know. I wonder how I will find him a free room, let alone an occupational position."

She spotted an open slot in the lot and pulled her old banger into position. As she did, Kyla noticed Mr. Pem standing awkwardly next to her passenger side window, and wondered where he had come from. "He must have seen me pull up," said she to herself.

She was quite happy to see Mr. Pem for an unknown reason. Kyla thought perhaps to tell him of the strange lapis occurrences, how for one

Chaotic Ocean

minute it seemed as if boiling with heat, and in the next was but a cold remnant of a forgotten memory. She vacated the vehicle and began to approach him.

"Ah, Miss Demark, it is so wondrous to see you. I have indeed been looking forward to your presence."

Kyla was inveigled. She became dumbstruck with a feeling of forgetfulness and could not think to bring up the stone. She could not utter its name, as if powerless to the most inanimate of objects. Kyla could not understand why it was that this was happening, though, at the same time, could not organise with cognisance the actuality of not having been able to understand as much, and subsequently, was not bothered greatly by the event.

"It is good to see you, Mr. Pem. I hope you've kept well since our last encounter," remarked Kyla.

"Oh, I keep quite well, Kyla. It is only by our external desires and passions that which we harm our being. The human body needs very little to actually survive. However, I am able to find quite warm dwelling even in the most bitter of colds. I am able to find the most powerful protection from the cruelty of the snow."

Kyla, of course, wore the polar opposite opinion on her sleeve of the snow, as she often thought it to have been the most beautiful of natural creations. She had wished to convey this to Mr. Pem, though again, for an unknown reason, could neither find the words nor the might to do so.

Kyla was curious of Mr. Pem's nature, in regard to where exactly it was that he "dwelled." Though, she did not wish to come across as rude or crass, if he in fact was without a home.

"Mr. Pem, if I may ask, and in asking please do not reach negative conclusions about my curious nature, because it is just that, curious, without implied insult, without cynical connotation, without..."

"Kyla, do not fear me, or yourself, or the questions that spark your mind's interest. Do as thou will'st, and please ask freely with no hesitation," interrupted Mr. Pem.

"Thank you," remarked Kyla. "Where is it that you reside? I would imagine that it might be somewhere near the hospital?"

Mr. Pem understood what Kyla had asked and could recognise the disguise in her query, even after having given permission to speak as indignantly as her imagination could have afforded. He decided to mock the moment and swell inside of it.

"Reside? Actually, I own four mansions just beyond the nearest pasture. Most nights of the week, I decide which to stay in based on my mood, the weather, and the stars. Most nights though, the third mansion ends up victorious. It is able to receive all of the U.S. television channels, thus, I enjoy being kept alert on the U.S. culture. Apparently, the news stations are owned by the largest soft drink producer in the country, and wouldn't you know, report a uniquely bulbous amount of stories in regard to consumer enjoyment of said soft drink."

Kyla easily detected the sarcasm in Mr. Pem's voice.

"Mr. Pem, I..."

"Miss Demark, did I not inform you to speak candidly to me? This hesitation, this holding forth of wills and urges is only useful when being admitted into Heaven. Do you understand?"

"Yes. I apologise," remarked Kyla.

"Do not," quipped Mr. Pem. "There is no need to be anything but brutally unyielding and unwavering."

She felt as if Mr. Pem had been two to thee paces ahead of her in each mental gesture, and as such, felt somewhat infantile when in his presence.

"I keep a room that two old commoners rent me, just a few kilometers down the road. That's what you were getting at, I'm sure. I am not homeless, nor if I were, would I feel the need to deny it. I appreciate your concern, even if it was at the cost of underestimation. Again though, do not apologise."

Kyla desired to change the topic quickly, as she was feeling quite vulnerable and of little intelligence.

"Mr. Pem, I'd overlooked the fine lines of your appearance in our prior meeting. You are quite a distinguishable man. Though, maybe it's that silly, little sense of wiliness about your person."

"Ah, flattery will get you everywhere worth getting. Triumphant over hounesty and good will, it often seals one's position in this world. Many thanks for the ego-building bricks. Though, somehow I doubt you're interested in discussing my appearance. After all, it is quite cold out, and perhaps I've underdressed as well."

She glanced quickly at Mr. Pem's attire. It was the bitterest of days and, he barely dawned a vest, let alone any real kind of self-shelter. Kyla did not understand how it was that he did not freeze to his tomb in such conditions. Again, as if a pace ahead of her, Mr. Pem quickly spoke the true subject.

"Kyla, was it not today that you'd promised to search out a position in the hospital? I realise I am perhaps little trained or educated for most positions, but any form of work that you can spare would be greatly appreciated, and surely, the effort would be rewarded kindly with whatever worldly gifts I may have to offer."

"You will owe me nothing, sir. I hounestly am unsure of my clout in such a regard, as I am merely a psychologist. Obviously so, I do not run the institution itself, nor am I in charge of any kind of hiring. But, I will speak with those in charge of openings, so to put in a great word for you."

"Kyla, that is all I ask. Nothing more do I seek. You're a devoted soul, and surely, that quality will come to be the making of your greatness," remarked Mr. Pem.

Kyla thought oddly on the man's choice of words, but was too timid in his presence to question his remark, as surely she was to understand them with absolute clarity, she thought to herself. The fact that she did not, or at least, had enough afterthought to have thought strangely on them, was to her a sign of weakness. And undoubtedly, this she could not further reveal to Mr. Pem, for she was developing a quick sense of respect and awe for the man of whom she knew little.

Kyla took Mr. Pem by the hand and quickly shuffled to the front door of the hospital. His hand was warmer than she had expected.

"Please wait here while I go and speak with the receptionist, Mr. Pem. I will be back in a short while to speak of the results with you, alright?"

"That sounds completely satisfactory to me, Kyla. Do not stress yourself over this, though. You're helping me more than you could ever know. And that is what remains of importance. If there are no openings, I will find another. Now go."

*

Kyla went through the door, glancing back at Mr. Pem. She soon walked up to the front desk and peered once more back before speaking to the receptionist. Mr. Pem had vanished. Or, as perhaps she thought, maybe he had paced to a difference spot. Kyla turned to the receptionist.

"Hello there, Miss..." as she paused to read the name on the tag, "Kendra. I'm looking to inquire about any positions that may be un-held."

"Gotta fill out an application, but I doubt they're lookin' for more pukka prats," the woman said in an obviously caustic tone of voice. "You might try one of them agencies or shelters."

"M'am, I am not a vagrant. I work here, as a psychologist, and I am not pleased with your tone," remarked Kyla.

"Sure, sure. I'm a psycho too. We's all are psycho's."

Kyla showed the woman identification. The woman, obviously embarrassed at her mistake, apologised vehemently.

"I'm so sorry, dove. What can I do for you?" asked the woman in a somewhat paranoid voice, in fear for the security of her job.

"I have a friend who needs work. I need you to tell me if there are any low level positions free that he can fill. His name is Mr. Pem."

"Umm, it seems the only thing we got is for one of them janitor positions. He can have it if he wants without a screening or application or anything. Please, just don't get me fired. You probably think I'm rat arsed or something. I just been havin' a bad day is all."

"That will do just fine," smugly remarked Kyla. "When may he start?"

"Umm, looks like as soon as he wants."

"Thank you," said Kyla. "I will notify you of the decision upon speaking with the individual."

Kyla confidently walked off in the direction of her office. She then remembered that her mind had gone absent, and she needed to inform her new friend of the good news. Quickly dashing outside, Kyla noticed that the man was nowhere to be found. This befuddled her greatly. Where could he have gone to, perhaps she thought. After some moments of failed searching, she realised that she had not the time to devote, and decidedly marched back into the building, still fairly confused.

Chaotic Ocean

Nevertheless, she was proud that she had been able to locate work for the man, even at the price of having been offended by an unruly desk attendant. Kyla was looking forward to seeing her patients now, so that her mind could be free of its own hardship, and instead, could focus solely on the hardships of others. She resolved to inform Mr. Pem upon their next encounter.

*

Laurna Tangly sauntered into Kyla's office and was bundled up like an Eskimo. The cold had stayed with her, and were it physically reachable in some other form of existence, her breath might have been visible despite the heated conditions of the hospital.

"Hello Laurna," said Kyla, "It's quite nice to see you."

"Yeah, you're not bad yourself. Of course, I'm sure I could find better ways to fill my time, but as I said, you're not half bad, for a shrink and all."

"I must hounestly admit that I've still been thinking about our last session. You had been speaking of subjectaphors. You had said that they were pamphlets or sorts which were means of distributing information, written by some man."

"Oh yeah. Ziggy Sardoce. Why have you been thinking about that? That doesn't really relate to me or my issues, does it?"

Kyla felt stupid, as if her questioning had been but thinly veiled, and surely was spotted as having been nothing more than something out of self-servility. Though, Kyla needed to press on. A feeling of unease continually coursed through her mind. She did not understand why this was so, though, willingly adhered to it.

"Well, everything that you bring up in here is of course in some way related to your case, whether it's outwardly obvious or not, is perhaps not for either of us to say. So yes, it is important to dissect many issues such as this," rationalised Kyla.

"Oh, okay then," agreed Laurna.

"Have you received any more subjectaphor pamphlets, Laurna?" asked Kyla.

"Yes, I have. I think the old chap had some pretty good ones, if I can recall. I know I've been using them a lot when talking to my stupid family and whatnot. They don't understand or care about me anyway. I figure, might as well give them some of their own treatment back."

"Were the pamphlets any different? Or were they pretty much the same as before. What did this last one say?"

Kyla was worried that her questioning was too intrusive and would somehow damage the session.

"Oh, it said something like: 'If you're free, than an already emancipated fat man can only speak in riddles of yes and maybe and orange duck sauce.'"

"And, is the purpose to find any true sense of meaning, Laurna?" questioned Kyla.

"Meaning? Didn't I tell you that the whole point is to be subjective and metaphorical? There is no meaning in these words, and those who try to figure any kind of such meaning are pretty hopeless. What's the big deal anyway?"

Kyla could sense the tone of the conversation changing from casual to something resentful.

"Laurna, please, it was never..."

"I mean, what's the point in figuring anything really?" interrupted Laurna. "It's not like anyone gives a damn in this world. It's not like anyone actually communicates with you, and even if they did, be it a bastard father or pissed arsed mother, who really cares? Nothing they or anyone says means a lot, if anything. People spend their whole bloomin' lives trying to figure why we're here, what our purpose is, all that nonsense."

Laurna's native tongue was more prevalent when she was angered, and as such, was not self-conscious about speaking properly.

"I mean, what if we are only some grand arsed accident, hmm? I'm not saying that's true, but what if? Did you ever question? Why then are people spending so much time looking for something, some answer, that never can or did or will exist?"

"Well, Laurna," calmly interjected Kyla, "you make valid points. But not everyone sees it how you are claiming. Some people understand the vast uncertainties of life and make their own meaning. It seems that is what's most important, no?"

"Oh you're such an optimist, sometimes I don't know about you," rudely stated Laurna. "It's like the pamphlet said, nihilism is the only ism that's not an asylumism."

Kyla thought to herself, "This is surely the influence of Zigmund. Never could a twenty-year-old girl, no matter how disturbed or fragile, have such a completely negative outlook on life. Why in the name of Heaven would he wish to do such a thing, to poison so many minds?! And this is but one of them! I must discover why he has taken to this form of diseased information integration."

"Laurna, please calm yourself. I did not wish to evoke such emotion from you."

"Sure you didn't. I'm sure that's exactly what you wanted to hear. Now maybe you can recommend me to some pill prescriber so he can put my mind on ice or something, so the Demons can't get me, at the same time blocking out the sunshine and wind and sweetness too. Right?"

"Not at all. You're going to have to trust me one day in order for our sessions to provide you any kind of help."

"Trust? Trust you? No thanks. I find I'm much happier when I trust only the two eyes betwixt this head and the heart inside this cage. Because, I know that those never lie, never cheat me, never kill me, never expect me to do anything out of my nature."

"That's a very unfortunate way to have to live, Laurna. I am so sorry that you feel as you do. But I beg of you, and this is truth in purest form, do not assimilate your thoughts with the pamphlets you are receiving. They only are affecting you in a negative manner, and can only do so. They are reinforcing your negative ideas about the world, and if not that, then are reducing your positive ideas."

"We'll have to see," jadedly replied Laurna.

"Would you do me a favor, Laurna?" questioned Kyla.

"What now might that be?"

"Bring me one of these pamphlets. We may look over it together. We can dissect it. I will show you why it is not a good way to live or a good source by which to be influenced. There are so many positive influences in the world. So many authors have battled with so many of the same issues that afflict you present day. Read their works. Be influenced by the great minds of history. Do not choose to be influenced by a random, unknown writer who might as well be the epitome of everything you despise. You know nothing of this man. He who distributes poison freely, distributes it for a reason. Remember that."

"Well, I will try to remember to bring one for you."

"That's all I ask."

"Anyway, I think I've reached my maximum pleasure level for the day," sarcastically remarked Laurna.

"Do not depart so abruptly. I did not mean to disturb you," said Kyla.

"What would you have us talk of?"

"The weather?" jested Kyla.

The two passed the time informally, each attempting to put on the best face possible.

"You may leave if you wish now," stated Kyla.

"Sounds like a plan. Till next time. Sorry to have been such a bitch arse."

"I am used to it," informally jested Kyla.

"Au revoir, dove."

"Stop and let the rain soak over you every once again," quickly added Kyla.

"What's that?"

"I think you'll see just how meaningful life can be if you smell the sky right before it pours, and once it does so, do not run like a mouse fleeing from a great piece of cheese. Let it bathe you, for, after all, water is life. Do not flee from life."

"Thank you," remarked Laurna, as if actually appreciating, for once, what Kyla had been trying to convey.

She was off.

Kyla felt conflicted. She did not wish to abuse her relationship with the fragile Laurna, yet needed the information about Zigmund's publishings. She dismissed the thought, as she prepared for her next patient.

*

Dorian Knots was slightly early for his session. He seemed to be wearing an even-tempered expression upon his countenance. Kyla generally knew to treat each patient differently. She felt that some needed more guidance, and some needed less. Dorian was usually swift to strike up the conversation, as perhaps he looked at the session as nothing more than a new debate, a new verbal confrontation of which he could triumph over. Kyla's role was not that of a debater though, so, perhaps this frustrated Dorian on some level. He was extremely competitive and would argue till the ends of the Earth to prove that he was the most knowledgeable on any given topic, on whim alone, even if he knew nothing of the subject at hand.

"How's it smellin'?" chirped Dorian.

"I'm doing quite well, thank you. And yourself, how are you, Dorian?"

"Whateva, whateva, like you care. You just wanna see me naked. So, uhhh, what are you doing later, tonight... if ya' catch my drift and by drift I do mean completely obvious references to sex!" joked Dorian.

Kyla chuckled at the remark.

"I guess you want me to start?" asked Dorian.

"Well, I've never tried to stop you in the past," warmly smiled Kyla.

Dorian had no trouble bouncing from casual back-and-forth to actual conversation, and ideas that he would himself consider important.

"To be hounest, I've been thinking a lot about the objectification of my body."

"Oh? Do you feel like a piece of meat?" jested Kyla.

"Well, okay, so I lied. Not really of my body, but of the collective body, if you catch me. You know, in pop culturedom, how we see all the time these super models, scantily clad, working to sell us all sorts of this-and-that."

"And... you're offended by this glaring objectification?"

"No, quite the opposite. I'm offended by those fools who call it objectification, by those who say it is immoral to use a woman's body for one purpose, for sales, for whatever."

"I'm not quite sure I get you, Dorian."

"Well, basically when conversations happen, the talk is of objectification in general, no? However, the specifics are completely unspoken. This is, specifically, the objectification of gender. Though, you never hear any bloke or femme talk about the objectification of intelligence, or say, the objectification of humour. Are those not objects as well?"

"Well, not physical objects, but I suppose," remarked Kyla, unsure as to where Dorian had been going with his banter.

"People talk about objectification, i.e. the use of, say, a woman's body for any purpose. I mentioned it in the use of sales. However, all the time you hear talk about womanising and only wanting 'one thing' and these sexual fiends being completely wicked, for they objectify a woman for her body, and for her body only. Well let me tell you something."

"What's that?"

"Every single day we act on our uses for people. We use some of our acquaintances for stimulating conversation. We use others to set ablaze our sense of humour. Some we use for recreation, and others we use to further our economic goals. Every single time we reach out to another human being, we are reaching for a use. However, when the reach is sexual, we become enraged with a sense of wrong. To use a human for sexual desire, to placate one's libido, to soften our natural human urges, we call this immoral. Sex without love, sex without family, sex without relationship, it is deemed. However, if one has no qualms about the morality of sex, to think of it as simply another act, another use, such as conversation or laughter, one can surely place no blame or label upon such a use. Why is sex as a use any more immoral than a stimulating conversation? Both involve sensation. Both involve a mutual personal gain. So long as both parties understand this, is morality even a question? I have acquaintances that I keep for the sole purpose of letting go, of having an entertaining evening and nothing more. We do not speak politics or religion. We do not speak philosophy. Is having a relationship such as this immoral or underhanded? If the answer is no, then having a sexual relationship of that magnitude is no different. If the answer is yes, then we would all be guilty of immorality on every level, and as such, one would not have to worry about the labels that which others grant about sexuality, for they themselves would have not a right in the world to toss that first stone."

"So, this bothers you to a great extent, Dorian?"

"Hehe, nah. I probably don't even believe it myself. You know me, I can argue with the best of them. Feel free to use any of that as self-rationale if you're ever in a situation you're unsure of, like in a pub with a handsome Devil such as myself."

"I will keep it in mind. Thank you, Dorian."

"So, we talk so much, and much I feel is one-sided, since of course I am the patient, but just the same, you see what I'm getting at, I trust."

"Well, Dorian, I've never really talked about my personal life with any of my patients. I simply don't feel it would be advantageous to either party."

"Yeah, you're probably right. I absolutely agree. So... what's been going on in the home life?" jested Dorian.

"Dorian, you're a truly unique individual. Or is it a uniquely true individual?"

"Eh, same indifference," remarked Dorian.

"I'm not sure what you'd like to know about me."

"What kind of company do you keep?"

Immediately Zigmund flashed into Kyla's mind. Though, she was incredibly embarrassed to have been associated with such a notoriously pretentious individual. However, she found a certain charm about Dorian and did not feel uncomfortable around him. For whatever reason, she found herself divulging the information, as perhaps she had secretly wished someone to ask of her.

"Well, I keep company with a man by the name of Zigmund Sardoce. You probably wouldn't know..."

"Oh yeah, Ziggy Sardoce, who lives in the Sardoce Estate, right?"

Chaotic Ocean

Kyla was shocked that her patient had known Zigmund. She was not shocked that he would have heard of him, but just something about the way he so quickly recognised the name, seemed to indicate some form of familiarity with him, and this she could only recognise as negative.

"Dorian, do you know Zigmund personally? Or have you merely heard of his name, since he is somewhat of a known character?" questioned Kyla, hoping that the answer would be the latter.

"Well, no, I don't know him personally."

Kyla was greeted with a great feeling of ease. She felt truly comforted that Dorian was in no way under the influence of such a man whom she increasingly viewed to be quite pernicious, for whatever reason.

"I have just read his work. You know, the doorstep pamphlets that he's been publishing. Quite good I must say. I'd never heard of him before then, but he has some real gusto."

The words were crushing, biting into Kyla's mind, as if a sea serpent pillaging a defenseless village. She felt weak, and above all, confused. To herself she thought, "Why would Zigmund have lied when the evidence is utterly obvious?"

She felt somewhat defeated and did not know how to address Dorian on the matter, since she herself had no concrete answers as of yet.

Kyla and Dorian continued on for nearly half an hour, as Kyla attempted to repress her anger and confusion.

"Kyla, can I be direct for a moment?"

"Certainly," responded Kyla.

"Sometimes I look, and I truly fail to catch the grand meaning," began Dorian.

"How do you mean?"

"Well, for instance, with each session, I travel this city, watching all the citizens nearly trample one another just to catch a minute or two, just to get to a destination a split second quicker, likely related to occupation. And then they trample to get home."

"Go on."

"Well, then it repeats the next morning. This is civilisation? This is meaning? Integrating ourselves into the economy, never twice thinking about what might make us happy? We're supposed to be an advanced species, but it doesn't seem we're much above ants, dutifully carrying out our predefined tasks, merely to fit in the pecking order of existence."

"The point is a valid one," replied Kyla. "I will not debate you on that. Meaning is often out the window when in the context of the work week."

"But doesn't this make if difficult, this knowledge? Granted, I'm a wise and happening guy, so maybe I can deal, on the basis of the goodness of being me. But, harrowing as it may sound, not everyone is me, Kyla. How do they deal?"

"My belief is that most do not consider the idea you've put forth. We are instructed from youth in the order to which we must conform, in order to be 'productive.' Leisure becomes but a luxury."

Chaotic Ocean

"Well," Dorian started again, "I don't think that's fine and well, even for someone as myself. And I'm not afraid to say it like it is. What in life has meaning: nothing, except for the simple and fundamental aspect of nature – procreation. All else is without meaning. We were not made to contemplate. We were made to reproduce."

"Rather negative, no?" questioned she.

"Negative or hounest. One of them. Don't worry, though. I'm sure it will pass once I reaffirm myself a few more times. I'm just talking from my arse again. Oops, looks like it's time to fly. Sorry. I'll see you next time, Kyla."

"Okay, Dorian, till next time."

"Lates."

She plainly sat there behind the desk for many minutes, putting the most recent debate behind her. What troubled Kyla was Dorian's acquaintance with "Zigmund's work," which much confounded her. She could not see why Zigmund, a part of her life that was once only for recreation, had now penetrated through the deepest layers of her mind, and had now manifested its presence into her very workplace.

*

Cecelia Greene, her third patient, was a few moments late. The young girl walked in, and more positive than usual, was wearing a half-smile of sorts upon her countenance. Kyla felt somewhat uneasy since, here before her, was a young, misguided youth, who truly, perhaps more than Kyla's other two patients, needed her help, and all Kyla could selfishly concentrate on were the publishings of which her other patients had prior spoken. She felt wretched to have been so narrow-minded.

"Hi there," timidly greeted the girl.

"Hello Cecelia, it's very nice to see you again," remarked Kyla as she attempted to suppress her other emotions.

"So, what might we be discussing today now? Maybe a few more of the chef's specials, insecurity, self-image, pasta and peas?" joked Cecelia.

Kyla was actually quite delighted to see Cecilia in such a mood. Their last encounter was filled with mistrust and negativity, which directly opposed the nature of the current session.

"Not to sound, umm..." she searched for a younger word, "barmy, but why the great mood, Cecelia? I mean, I love it; it is really nice to see you looking and acting so wonderfully."

Before the girl had a chance to respond, Kyla thought to herself, "Wow this is quite a treat, for Cecelia and for myself. Maybe this day is not as wicked as it was earlier looking."

Cecelia remarked, "Oh, it's nothing much, I've just been enjoying some new reading material."

Kyla's soul seemed to escape her body, as she was in utter fright of the next words to come from Cecelia's mouth.

"It's this old ancient Chinese poetry. Some of it is really, really, ummm poetic."

Chaotic Ocean

Kyla was relieved, like some dying desert vegetation greeted by a monsoon. She tried to show no change in emotion.

"Ah, so it's quite beautiful?" questioned Kyla.

"Yes, that's it. Some of it really applies to my life, as if the author then had intended it for a contemporary troubled teen. Isn't that very odd?" asked the girl.

"Great literature and poetry is ageless. It lives not in the confines of the year it was written, nor in the lifetime of its author, nor even in the general time period that he lived and related the ideas to. It lives universally, through the ages, through time and space, as it is magnificent enough to be related to persons of all eternity."

"Well, I think that's what I have. It is an anthology, I believe, of all different poems. So, it has kept me busy, Kyla love."

The two departed the topic of reading for some time, and began to discuss some deeper issues, such as the girl's relationship with her family. Since Cecelia was so young and malleable, Kyla thought not to exploit her hounesty for long bouts. Kyla then decided to return to the prior conversation, perhaps for some kind of closure.

"I'm just glad that you've placed your reading in valid writing, as opposed to here-and-gone insignificant, pernicious authors who seek to misguide in the most subversive of manners."

Kyla's words had been too specific to go unnoticed.

"Umm, do you have someone in mind, Kyla? I mean, you sound angry at someone. Just curious."

"Angry?" Kyla asked as she tried to buy time to form a response.

"Yeah, an angry bugger indeed!" laughed Cecelia.

"Well, I have this friend, he..." she let slip.

"A friend?"

"I," as she regrouped her thoughts, "don't think it's very important. Don't worry about it. Merely a man I know that lives a bit too awkwardly to be of any good to this world."

"Well, okay."

Cecelia was unsure how to respond. Kyla felt, once again, that she had let her personal world and troubles penetrate into the world of her patients, which for her, was completely unacceptable. Though, she decided that even at the risk of cutting a session short, it would be ultimately healthier to the patient to see her when she herself was of sound, cleared mind.

"I'm very sorry, Cecelia, but..."

"You're leaving me? Like everyone else? Cutting me?"

"No, I'm..."

This was exactly what Kyla had feared: losing trust from the one patient to whom trust was the most important issue.

"I'm just going to end this session for the day, as I have personal matters to attend to. It has nothing to do with you as a patient. I have enjoyed this session, and am truly happy to see you with a smile on your face. Keep reading that poetry, and next session, perhaps you can give me

Chaotic Ocean

some specifics on it, and we'll discuss it more deeply. How does that sound?"

The girl looked disappointed, but somewhat compassionate at the same time.

"I guess that will be alright. Maybe we can make up the time lost in our next session?"

The girl looked as if Kyla were her only companion.

"Sure, we can do that, dear," replied Kyla.

"I guess I'll be off. Bye Kyla. Have a good one."

"You too, dear."

The girl began to walk off, and Kyla could view a rectangular object protruding out of the back of the girl's pants. The girl stopped to wave good-bye as she stood in the doorway, and as she turned, the object swiped against the wall and fell to the ground.

"Oh Cecelia..." called Kyla.

However, the girl was already down the hall and could not hear the call. Kyla slowly stood up and walked over to see what the girl had been carrying with her. She bent down, and as the object came into view, was disgusted.

It was a subjectaphor pamphlet.

"What God in Heaven could allow this reach to be so vast, and surely, so crippling? What God in Heaven could allow the minds of the young to be affected even in the slightest by Zigmund Sardoce?"

She began to open the pamphlet, but the pages had been stuck together. Kyla managed to pry it open only to discover that the ink was faded. It must have had been washed with the girls clothes.

"Confound it!"

This she could stand no longer. She decided to retire home for the day in hopes of reaching Zigmund. Kyla had planned to bring him the pamphlet, which, while it was faded, still donned his name.

"This is a tangibility he cannot subdue or obfuscate. He cannot deny the piercing evidence of actuality," she thought.

With a feeling of vengeance, as if some beast tasting its first drops of blood, she was off. This was a fresh feeling that she had never experienced. Kyla enjoyed the newness and freedom of the moment.

As she started her old banger and began to drive away, she thought she had seen Mr. Pem in her rear mirror. Halting the vehicle before exiting the lot, he was absent. As she drove off, far from view of the compound, Mr. Pem stepped out from beside the building, wearing a curved smile upon his face.

CHAPTER SEVEN
☦

THE ABJECT OBJECT

*

Zigmund had not slept since having witnessed the horrific crime in the park. He had not ceased thinking of the grand implications that he perceived Kyla to have had in the matter. The man had been poisoned with a purpose – to expose to himself and to the world what Kyla had become. Zigmund paced around the pond, stiffened by his own trepidation, utterly convinced that he had to consult it on Kyla's nature, yet utterly wavered in so doing, as if fearful of the actuality of what was to be answered.

"I must summon this haven of pure truth. I must reach out so to be included on all that is fact in this world. Why did Kyla lead me into the park, only to witness such a vile and wicked crime? Could she have possibly had no foreknowledge? Could she have possibly had no hand in this perfectly timed, not quite random occurrence? I wish it were so, though, I cannot believe such a tale."

Zigmund, for the first time, prepared to make a conscious and concerted communication with the pond. Liveliness coursed through his veins. He felt powerful, like the champion of some magnificent past epoch. The sky was distasteful and putrid-looking. Thick, brown clouds had formed over the city skyline. The Earth seemed to gnarl, as the slow, subtlety of underlying thunder formed in the air. As if a steady vibration, the sound grew louder. Passersby increased their pacing speed, as a dark feeling seemed to entrench existence.

Zigmund intrinsically understood, without practice, how to summon the pond's knowledge, as if having only awoken an archaic archetype within his own self. He knelt down beside the thing, closed his eyes, and cupped his hands together. As if an ancient ritual, he reached for the pond's water. It was warm and smooth like freshly blown glass. He dripped the liquid over his head, as if some kind of baptism. Zigmund quickly became electrified with feeling, emotion, and thought. His tears wept violently from his body, as if trying to escape an unholy torture. His joints stiffened like stones, and his spine writhed in contortion. He could feel a spirit other than his own swimming through his entire body. Zigmund felt like he had been possessed.

His eyes began to open, completely independent of his free will. He was the vessel, but was no longer the controller. His head tilted downward to the pond. The water, once again, as such was the occurrence with his first experience with the pond, turned murky, like the palette of some artist mixing colours at random. Zigmund attempted to make out anything he could, yet his body was too much in utter shock for his mind to care. It was as if he had been struck with cerebral edema, high upon some great mountaintop. It seemed like his brain needed oxygen, but was too famished to have been bothered, too famished to make his body move to obtain it.

Then, a compromising process of sorts began to take place. The pond had surely been too much for any man to harness, so it seemed. Though, an assimilation began, whereby Zigmund started to regain parts of his senses, as the utter power of the pond eased out from his body. It was in this moment that revelation was greatest. It was in this moment that the pictures seemed clearest, so it seemed.

He gazed at the pond in wonderment. Zigmund saw Kyla's image appear. He almost dreaded the forthcoming pictures. In one moment, he could see Kyla with a man standing in the shadows. She appeared to be handing the man something, which most closely resembled a large amount of highly marked notes, as if a payment. The next image flashed into the pond. The same man whom Kyla had paid was to be the man in the park, the one whom they had together witnessed wickedly murder an innocent woman. The final image flashed through the murky waters of the pond. It was simply that of Kyla smiling Devilishly as she stood outside Zigmund's mansion after the night had concluded.

Suddenly, Zigmund's body was arched like a curved beam, each side sinking to the ground, weighed down by respective objects. He felt like his back was going to break in two. Zigmund could no longer feel the ground beneath his feet. He was elevated, or so he thought. Then, as rapidly as the power had come to him, it vanished.

There he lay on the ground, feeling empty, hollow, as if one of his internal organs had been ripped out by force. His body was weak. His mind was numb. His eyes were watery. Zigmund could not muster the strength to pick himself up. He longed for the comfort of his mansion, of his bed. He longed only to rejuvenate. Though, Zigmund fell prisoner to the pain. He could be nothing more than inert, and as such, was forced to suffer the cold conditions of nature. His body did not seem to care, as sleep was its only guiding force. He quickly dozed off and entered the world of the subconscious.

Zigmund found himself in a courtroom, shackled in heavy, metallic chains. The judge was speaking to him directly. Apparently, he had been on trial for some great crime against humanity. The judge's voice was coarse and bellowed throughout the hall.

Zigmund could see a sea of faces, all directly peering at him. He felt small, belittled, as if guilt had torn a hole through his soul. For the life of him, he could not understand why he was being held. He was but an actor playing a role, though, could gather no prior information about the script.

"Why am I being held?" he whispered to a man behind him.

"Silence!" shouted the looming judge. "You will not speak till you have been granted permission to do so. *Incontrovertible* is the evidence before the court. Woe is you, Mr. Sardoce."

"But what did I..." Zigmund began to ask.

"Have you no penance for your actions? Could you be so bold to deny them at this point?" asked the judge.

"But, judge..."

"Once more will I explain to all, the charges brought against you, Mr. Sardoce, for the mere humour of the court. You are charged with, and found guilty of the following – making your fellow man, your fellow brethren, feel little and insignificant. This is the highest dishonour in the land and will be punished greatly. You sir, are nothing better than the fellows whom you've brought down. You are not divine. Their intelligence does not pale in comparison to yours, as you have made the case time and again in your life."

Zigmund was no longer in control of himself in the dream. It was at this moment that he was relegated to omniscient spectator.

"You, Mr. Sardoce, have one last comment to make before sentencing. You may use it however you wish. I would, though, lean toward humility," spoke the judge.

Zigmund felt no sin for his pride. He felt no sin in belittling others. He spoke not humbly, but boldly, as was perhaps the only plausible outcome for a man such of his nature.

"The only common ground betwixt extreme intelligence and extreme inanity is that both wish to reach the other's plateau with no concept of how to do so. The means to an end is similar, but not the same as the process and journey itself. Who is more advanced? The 'unknowing' journeymen who travel to the end and arrive at the beginning, or the 'knowing' campers who stay in their true first and last destinations. I seek no compassion in sentencing, for I have only spoken candidly, what every man believes in his heart, but is too shy to speak. I leave you only with the question that I have so eloquently already given. Were the lot of you not imbeciles yourselves, you'd see that there is worth in men such as myself. Ponder the question, and you will see maybe that I am not who I have been made out to be. That is all."

The judge stopped for a moment to gather his final statement to Zigmund.

"You will be punished for your pride, Mr. Sardoce." The judge paused. "Intelligence has not much a distinction from height or hair color. Yet, we praise it to no end, celebrate it in every possible manifestation, and wave it around as a flag of accomplishment and honour. It is no better than height. There is no more a process than the simple random crossing of parental genes. This though, as a society, we cannot accept. We must punish the ones of ill-intelligence and attribute it to predestination or lack of schooling or laziness or willpower. We force our false ideals on a system that couldn't be more sporadic. This, of course, all along, is preached by the ones who did happen to randomly receive a mental blessing. Make no mistake about it. When power surges within our bodies and our lives, we can attribute nothing to luck. Humility escapes our very vocabulary. But, when we are on the bottom, we say it's the market, it's the time, or it's the weather. A double standard would be understating the issue ten fold. Your are sentenced to eternal discomfort."

The two opposing arguments seemed awkwardly juxtaposed against one another. It was as if Zigmund's inner character was becoming permeable, even from sentence to sentence. His statement had not been that of a cruel and snooty man looking down upon his brothers. Surely, it was misguided, and filled with a sense pride too pourous and obvious to be veiled, though, it was not as it was made out to be. The judge's remark did not seem to reflect any kind of understanding. It spoke to the idea's for which Zigmund was on trial. It spoke to the insultory remarks spoken by Zigmund toward the end of his confident statement. Though, it did not speak to the statement itself. Perhaps the judge cared not, or cared not to observe the validity of the statement that Zigmund posed to the people. Perhaps the judge too was not free of criminality. C'est la vie. So is inadequately put together literature. One must rationalise when one's ideas do not combine precisely. Though, this is no new concept to the reader. Let us depart from this rant.

*

Zigmund proceeded to dream on into the night. His next dream was that of a political debate. He was the prime minister or something or other. Zigmund was told to prepare a three-minute speech on whatever topic he so chose. He found himself before a large audience. Once again, all eyes were fixed on his. The crowd seemed anxious and willing to listen to Zigmund's remarks with respect. It was as if he had been presented with a riddle, and eight of nine parts had already been solved. The giving of this speech would complete the ninth part and solve the greatest mystery, cure the greatest illness, or fill the largest information loophole in the world. He was not anxious at the podium, but poised, and once again, ever confident in his words.

"Over the years I have acquired a great discord and discontent for science. It is merely a system created to put order on to, and an attempt to rationalise different beautiful mysteries of life. We in turn take this man-made invention and name it logic. We are players, and yet we also write the rules to the game, therefore, it must make profound sense. No one denies the genius of the system, just the lock and key hypocrisy that dictates it.

Is this not merely our attempt to understand the incomprehensible world around us? Our modern day knowledge seems no better than the ways of the Romans in naming spiritual suns and moons, and yet we look back to them as having been simplistic. It is clear that we will share the same fate; we will be looked upon in the same fashion in which we look upon them.

Practical application aside, it seems to me that to theorise about voids of information we know not about is foolish. How the universe began is an ongoing question that haunts some people even when in deep slumber. We, as a race feel the need to know, to explain everything that is above our present understanding, simply so we will have an answer for the history books, merely so we can sleep.

The greatest clarity is in admitting the unspeakable, the uncomfortable, that we do not know who we are, or where we are going. No theory of life seems to be of any importance compared with life itself, said the great Oscar Wilde. Though, said many times before, the fact of life, the only tangible and concrete idea, the only exacting truth, is that we as a species know very little if anything, and that there is always more to learn. The only way to learn is to explore and experience life, rather then compute and normalise its wonders. It is impossible to gain anything from life, or to understand it at all, by merely experiencing it from afar, or equating it to some artificially shaped idea of truth.

Overall, it merely seems that attempting to figure out the 'large picture 'or even the small picture on some sub-atomic level, is less beneficial than seeing it, smelling it, and touching it. There is value in everything of course, but a life has a certain number of years with it, and you may decide how to use them. Lastly, it has been said, 'We cannot appreciate that which we do not understand.' I do not proclaim to understand all scientific concepts, but I do know that putting oneself in a state of open mindedness is the key to new experience.

On a side note, science is the very device that has led humanity to its current state of comfort and convenience. While I speak and rant and ramble of its lesser qualities, I also realise and understand how beneficial it is as well, and how it surrounds me always. I appreciate it and its creators who sacrificed life's experience to give us the gift of technology. Let me further that idea. Forget experiencing life. Become a scientist and create. Create and create and create. Make the world your technological playground, and I will heed my own prior advice, that is, of course, with a little help from my scientific friends."

The audience instantly morphed into a sea of Kyla Demark's chappering on and on.

"Whop whop, choppa choppa, whop whop, choppa choppa, whop whop!!" they cawed.

"Kyla, your games do not fool me!" Zigmund yelled from the podium. "I am onto you, and have been for quite some time. Do not invade the innards of my mind and attempt to reprimand the deepest most manifestations of my being. Gladly, I will debate the validity of this argument in conscious awareness, though, that time is not of the present."

He became increasingly infuriated with the audience. His distaste for Kyla increased almost as largely and quickly as his ego had. For whatever reason, he could think of nothing but Kyla, and was drawn to completely wrapping his mind around her nature.

The speech seemed to have been for not. He was quite proud of himself for admitting his own hypocrisy, and for this, assumed that since he had done so, it was a canceling factor of sorts. Perhaps, so long as he figured to recognise his own flaws, it was quite noble to have had them in the first place, and needed to change little of his thinking.

Chaotic Ocean

The latter part of the dream turned his anger aflame, as Kyla seemed to replicate every few seconds. Soon there was a population cawing at him, and he could see this only as insidious.

Zigmund awoke in a cold sweat, remembering precisely the ideas from the dreams.

He thought to himself, "How has that wench penetrated into my mind? What has she done? What power has she?"

His only resolve was, "She will not get off with this trickery. Surely not."

Zigmund was able to gather enough strength to walk inside the mansion.

*

Meanwhile, Kyla had been driving along the road to Zigmund's home. She was filled with purpose, not completely unlike Zigmund, and could not bear her friend's lies a moment longer. She felt in her heart that there was no chance of Zigmund's innocence on the issue of having created the subjectaphor pamphlets. Kyla thought he was as guilty as Napoleon and deserved no sympathy on the matter. She desired nothing more than to present him with the irrefutable evidence that she had found on her patient.

"His Goddamn name is on it. Surely, he will not have words for me. I cannot wait to see a smile fade to guilt. I cannot wait for this, to see the cowl shed and the cower to set."

Kyla's own predicted satisfaction from the forthcoming confrontation was a feeling almost entirely new to her. She did not feel good to have had this feeling. It was as if a shark tipped off to chum. The idea of feeling anything but pity for a man such as Zigmund was harrowing. The idea of extracting joy from his negativity, from his lies, was completely polar in nature to Kyla's normal demeanor. She could not fathom why this instance was different from any other. And yet, somehow, it *was* entirely dissimilar.

Somehow Kyla had changed. Somehow this satisfaction bothered her less and less as she thought more about it. She even began to rationalise her desires, freeing from her usual sense of goodness.

The city was filled with an atypical motorcade of congestion. It was as if a parasite had attached itself to the walls and streets, the blockage its web, as diligently doing the ill-advised deeds of Zigmund. Kyla imagined him buying time, so to speak.

"The audacity of the man!" thought Kyla. "Not only has he a liar's soul, but now also that of a procrastinator, stalling and slowing the inevitable. I ought to give him a mouthful."

The automotive blockage continued on for what seemed like days. Kyla could imagine the sun falling, the moon rising, the rains passing, and the snow piling up in the span of a few hours. She could have probably walked to Zigmund's home in a shorter span of time than sitting in unexplainable congestion. It had no reason for existence. It existed, perhaps, purely to exist. Kyla took personal offense to inconvenience of this nature.

"Confound it!" said she aloud.

The negativity was boiling inside of her body. She could feel her anger rising and her reasonability decreasing. Kyla could no longer focus on the joy of exposing Zigmund for his lies. She now could only think of the wickedness of the man, of Zigmund, whom she simply knew was somehow to blame for the sudden and malicious congestion that had swept her in, as how perhaps a sales person might do to innocents.

Suddenly, Kyla realised her own internal change, as if having been freed from possession for but a brief moment.

"Oh dear, what has become of me? I've turned into an enraged being with little knowledge, only driven by a motive of finding pleasure in another's pain? Who is the hunted here? Have I truly allowed Zigmund to invade the space of my mind this much? This cannot be, will not be. I must calm down. I must find peace within myself if I am to speak candidly to Zigmund."

Kyla quickly inhaled a few deep breaths and let her mind wander. The negative thoughts soon faded, and she was able to once more regain control of her emotions. The congestion quickly dispersed, as if in accord with the web of hostility Kyla had been weaving. She swiftly drove onward to her friend's estate, now feeling better about herself, and looked forward to conversing.

*

The congestion had literally lasted for hours. It was very late at night, and Kyla contemplated leaving the deed for the next day, though could not. As she approached the estate, Zigmund was simultaneously awakening. Sleep was no more as he could sense something strange in the air. He decided to walk out onto his property, and in so doing, witnessed Kyla opening the gate and pulling into the drive.

"I could have guessed," smugly remarked Zigmund into the sky.

Kyla did not see him till she had parked her old banger. She exited the vehicle and could too see Zigmund glowering at her.

"Why am I not surprised that he has been waiting for me?" she thought to herself.

The two dropped their preconceptions for a moment, or at least, each respectively erected a façade quickly enough to resemble civility toward one another.

"Kyla, dear. What brings you to my estate at this hour of the night? I thought you fancied day meetings? Then again, our last nighttime meeting was quite *interesting* to say the least, so why *wouldn't* you come back to explore another?"

The tone in his voice was obviously sarcastic and offensive.

"Zigmund, you must know me too well," remarked Kyla.

It was an awkward juxtaposition for the two: each had an incredible deal of which to accuse the other, but neither wished to fall into the trap of tactlessness.

Chaotic Ocean

Nonetheless, Kyla was first to strike.

"Zigmund, I came her for a simple reason. I came here for a simple answer and to expose a simple mystery. There is no sense standing about without walking. There is no sense in having one's eyes open without seeing what is directly in front of oneself."

Zigmund thought to himself, "The insidious witch."

"So what is it, Kyla? Do tell of what is on your mind."

"I asked you once before, Zigmund, if you had been behind some wretched pamphlets called subjectaphors. You denied this vehemently in every possible manner and went so far to say that you'd investigate the idea yourself. Well, the investigation is over, my friend. Do you wish to say anything before I go onward?"

"Say to you? A witch?" thought Zigmund. "What is she babbling about?"

"I've nothing to add, sorry. Get on with this," he replied.

"Three of my patients each had knowledge of your subjectaphor pamphlets. Each expressed the ideas that had been written about in these harmful papers that you distributed. Furthermore, I have even acquired one of these silly little things. And the proof is *incontrovertible.*"

The word rang inside of Zigmund's head as he thought back to his dreams, the judge who had used the same phrasing, and the many replicated Kyla's barking at him. This shook him visibly.

"Your name is printed on the inside cover, Zigmund. You published these pamphlets. Now admit to this. There is no other path. Gather up some dignity and admit what I already know."

"Kyla, I am sorry," Zigmund started, as he collected himself. "but I am guilty of no such crime. I believe you are..."

"I am not mistaken," Kyla interrupted.

She proceeded to take the pamphlet out and handed it to the man.

"The writing is faded, but clearly, you can see your own name on this abomination of literature."

Zigmund took the paper. He seemed quite taken back by the whole idea. For a long while, he said nothing. He did not question the validity of the pamphlet, nor did he remark about the washed out print. Seeing his own name on a creation that he had no knowledge of was entirely shocking. The writing seemed to call to him, causing electrons to fire about his brain.

"But I..." timidly remarked Zigmund.

"*Do not deny the woman of truth, Zigmund. She has come so far for her answers.*"

"Who is that???" Zigmund yelled.

Kyla did not know what was happening to her friend.

"Zigmund, what's wrong? What's the matter?" asked Kyla.

"*She's onto us, friend. There is but one way out of this. Perhaps you already know such,*" spoke the voice inside of Zigmund's head.

"Leave me alone!!!" shouted Zigmund to himself.

"*But one way. You know the nature of this woman. You know exactly what she has done, what she has orchestrated. You know exactly that all your fears of her are entirely true. She, so holy, has come to accuse you? There is but one solution, Zigmund."*

"Zigmund, are you okay? Do you need help?" pleaded Kyla.

She could see her friend enwrapped in some kind of inner turmoil. Such an adverse reaction Kyla did not anticipate and consequently felt horrible. She felt as though her accusations had caused Zigmund to go mad. He was visibly disturbed and battling some kind of unknown force.

"*There is but one way,*" spoke the voice to Zigmund. "*Kill her.*"

Chaotic Ocean

CHAPTER EIGHT
✝

PERNICIOUS EVENTS?

*

Zigmund stood about with his head to the ground. A brown dusting of snow began to fall, as if it had been passed through a dirt filter after falling from the Heavens. A cool wind swept over London and through Kyla's veins. Zigmund was still. He was no longer shouting or ranting, and Kyla did not know how to react.

"Kyla dear," remarked Zigmund, who had regained composure, "this whole pamphlet accusation is very troubling."

"Zigmund, are you sure you're okay?" asked Kyla in a concerned manner.

"Quite," snapped Zigmund.

Kyla was taken back by the coldness of the remark.

"I still must completely deny all of such accusations, Kyla. Obviously, this is a forgery, some hooligan using my prestigious name to gain notoriety. I tell you again that I have never seen this piece of paper before in my life, nor have I published it or sold it or spoken the faded words."

Kyla did not believe Zigmund. She thought this to have been yet another lie.

"Can this man truly fib so freely with no conscience to hold him back?" thought Kyla.

"And you don't find it odd that the ideas presented inside are much like ideas that you might have?" she then questioned.

"Well now, as you can see, the words are faded beyond recognition, all conveniently but my name. I cannot see or make out a single sentence, let alone enough to say if it is at allakin to my own thinking. Can you?"

Kyla took the subjectaphor pamphlet. It truly was unreadable. Yet, she had discussed the ideas with her patients. Though, she had no concrete evidence to give Zigmund. Kyla figured he would not take the word of her patients as truth enough to admit to the sin. And for this, she resented him. She loathed his dishounesty and was bitter that her old friend could not concede to even the obvious truth of the matter.

"Yet another useless verbal confrontation," she thought inside. "I don't even know why I bother anymore. Why am I drawn to this pernicious man? Why am I drawn to this place of pomp? I should care not an ounce, but I care an ocean. For this, I am ever in turmoil."

"No, Zigmund," said she aloud, "I cannot read the words."

Chaotic Ocean

Zigmund felt proud. He felt that his words were beautiful and Kyla had not a bone in her body with wit enough to combat them. Then however, the hubris soon turned to realisation.

"This woman is evil. Perhaps I know what I must do. No longer is this about an accusation. This is about justice and piety. Must I kill though? Is there no other way from this fortress of omniscience?" Zigmund thought to himself.

Kyla could notice the brief pause inside of him. She knew there was more than what he was letting on and interpreted this pause to have been his further concoction of lies with which to spew.

Finally, Zigmund spoke and said, "Then I suppose that is all there is to it. Perhaps I will still investigate, Kyla, if that would make you feel better at ease. Though, surely you can see now that this is not something to accuse me of, but rather, a crime that some fool has committed. Perhaps you can use your powers of accusation to find that young individual."

Kyla understood the insultory tone that he had inserted into his statement. She did not enjoy it. At the same time though, she was tired of arguing, and her desire of extracting a grand expose had long ceased. She wished to leave such revelations for another day.

"Perhaps," chirped Kyla with causticity.

"You don't seem your usual self. You seem somewhat different. Would not the Kyla I'd known just shortly ago argue this point to no end to prove that I am in fact the phantom publisher?"

Kyla did not fancy the casual tone the conversation had taken. She wished nothing more than to deflect its direction, and knew that she would have to dig down to find a satisfactory remark to appease Zigmund, but now, no longer wished to speak of the pamphlets or his involvement. Kyla actually wished nothing more than to vacate the estate, though, figured she would stay to humour herself, to see what Zigmund had been mentally concocting of late.

"Kyla," again stated Zigmund, "no retort to offer? Do you not have a guiding argument for me?"

Zigmund seemed somewhat offset that Kyla had not been giving in to his demands. She could notice this too. Decidedly, she spoke perhaps the one thing that she knew he would detest.

"I've increasingly come to view all debate as quite useless: two opposing forces egotistically arguing a point all to further their own self-hubris. I've found that the man who truly wishes to learn is more apt to listen than to challenge. The man who knows he knows not is much more willing to be open than he is to chastise or counter. Thus, the man who does debate, who does challenge, wishes to know nothing more than that which he already knows. The man who debates has a fixed idea about the world and is therefore unwilling to alter his idea, thus giving little if any worth to opposing beliefs and values. This man knows himself only through his own cognition, and such is a shame. Accordingly, such mentality as this breeds nothing but ego, disdain, resentment, and hatred. Exchange of positive, mutually respected, open information is how the world grows. It is not through thuggary or through forceful and nearsighted bickering. All debate is useless."

And so this did in fact infuriate Zigmund.

"That's hogwash, Kyla! You know as well as I do that even you do not believe the contrived words you've just spoken. It's as if you'd thought of it before and have been merely searching for the proper conversation in which to insert it your dribble."

"I am sorry if my remark displeases you, Zigmund, but that is the truth. I no longer wish to argue with you, today or any day," added Kyla to further infuriate her friend.

"Bah, just leave, Kyla. You come here in the middle of the night, accuse me of a crime I am obviously innocent of, and then speak this hogwash to me. You've changed, and you should go. Do not think your cowl will stay on in the harshest of winds."

Zigmund's last sentence disturbed Kyla, though she was willing to dismiss its meaning for the opportunity of departing home to forget all that she had come to do.

"As you wish, old friend. Good-bye."

"Good-bye."

And with that Kyla walked over to her vehicle with a renewed sense of hope. She was entirely angry that Zigmund would not admit to the publishing, but on a different level, entirely happy that her comment had upset him to the point of asking her departure. She drove off.

*

The brown snow fell more as she road along the cobblestone streets. It was difficult to see out of her dirty windshield. She made it home at last and figured she would retire for the night.

Now inside of her home, Kyla decided to walk to the back doors to look out upon the land that stretched on for miles. It seemed always snow covered, but now, the snow seemed browner than ever; it looked squalid. It had not been white for some time. Kyla was puzzled, but gave the fact little thought.

The morning brought with it a sense of optimism. Kyla gave little consideration to her conversation with Zigmund. She was up and about, and while strolling through her flat, recalled the trouble of the lapis.

"Dreaded stone. Was this a gift or a curse? Could Mr. Pem have known about the nature of the object, of the strange feeling one acquires when in physical contact with it? Could I be imagining the whole thing? I have so many questions to pose, so many questions that need answering. Yet, I've no one. I've not even Zigmund anymore."

At that moment, the homely church-going Horris popped into her mind. She recalled how he was so utterly exacting in his heavily Londonised vocabulary. Kyla recalled how with one whisk of a sentence, with almost no thought, he could break through the thickest armies of her mind and take total control for moments, seconds, and possibly, however long he so desired. This was not a comforting feeling, though, was very curious a sensation. For one reason or another, she felt Horris was the

Chaotic Ocean

man to speak to again. She felt as if everyone else had abandoned her in her time of need, as if some cancer patient in late stages losing a mother to daytime television. Kyla was drawn to Horris for his simplicity, for his ability to listen and dissect, and perhaps most of all, for his hounesty.

She quickly scurried to put on her face and darted out of the flat. Within minutes, Kyla arrived at the church where at she had prior met Horris. It looked brighter on this day, brighter than it had in the past.

"Perhaps they've just given it a cleaning," she thought as she pulled up.

It seemed more inviting on this day as well. Kyla felt good for the first time in a few days and was looking forward to seeing the man.

"I only hope the guy is here. I mean, I know he can't be here all the time. After all, the church does have hours like any other place in London. So, we'll just have to see."

She opened the magnificent church doors and peered inside. Kyla was surprised at the result. Unlike times past, the church was not filled with a slew of goers. The rush-and-tumble mentality seemed to not exist on this day. It was quiet, almost peaceful. She peered around some more, noticing there was hardly a soul in the place, as if it had been condemned. This was unusual. Along the second pew from the altar up front, Kyla saw a single man sitting in prayer. He had his head down and seemed deeply involved. She was about to close the door when the man suddenly called to her.

"Kyla, Gawd blimey, good of ya' ta come. Please, come, come, sit with me," yelped Horris from the front of the church.

Kyla gracefully walked down the centre aisle and approached him. He again looked similar to days past, and this provided Kyla a small amount of comfort and familiarity.

"H...h...how did you know it was me?" she questioned timidly in a hushed voice.

"Aw com'on, dovey. The whole world is going pear shaped. What makes a man like me think yer life is gonna be any different from the rest of prats 'hat roam this vast planet?"

"I suppose you have a point," she quietly added.

"And there's another thing, dove, why are ya' talkin so Gawd chirpy low? This is a house of God, not Heaven herself. Have some life in yer bones for once."

Strangely, Kyla felt good to take Horris' barking orders. She felt good again, as if Horris would steer her in the right path.

"Horris, I..."

"No need ta explain, Kyla dove. I'm here for all of whateva' it is ya' gots ta tell me. I'm not a doctor, thank God herself for 'hat, but maybe I can put-paid-ta whateva it is ya're not thinking is good about yer life."

Kyla did feel relieved at Horris' willingness.

"So many things, Horris, so many things. My friend, Zigmund, he, he's..."

"Don't worry, dove. He knows not what he does," he remarked before hearing the rest of the sentence.

"He's a liar. He's created these disgusting philosophies, if you can call them such, and now he's propagating the material to the young and innocent."

Horris' premature answer registered in Kyla's brain then.

"Wait, what did you say?" she asked.

"Never mind about a mind who says never, Kyla; it just don't make no sense ta bother. This Zigmund fellow, I'm sure he's more innocent than for which ya're giving him credit. He's just a man, just a rat-arsed-pisser like all of us. Why should he remain so special?"

"This is what I am truly confused by. I should not care for such a man. I know the man's nature, the man's past history, and I know that our friendship is for nothing more than jest, in hounest. Yet, he is exacting when driving the nail. He is exacting when getting under my skin. And furthermore, lately I have been dismissing all of this. I am drawn to him. And I am weak, and I don't know why. It is as if he has some hidden power over me that cannot be defined, or is so hidden that I will never solve the puzzle. As I told you last time, I simply feel one step behind in everything I do or think; I am seeing only portions of a picture. The curtain remains over most of the stage, and I am left to interpret."

"And what of your friend, Mr. Pem, was his name?"

"Why, yes that's his name. But I am speaking of Zigmund, Horris, not Mr. Pem," snapped Kyla, as if the man had done something horribly wrong in asking.

"Yes, this I know, dovey. What of Mr. Pem though?"

"What of him?"

"Where is he? When did ya' see him last? Have ya' had any strange encounters with him?"

She did not understand why Horris would care to divert the conversation so entirely much to Mr. Pem when clearly she had been speaking of, and had been having trouble with, Zigmund.

"No, no. Mr. Pem is a kind, old man whom I found a job for at the hospital. That's all."

"And he's asked nothing of ya' in return?" insinuated Horris?

"Of course not, Horris, what kind of person would you have me for?" she snapped again.

Horris looked into her eyes. He said nothing. He peered into the glassy surfaces that seemed to be trembling. He said nothing. He could see fear and anger inside Kyla. He could see a defensive mechanism working on its own will. He said nothing. The man peered on for a few more moments.

"I am sorry. Ya're right, Kyla. We will move on, dovey. Sorry for digression," apologised Horris.

Kyla had not expected an apology.

"Quite alright, Horris."

She went on rambling.

After a few minutes, Kyla noticed his attention to be elsewhere.

"Am I boring you, Horris?" asked Kyla in a concerned manner.

"Not at all, dovey; I was just waiting ta put mine in, ya' know, for the moment, so ta speak, dove," he replied.

"So what do you think? I know these are my problems to solve, and I am selfish to seek advice from you, but I feel strangely at peace when we're talking, Horris. I feel good, and I am sorry, but I enjoy the sensation."

"Don't be sorry, dove. Everyone's just trying ta get his or hers. Feeling good however ya' can is always right. As for yer friend, Zigmund, pardon the harshness, but this chap sounds like he needs ta don some self-deprecating lubricant. Sounds like a pompous human with the worth of dogs' bollocks. I can lend ya' some of this lubey if ya' want to give it a try," joked the old man.

"Self-deprecating lubricant, ey?" encouraged Kyla.

"Oh yeah, for sure, dovey. I keep a spare supply ta keep myself in check when I'm feeling too good about something I've done. But it sounds like yer friend could sure use a few drops. Rat-arsed-pissers always need ta don this kind of potion."

"Well, it sounds divine," she joked.

"Got 'hat right! Nothing short of God herself could have invented something so deliciously humbling as this. Even got a nice smell ta her, the lubey 'hat is, not God. I can't say for sure about God, but if ever there was a fine smelling ambrosia, God herself probably is advertising it as we speak."

"Well, thanks for the advice, Horris. I think maybe Zigmund is in need of the product. Maybe it could also be helpful in removing the pomposity from his lower region."

"From his arse? Ya' folks and your propriety! Eh, ta eat his own."

"Don't you mean, to each his own?" asked Kyla.

"Hey, whatever turns yer knobs, dovey; just don't lay yer rules on this tired body."

Kyla smiled and felt joyous to be joking back-and-forth. She did actually forget her troubles while speaking with Horris. Even if she had been speaking about the ills of her life, it was still unlike having been pained *by* them.

This was the longest conversation that the two had partaken in, and Kyla did not wish for it to end. She decided to continue onward about other topics, as discussing her personal life had become tiresome.

"I've only been here a few times, Horris, and it seems I know little about you. It seems always that I am the one working with Demons. Tell me something of your interest."

"Ideas be the best tellers. Lotsa pissers can say this about 'hat or 'hat about everything and all while ya're getting nothing about nothing. Ya' don't know 'em from a hole in the pub. So, I'm not really in 'hat business."

"Fair enough," remarked Kyla.

"But if ya're interested in ideas, then surely I've got one," he responded.

"Over the past days all I've thought about is myself, so yes, I would love to hear one, Horris, about whatever you wish."

"Ever hear of eternal recurrence, dove?"

"Can't say I have."

Kyla seemed intrigued.

"Ah, it's just this rat-arsed theory 'hat after mother Earth is destroyed, life will repeat again in many eons. So many ideas like this rat-arsed one 'hat ya'll never get ta witness, just have ta accept or deny. Seems such a narrow way, 'hat's all."

"Well, that's not incredibly far fetched. Even today we see patterns and cycles of nature that occur. Of course, humans are impacting mammals and are somewhat transcending the set course of nature with all their doings, but so it happens. So to think that I could again exist in eons, or humans, to say, is in my opinion quite probable. We have an environment and conditions, and so did past creatures, and so will future creatures. What's to say the same sorts of creatures won't always thrive in similar conditions?"

"For sure, dove, but, we'll never know more than a glimpse, so no sense jarring yer marbles on it, ya' know?"

"Of course," responded Kyla, though perhaps she did not fully believe that one should not contemplate solely because a definite answer could not be found.

"Dovey, I've got ta get back to some things now, if it's all the same," spoke Horris.

Kyla did not mind.

"Of course. Thank you so much for cheering me up. It seems to work every time, old friend. Maybe I can go home and relax now."

"Hopefully so, dear."

"Okay, Horris, good journey. I am sure we will meet again. Maybe one day it will be under less self-serving conditions."

"Good day, Kyla."

"Good day."

She walked back through the centre aisle and forced the church doors open. She looked back to wave good-bye to the man, though, he was nowhere to be found. Kyla looked about the church to see if he had moved, but she could not spot him.

"Must be in the bathroom."

*

The drive home was fairly pleasant. It was pleasing to see her familiar flat as she pulled up into the drive.

While walking in, there was a stale stench about the place. It was as if something had died, perhaps an emotion inside of Kyla. She opened a few windows to let out the unpleasantness. Within literal moments, Kyla had forgotten about all the good memories of Horris. Her mind was like a machine that could be turned on and off by a mechanical switch. Part of the time was ordered for contemplation and sulking. Part of the time was ordered for figuring out the day's events. And it seemed, to Kyla anyway, that a large portion of the time was devoted to desire, to hunger, to some form of satiation that could not be defined or appeased. Whether it was Zigmund, Horris, Mr. Pem, or the stone she had hidden away in a chest, the hunger existed. It was ceaseless.

This she could not comprehend, nor could she even attempt to make sense of. She did not enjoy the toying of her soul and much detested the uncertainty. Kyla despised any feeling that made her less sure of herself, especially those feelings that she could not control, let alone identify.

She lay on her bed in a hurry, as if to say 'to Hell with it all.' Kyla could sense a strange energy surging about the flat. It was as if it had a life and will of its own. Her hair began to stand up in a few places. She started to hear noises that were perhaps not there. Kyla could think of nothing but the lapis beside her, a magnificent stone.

"I must not dissect, must not attempt to hold it again. On last attempt, it did nothing for me. It is nothing more than a tease, nothing more than my imagination running wilde. This stone is merely a stone, a selfless gift from my friend, Mr. Pem. It has no significance outside of representing a token of a giving man," said she aloud.

A fervor began to boil. The rationality of one hundred Gods could not have held her emotions in tact.

"You are nothing!" she began to shout in the direction of the stone, now standing back from the bed.

"I will not concede my sanity to the most inanimate of objects. You have always been a lifeless object, and when I thought I felt sensation through you, it was surely the weather or the environment or the moment!"

She could hear her own words, and they were frightfully nonsensical to her. Kyla felt embarrassed to have even spoken them.

A rumbling of the Earth began to form. The sky barked angry cries of disapproval, as if sharpened metal colliding against a barricade of bricks. Thunder shot through the air, as if having been thrown by the Gods. The natural colours of day and night seemed to blur, as if a spiral of oneness presiding over all existence.

"Dear God," Kyla thought to herself.

An unknown energy continued to surge throughout the flat. She could feel it inside of her mind and inside of her eyes. It was as if nature herself had been coursing through the body of Kyla Demark.

"What is happening to me?!" screamed Kyla in horror.

She found herself in the front room, closest to the front door. Kyla had somehow been drawn there, or pulled to the position. The haphazardly placed stone had eerily been drawn to the front room as well. A force beyond her cognition was playing a hand of cards and her body was the ante.

The door blew open from a terribly forceful wind. Kyla could see outside for the first time now. It was not night, not day, but a bitter blue, frosted colour, as if life had been set through a filter. It seemed entirely surreal.

Chaotic Ocean

"In the name of all that is worth knowing, by God or whomever, what is this creation? What world is before my eyes? What existence have I been cast into? What is happening?"

Kyla screamed deathly screams. Alas, they were in vein. Not a word was responded. She was entirely frightened, entirely engulfed in the moment. She closed her eyes, as if to hope a dream, though once again, the same blue, odd reality shaped before her eyes. It seemed too incredibly unnatural for Kyla to even accept the occurrence. Nature had created a violent storm, had formed an angry and abusive hand, all the while drawing her closer to the stone, which had grown increasingly detestable to her. And yet, somehow, in the midst of all the chaos, there was a calm of sorts taking place. The outside world was oddly unchanged, almost unaffected from the sky, from the Earth. The blue seemed a shield, as if all those under its protection could live peacefully, happily, and with no thought of the troubles existing everywhere, omni-presently.

Conversely, the innards of Kyla's flat were in total disarray. Tiny objects were strewn about the floors in hysteria. Papers were blown about in frenzy from the continuous wind. It seemed to her that the flat was the only piece of land under scrutiny, under attack even.

"What am I to do? How am I to attain a calm!" barked Kyla into the air.

The energy now surged more intensely than ever. She could feel it through her legs and through her limbs. It seemed like a symbiote attempting to seize control of Kyla's actions.

"What is happening to me?" she was able to get out. The battle for control of her actions seemed as hopeless as the battle to deny the sun its rising. It seemed as hopeless as the battle to deny the rain its falling.

All she could do was guess, was wonder, and was fear the actuality that had been shaping in the minutes since the storm began. Her body started to stiffen like a frozen tree branch and she fell to the floor. The thud was heavy and painful.

She could no longer stand the turmoil and could no longer fight the will of the unknown. No longer could she maintain any sanity in a world so entirely full of insane events. Kyla could no longer deny that perhaps this was beyond the will of mortals, the will of mere men and women like herself. Finally she gave in and conceded to the strife.

At the moment of so doing, it was like some bliss had taken over. She no longer was fighting a nameless battle; no longer did she desire to know, to win, or to have control. And in this way, her actions unfurled before her eyes. Kyla was like a spectator: she had little control of her actions, but had an incredible grasp on her thoughts for the first time in what seemed like an eternity.

Her hands gracefully moved over the perimeter of the lapis beside her. It was like a dance, or a partnership, as if this event had been set in motion long before any thought she had ever conceived. It seemed incredibly right, incredibly soothing. Her mind was in a fervor, curious beyond the most questioning of philosophers. The outward action led to the greatest of inner predictions.

Chaotic Ocean

The once lifeless and innocent stone was no longer a shroud. It glowed the deepest of reds, as if drenched with a spectrum and colour of wine. The energy that had engulfed the flat was surely surging from the stone. It even seemed to have a hum to it, like an aural nimbus.

To herself she thought, "Of all the wonders, this is surely the most wonderful. What is this object? This gift? What is this stone? Surely I've not gone mad, but rather, extremely sane. Share with me your life; share it all with me. Share the secrets of now and forever."

Her hands were drawn to the stone, as if magnets. They reached delicately, caressing its surface. It was a warm feeling that ran through Kyla's body, as of the warmest of hot chocolates on the bitterest of Winter days. She felt good all over and inside.

Suddenly, her hands began to tremble. The stone had seemingly attached itself to them. She could not force herself off the object, nor did she care to. The stone rose into the air like a phoenix finding life, and with her hands still attached, she could do nothing but hold it high above her head, as if calling to the Gods.

The flat had become a reflected pinkish colour. The stone continued to glow and to surge. Kyla could feel it continually lifting as it pulled on her entire body. It had lifted her to her toes. She could still not let go of the stone. Within moments, her feet no longer could feel the floor of the flat, and she was raised like Christ in the centre of the room. Kyla was elevated by and attached to the glowing stone.

She could not focus on a single thought. Thousands of thoughts seemed to run through her mind every millisecond. While hundreds came, hundreds left, and she could not hold onto a single idea. Her mind was injected with pure cognition, and for this, she could do nothing but remain slave to the stone. She could not think of the ramifications, of the possibilities, of anything. Kyla was so incredibly entranced in thought, that no thought made an ounce of any kind of rational sense.

For a thought to be rationalised, one must put it into context. One must relate and formulate about it in order to forcibly fit it into one's reasoning. This process was unlike any rationalised idea. And perhaps, so is the nature of truth and purity.

"I...I...I...," she tried to think.

It was to no success. Many minutes passed while Kyla was raised like a balloon in the centre of the room. Outside, the storm seemed to rage on. The thunder was now more vocal than ever. It seemed watchful of Kyla's actions, responding accordingly. Lightning began to thrash on and off as it lit up the frost-blue sky.

Kyla could see what was happening outside, but again, could not formulate a single idea about the weather. Though, while Kyla could not think, she could certainly feel. She was frightened of the power surging through her body and did not know what it was, and this was very unsettling. However, perhaps more than being frightened, she was anxious and hungry. The power excited her and made her feel good, something that had been lacking for some time.

Chaotic Ocean

The stone began to heat more intensely. It was deathly hot in Kyla's hands. It was burning them, as if searing its impression into them so Kyla would never forget the experience. Kyla's hands were being branded.

The weather began to go wilde, wilder than it had been. The wind became chill and harsh. The thunder became loud enough to harm the human ear. Lightning seemed to crash in all directions, in an almost chaotic manner. It had nothing to do with reason or normal storm patterns; it was simply striking again and again in various positions and spots on the land. It was like a magnificent centre of the most important and impacting of events.

As Kyla's body had almost been pushed to the edge of its limit, a lightning bolt seemed to crash down to Earth, meander into the flat, and strike the magnificent lapis stone. Kyla was violently dropped and thrust to the floor. She fell hard, and there was a painful thud. The stone quickly levitated into the chest in the back room, and the impact caused it to close upon interaction.

Kyla was left drained and weak. She could barely move.

"Water... water..." said she aloud.

She needed water; her thirst was greater than any thirst she had hitherto experienced. Her mind was completely one-dimensional and could think of nothing save for satiation, for the appeasing of her body's need.

Kyla slowly crawled and inched toward the open front doorway. It seemed silent outside now. As she slowly approached the door, she could see that the lightning storm had ceased. Not a decibel of thunder existed anywhere across the land. The frost-blue world had returned to normal colour. All that remained was the night, the dark, black cool of the night. That, and a light, and the fine flow of calm rainwater steadily falling to the ground, like the conclusion to a great event.

She cared not to think of what had happened in this moment. Again, Kyla could concentrate on nothing but water. She inched closer to the door. The rain was falling in the direction of her flat and was almost drenching her inside carpet. She inched closer again, entirely exhausted from the event, and could do nothing but fall to her back.

Kyla had inched near enough for almost half her body to reach outside the door. She opened her mouth and let the light rain pour in, lying there for some time.

*

The rain continued to drop into her mouth, and she swallowed it down ever increasingly in pace. Her body was limp. The rain washed over her face, and the cool droplets felt good on her warm skin. Her hair became drenched with rain, though this felt better than the prior sweat soaked existence. Kyla continued to gulp down water. She cared not that this was perhaps not the healthiest of waters to be putting into her body.

She closed her mouth and did not move from the position for a long time. Kyla simply let the rain descend and drop all over her upper half; it felt good to her. Her body was extremely famished and had soaked in a great deal of warmth from the stone. She felt the rain was a rejuvenating factor.

Kyla, for minutes, had made a conscious effort not to think about any of the events that shaped the course of her evening. Deep inside, she knew that she would not be able to make any discernable sense of any of it. Kyla knew that something powerful was happening, and maybe for the first time in days, she felt that perhaps all the nonsense and mystery of her present life had something to do with all of this, and while she could not figure how, she could certainly figure that a 'how' did exist. This gave her great comfort. She did, however, have one foremost thought.

"Rain, snow, rain, snow. What happened to sun and shine?" she thought to herself. "The weather has been so entirely back-and-forth that I cannot even figure what season this is."

The rain continued to pour on. Strength slowly returned to her body. She had been lying there for some time and had not moved a limb since inching into the position. Kyla imagined she could see the white stars in the sky; they were magnificent.

"So much is out there," she thought. "So much is in the would-be stars. So much knowledge. So much history. So much future."

Kyla's thoughts slowly began to return to her mind, as if she could no longer suppress the desire to question everything that had happened, as was her nature.

"I do not even know where to begin," said she aloud, in almost humourous tone.

"Maybe I should not at all," she thought. Though, obviously, this was a complete and utter self-delusion.

She finally garnered enough strength to slowly stand up. It felt incredibly satisfying. The movement of her limbs, something so simple, she could have never guessed would have provided so much pleasure. Kyla slowly dragged the chest back into its normal room. This task took a good deal of strength from her body, due to the weight of the cumbersome holding.

She walked into her bedroom and fell face-first into the bed. She lay there silently. Kyla Demark was confused and excited and worried and weakened all at the same time.

"Why... How..."

She began to question for a vast period of time.

CHAPTER NINE
☦

WONDROUS WATERBEAR

*

The morning of the next was a particularly pleasing one. The skies looked clear, and the passersby seemed content in their respective actions. Kyla had regained her strength, and had allowed for her mind to recuperate and gain perspective on the events of the prior evening. Halfway across town, Horris was likely chitchatting inside of the church to a local about how beautifully crafted the objects inside the building were. In the middle of somewhere was Sean, the cabby whom had given Kyla a ride to her flat. A pretentious man was likely speaking to him about an idea designed to belittle. In his usual way, Sean likely deflected the ideas and humbly gave his own impressions on the subjects at hand. Across the other side of town, near the hospital compound at which Kyla worked, Mr. Pem was likely pacing about back-and-forth with his hands tucked deep in his pockets, seeming rather pleased.

Zigmund Sardoce, residing on the opposite side of town (from Kyla's flat and the hospital), had awoken early on this day, most assuredly (this, reader, is a fact, not merely a likelihood as had been the above literary supposition, if you can indeed distinguish betwixt fictional imaginings). He had been awake since the first noises of the morning. Our notorious character could not sleep, but and furthermore, could think of nothing but the utilisation of his pond. Zigmund could ponder nothing but the supremacy of his own character.

"My God, is there no secret to be left untold? Is there truly nothing that I cannot see?" said Zigmund aloud, as the pride seemed to set in like thickening mortar.

He felt a hand-up to any man on his level, and moreover, felt that beyond all the unease of his ideas regarding Kyla and her nature, he should be rather well in the revelation of his fortune. Zigmund perceived the pond and its images as glorious gifts, hand-picked for him alone from time immemorial.

"Perhaps it has been fated. Perhaps the centuries and civilisations have been passing only to give way to me, to this moment, to this time. Perhaps not a fool in the universe could harness the pond till this moment. As if the sword in the stone, I have been destined to control this power, this knowledge."

As Zigmund proceeded to stroke his ego, he anxiously walked outside to discover the day was quite calm, and the sky was clear.

"Hmm, first clear sky I've seen in about five to ten," he thought.

Chaotic Ocean

Proceeding onward, he meandered casually over to the position of the pond.

"Why can I not remember how to summon this knowledge," Zigmund thought, frustrated at his ineptitude.

He knelt down and placed his hands on the ground. Zigmund tried muttering some different words to conjure up the image. Nothing resulted. He next placed his hand into the water. Again, nothing resulted. Zigmund became infuriated.

"Speak to me, show me!!!" he yelled.

Nothing resulted. It was as if the pond had been toying with him. He waited for many minutes, sitting beside the stubborn water. Thinking of nothing to do, he decided to feel sorry for himself, as many minutes then passed. Zigmund was stone-like.

"Pathetic being," whispered into his mind.

He jerked and fell about, confused.

"Who, who is that? What do you want from me?" asked Zigmund into the air.

"You're entirely disappointing," said the voice. "It's not what I want *from* you, but what I wish *of* you."

"This is not a joke anymore. Name yourself," he ignorantly shouted.

"You are not worthy of this power," stated the voice.

At this moment, Zigmund could understand that the voice inside of his head and the pond's image were interrelated. The voice spoke the perfect sentence of motivation. He became frightened; Zigmund did not wish to lose the power of the pond.

"No, I am exactly the correct individual, please," he proclaimed.

"Baptise yourself with the water. Then you will see all that there is to see, Zigmund. Baptise your head, your skull, your brain. You will see what is imperative to see."

Zigmund seemed confused at the simple instructions.

"But, how... why?" he again asked.

There was no reply. The voice ceased to exist. I suppose its existence in the first place is debatable, but that is a literary argument you will have to discuss later with a fellow reader.

Zigmund, as if instinctually, did as told. He knelt down beside the pond again and put his hands in the water. Dripping the drops over his face and head, he felt somewhat strange in so doing, though, did not dare deviate from the instructions that had been given.

At first, he felt nothing. He felt as if the whole process was somehow a sham and this would bring about no image.

"Oh, the things that I do and the people I listen to. How learned am I after all?" he thought to himself.

Zigmund decided to go for a walk around his property. He strolled over to his magnificent carvings and to the meticulously kept garden.

"It is truly amazing."

*

Chaotic Ocean

The weather, having snowed, rained, should have crushed his garden, should have crushed the flowers and killed every living plant that Zigmund had set to Earth. It did not. His flower garden looked more splendid now than it had in the past. The rain seemed to have overlooked his work, his flowers. The snow did not only overlook the destruction of the delicate flowers, but the frost and flakes seemed to add to the beauty. The snow had become a lining of sorts, ever accentuating the garden's delicacy and majesty.

As he knelt down to stroke one of the more magnificent flowers, a jolt of energy ran through him. He felt as if he had been having a seizure. It was the pond image running through his bones. It seemed that proximity was no longer a factor to the pond. No longer was there any set protocol for the impressions that the pond had wished to give Zigmund, it appeared.

His hands began to shake. His body gave out, and he lay flat on his back. Zigmund was conscious, awake, but could see nothing but blackness. His hearing was slowly fading to silence, and this frightened him, for the image had never come to him in this manner.

As his hearing became all but nonexistent, the image slowly revealed itself. He had prior expected another revelation about Kyla and her supposed actions and nature. This he did not receive. Zigmund began to see flashing images of hangings and firing squads. He saw lethal injections and executioners in black, daunting masks. In betwixt these flashes, he began to see images of the local fuel chains. Zigmund witnessed food market chains, large, publicly known corporations, and universal consumer symbols known all over the globalised world. The images seemed completely nonsensical to him, and he could not figure how they related, or how this would help him in any way.

"Good God!" he screamed aloud, as if wishing to be set free from the imprisonment of the image.

The interchanging deaths and product symbols continued to rage onward, always flashing and blinding. The images soon became too much to endure. He was slowly slipping into a trance of sorts with little control over any of his sensory functions.

Death
Corporation
Death
Corporation
Death
Corporation
Death
Corporation
Death
Corporation

The images continued to assault Zigmund's mind. As each new image flashed, it was as if the prior had become nothing more than a daze and confusion of colours and tones. The images soon repeated with increased rapidity. There was little time for consideration of the actuality

Chaotic Ocean

being presented before his eyes. Images occurred at distractionary intervals, such that his mind was not allowed to deviate, to wander for even a moment.

Death
Corporation
Hanging
Food Merchant

As one image was permitted to leave, a new image appeared just as his consciousness was returning.

Firing Squad
Fuel Chain
Lethal Injection
Pharmaceutical Supplier

This pattern continued on for some time. He lay there like a wondrous waterbear, completely vulnerable to the environment, and yet entirely powerful enough to survive the turmoil and hope for a better day. His body was limp and stiff like a corpse in the cold. To any passersby who may have accidentally witnessed some portion of this event, be it from a higher physical position or simply from an auditory stance, Zigmund appeared comatose.

Inside his mind, though, a clearly different story presented itself. Alas, he could stand the battle no longer. Zigmund decided, as much as was humanly possible at the time, to submit to the repeating and senseless images. He could certainly not discern their meaning, nor did he wish to attempt it any longer.

Death
Corporation
Hanging
Fuel Chain

Still though, they continued on, as if intending to brainwash the man. The images were relentless. This was unlike Zigmund's prior pond image experience. It seemed then that there was a message attempting to convey itself through self-realisation. It seemed clear, though, and less invasive. The image of old seemed up for the taking, so to speak. Zigmund was the orchestrator and could seemingly choose to accept the knowledge or to decline it. This, however, this new experience, was completely alien to Zigmund. Had he been able to question at this moment, surely he would have done so.

Death
Corporation
Firing Squad
Food Merchant

*

A large amount of time had passed. Though, perhaps it only seemed like minutes. Zigmund slowly regained his awareness, and his neck felt stiff. He could not figure how long he had been out. A day seemed like a moment, and without memory, everything seemed completely blurred and confused. He did not move from his position on the bare ground, and found himself looking up into the sky. The land was hard like a piece of iron. His head trembled with ache.

"Ouch," said he aloud.

Zigmund slowly moved his hand across the surface of his head to check for physical damage, as a possible reason for the pain. He found nothing. For the life of him, he could not remember a thing. Zigmund recalled having wished to use the pond, though, could not recall any such occurrence ever having materialised.

"By God, what has happened?" he thought to himself.

He considered it best to move from his prone position, gathered what strength was left inside of his body, and pulled himself to a sitting position. Zigmund looked all over his property to see if he had been attacked.

"If anyone is out there, leave from your place. I will call the authorities," he threatened.

There was no response.

"How long have I been out?" he wondered. "What time is it? What day is it? What *year* is it? Why can I not determine? The sky looks only slightly darker than it did earlier in the day, this day, the day I feel I have started and had hoped to end... I think."

The contemplation awarded him no comfort. The one thing a man has in life is an account of his own time, of his own existence and actions. This very thing had now been stripped of Zigmund, and he felt completely insecure and estranged from the reality he had proclaimed to know so well.

After some moments, our anti-hero garnered the strength to stand up. The city seemed quiet outside of his property. Zigmund could not hear one authomobile on the street, let alone the usual hustle and bustle of London. He walked around the exterior of the property, so to check for any noticeable changes. Zigmund had still not ruled out the possibility of a mugging.

He meticulously checked under, in, around, and about each portion of his dwelling. After a long while, with no result, he headed back to the canopy and into his mansion. While approaching the door and instinctually removing the key from his robe, he noticed that it was already ajar.

"By God, the scoundrels are inside!" Zigmund instantly concluded.

He approached with apprehension.

As Zigmund slowly moved the door with his foot, a great creaking sound formed.

"Shhhh," said he aloud, as if the door had been alive and could respond to his demands.

There was no response. Once the door was fully open, he could notice some papers strewn about the hallway floor. His eyes became large with anticipation. "Stay calm."

Moving forward into the hall, his heart seemed to beat with increasing rapidity. It was like a fist beating against the inside of his rib cage, as if forcing its way through the interiors of his chest. Zigmund moved further still.

For the most part, the rooms seemed in tact. His bedroom was the last portion of the inspection. Perhaps he left it for last because he feared it most. His heartbeat continually increased, and this stressed him greatly. Zigmund's bedroom door was open just a bit.

He thought to himself, "Did I leave this so? Or is there something much more dire to the tale?"

He again proceeded with trepidation. Upon opening the door to its full capacity, an act of utter courage to Zigmund, there was surprisingly little disturbance to the room. A few objects were scattered about, as if someone had been looking for something, but in all, the room remained well kept. This gave Zigmund comfort at first. Though, after a few moments of contemplation, this made him uneasy. He decided to search no more for the time.

An oddly placed key partially revealed itself after a paper suddenly shifted from the middle of the bedroom floor.

*

It was time for Kyla to return to work and meet with her patients. She gave little thought to the fantastic events of her life. It simply would have done no good, perhaps she felt. Kyla needed to get away from her flat, and looked forward to the break from her own life, as she was anxious to see what her closest patients had been up to.

Kyla wished for a change in routine. Instead of dragging her rusted, old motorcar out of the drive, she called up for a cab. It took nearly twenty minutes to arrive. Kyla was somewhat surprised and elated when some familiar events unfolded before her eyes. She saw the corrugated writing on the side of the memorable automobile.

"Ah... I cannot believe the coincidence. Still, I really should not make assumptions about my beliefs, considering what has been happening to me."

The cab pulled slowly into the drive. Sean the cabby rolled down his window, as he too noticed the address and familiarity of the situation.

"Hey there, Miss, where to?" he joked in an unnecessarily formal tone.

"Sean, it is absolutely wonderful to see you again, and I truly mean that."

"Yeah, yeah, get in lady," joked Sean.

Kyla opened the door and entered the cab. The environment, the smell, it all came back to her, evoking the vivid image of the rainy day that Sean had previously driven her home on.

"So, I feel kinda odd," said Sean.

"How's that? No need to feel odd," replied Kyla.

"Well, I feel like last time, me and you, you know, it was friendly and whatnot. I know we only met once and talked for a brief while, but since you lady, I ain't never had any customers who asked me personal questions like you did. And I guess, I guess I just kinda miss that. I know my job is drivin' and your job is sitting back there, but still, you know? I don't know if you get me or not, so maybe I'll just shut this yapper and make like a cabby and do what I'm supposed to."

"Please don't do that, Sean."

Kyla's kind words surprised and relieved him.

"I've had such a sprinkling of obtuse days that a conversation with you would surely brighten my sun."

"The way you folks make bad days sound like courses in speaking well is beyond me."

There was a moment of silence. For the first time, it occurred to both that sitting in a cab while remaining still, was quite the oddity indeed.

"So eh... where to?" asked Sean.

"Am I boring you, Sean?" responded Kyla.

"Nah. No. It ain't that. I just gotta make a living. You know how it is. And while I'd love to talk and all that goes with, I also need to bring home food for my family."

"Start the clock running. It's fine."

"You got it lady," said he excitedly.

Kyla felt good to have been in Sean's company. She could not figure why a perfect stranger would provide feelings of goodness, but she cared not for the mystery.

"So eh, why have yer days been so awkward lately, lady..., Kyla?"

"It is completely impossible to describe, and likely, it would be difficult to convince even the most sane of men that my words are not fabricated. So, I won't put that burden upon you, Sean. Let me just say that I have had a fantastic turn of events, and I do not mean fantastic in a satisfactory way."

"Well, least we're both still breathin'. Whateva' happened, Kyla, you look fine to me on the outside. The sun still comes up each morn, and the moon still replaces it in the night. The wind still blows, and all the buggers of modern life are still breathing with the lungs that God almighty gave them."

Sean's simple words did actually bring some solace to Kyla's mind. She was fascinated with his ability to find the point of goodness in everything that she said, in every problem that existed. He was a good man, and she was thrilled to have been speaking with him again.

"Maybe you're right, Sean. Maybe I should think of it, of life like that. Perhaps that is truly best."

She did not believe the words she spoke. Though, she wished to, and perhaps was even convinced at present that she actually may have.

"There, that's the spirit. I mean, hey, I don't really know nothing worth knowing like educated folks like yourself, but I know a lot of blokes going around lookin' unhappy who all gots lots to be happy for in this world. That's all."

"Indeed there are," said she softly.

Chaotic Ocean

She looked down, having accurately read Sean's statement as directed entirely toward her. Sean immediately noticed the change in her tone of voice and quickly jumped in with a further comment.

"Hey Kyla, I didn't..."

"No, it's okay," interrupted Kyla.

"No, I didn't mean that you, that I was, you know, implying something about you or *your* kind, nothin' like that. Hounestly, I didn't. You are completely lovely. And I'm sure when you sort out whateva' 't is that needs sortin', that you will always smell the flowers in Spring."

Kyla believed him.

"Don't mind me, Sean. Don't apologise either. I am fine, and will be fine, as you say. I only hope this sorting process that you speak of happens relatively soon. If not, with not many souls to spcak with, I don't know how I will subsist going in the path that I am."

"Ain't you got friends, loved ones, family?" sympathetically questioned the cabby.

Kyla laughed. She laughed hearty laughs for some thirty seconds. Sean seemed confused.

"Erm, did I make a funny?" asked the confused cabby.

"Heh, no, Sean. It's just, you're right. And it is extremely funny. No friends, no family, and no loved ones. I don't know what I've been doing with my life. It's as if my patients are closer to me than any others in this world. I find comfort in complete strangers such as yourself, in bums in churches, and in little odd men that would appear nothing more than loiterers."

She began to laugh again for some time.

"And now it all seems purely hilarious. How could I possibly *not* look forward to the rising of the sun or the cool breeze of an ocean? Seems like it's all I have in this world. How could I not cherish these things? Oh, the humour is terrific, Sean."

She laughed again for a few moments. This time, however, the laughter soon morphed into tears. Kyla pressed her hands upon her face, and Sean could notice that she was entirely embarrassed to have spoken so many inner feelings to a stranger. He felt responsible.

"Please don't do that, Kyla. Don't do this to yourself."

"Do what?"

"Don't beat up on yourself with the will of a prize fighter. It just ain't worth it. You know? It just ain't. You'll get through whateva' it is that is happening to you. I know you will. Please don't cry. I'm so sorry, lady. I am. It was never my meaning to bring this out of you. I was really just tryin' to help, to offer up some possibilities. You know? Please don't cry."

"It is not your fault, Sean. I know that you were trying to help, and, perhaps you have."

Kyla's words were hounest.

"Doesn't feel like helpin'," responded Sean.

"Sorry to drop my tears in your cab. Sometimes I feel so utterly alone, though. And that is pretty darn ironic. I'm supposed to be the one person in complete control of everything. I help others with their problems. I am not supposed to need the shoulder. I *am* that shoulder."

"No offense, love, but even Atlas needed a shoulder to cry on sometimes. Men ain't perfect. Nor are women. We're all just here tryin' to make best, tryin' to do what we feel is right. And you're doing something noble, helping people. You're human, and you know what they say..."

"What's that?"

"Humans step in shit sometimes. But, it washes off."

Sean's comment made Kyla chuckle.

"I'm pretty sure even Zeus needed a shoulder. I mean, I don't know for certain or nothin', but God or man, I'm sure we're all not too different. I'm sure we all ain't as different as we think."

Again, Sean's comments did bring a smile and a feeling of comfort to Kyla. She felt as if her conversations with Sean meant more than the most important of philosophical mysteries.

"To the hospital," stated Kyla.

"How's that?"

"What, you're used to not working today? We all have to make a living. So get off your stagnant bum and do your job," joked Kyla.

"Oh, I see. Now you want to get some bang for your money? That it? I thought you'd be happy just lettin' the meter run. Maybe you got too much money or something and you need me to get rid of it for ya'. Okay, I suppose I can take you to the hospital. Bill's gonna be more than you can afford though, so you sure you don't wanna just get out now, before we start moving?"

"Quite sure," she replied in a lighthearted manner.

"Okay, to the hospital it is, lady."

*

The cab ride was fairly pleasant, and Kyla was able to forget her problems for the short while of the drive. The two continued to speak onward about various topics. Sean spoke of his family and Kyla spoke of her job at the hospital, specifically what she did and who her patients were, breaking formal regulations of privacy. Sean was truly interested in her work, and it gave him pleasure to hear Kyla speak of it. He thought her to be a kind and giving woman and wished that he could help people in the capacity that she did. Sean did not speak these thoughts though.

The cab pulled up to the main entrance of the hospital. Neither Sean nor Kyla desired the company to end, but both realised that it was inevitable.

"How much do I owe you, Sean?" asked Kyla.

Sean looked at the meter, and it was a very high number. He thought for a moment.

"Whateva' you got on you. Never mind about the actual price. The price of good conversation is payment enough."

Kyla was impressed at Sean's selflessness. She could see the meter price, though, over Sean's shoulder. Reaching into her purse, she

Chaotic Ocean

pulled out an amount higher than the true number and placed it in a white envelope.

"Here you go, Sean, enjoy. I hope we can do this again sometime. I truly enjoyed it, and maybe I truly needed it."

Sean did not open the envelope to count it, as he assumed such actions would have been inappropriate.

"Of course, of course. Was really great. I had a blast. I consider you a friend now, lady, Kyla, so I hope that's okay with you."

His eyes were anxious, as if frightened that she would feel differently and embarrass him. He seemed to slouch a bit. Kyla could recognise this and felt sorry that any man as noble and goodly as Sean would have ever had to bear such feelings of insecurity.

"Certainly, Sean. You're my friend. I love speaking with you. You're one of my better friends in fact, now. So, I truly feel good in the knowledge that you feel similar. It was a *blast*, as you said."

Sean laughed with Kyla's usage of the word 'blast.'

"Now that's more like it!" replied Sean, referring to the contrived word choice.

"Well, again, thank you, Sean. Thank you for a wonderful conversation and a wonderful ride. Maybe I will have to start taking the cab more often, so long as I know you're on duty."

Kyla smiled, and Sean smiled back.

"Well, I work most days, but if you want to ensure that 't is I who be the driver, when you call the company, mind ya' there is only one big company 'round these parts; all you have to do is ask if a specific cab is available for pickup. They know where all the cabs are and can call in an order to me."

"Sounds wonderful," replied Kyla.

"Okay, let's see, number is 0037."

Kyla quickly jotted it down.

"Good-bye Sean. Hope to see you soon."

"Have a good one at work, Kyla."

She stepped out of the cab and proceeded toward the entrance of the hospital.

Sean decided to open the envelope Kyla had given him. The exaggerated payment made his eyes widen, and he quickly looked up to see if Kyla had gone inside yet, hoping to give back some of the payment. She was nowhere to be seen, and the cabby drove off.

*

Once inside her office, Kyla plopped down into the seat and kicked her feet up to relax. She sat there for some time trying not to think of anything. This was an extremely difficult task. She soon started to prepare for her three main patients, as she did on most days.

Laurna walked into the office in a timid manner.

"Hello Laurna," greeted Kyla, "it is very good to see you. I hope you've been well."

Chaotic Ocean

"Hey, you know how cheeky London is. Can't keep well all the time with every bloke always looking at you, judging you on how you keep your appearance. You know."

"Well, I don't think everyone does this, nor do I think the majority of men are cruel-hearted individuals."

"There's that optimist in you talking again, there it is. Never seems to waiver or go away. That's pretty impressive," responded Laurna.

"Laurna, I'd like you to know that just because I am a professional and you a patient, that this does not mean that we are not entirely similar, with even many of the same issues and problems. I have grown and hopefully have learned to deal with my problems, and in the process, have learned how to aid others. That is the only difference."

Kyla could hear her somewhat hypocritical words floating in the middle of an ocean. Laurna looked into Kyla's eyes for a few moments, saying nothing. Kyla thought perhaps the young woman had seen right through her, had seen right through the empty words of a professional clinging to past glory, past conclusions, and all the while, swimming in the midst of terrible chaos and disarray.

"Well, you're the doc," replied Laurna.

"Is there anything in particular you'd like to discuss, Laurna?" probed Kyla in a relieved tone of voice.

"Well, them blokes ain't paying me to do the figuring, are they?" half-joked Laurna.

"Okay then, perhaps then I will do the guiding. I only figured it would be more enjoyable, and even easier, if you were the one who spoke of what was on your mind as opposed to me walking through every single alley only to find the one of one hundred with a flaming trash can in it."

Laurna understood the statement.

"Well, I don't really feel like talking much today about my own arse, but maybe you'd want to talk about what you told me last session."

"What was that?" asked Kyla.

"You told me to bring in a subjectaphor pamphlet, by that man, Ziggy Sardoce, did you not?"

Kyla's heart dropped to the floor. All of her forgotten worries seemed to immediately rush back in an instant. She did recall asking Laurna to bring in a pamphlet, as Laurna was the first person to alert her to the pamphlets' very existence. A feeling of sickness sunk into Kyla's stomach.

"You don't look so hot," said Laurna, as she could see Kyla visibly writhing with some kind of pain.

"I will be fine, dear. Thank you for your concern," she was able to mutter in response.

"Well okay," Laurna went on, "the pamphlet is right here. It's a brand new one, with some really funky words in it. This one is a lot different than the others. I don't know if that Ziggy is changing them or something, but it seems more direct or something. But who knows with Ziggy; he seems like a genius. So I'm sure even if I think I understand it, I truly don't. Who knows?"

Chaotic Ocean

Laurna proceeded remove the pamphlet from her back pocket. She delicately placed it on the desk for Kyla to take. It seemed to peer at Kyla, and for some moments, she made no movement. She simply stared at the thing, as if time had ceased and the world had faded away. The last two survivors were she and Zigmund's ideas. Looking upon the object in disgust, Kyla contemplated burning it or tearing at it. She wished not to read the ideas, and furthermore, did not desire to poison her own mind. Though, Kyla felt that perhaps, if she could read his words, perhaps she could undo whatever influence they had had on Laurna, or on her other patients.

"Whatchya' waiting for there?" asked the girl.

"I suppose nothing."

Kyla slowly caressed the subjectaphor pamphlet. She found herself fooling with the thing, twiddling it betwixt her fingers. Wishing deeply to view the words written on the inside, at the same time, Kyla dually feared the rotten ideas contained, searching to be discovered. She decided to fool no longer and jolted the pamphlet open. Her eyes grew wide.

Blokes and Fools and Thinking Men Alike,

If all the pearls in the world could speak and convey one idea, they'd collectively roar out to preach the worth in the flight of an elephant. Think not about the everythingness of nothing. We live in a time of civilised men. We live in a time of exploitation, and we love it. We live in a time where there is a fine line betwixt fun and fascism. We live in a time where the success of one man might mean the failure of another. This just happens to be the time. No criticism, no complaints, this just happens to be the time. The time is now and will always be now.

Most importantly, we live in a time where men are still held to Hamurabi's code and still die for their sins. Kill and be killed. You see it in the States, in other countries alike. This is our time, no criticism, just happens to be our time. We're moneymaking mammals. This is what we toil for, no? The world goes around. Allow me be the first to propound a monumentally sound idea. No one is saying it, because they are afraid of the utter sense of the thing. They fear the complete logic of the idea. Many could have had this idea but had been not strong enough to bring it forth.

Fact one: we put to death those who wrong our loved ones.

Fact two: we watch programmes on the tele that exist for the sole purpose of commercialism; commercials sponsor the programmes that interest us. We view the commercials because we have no choice, really.

Fact three: we enjoy the suffering of others, as it makes us feel good about ourselves, real or fictional.

It seems to be that every bloke has overlooked these glaring, GLARING I say, facts and truths about how we live. Come now, throw your naivety to the wind and fear not the words that everyone wishes to bring to fruition.

COMMERCIALLY SPONSERED CAPITAL PUNISHMENT.

Chaotic Ocean

It is genius. Everything is satiated at once. The commercialism that dictates existence gets its primetime programme. People have to watch as the human spirit wishes nothing more than to feel good about itself, and what way better than that of the death of vulgar criminals. And of course, them damn wrong-doers get what is justly coming to them. The guilty are hanged. The suits make their profits. The locals sleep better than usual at night. No regrets.

And if questioning the monumental soundness of this idea, one has not far to search. One need only search as far as one's own heart. One must simply ask oneself, when deciding if this programme would sell, would 'I' watch it? If the answer is yes, congratulate yourself for the magnificent hounesty you've just displayed. If the answer is no, either you're truly hoping to get points with the Big Man to get into that glam hotel up in the sky, or you're in utter denial. Unfortunately for you, God don't like kiss-ups, nor does he like liars, so you're going to Hell anyway. Once you realise this, you'll watch the programme.

I suggest you write the Prime Minister himself to suggest this idea. Feel free to take it as your own. I can't change the world, but we can.

Yours truly ill-advised,
-Ziggy Sardoce

Kyla immediately shut the pamphlet in disgust, having finished the last line. Laurna could see that Kyla seemed upset in some way, though, could not figure why a piece of paper, a flyer, a mere pamphlet, would have bothered her to such an extent.

"You okay there?" asked Laurna with concern.

"You don't understand. This is not right. Zigmund Sardoce is a sick and twisted individual. He has not the right on this Earth to freely distribute his diseased ideas to the youths of tomorrow!"

"But, it's just reading. I thought the more you read the more you learn. How is any reading bad?"

Laurna looked confused and was unsure why so much chaos had entered into the normally professional environment of the session.

"You don't understand, Laurna! This man is not a good man. He has no good intentions. His ego is the only thing worth living for, he feels. He wishes to help no one but himself. He wishes to do nothing positive with his fortune. He can only spread negativity and sedition. Do you not see this?"

"I just know what I read in the pamphlets."

Kyla could see that Laurna was confused. She could see that Laurna was a patient in need of stability, not a soldier in need of a war. Kyla felt selfish in allowing her own anger, her own fears and worries to cloud the session.

"I am sorry, Laurna. I did not mean to go off. I just happen to know the man personally. And it is my professional opinion, in your specific case, that the continued reading of these pamphlets will be of no value whatsoever to your health or well-being. It is my opinion that the pamphlets will have quite the opposite effect."

Laurna did not know how to respond. She was an intelligent girl though, and while she did not actually believe Kyla's contrived advice, decided to appease her doctor.

"Bonkers, I didn't see that one coming. I guess I won't be reading any more of these things. That's what you think is best, right?"

Kyla did not pick up on the fabricated response. In fact, she was too blind with distress to see anything except for what she wished.

"Oh yes, yes, Laurna. You have it now. These are not good to read anymore. Thank you for understanding it as I have spoken it."

"Not a problem," replied the girl.

"Do you mind if I keep this one pamphlet, Laurna? I figure, since you won't be needing it anymore, there is no harm in me taking it to examine further and whatnot."

Laurna thought for a moment.

"Course not, you can keep it. As you said, it won't be doing me any kind of good. If I see another one, I'll just throw it in the trash. End of story."

"Very well," replied Kyla.

Kyla attempted to level her composure, and failed in attempting to keep the girl for any longer. The conversation became contrived, and it was obvious to each that they had exhausted enough time for one day's work.

"Okay now, I will be off. See you next time, doc."

"Good day, Laurna. Stay well."

And with that, as have many previous departures have been worded, Laurna was off. Kyla was left alone in the office, perplexed. She decided to re-read the pamphlet.

"Curious that this pamphlet would be so different than the others, so direct in its message. Why the change?"

*

She sat there for some time, waiting for her next patient, Dorian, to arrive. He was absent for the time of his appointment, and Kyla decided to stand up and pace the office. She seemed unnerved. Kyla wished to help her patients to the most of her ability, yet could not help thinking of the personal matters of her life that seemed to be infecting the professionalism of her work.

Dorian finally strolled in, walking in such a manner that could only be described as somewhat of a strut.

"How my smellin'?" asked Dorian in his usual way.

"Smelling just fine," responded Kyla in a tone that seemed to say 'please, no nonsense today.'

"How's it been?"

"Dorian, Dorian, it has been, to say the least, interesting. And I suppose that's not an entirely bad thing for it to have been."

Chaotic Ocean

Dorian could sense the perfunctory manner in which Kyla had replied to his question. He did not sense the air of a woman in control, nor did he sense a woman with a plan. Dorian was a perceptive individual when he chose to be. He could now sense a woman in distress, replying to his meaningless, ritualistic question, as if with no tact, no power... an answer formed in a foreign way by a woman for whom he had an immense deal of respect. Again, it seemed Kyla's emotions were clouding her work.

"Well, maybe you've just missed this young, virile, pleasure-playground body of mine," joked Dorian, as he attempted to bring a smile to Kyla's face with his awkward sense of half-feigned vanity.

"Somehow I doubt it, Dorian."

"Whateva' lady, I know how it goes."

"At any rate, Dorian, how have *you* been? This session is about helping you, not about discussing my personal life or feelings or anything of such nature."

Dorian was glad to see the change of tone.

"Yep, I was right, you did miss this pleasure-playground!"

The two smiled.

"I try and guide you less, as opposed to my other patients, Dorian, as I can recognise your soundness of mind, can recognise your needs. Is anything on your mind that you'd like to get out?"

"Beside the pleasure-playground and all?"

"Yes, beside that."

The conversations betwixt Kyla and Dorian had always gone something like this. There always seemed present an extreme polarity, whereby the conversations drifted quickly from casual nothings to solid and directly stated ideas.

"Okay, here's something," started Dorian.

"Yes..."

"We are born as equals. We die as equals. We have nothing when we are delivered into the hands of the magnificent world, and it is a similar experience when we finally check out."

"This is all true."

"Yet, somewhere from birth to death, people get this idea that we're extremely different. They get this righteous idea that because of your last name, because of family fortune, because of what neighborhood you live in, that we are all extremely different animals. They get this impression because of how you're born or how you're raised, or what special talent you have, that there exist appropriate class distinctions."

"Unfortunately, Dorian, men will always find whatever excuse suits best to rationalise the subjugation and poor treatment of the less fortunate. This is how it has always been. Men have used religion, skin colour, and every noticeable difference under the moon to differentiate betwixt the blessed and deserving ones and the unfortunate and undeserving ones."

"It's all such a crock though. No human has that right, that right to look down his nose at another. It's all Goddamn ideology. As you said, we'll match any possible idea of hate to some ideology, and since it's an ideology, people accept obtuse theories for irrefutable facts. It's a crock."

"I agree," replied Kyla.

"Maybe it would make me feel better if you adopted a different viewpoint on the matter. We could argue it then."

"I am sorry, that's not exactly what these sessions are about or what they aim to achieve. Even if I thought the opposite, I would still listen with the most compassion possible."

This slightly agitated Dorian. He was an individual who thrived on arguments. In his personal life, whatever innocent statement was made by another, he automatically adopted the opposite view, if for nothing more than to argue a useless point and come out triumphantly. This was his way. He needed to be knowledgeable and seem adept in almost every field. Though, while he was a very intelligent man in his own right, perhaps this facet of his personality was for the pure stroking of his ego. Perhaps, in this, he knew something about everything, but much about nothing.

"We are born, and we die as equals. Why is it impossible to live as equals, Kyla?"

"Because men have pride and egos, and perhaps are the must stubborn animals to have ever lived. We enjoy the feeling of being supreme, and enjoy that power over others. And in this, we are surely too proud to admit that this fortune was had in any other way than by extreme deservedness."

"Perhaps."

"And most likely, Dorian, you and I are no different than the people whom we speak of. I am certain we would like to be, but maybe deep down inside, we know we are not, and this bothers us. So our only means to restitute our consciences is to point out the very ideas that we have been."

"I disagree. I don't think that is so. Just because a man points out something he notices in another, does not mean that the man has that in himself."

"Dorian, you are amazing, but I will not argue with you. I have told you this before. But, as they say, we can smell our own better than anyone else's."

"Ra ba ba," dismissed Dorian.

"I am sorry if my manner is not what you had hoped for, however, this is my profession, and I must do it professionally," replied Kyla.

Though, in a way, Dorian was overjoyed to see that Kyla had regained her stern position, that position which he had earlier perceived absent.

The two went on to discuss current events for the next forty minutes or so. Dorian, in his usual demeanor, had been raving about something reported through the news. Kyla listened as attentively as she could, knowing that Dorian's heart was at times in question. He seemed to delve quickly and deeply into subjects, only to later dismiss his interest in such ideas. Was it that he merely enjoyed the sound of his voice, or that he enjoyed discussing ideas in general? Or was his halfheartedness farcical – a shroud erected to further a kind of emotional armour? Kyla quite understood the idea of armour, and perhaps sympathised with Dorian.

"Well, I'm spent," said Dorian.
"Okay, I will see you next session," replied Kyla.

"Just one thing to think about..."
"What is that, Dorian?"
"Commercially sponsored capital punishment. Something to give some consideration to. Everyone wins."

Kyla's heart sank to the floor. She hardly had the strength to question him on his comment.

"Dear Dorian, you don't truly believe that trash, do you? It can't be that a man such as yourself would really be influenced by an idea so completely vulgar."

"Heh, just messin' with you," replied Dorian.

Kyla was relieved to hear Dorian's words, though, at the same time, could not help but think that on some level Dorian was certainly affected by the idea put forth by Zigmund in the pamphlet. She thought that perhaps Dorian was too proud to admit that he could have been affected by such an idea.

"I am glad you would not be influenced by that garbage," reinforced Kyla.

"Okay, I am outta here. Peace and oneness."
"Good day, Dorian."
"Lates."

Just as he had upon entering, Dorian strutted out of the office. He looked back once at Kyla before closing the door, as if to say good-bye for another time. She gave no motions, staring in some sense of pity, and soon shut her eyes. Work of this nature had become trying for Kyla. When at home, she worked to ignore the oddities of her current life. When at work, all that which she had wished to purge from her memory suddenly came flowing in like a monsoon.

*

To herself she thought, "Is there no peace for me? Is there no corner left for silence? Is there no man left with the decency enough to allow me my own delusions? Why is this happening? That wretched stone. That wretched, abject piece of rock. There is no peace. What of the days of yore? What of brutally perfect conversation with Zigmund under the canopy? What of my sense of right and his sense of ignorance? London has changed. Something is different. I am different."

Cecelia walked into the office. Kyla was too self-absorbed to notice. Cecelia took a seat and waited silently for Kyla to greet her.

"Goodness girl, you almost scared the soul out of me!"
"I'm sorry. This is the time of my appointment, is it not?" asked Cecelia.

Chaotic Ocean

"Of course, honey. I apologise. I am a little off today, a little wrapped up in other matters. The lapse will not happen again."

"Oh, you don't have to be so formal."

"So, how have we been?" asked Kyla.

The girl, in her usual way, found objection to certain questions and lapsed into her defenses.

"We? How the heck should I know? I just know me. Better than you do, doc," stated Cecelia in a caustic tone.

"Please, Cecelia, you know as well as I do that these sessions are for your benefit. Lashing out at me will do nothing. How are you doing today?"

"I suppose I am fine."

The girl seemed reluctant to converse.

"You're looking very well today," replied Kyla.

"I am? You really think so?"

The girl's eyes seemed to brighten up with the slightest of complimentary comments.

"Of course, dear. You're a lovely young child with a lot to look forward to, and I am positive you will feel better after the conclusion of our time together."

"Well, if ya' think so. I didn't know you could cure what the world forces on you."

"Maybe not cure, but readjust, re-appropriate. The world is a harsh place to exist in, but it's also a beautiful place, filled with mystery and goodness alike."

"You really think that?" asked the girl.

Kyla paused for a moment with hesitation. Cecelia could see this.

"Of course. The world is wondrous; you just have to embrace it when it gives to you, and deal with it when it seems like it is doing the opposite."

"Good advice. Who's it for, me or you?"

"I beg your pardon," replied Kyla.

"Nothing."

"How's your reading coming along, Cecelia? I recall last time we spoke of your having new reading material that you seemed interested in."

Kyla thought her own words had been sly in attempting to get Cecelia to reveal Zigmund's latest work.

"Hmm, nope, not that I can think of. Don't think I've read anything new of interest," replied the girl.

"Lies," thought Kyla.

"Come now, dear, you don't have to withhold from me. I am not here to judge, simply to discuss."

"Truly, nothing of interest worth speaking," again replied the girl.

Kyla could think of nothing but the malicious nature of the girl. She could think of nothing but the direct lies that she perceived Cecelia to have been telling. She was on the verge of erupting when suddenly she was overcome by a feeling of rationality.

Kyla thought to herself, "Goodness, what am I thinking? This is an innocent, young girl. What are these notions entering my mind? Good Heavens."

Kyla was disgusted with her own thoughts. She desired nothing more than to comfort Cecelia, to make the young girl feel good about herself. And here, she was thinking negative thoughts without cause. Kyla decided not to bring up the pamphlet that Cecelia had dropped on the way out of the previous session. She figured if she had, it would be a way of further accusing Cecelia of fabricating the truth.

"How about yourself?" asked the young girl. "You read anything of interest lately?"

"Read, experienced, done."

"What's 'at supposed to mean? That like some psycho-babble speak or something, doc?"

Kyla warmly smiled to the girl, lowered her head for a moment, and took in a deep breath. As she exhaled, she replied, "We work a long day."

Cecelia could see that Kyla was disturbed in some manner. She could notice that this back-and-forth was helping not a soul. Cecelia decided to concede for the sake of disturbing the discomfort of the atmosphere that had manifested.

"Well, if you wanna talk about readin' and all that, I can. I'm not sure how such and such is gonna make me cured, but you're the doc, right?"

"Thank you," warmly replied Kyla.

"Well, sometimes I fancy the local papers around these parts. I don't think enough young people keep up with the news, and I think I wanna be the one to buck that trend. Plus, it's always nice to see a familiar name doing something worthwhile who's actually made something of himself."

"How do you mean?"

"I got this uncle. He's sort of an independent writer, you know, like freelance. He writes articles here and there, and then if the papers like what he's done, they pick 'em up, you know, commission him. And as I just alluded to, the local papers 'round these parts generally pick him up a lot. Frankly, I don't know why he just doesn't try for a full time job with 'em."

"Well that's great, a writer in the family."

"Hey, I don't wanna get involved in the crumby world of writing. It's all just one big lie anyways, selling your art, catering to the masses so you can put some pounds on the table and support yourself. That's not writing; that's not art. That's hogwash, pure rubbish. Someone said once, the second you change your art in order to cater to someone else, to cater to any kind of guideline whatsoever, then it ain't art anymore. It's hogwash. You think the masses would well-receive true art if it weren't homogenised to their every little ignorant desire? Nah."

"Well, do you think the public would be ready for the art, in the sense that you speak of it, if it were an option?"

"Who cares? Who cares of anything for if they are ready? The great writers and painters who are recognised today were often thought of as fools in their own times. A lot of these guys didn't make nothing for their contributions. But at least they were true to themselves. They created art, not hogwash like today."

"So this uncle of yours, you do not hold him in well-regard for his writing?"

"He's a story writer. I respect that. He earns himself a decent keep. He doesn't proclaim to be Voltaire. Does he inspire me? Course not. Is he a good person? Probably. I know I'm young to the world, but what I do see is that whatever you do, whatever job you take, you gotta know what it is exactly you are creating, what you are affecting. So long as you don't make misconceptions about the gravity in your head, you'll be fine."

"And what of your uncle's conceptions?"

"I think he knows where he stands. And if he's okay with that, which I suppose he obviously is, then great."

"Well, it sounds like you've given this a great deal of thought, Cecelia. That's a good thing. I don't consider there to be such a thing as too much contemplation. It's healthy, and it will lead you on a road back to happiness, I am confident."

"Well, I don't know about all that. All I know is I don't wanna be no stinkin' writer."

"Fair enough, dear."

"So am I dismissed now?"

Kyla thought not to let the girl off the hook so easily.

"Well, not quite yet. If you do not wish to be a writer, or a modern artist, what is you wish to do?"

"Oh, come on now. I'm a young girl. Who knows? Half the bloomin' world don't know, even those who got jobs already. Buggers don't pick occupations based on, as you say, want they wanna do. They go for what's most profitable, what they are most skilled at. That's the motivation, the driving force. As for me, who knows what I'm good at. Likely nothing."

Kyla shed sympathetic eyes upon the girl.

"Do not be so cynical at so young an age, dear. We all have some talent."

"I don't," started the girl, "really wanna talk about it anymore. I mean, maybe you're right, maybe not. Who knows. Probably not even you."

As a few more minutes passed in the conclusion of their conversation, Kyla felt satisfied to have extracted a bit more than the girl had planned on offering.

"Have a great day, Cecelia. Keep reading; keep thinking. We'll talk more during our next session."

"Sounds like a plan, doc."

"Okay."

"See you later."

Chaotic Ocean

Cecelia strode lightly out of the office.

*

Kyla kicked back as she often did after the sessions of her three main patients had concluded. She seemed especially exhausted on this day, as one may have been able to guess. Kyla was still a tortured woman with supernatural ideas running in and out of her mind. Her life had become entirely alien to her. The once static map of everyday life had now become a maze filled with tunnels and shortcuts.

"Indeed, we do work a long day," repeated Kyla aloud.

She got up to stretch her feet and noticed that a paper had been delivered just aside the entrance to the office.

To herself she thought, "Ah yes, now for the entire perversity of human nature, all that is fit to print anyway!"

She scooped the paper into her arms and strolled back toward the desk. Kyla began to think that this routine had become old.

"Ahh, none the less, perhaps some routine is just what the doctor ordered. Routine with a side of chips, hold the pickle," she joked. It was a bad joke. With that, she delved into the paper.

An Exercise in Fertility
By: Timothy Sleiney

These quirky Londoners... they'll bark, scrap, and fight all just to get what's coming to them. Though, through it all, I for one commend them. There are few maxims in life that are worth knowing, and perhaps even fewer actions in life worth performing. But these people, the cheeky lads, year after year, live with a common mantra that only God herself could find any kind of flaw in.

Pardon the suspense. Most folks you'd come across in everyday life are so incredibly timid, either out of fear of God, fear of morality, fear of the law, most often though, out of fear of self-hypocrisy, self-condescension folks! Ain't that a way to live? Most people's tongues are held tight enough to play string symphonies on. Most people have a million thoughts a moment, but say nothing out of this fear, out of this pitiful, destructive fear that cripples every single one of us. Sure, not every sentence is going to sound like a profound ideology (thank God), but at least every sentence would be true, would be hounest.

How is it that humans learn? Through error. When there is no daring, no insecurity, we will all be a very sedated group, wouldn't you say? There must be this insecurity, this daring. And I say, hands down, these cheeky people of London have it and are not afraid to use it! These people have it. I assure you.

The boldness and conviction to actually make comments, statements, without second guessing yourself, without using qualifiers like 'if,' 'but,' and 'maybe.' When you run into a London bloke on the street and ask how the weather is, he doesn't respond with 'I'm not sure, looks like it might be a'brewin' out.' No, he responds with 'Looks bloody as Hell out! Horrible day.' And he doesn't apologise, doesn't think of the repercussions. He has the conviction to say what is on his mind even if there is a chance that it will bite him in the cheeks later on.

That's truly what this is about. Not being in fear of being bitten in the cheeks later on. The people of London know this and are not timid beings. This entire existence we are renting out is one huge exercise in fertility. Treat it accordingly and live it up like we do in London!

"Timothy Sleiney?" questioned Kyla aloud. "Do I not recognise that name in its entirety?"

She thought for a few moments as the name struck her with an unusual sensation of familiarity. Alas, she could not figure anything. Kyla chalked it up to chemical imbalance or any other kind of justification that would suit the moment. This kind of reasoning did not please her, though, she found herself clinging to it more and more often of late. Her once clear perception of the occurrences around her had quickly faded into a shroud-like fog that perpetually dampened and confused every sense she had known. Kyla's warm and comforting relationship with the world had turned cold and barren.

Through the odd mist of feelings, she continued onward into the paper.

Elastor Plastors for Sale, You're Gonna Need 'em for Your Conscience
By: Berg Daye

We've all used elastors before, isn't that right? We've all been piss-arsed enough to have fallen down and injured these expensive and irreplaceable carrying cases that we know only as our bodies. When you're just a little tot, you've got your mammy's and pappy's all about, on this stalwart and watchful command with their elastors in pocket.

Little one has a malady, hey well let's just elastor plastor it up. Fixed. Done. Thing of the past. Right, blokes? That's how she happens. It's a simple kind of procedure that doesn't even cross our minds.

But that's the past. That was a time. Now is a time. A different time for all of those blokes. The cuts and bruises have escalated into something much different. We've all become slave to injury. In the adult life, we kill, maim, and torture, and we don't have elastor plastors to cover up for our acts. That's the truth now.

This is the natural progression of man. Innocent at first, making use of the elastors for the injuries unjustly, perhaps, put on him by the world. Then, bam he's all grown up, and now it's his turn to place some blame, to put some injury onto something else. And he does. He kills, maims, and tortures, as I have mentioned. Elastor plastors of old are now laws and bills and acts of legality to cover up for what we've done.

How's our conscience to respond though? How's our mothers and fathers to respond? This is our world; this is the now. This is how it goes, just like how it went when we were young. Just now you got a bigger picture, a bigger piece of that puzzle. You maybe see a little more, and it takes you back, it frightens you. You're thinking this is too much. And it probably is. But this is the now.

Brothers and sisters go to that shop on the corner and stock up on the best brands of elastor plastors. Get the big, sticky ones, the ones that cover more surface area, because you're gonna need 'em for the restitution of your minds once you realise exactly what it is that you do in this life, to this life.

"Now, I know this man, I must. I recognise the style. I recognise the name, mustn't I?"

She thought for a moment.

"Ah, I surely recognise the name, Daye, for I read an article by him just recently. I recall sitting at this very desk, in perhaps this very position, reading, and looking over an article by Daye. That must be the reason for the familiarity."

Though, this line of reasoning did not truly appease Kyla. She felt there was still something more, something more deeply shrouded that was yet uncovered. Not only did she know the man's name, but felt that there was a much greater connection. This frustrated her. This made her uneasy and discouraged her from reading onward. She felt as if many steps behind in everything that she did. This was entirely foreign a feeling to her, and she detested it.

"Have I not given enough in this life?" she began to wail. "Are these articles tailored to me? Am I to speak out more? Have I done something horribly wrong, or horribly right? I am greatly confused."

Just as she began to wallow in her self-loathing, she heard an urgent sounding knock on her office door. It was hard against the wood and repeated with extreme rapidity.

"Curious," she thought. "I don't believe I've any more scheduled appointments today."

The knock continued and seemed to gain strength. It was as if the urgency of a dying soul had manifested its cries into this knocking.

"Yes, yes, come in," she replied to the sound.

A man quickly jolted open the door and appeared out of breath. He was a slender man of medium build. A dark, navy blue cap pointed downward covering most of his countenance. She could notice untrimmed hair screaming out of the sides of his cap though, and the man also seemed unshaved. He appeared to have been a commoner, and Kyla was unsure of his purpose in this instance.

"Who are you sir?" questioned Kyla with a girlish curiosity.

"I have been told to give this to you, madam. That is all there is to the story."

He avoided her question.

"Give me what, sir?"

He walked quickly over to the desk, placed a milky white envelope on it, tipped his hat, and then hurriedly walked to the door and escaped.

Chaotic Ocean

"Sir, I do beg of your pardon; please do not leave in such a way. What is your name, what is this that you have given me? Do I need to sign for something? Sir?"

Her attempt was of no use. The man had ceased to be near enough to have heard Kyla's faint cries. She was alone in the large office. The lettre stared at her, and Kyla seemed to detest it as well.

Kyla slowly moved from her seat and walked to the office door to shut it. She was confused by the sudden event. Though, she tried to take it in stride. Walking casually back to the desk, she sat down and stared at the envelope, as if unsure of what to do.

"Okay, let's see what the unknown has to offer up for today."

She quickly sliced open the envelope and unfolded the piece of paper. It was a lettre.

Dearest Kyla,

Consider this your very own death promise. I promise the death will not cause too much discomfort.

Chaotic Ocean

CHAPTER TEN

☦

A PRIMORDIAL FERVOR

*

Kyla was obviously taken back by the lettre's opening remark. She slithered in her seat, as if completely uncomfortable. A bead a sweat rolled down to her cheek and dripped onto the words of the lettre. She was too frightened to stop reading and went onward.

Threats are for the weak, for those individuals not entirely committed to the act that they bark in harsh, ill-educated words. Threats are for the timid, for thugs who wish to dampen one's mood or send a few insignificant chills up and down the spine of the reader. Such writing is not what you have before your eyes.

This is not a threat. Your death will come soon, I can promise you that. And hounestly, I cannot make the promise that I attempted in the second sentence. It may cause pain; it may cause a river or pain. Hopefully you've not let that run from your body. Hopefully you've not let the built up negativity escape at no price. I intend to bring that out of you, and it will frustrate me to a great extent if you have allowed some thug to get the better of you, to capture your better screams, your better true-life nightmares.

If so, the pain will be immense, surely, as you will have no shrieks to unleash that are candid. Manufactured pain from an empty body is the most horrific of all.

"Good God," she thought. "What do I have before me? Is this truly what it appears to be? Am I being informed of some nefarious plot to end my days on Earth?"

The wilde thoughts seemed unreal. Nonetheless, they ran as if professional athletes would, to the farthest and fastest extent that one might imagine possible. Kyla began to perspire more, and her forehead began to twitch. She had not been used to the drama that had seemingly unfolded itself before her life. The death promise seemed to affect her deeply, and she took it quite seriously. She again continued to read further.

You will be uncovered for all that you are and have done in this life. That is a promise too. Your actions will not go unpunished in this existence, and certainly not in any future ones. Think to yourself, and all whom you have touched, and all of your dishounest and manufactured feelings, shrouded behind a wall of pride and stubbornness. Certainly you can see the guilt that swells around you like a cloud of fog.

Chaotic Ocean

The day, is it important? The time, is it not even less important? You need not know the precise moment of your doom. It will arrive on a perfect day, so that the act is carried out in perfection. Your life will be over, and perhaps you will finally be able to rest in some kind of truth. The rains and snows will come and go, and your memory will come to pass from all of those whom you've affected. You will be and remain just another human to have crossed this world, as if on a journey, only to find out as all have, that there is truly nothing of ultimate meaning or purpose. And in your final state, you will realise that you had one of the most wonderful gifts, were truly blessed, and chose to waste it, as most do, on a fruitless search.

You are a piece of work. We all are. You will die soon, this I can promise, Kyla.

Signed,

The chill wind that blows over every man when he notices his own unimportance

Kyla was frozen in fear. There was no comfort in trickery, for this lettre expounded verily on the fact that this was no act of make believe. She found less solace in the anonymity the writer chose to keep. The words seemed to haunt her, as if they had been meticulously chosen for the greatest inner impact.

"The chill wind that blows over every man," said she aloud, in a state of disbelief.

*

She could no longer remain calm. Kyla hurriedly packed her belongings and was off, as if in a race with a transparent ghost. She shuffled quickly past colleagues and exchanged no pleasantries. Her demeanor was extremely obvious. The woman at the front desk in the main lobby of the hospital barked at her as she strode past without making any eye contact. Kyla cared not for the habitual greetings that only superficially made existence more warm and cordial. On this instance, her thoughts and actions were magnified due to her troubles.

"Miss Demark..." echoed through the lobby as she burst out through the main entrance. She did not care to explain herself, nor could she have in her state of being.

"Kyla, off to a better place?" asked a voice.

She stopped suddenly with great apprehension. The unknown on this particular day was more eerie than on others. Kyla was frozen with a dread too transparent to have been anything but childlike.

She turned swiftly to identify the voice.

"Dear, you look deathly ill," remarked Mr. Pem.

The sight of Mr. Pem seemed completely comforting to her. Sweet relief rushed into her body as she recognised the man's familiar countenance. However, she likely resented having been described as deathly ill, especially now.

"Ohh dear, Mr. Pem," responded Kyla. Her mouth was dry.

Chaotic Ocean

"Apologies if my presence disturbed you. It was not my intention to shock you into any kind of submission."

"You did not. I really have just had a magnificently horrid day. I was rushing off and hadn't expected to be stopped in mid step."

"Ah then, has someone else shocked you into submission?"

His question seemed almost eerily omniscient, and she did not enjoy the accuracy of the remark.

"Mr. Pem, I do not get shocked into submission. It was merely a bad day. We all have them. I trust you have."

"Of course," replied the man.

Thoughts of Mr. Pem's disappearance ran through Kyla's mind. She recalled his having been oddly absent the day she had attempted and succeeded in fetching him a position at the hospital.

"I am fine, Mr. Pem. There is nothing much more to the matter."

"Well, that is a good thing to believe," replied Mr. Pem.

"There is nothing more."

"You need not convince me, Kyla."

"Pem, where did you go the other day?"

"Pardon?"

"The other day. Come now, surely you remember. You had enlisted in my aid to procure a position for you at the hospital. We discussed this perhaps in this very spot. I was to go inside, find out about the position, and was to return to you with the news. I attempted to do so, and you were nowhere to be found. I could not tell you of the news, good or bad, either way since you'd vacated the grounds, or so it seemed."

"It is completely valid for you to be upset. All I have to offer is an apology. Something turned up that I was forced to attend to, a matter of personal business. I was entirely apprehensive in so doing, as I foresaw these kinds of feelings. But so is the way, and so was done."

She looked into the man's eyes, and he had truly a look of sorrow. She could not hold the resentment for long. Kyla was curiously drawn to Mr. Pem and wished to continue residing in his company.

"Well, it has been forgiven. No great injustice has been done, Mr. Pem."

"I thank you for your understanding. Many do not have the capacity. And that is a truthful comment. Historically, we can point to dictators, to murderers, to the poorly treated, and yes, maybe even to some good individuals, those who have pushed the limits of knowledge, even a few here and there who stood up for their beliefs, but how many can we point to for sheer compassion and forgiveness? Christ perhaps, but beyond that? I can't think of one. Compassion is simply a neglected human emotion. It is not taught. It is not passed down. It is not preached. And most harrowing, it is not expected. This is unfortunate."

"Certainly I do not beg of comparisons with Christ, Mr. Pem, for I do not wish to have that kind of responsibility, but, thank you. Perhaps I have not had the good feeling of praise in a long while. Modesty can only go so far. I will not lie and say that a complement from an individual whom one respects does not reach the warmest regions of one's soul. Thank you."

"You seem to have calmed down," remarked Mr. Pem.

Kyla had not noticed the change in her body till the man had verbalised it.

"Yes, apparently so. It is odd, but as I said, apparent."

"Well then, I must ask how it went. Have you returned to me a saint or a sinner?"

"I beg your pardon."

"The meeting to procure a position with the hospital. "

"Oh," smiled Kyla. "Yes, actually I was. I spoke with some people, and it didn't seem that there were many open positions. Though, I was offered a janitorial position on your behalf. I replied that I would discuss it with my friend, you, and get back with an answer as soon as possible."

"A saint! Oh my, that is wonderful news. I am greatly indebted"

"Well, I understand that a janitorial position is perhaps not what you'd intended. Thus, I wished to discuss it over before assuming that you'd jump for the position."

"Kyla, a position is a position. There are no such positions which are above or below any particular individual. The days of nobility and noble occupations are long gone. Perhaps the mentality still exists, but the presentation is but a dream. I gladly accept the position. I will do the work proudly. I owe you my deepest gratitude."

"Well, it is not necessary. It was well within my reach to do, and it seems we should help others when it is possible."

"Again, perhaps a dead theory, but one of the most magnanimous nature."

"I hope it is not dead."

"If not dead, then at least archaic or dormant."

"Whichever, the position is yours. I imagine that you can start tomorrow. I'd suggest going in around nine in the morning to fill out any necessary paperwork and obtain your work detail."

"Surely, I will do so," remarked the man.

The two stood there for a moment exchanging glances.

"Alright, Kyla, I have matters to attend. It is my hope that we will meet again soon."

"As it is mine."

Mr. Pem walked off from the parking lot into the distance. Kyla watched him the entire way. He walked at a medium pace. She perceived something of an odd effect taking place. It seemed with each step Mr. Pem took, the distance betwixt she and the man grew. The warmness that she felt while in his presence, which provided for her calm, seemed to dissipate, to fade more and more with each step as well. Kyla was confused. Mr. Pem could no longer be seen, and she was left alone.

*

Chaotic Ocean

"Oh dear," she thought to herself. "I am entirely absent in the mind. I did not drive that ol' banger here today. I rode with Sean in the cab. I must ring for him."

She walked over to the payphone and dialed the cab company, asking specifically for Sean's cab number, as he had prior informed her to do. Kyla was put on hold for a handful of minutes. When the voice came back to the phone, she was informed that Sean's cab was in the area and would arrive shortly, probably within ten or fifteen minutes.

"Thank you. I will be just outside the main entrance of the hospital," she told the man on the line. The two hung up.

It seemed longer than ten or fifteen minutes while she was standing there. The air was brisk. Her excitement again began to increase, as she thought back to the lettre she had received. Kyla was amazed that, while speaking with Pem, she could maintain so much control over her actions. She wished to tell Sean of every detail, of every biting word of the lettre. For a reason unknown, she did not feel comfortable enough around Mr. Pem to divulge such information. Kyla felt good while in his presence, but paralysed from speaking too personally. It was an odd dichotomy.

The cab pulled up suddenly, and Kyla's eyes brightened. She was very glad to see Sean's familiar motorcar. With each meeting, she felt closer with Sean, and enjoyed that sensation.

"Hop in lady. I got a schedule to keep here. I ain't working for free, lady!"

Sean's joking demeanor was welcomed.

"Yeah, yeah. I've been waiting here for four hours. What happened to ten minutes? Seems like this ride should be free," she responded.

Kyla quickly stepped into the side door and into the back seat.

"So, how's it been, Sean?"

"It's been rosy, love! Thanks for askin'."

"Any time."

"Where to, Kyla?"

"Where am I going, I don't know, Sean? It is entirely difficult for me to say at the moment. I am feeling quite awkward."

"You want I should just run the meter again?"

"Yes, please."

"Okay, done. So what's on yer mind, Kyla?" asked the cabby.

"Many things. Many, many, many things, Sean. Dear God, I have a story to tell. What a day I have had at work! The things one comes across in this life are just utterly surprising sometimes. I suppose I will cut to the point. I received a lettre today."

"A lettre, ey?"

"A lettre of grand implication, no less! I don't know what to do, who to tell, where to go!"

Sean could hear the fright in Kyla's voice.

"Grand implication?" questioned Sean. "Come now, it can't be all that bad, Kyla."

Chaotic Ocean

"It is all that bad and worse, Sean. I've tried to live a pretty helpful life, tried not to take advantage of my fellow brethren, tried not to stampede over those whom I could have. And yet, and yet I am the victim here. I am the one trying to forge an escape, and from whom I do not even know!"

"Okay, take it easy there, love. What has happened?"

"The lettre I received was a death promise. I've no clue who would wish to harm me. I've no clue what to do. Should I take the lettre to the authorities? Should I shrug it off as some pitiful perverted prank? Should I run? Should I remain calm and reticent? Should I be frantic?"

Kyla's eyes seemed to bounce about, as if she'd been completely devoid of stability. It remained quiet outside of the cab. The hospital seemed discordantly serene. There had not been a passerby for sometime now, which seemed odd at a main hospital.

"Kyla, I know only what you tell me of the situation at hand, love. It may not be safe for you at your flat."

"Not safe?" she barked, as if to presume Sean a possible suspect.

"That's exactly right. Confound all the dogs' bollocks in the world, Kyla. Think deep down. You know I'm right. Where would you have me take ya'? The workday is done. Now you wanna go home? You've just received a sinister sounding lettre, and now you wanna go to the one place where everyone knows you'll be? Everyone!"

"Sean, but…"

"No, Kyla. I won't have it. I may be a simple cabby, but I know what sounds like rubbish and what sounds like sense. And goin' home would be rubbish."

"Perhaps you have a point. Maybe I should put up for the night somewhere else," conceded Kyla.

"Now you're thinkin'. The only place I will allow is with me and my family. Come stay for a few days. Maybe this whole thing will blow over by then. And if it doesn't, you can stay longer. I don't know what to tell you now as for a plan of action, love, but I know you could think better knowin' you're safe. Come stay with me and the fam'."

"Sean, I am touched that you would be so kind to offer, but…"

"Nah. None of that," replied the cabby.

"But Sean, I feel it will be safe in my flat. If I cannot reside in the most secure of places in my life, then have I not already lost this game? Have I not already submitted too heavily into the fear? Have I not already given them the greatest edge one can give over oneself? I do not wish to live in hiding from a threat or promise, no matter how grim the sentiment."

"I thought you might say some rubbish like that. But this ain't no time for your head to be filled with heavy stones. This is a time for you to get your act together, leave your cheeks in the seat they're in, and let me take you to my place."

Kyla thought for a moment. She rationalised and theorised and debated the risks of the situation. She thought to herself that staying at Sean's would be awkward. Kyla felt it was almost unnecessary to take such a precaution when she knew so little of the legitimacy of the lettre received. Though, at the same time, she felt as though Sean had been kind enough to offer, to do so much for her really, that to turn him down would have been entirely rude and thankless.

"Alright, Sean, I will agree to reside at your place for a short while. Don't get used to me though, as I will be out of there before we even arrive, so to speak."

"Now you're talkin'! I will buzz up dispatch to learn 'em that I'm takin' the rest of the day off for a personal matter. You just relax back there. We'll be at my place before you can say bob's your uncle."

*

The two drove for some time in silence, and Kyla rested her neck on the back deck of the cab. She felt somewhat relieved in allowing someone else to make some of her decisions. Though she could not fully formulate the forthcoming idea at the time, sometimes the greatest satisfactions are found not in the complete control of oneself, but in the willing submission to another. Kyla was fatigued from emotion.

A light sprinkling of snow dusted the streets of London as the cab drove onward. Nothing significant amounted, but the white seemed to glaze the buildings like pastries.

"The weather is completely queer," thought Kyla. "Rain, snow, snow, rain. Is there ever an evening of shine or a night of clear, cloudless skies?" She felt as though the weather was like her life, enormously habitual and yet almost utterly chaotic of late.

The light frosting made the trip seem like it went on for hours. Kyla thought back to wonderful childhood memories of dancing and frolicking in the white powder. The past seemed like a time so long ago, as ancient as the pyramids. In a way, she longed for that time, those memories. She felt as if she had been unfairly thrust into the world, ripped from childhood with almost no warning. It was unfair. Perhaps that is the great misfortune of modern life. As the naivety of youth fades, the cruelty of adulthood, of war, of hatred, of toiling a good portion of one's time away for false fortune sets in. Each is forced to deal with the pattern in his own way, with little guidance or solace. The pattern repeats, and life becomes more degrading, more of a perpetual habit of actions that one lowers oneself in doing over and again till death. Everyone is forced to sublimate himself into the tried and true blueprint that those in power have set forth, regardless of what the individual wishes. The snow continued to dust the streets.

"Almost there, love," said Sean from the front of the cab.

His voice almost shocked Kyla, who had been deep in thought, as if in a trance-like state. Her body jolted at the sound.

"Oh, okay, sounds good, Sean. Sorry I have been so quiet. I was only thinking to myself, contemplating."

"Hey, you don't gotta make excuses for me. Each should be allowed his or her own contemplation. We take that away, what do we got?"

"Thank you for everything, Sean."

"Hey, you don't need to be doin' that now. It is my pleasure to help out someone whom I consider a friend. From the moment we met, you seemed different than most Earth-walkers. You intrigued me. And you've turned out to be quite a kind woman. So, again, nothing is required of you to say thanks or grace."

"Exactly how far away is it now?" questioned Kyla.

"Faster than you can say bob's your..."

Sean stopped in mid sentence once he pulled into the drive of his home.

"See, told ya' it be faster than the expression."

Kyla smiled warmly back at Sean's quirky sense of humour. She enjoyed it and looked forward to kicking back for a while.

*

The two got out of the car and slammed the doors shut. She looked around for a few seconds at the surrounding area. Sean lived in the less affluent section of London. The homes were packed very tightly together, each having almost no property attached to it. The flats were smaller than even traditional tiny residences. Sean's home, along with most of the others, was completely rundown and rusted-looking. There was a foul stench in the air that Kyla could not identify, and surely could not ignore. The town seemed loud and awkward. It was as if it had been out of place, so to speak. Perhaps that is why Sean lived there. Kyla perceived him a man out of place, and thought him a good and kind man who deserved more than he had, though, she knew deep down that he had more than she.

"How's it look?" he asked.

"It looks wonderful," replied Kyla.

The home seemed only a few feet taller than Kyla. Bits and pieces of the paint had peeled away, pointing to low maintenance and antiquity. The colour was almost unidentifiable. It seemed a putrid kind of yellow had merged with a light, washed out brown. Though, most of the houses in Sean's neighbored looked nearly identical. Kyla could not figure if it was the weather over this particular region of town, or if it had been something else that cursed these residents into a filthy sort of living. She could feel a certain insecurity in the wind, as if the neighborhood itself had taken on a personality. Kyla thought to herself that this was the kind of place where doors are kept locked at all hours of the day, and not just out of habit, but out of necessity.

"Hmm," she ironically contemplated, "this is my safe haven?"

"Come now, love," said Sean aloud. "Let us go inside."

"Alright, Sean."

The two shuffled about quickly. Kyla followed Sean as he led the way into his abode. She watched his hands, noticing the moment they were in the door, he shut it tightly and locked it.

Kyla stared into his eyes for a brief moment, as if to say, "This is your security?"

Chaotic Ocean

"Come here, Kyla, meet my family. I've told them about you before, but they don't know you're gonna be stayin' here a few days."

The innards of Sean's place seemed cluttered, as one could have imagined from the exterior. A small dining area situated itself adjacent to what appeared the main family area, though this section was filled with boxes and various items that looked destined for storage. The walls were lined with many pictures of the family. It was the trait that gave the house the most character. Beyond the first two tiny rooms, there was a short hallway that stretched into the rear portion of the flat. Kyla could see a few doors off the small hallway that she assumed to be bedrooms. To Kyla's surprise, a few children then ran out in excitement to hug Sean.

"Daddy, daddy!" the little ones shouted, as if their lives had been entirely empty without their father. It was an alien feeling to Kyla, but she knew that it was one she envied. The two children attached themselves to Sean's legs like little parasites. They seemed no older than four or five years of age. Both had an incredible innocence about their eyes. There was a boy and a girl, and each had clothes that appeared aged and unclean. They seemed as if bathed only every handful of days. The children looked in one way sickly, though in another, magnificent, which Kyla could not reconcile, completely happy and filled with all the satiation in the world. Both the boy and girl had ocean blue eyes. They were like crystals or diamonds, without an ounce of impurity. The light reflected brightly off the their faces.

Shortly after this, a tall, slender woman stepped out from one of the rooms and ran into Sean's arms, as if a child herself. She kissed him passionately for what seemed like a minute straight. The woman hugged him and grabbed at him. Words like "darling" and "dearest" were exchanged, and Kyla was bewildered that people actually existed like this. She thought back to her initial conversation with Sean the cabby, how he had explained the contentment of his life, how he had even detailed this very situation. At the time, she recalled understanding Sean's words, and even envying them. Though, in all likelihood, she probably had difficulty imagining such a life, such a situation, and therefore, could easily idealise it. This, however, was the reality of which Sean had spoken, and it was almost entirely too much for her to bear. Kyla thought silently that Sean had acquired perfection. This made her feel unfortunate, and her eyes drooped.

"Angela, I'd like you to meet Kyla," said Sean to his wife. "She'll be staying here for a few days if it's alright. She's kind of in a bad way, and is scared for her life. Ain't no worries though; we're in no danger."

Angela walked warmly over to Kyla and shook her hand. Kyla smiled back and was relieved.

"Any friend of Sean's... Well, you know the saying. So how do you know my Sean?" asked Angela.

"I work at the hospital, and Sean has happened upon me with his cab a few times, Mrs...."

Chaotic Ocean

"Oh, just call me Angela, or Ange, whichever. Not Angel though, don't really like that one. Sean calls me it sometimes, but you know, it's Sean, but Angela or Ange are both really fine."

Angela had red hair and was a very pretty woman. Her smile was warm and her actions seemed true. Kyla could understand why Sean seemed so taken by her. Angela exuded a kind of sanguinity in her words when speaking. She was bubbly and fun, and Kyla thought her to have been the perfect match for Sean.

"Now dear, Kyla is it? These are the little ones," said Angela referring to the children. "This here is Liam; he's four years old. Isn't that right bubby? Isn't that right? Four years old, or are you as old as Daddy? Hmm? Hmm?"

Angela seemed sidetracked, acting playful with Liam. One could tell that the child loved her immensely, as much as four-year-olds can actualise love, anyway. Liam responded, "I'm fouw!"

Angela went on.

"And this one is our other little darling, Maggy. She's a year younger than Liam, three years old. She's so smart for her age."

"Well the children are lovely, Angela. It seems like you have a wonderful family here," replied Kyla.

Angela could hear the emptiness in Kyla's remark. It was not empty in sentiment, but empty in that Kyla obviously had nothing close to this sort of life, and it appeared that she wished for it greatly.

"Hey dear, thank you, and I'm sure your little ones won't be too far off," tried to comfort Angela.

"Thank you," replied Kyla. She could pick up that her own feelings had become entirely transparent, and that being the good woman she was, Angela was of course attempting to make her feel better.

"How long will you be staying with us?" asked Angela.

"Well, I hope not too long. As Sean said, I am in an odd situation that I'm hoping will work itself out soon. I hope to be gone as soon as possible. Whether that is tomorrow evening or three days from now, I do not know. I hope I am not too much of a burden. Please just let me know; just say the word and I will be gone with no resentment."

"Nothing of the kind will be done," replied Angela.

"That's exactly right," echoed Sean.

"You will stay here as long as you are in any kind of danger. What would be on my conscience if I were to let you from my home and something happened? Beyond conscience, that would just be wrong, wrong for everyone. You will stay here while it is dangerous out there, for whatever reason," barked Angela.

Kyla was impressed with Angela's selfless demeanor. Her actions and words were entirely magnanimous, and it was difficult for Kyla not to like the family. Their company was pleasant, and they were good people. Kyla had been used to the self-serving company of her friend Zigmund Sardoce, hence, this was quite new to her, and she enjoyed it.

Chaotic Ocean

"Ange, could you make Kyla up one of the rooms? The kids can stay in our room, and Kyla can stay in their room. Do you fancy that an okay solution? Not sure where else she could put up."

"That's fine," replied the wife. "Come along, Kyla, you can help me transfer some things. And then your room will be ready."

The two went off. Sean was left behind in the main area playing with Liam and Maggy.

*

Zigmund slumbered at his mansion. Not unlike Kyla, he was a confused man. Terrible, paranoid ideas took up the better portions of his days. Perhaps more cruel, the ideas took up the entire portions of his dreams.

He continued to his unconscious reverie. Inside of which, Zigmund found himself in a barren graveyard. The moon shined brightly on the headstones, as if a flashlight illuminating all of the forgotten names and memories. It was cold, and he found himself shivering, listening closely for the faint sound of voices, though, he could hear nothing. Zigmund looked all about, as if to find comfort in the company of others, though not a soul could be seen within many miles. The stars in the sky were piercingly white, almost like purity in a physical manifestation. He concluded that had the moon gone mad and shirked its duties for the night, the stars could have filled in aptly with no noticeable difference in brightness.

"What time is it?" he thought to himself. "It must be late, for there are no passersby, no children, no adults, not even an auto engine kicking out pollution and barking like a wilde beast, as so often is the case."

He had not moved from his position, continuing to take in the surroundings. Zigmund could not figure why he had been placed in such a scene. It was then decided that he should move about, so to further inspect. His footsteps were heavy, and the ground beneath him was cold. The steps were loud as Zigmund's feet created crunching sounds, the leaves and debris depressing beneath him.

Zigmund suddenly found himself stopped. He could no longer move his legs. A headstone seemed to uncover itself before him, the words on the stone reading:

R.I.P.
Zigmund Sardoce
Born Insignificant, Died Insignificant
Father to None
He Kept to Himself, and to Himself the World was Kept

"Goodness! What is this, some means of trickery?" said he aloud.

His voice seemed to boom and echo throughout the empty graveyard.

"This is just pure nonsense," said a frightened Zigmund as he started off from the headstone.

As he turned his back, the ground began to shift. He could hear a rumbling noise under his feet. Zigmund was stiff with fear and could not figure the supernatural event. The Earth uncovered itself, and before his eyes was a corpse, standing eye to eye with him. The thing was half skeleton. The other half seemed like flesh, as if it had not yet fully eroded. The smell was putrid that the corpse gave off.

"What is it you desire?!" barked Zigmund out of terror.

"Zigmund, cannot you see the obvious? Did not you read the headstone? Are you mentally blind as Tiresias was physically?"

Its voice was only half human. The other half seemed almost animalistic, as if two spliced into one, making for a horrid sound.

"I must go. I do not have time for ghouls! You cannot be real; it simply cannot be!" shouted Zigmund.

"Real so far as affecting your reality, is there truly another requirement, Zigmund? You are a piece of work. You see your own name on a headstone, meet your dead self, and all the while, choose to deny that it is at all happening. We are both dead and alive at every moment of our lives, Zigmund. Perhaps you will come to realise this."

"I just don't..."

"Step outside for one damned moment of existence, you foul creature! It is you, not I, who has no peace in rest!" shouted the corpse.

"Step outside to go where?" inquired Zigmund.

"You'll never know anything if you don't step outside of yourself, Zigmund. I am here to guide, not to frighten. I am here to bring some lasting impact on your pathetic existence. All that you think you know, all opinions formulated, all of that, means nothing while you are inside of yourself. Of course, every opinion makes sense because it is guided by your own emotion, by your own biases, by your own experiences. It all will make sense in this manner. Step outside yourself; step outside to see your opinions from another angle. This other angle is the only angle that one can put any kind of sense around. It is the only angle that is not entangled in one's own superficial stupidity. One must step outside of oneself in order to know anything *of* oneself, and of the world for that matter. This is a lesson you are far from learning."

"When am I to do this? On special occasions, holidays?" joked Zigmund.

"You are a piece of work. I should know, since I am you. And I suppose I shouldn't be all that disappointed either, again, since I am you, since I was you, and since when you have long ceased to exist, I will still be you. Sardoce, I say to you one last time, you have learned nothing that you think you have. It is not too late to alter the sands of time. Do so, and perhaps some happiness will find its way toward you. Good-bye. All that we see or seem is but a dream within a dream...."

The corpse's voice trailed off, as if an echo reverberating many times and then ultimately losing strength with each replication.

Zigmund woke from the dream. His head was pounding.

"Goodness," thought he, "a graveyard. I should have known it was another blasted dream. I'll step outside this bedroom to grab some medicine for my headache. I suppose that's what it all meant. My head must have been hurting when I slumbered. That's all."

Zigmund decided to quench his confused state of being with a glass of water. He walked slowly and timidly into the kitchen area of the mansion. His curiosity still had not been appeased as to the displacement of objects in different areas.

"I wonder if my mind is sound, for no intruders did I find upon my search. Why would some scoundrel take the risk of breaking in only to mess a few papers about? And yet, no trace was left."

Zigmund continued to contemplate the confusion that he had earlier felt. He indeed had searched and indeed had found nothing as to evidence of foul intentions.

Our colourful antihero persisted through the mansion and then into the kitchen. He filled a glass halfway with water as cold as the arctic and swallowed it quickly. It was pleasing to the senses. Water, which brings and is the basis for so much life, can perhaps too bring life back to its base. Zigmund refilled the glass and repeated his actions. His thirst was immense. It was as if he had awoken from a hibernation of sorts and needed to replenish his body with fuel as quickly as possible.

"You're doing it all wrong!"

It was a voice familiar to the prior voice he had heard upon last use of the pond. Once again, his body jolted. The glass fell from his hand and shattered on the marble floor. He instantly attempted to reject the voice, almost instinctually, as if his immune system had prior created antibodies and now was attempting to make use of them. He could not resist, could not reject. The force was too powerful. After many moments of defiance, the words echoed again.

"You're doing it all wrong."

"By God, leave me alone!" shouted Zigmund.

"You will not be granted such a request. Especially not when you're doing it all wrong, making every possible wrong choice, leading yourself up and down every wrongly lit path."

Zigmund wished not to fight with the force, or perhaps realised that he could not. It was almost as if a submissive acceptance had overwhelmed him.

"You speak in circles and rhymes and expect that I should decipher your metaphors, as if a scholar interpreting Keats," replied Zigmund.

"Come now, do not wish for the boredom of simplicity. Life has far too much cunning in its nature for that," reverberated the voice in a caustic tone.

Zigmund seemed fed up. He almost seemed unsurprised at this point, having experienced odd feelings in his recent days.

"Phantom, apparition, whatever you are, whatever impression you wish to impress upon my mind, upon my being, please simply do so; please do not elongate the process under the tasteless veil of art. What have I done that is wrong?"

Chaotic Ocean

"Kill Kyla. Do it swiftly. Do it immediately. Kill without hesitation. Kill without thought or conscience. It is your fate."

Chaotic Ocean

CHAPTER ELEVEN
☦

SELF-FULFILLING PROPHECIES

*

Zigmund seemed stunned at the haunting request. He attempted to gather his thoughts in order to reply, but found incredible difficulty in such a task. While it was true that he suspected Kyla of some malicious shroud, of some sinister involvement in the park murder that the two had witnessed together, the thought of ending his best friend had never come into his darkest of dreams!

"Internal spectre of the mind, surely you are mistaken in your wishes, or if not, mad in your intentions! Kyla I hold in my dearest of involvements. Never would I dare bid an ounce of harm to her, regardless of who she may be or what she may have committed in her days on Earth."

"Ah, but there it is! Your logic combines with your desire to make for a curtain you cannot seem to pull down. She is your friend, a human being. Obviously, to kill would seem wrong on any plane of thought. Though even now, even in your defensive, shaking words, you choose to bring out the worst in her, the villain, the savage, the soul who needs rest from its eternal and misguided actions. Logic and desire are like oil and water my friend. They do not co-exist."

"Your words do not convince me. I will not kill. It is not in my nature."

"It is in everyone's nature. Do not mistake that truth. Logic is hypocrisy, for it can never be complete or exact in every sense. It is the poison of humankind. Desire however, our inner most essence, can never be obliterated or even repressed. It is omnipresent like the oxygen in the air you breathe. It is need. It is a healthy satiation. The laws and ethics of humankind will have you feel depraved in every possible desire. How moral, my friend, is a rule that makes you feel as if the basest of all creatures? Desire is all anyone truly is. It is unfortunate that the truest sense of humanity is veiled and hidden under politics and righteousness."

"Phantom, you are too human to be true. You are of my imagination, nothing more or less. It cannot be any other way. I once thought that my pond gave me all of the power, all of the knowledge in the world. I once thought it had elevated my ideas and perceptions. Now I know that such ideas were merely hallucinations! You are a hallucination, and I've nothing to give to you or do for you. Desire, logic, humankind... We all sell the shit every day of our lives, and we all buy it back at cost. Your ideas are not novel, and any humble man would not need them preached to him. I am not a humble man, but I know you are not man at all!"

"Ahh, so it is knowledge that you crave, is it?" asked the voice.

Zigmund felt uneasy in his lower intestines. He felt like a child again, as if with one swift sentence his hope in ultimate power had been restored. His eyes glistened, and his lips were moist. Zigmund could think of nothing, save for that this was the moment for which he had been waiting. He thought all of his inner voices to have been tests of his will and attributed the obtuseness of his doubts to human nature. Zigmund regained composure and once more spoke to the voice.

"I have waited anxiously for absolute knowledge. The pond is it; you are it! Am I not correct in my assumptions?"

"Assumptions are always correct, for there is no room for debate in a fact one already has concluded. Your ultimate knowledge will be had, Zigmund. Perhaps you are ready."

"I will do anything," replied Zigmund.

"Kill Kyla. Do it swiftly. Do it immediately. Kill without hesitation. Kill without thought or conscience. It is your fate. It is your fate and your glory."

*

Zigmund was disturbed from his trance by the piercing sound of a telephone ring. He found himself lying on the kitchen floor next to a fallen drinking glass. The phone continued to ring and to pierce the inner drums of his ears. It was screaming, as if for attention. Zigmund perceived the pace to have increasing rapidity. He lifted himself off the floor, placed the glass on a counter, and made his way toward the nearest telephone.

"Heh... hello?" he answered in a hesitant voice.

There was no response on the other end.

"Hello? Is anyone there?" asked he.

There were rustles on the other end. Zigmund waited patiently for a response. After the rustling noise ceased, there was dead silence for some time. Zigmund said nothing. He simply held the phone to his hear in anticipation, as if an eager student wishing to learn.

The voice began to speak. It was absolutely muffled and awkward sounding. The tone seemed a mixture, and at this point, Zigmund was very curious indeed.

"124 Edgmere Street," spoke the voice.

"Beg your pardon?"

For a moment Zigmund could hear a soulless dial tone on the other end, and then could hear nothing. He did not hear the slamming of a phone or clicks and rustles. Zigmund could not hear any background noise, simply the empty dial tone and then nothing, as if the call had not occurred but in his mind.

He hung the phone back on its bearing and stood confused for a few moments. Perhaps this feeling was no longer foreign to the lonely man. In barrenness seemed familiarity.

Chaotic Ocean

"124 Edgmere Street... By God if I know anyone at such a residence. A curious address given for no reason at all?"

After some moments, the old self-assured Zigmund Sardoce began to set in once again.

"I trust I'd better record the address while it is still fresh in my mind. Entirely curious, though. For certain, I do not know a soul who lives at such a place. To my recollection, Edgmere belongs to the London poor folk who cannot muster the good graces to pull themselves out of their current infestation of living. Entirely curious!"

Zigmund wrote down the address on a piece of paper and thought for a few moments as to his next action. He decided to ring the information directory of London and acquire the telephone number.

"Number for 124 Edgmere Street, please."

"One moment, dovey," responded the operator.

"I am no woman, Madame. I'll have you know that you are speaking to..."

"You want that numba' or what you piece of work?" interrupted the operator in a crass tone.

"Yes please," responded Zigmund with indifference.

The operator proceeded with the request, numbly rolling off the digits as Zigmund listened.

"Any way to procure the name of the resident?" he furthered.

"Procure your own bloomin' names, Mr. uppity talka'. You want for the name of that there home though, even if I wanted, I couldn't give it out. Ya' know, privacy and what have you. Can't just be givin' out names left and right. People need their identities to treasure."

The operator's tone was completely rude and sarcastic, and it was obvious that she took more time on this particular call than on others.

"Have a great day you fine creature you!"

The two parties hung up and went about their respective businesses. Zigmund was surprised that the call brought so much grief with it. Nevertheless, he had acquired the number of the residence, and too wrote it down next to the address. He decided to waste no time in his actions and lifted the phone once more.

4-3-2... Zigmund dialed the number, unsure what to expect. He had not thought of who to ask for or how to explain his curious situation. He could hear the phone ringing, once, twice, now three times, and with each ensuing ring, his mind grew more anxious.

"Hello?" replied the voice on the other end.

Zigmund said nothing for a few moments, perhaps surprised in the actuality of a man responding on the other end.

"Hello?" again asked the man, "Anybody there?"

"Sorry, hello. I am in sort of a precarious situation. I am not quite sure as to who I should be looking for, or as to why I am calling this particular number."

"Ya' lost pal? Dialed the wrong digits?"

"Not exactly," responded Zigmund.

"Well my name's Sean, you looking for me? Or maybe my wife Ange? Either one of us?"

Zigmund had happened upon Sean's residence. Sean's family and Kyla seemed curious as to the phone call.

"It's quite possible. You see, I came into your number by an unknown means and..."

"Sean, who is it your speaking with?" questioned Kyla in the background on Sean's end.

Sean placed his hand to the phone to muffle Zigmund's hearing.

"Not sure, some lost duck who don't know why he's callin' me. Maybe some loony, not sure yet."

Zigmund could hear Sean's comment and more curious to him, recognised something in the voice of the woman in the background, Kyla.

"Who is that woman I hear in the background?" boldly inquired Zigmund.

"Now pal, that's really none of your business. I don't even know who you are, and you're callin' me makin' requests. I think this talk here is over now."

"It's Kyla, isn't it!" screamed Zigmund.

"How did you...?" started Sean.

"What is going on there? Why is Kyla staying with you? Why is she not in her normal place of dwelling? What have you two conspired on? You must be hand in hand! Tell me, I demand it!"

"Now listen, buddy. You have no right," replied Sean.

"Put Kyla on the phone. I wish at once to speak with her. Put her on the phone and let innocence set you free. I wish to speak with her this very moment!"

Sean could hear the anger and madness in Zigmund's demanding voice. He looked over to Kyla and could see the lightheartedness in her eyes.

"I am sorry, pal. Nothing of the kind will happen. Do not call here again, buddy."

Sean immediately hung up the phone. Zigmund was left to himself with a feeling of disgust and anger.

*

Kyla began to speak to Sean.

"Sean, who was that? What happened? I could hear some screaming on the other end of the phone."

Sean thought for a moment.

"It was nothing to worry for. One of those fanatics callin' askin' for this, that, and the other way 'round about. You know the types of these blokes. They get yer numba' from so and so, and after that, you turn 'em down, they get all inspired and start pissin' their mouths off. Nothin' to worry about."

"That is a relief," responded Kyla.

*

Chaotic Ocean

In his respective home, Zigmund paced about in confusion and bitterness. He could not understand why the number would come to him so entirely naturally, and yet when he rang, his purpose, in so doing, was completely convoluted.

"Why on Earth and in Heaven would Kyla be at this man's house, this... Sean? She has not told me of such a man. Can there be any other possible explanation for this odd act, save for the idea that he is her sinister accomplice?"

Zigmund continued to pace about the marble floor of the kitchen. He scratched the back of his head every few seconds. The space behind his ears was warm, and he looked disheveled from the chaos that had befallen him. It seemed as if Zigmund had not showered in days.

"As God, the Devil, Allah, Buddha, and Mohammad are my witnesses, I cannot overlook the nature of this woman. Perhaps before, this idea, the idea of her wickedness was premature and unproven, though now how can it be? Is it not clear as the day that provides for our lives that she is nothing more than a creature of the underworld? I can come to no other conclusion. There is not an ounce of truth in the universe that would be kept were the truth not of a dark and shrouded nature. Has Lucifer himself employed this woman, this Kyla to destroy all the glory of who I am and have built myself to be? Is she not the sole cause of the confusion that has besmirched my days? I ask of you, of myself, of any force that exists past or present to prove my ideas wrong. I ask to be struck down in my obtuseness. Though, I know better. I know entirely better. Such an act will not happen for the simple reason that I am not obtuse. My ideas are not obtuse. I clearly see the existence that has been twisted into knots. I can clearly surmise that it is my happiness and sanity that Kyla wishes to fell, as if with a proverbial happy face. Yet, I know better. I know of the veil that is worn. I know of the murder that occurred in the park. I know of the sadistic nature of a woman who would wish one to witness such a crime of vulgarity. And this Sean, it appears that he too I know. If Kyla is Lucifer's servant, then Sean is her incestuous, malevolent brother. The two are in bed with one another, in bed and in death. How can it be that no man is sane to see what I have and do? How can it be that the spectre of my mind is the only clarity that exists among this city of sin? The phantom that speaks to me has ordered me to extinguish the flame that eternally fuels Kyla's existence. It has ordered me to do so in exchange for actual and absolute knowledge. I will do so, and will take pleasure in the act. The knowledge I will find comfort in, but it is now certain to me that I need no absolute knowledge to absolutely recognise the face of darkness that Kyla wears each day of the year. The act? The plan? They need not come at this very moment. I am here at this moment and for once, through all that I have done in this life and plan to do, can see without any veils, without any obstruction, that the one entirely true fact of life is one's destiny. It is my destiny and my glory to end the lies and sedition of my old friend Kyla Demark. It is unfortunate that a soul so promising is to end in such a manner as this.

Chaotic Ocean

However, the deed must be carried out. It must be carried out without hesitation. My conscience is in accord with my desire."

After Zigmund was through ranting his convictions, the actual idea of power began to set into his mind. The voice had promised him absolute knowledge, as he had longed for his entire life, and had once expected the water of the pond to bring him. The thought was delicious, as if an obedient dog slobbering at the scent of the food for which it had been conditioned. If what he had just ranted could have been classified as organised thought, then what was to come was the passionate portion of the dream he deemed so palpable.

"The power will be immense. If I am able to discern all that I can of present with no aid of any outside force, I can only imagine the clarity that shall exist once I am gifted with the vision of the ages. Nay, I revoke, I entirely doubt that I can imagine what life will look like under such a lens. I give my imagination far too much credit, for can one cardboard piece of a puzzle understand its purpose in a universe of endless realm? I dare not predict what I will see. In certain, it will be glorious, as if all mystery were science and numbers, and I were the only interpreter of the world.

It has somewhat confused me, the odd correlation betwixt my pond and the voice that speaks to me. Are they one? Are they separate entities guiding me on the same path? Do I need one for the other? Perhaps more important a question, does it matter at all? If absolute knowledge is in my cards, is it truly necessary to wrap my mind around a vagueness such as this? Perhaps not. Perhaps they are one or two. Perhaps I am the integral factor and not either of the two forces matters much. I am driven with motive at this point and care not of the correlation. It is of no use at any rate. Once the power is mine, all questions will be answered.

In this future, a future of endless possibility, I will make no mistakes, come into contact with nothing unpleasant, and certainly will see sin for what it is and will be allowed to stay far from the clutches of horrific individuals such as Kyla and this Sean. Beauty will be in abundance, and it will be for me to view alone. I will be a God who walks the Earth not in purpose or ambition, but a God unto myself, longing for the simplicity of pleasure. Though, to say I will wish or crave this is inaccurate. I will never *long* for this pleasure, as it will be omnipresent in my blood and in my brain at all moments. Pain will be a thing of the past, taking with it all the negative tears of one billion fallen soldiers.

Is it not right, not extremely just that it is I who have come to find this fortune, perhaps fissured in time till now? It must be so, for what other great men of the world exist? The great thinkers and innovators of all the arts and sciences have long ceased to be. As time stretches onward, the minority of brilliant men decreases even more to an infinitesimal amount. The thinking man, as I am, is an anomaly of nature. I look to my left and to my right, and I see none who are more prepared to receive this gift than I. It is my destiny and my glory. This seems entirely clear.

Chaotic Ocean

A new world will dawn once the transformation is complete. The world will be entirely unfamiliar to me alone, and yet in its new innocence, in this alien perception, there is to be something entirely familiar, as I will know all that was, yet see all that is. I cannot think of a more proper purpose for my existence than one such as this. And, as I well know, the act, the deed of blood is before me. I must kill to receive, must maul to benefit. And I look forward to doing so. Kyla will no longer walk the Earth fooling all of those whom she comes across. I will not allow this any longer. It simply cannot be. The Gods have beckoned me. They have wished of me, and I shall will of myself their every request, for it is just, and in this justice, reward awaits my spirit. My conscience is in accord with my desire."

*

Zigmund decided to vacate the kitchen and sauntered back to his bedroom. He intended to find some parchment paper and record some of his thoughts. Perhaps he wished to outline a possible plan of action. Desire and primordial passion had taken over his being. On the way toward a dresser in the far corner of the room, his foot glanced a fallen piece of paper. A key could now clearly be seen which had prior been partially covered by the fallen paper. Zigmund, however, was too driven and enwrapped in himself to notice. He continued onward, seemingly confined to the space of his own mind.

The key had a bright sheen and sparkled even in the dim lighting of the bedroom. It was like a diamond singing to white, crystalline light. It was not rusted or corroded, as perhaps many keys are. It looked as if it had just been pressed, fresh off the machine. It was medium in size and looked far too awkward to fit into any of the traditional doors of the mansion. The body was completely slender, like a tiny, metallic straw. The head was of magnificent design. The main section was circular and was hollowed out on the inside. Attached to the circle were artistic-looking grids and wing-type structures. The fact of Zigmund overlooking this piece of craftsmanship was astonishing in itself.

Even in its extravagant design, it had quite the air of antiquity about it. The key appeared something to marvel at, a true piece of beauty. The substance seemed rough and durable, yet also shared a good amount of vulnerability. The dichotomy was perhaps too human to overlook. While the head seemed coarse as stone, the slender body was smooth like the dance of a cobra. It appeared that this polarity was desired, for what reason only the artist perhaps knew.

Zigmund continued to go through the dresser, almost mindlessly searching. The key was a traditional golden yellow colour. It continued to sparkle. An object traditionally sparkles when light refracts on it in particular ways, though this object seemed different. It sparkled with no provocation, with little to no interaction with light of any kind. The glimmering key bounced its projections off the walls where Zigmund had been searching. It was as if the key had been calling to him, hinting at him, wishing of him to take notice. Zigmund noticed nothing of the kind.

Chaotic Ocean

The key seemed personified, as if in its strange and static placement, in its solidity, in its complete unanimated state, it was somehow oddly alive, somehow oddly human. The majesty of its appearance was like a pudgy woman wearing a fur coat and a large four-caret diamond ring. It was as if the key were calling for the attention of others, indeed, like the pudgy woman who perhaps needs to glorify and glamourise her outer being to compensate for the complete inadequateness of her inner self-image. A man cannot easily ignore a woman of such flamboyant nature. Perhaps he does feel pity for her, which the woman obviously overlooks, but he cannot ignore her presence, which may bring him a confused look or a half-hearted smile. Zigmund, though, a man, easily overlooked the overt behavior of this seemingly lifeless object. He did not glance in its direction when it first became visible, nor did he when his foot grazed the paper which then completely uncovered the object.

Zigmund continued to rummage. Finally, he found the paper for which he had been searching and began to write. He seemed deeply involved in his writing. It was as though Zigmund was fed up from the confined space of his bedroom walls, decided to vacate the room, and moved about the mansion, as if impermanently roaming.

The key was left behind on the floor. It glimmered and sparkled like the highest of Heavens for a handful of moments after Zigmund had left the room. Soon after, it suddenly lost its ability to do so, and seemed quite uninteresting.

*

The next evening, Kyla had become anxious and decided to address Sean about the current situation.

"Sean, you know how much I do truly appreciate everything you are doing for me, allowing me to stay here..."

"Kyla, old gal, I know what's comin' and I expected it. You can't keep a wilde animal in a cage for more than a few hours," replied Sean.

"Well, I'm not sure its quite that extreme, but, I do have to get to work this morning, as I am certain you do as well. After all, I cannot just drop all of my responsibilities to cater to the lettre of some madman."

"Don't overlook the severity, dovey. You got yourself in a bit of a honkin' bind. It ain't every day that one gets him or herself a lettre promisin' death. Now that's somethin' special!"

"Sean, don't..."

"Hey, hey, I ain't jokin'. I, more than anyone, think you gotta look at this in a serious kinda way. It ain't no hogwash. Whether the lettre you received was real or fantasy, some bloke certainly took the time to write it, and if for nothin' else, to send some shiver-me-timbers up the back of your neck. That in itself is a situation not to be overlooked."

Kyla could see the concern in Sean's eyes and felt comforted that a complete stranger would show this much compassion and caring to look out for her better interests. While she had long suppressed her fear of the death promise, Kyla could perceive that Sean was absolutely serious.

Chaotic Ocean

"Well, Sean, why don't we head out now? You can drop me at the hospital, then can report to the cab company for which you work. It would be a tremendous mar on my conscience if you were to lose your job over me."

"Okay," replied Sean. "Let's head out."

He turned to his wife Angela, kissed her passionately, and wrapped his arms around his two children.

"I will be home tonight. Hopefully Kyla here won't be too stubborn and she'll be with me," said he to his family.

"It was nice having ya', dear," said Angela to Kyla.

The two children also chimed in.

"Thank you for everything. I don't know if I will be back or not, so just please know that I appreciate all you have done. Hopefully I will feel safe enough to stay at my place tonight, and hopefully Sean will allow it. He's quite the bossy one when he has his mind set."

"Don't I know it," jested Angela.

Sean and Kyla left the small home and headed into the cab, which had been parked in front of the residence.

"Think it'll actually be safe there today, Kyla?" asked Sean in the tone of a naïve and wide-eyed child.

"I certainly hope so. We can't run for our whole lives, or for that, even for parts of our lives. Running will get you nowhere. You'll run from everything till there is nothing. That is not who I am or how I intend to live my life, regardless of some lettre that was written."

"Well, that's a very assured viewpoint, dovey. Glad you're able to maintain so well," replied Sean.

"Yeah, yeah, yeah. Just drive. You cabbies are all alike, always thinking that you're going to solve someone's problem. I often wonder if cabbies and bartenders are interchangeable. It seems that way," jested Kyla.

"So, straight to the hospital then?"

"Actually..." Kyla responded in a hesitant manner. "Actually, I would like to be dropped off at the church, if it's all the same."

Sean seamed confused.

"The, uh, church? I didn't figure you to be a church-going kinda woman. What for do you want with the likes of kneelin' and prayin'? And don't you need to be at the hospital?"

"I'd appreciate my own privacy on this one, Sean. I appreciate your concern though. No offense taken I hope. Please just drop me off at the church, and from there I will ring another cab to drive me to the hospital. Is that alright?"

"Yeah, sure. I can wait for you if ya' like? You know, outside the church while you do whatever it is that you intend on doing," replied the cabby.

"No, thank you, Sean. As I said, I will simply call for another when I am finished. I do not know how long I plan on being there. I would not wish you to be in limbo for a long amount of time. You have passengers to help in this little city of London."

Chaotic Ocean

"Well, alright. To the church it is. I didn't know this was to be a religious adventure, though. I think I might have to charge you twice of what I normally would. The Lord is an important man, thus making the ride over all more integral. Heh, just fooling."

Kyla enjoyed Sean's company and his quirky sense of humour. She enjoyed the fact he represented the whole of London more in one of his fingers than did Zigmund with the whole of his being. Sean was a real person with actual thoughts and feelings. He lived a normal life, and she seemed to have been able to identify with him much more easily than with all the baggage that Zigmund seemed to carry. He was not proud or egotistical, nor did he live in some unrealistic mansion and consider himself on the highest of mental planes. Sean was a man, a commoner.

"Okay, here we are, dove. No charge. I don't think I could charge a guest in my own home a cab fare. Just wouldn't be right; you know how it goes."

"Thank you, Sean. That is very kind of you. I will ring for you after I am done with my work at the hospital. At such time, we will further discuss what my plans are and if it is safe or not to stay at my home tonight. Is that satisfactory?" asked Kyla.

"Heh, you sure have a long winded way 'bout sayin' 'see ya' tonight.' But yes, cheeky as it was, that's 'satisfactory.' I will wait for your call. Have a good experience at church and a good day at work."

"Thank you. Good-bye Sean. 'See ya' tonight.'"

*

Kyla vacated the cab, slammed the door, and Sean was off. The church looked as it always had, like a picture of serenity. Perhaps there was something in this calm that affected her. She enjoyed it. Kyla also enjoyed the knowledge that Horris would be waiting with open arms as soon as she opened the giant double doors. It was odd for her to think why he was always there, always praying or snapping photos. She could not think of another individual who would cling to church so much. Often, Kyla would think to herself that Horris actually lived in the church. She would joke inside of her mind that he had somehow coerced the church people to employ him as a full time preacher, converting passersby to the Protestant faith.

Kyla waited not a second longer. She burst through the doors and expected a large crowd. Though, similar to her last visit, there were few people inside. Here and there some could be seen snapping stills, and there existed four or five men and women who appeared deep in prayer. Kyla searched the aisles but could not locate her friend.

"Horris?" she whispered every few moments.

There was no response. She began to doubt his presence and was oddly amazed in his absence.

"Hmm, maybe I have finally found the time when Horris goes home to sleep and eat. What an odd little man."

"Why don't ya' put yer cheeks in seats like everybody else?"

Chaotic Ocean

The voice surprised Kyla from behind. She turned suddenly, and sure enough, it was Horris. She had not seen him approach her.

"Horris! Why on Earth are you sneaking up on me like that?"

"Maybe I wasn't sneakin' up, duckey; maybe ya' was just too fascinated with all the idolatry. Gawd blimey ya' were!"

"Horris, you never cease to amaze, truly you don't," replied Kyla.

"And ya' never cease ta not show up here! If I couldn't tell better, I'd think ya' were in for some rogering! 'hat ain't the case, is it? Or maybe ya' just wanted ta take a shufti, see all the fine gents and blokes and dames here who are happier than ya', who ain't even shit-faced, and are findin' somethin' here in the hands o' Christ?"

"I somehow doubt that, Horris. And don't flatter yourself. I enjoy showered men for my 'rogering.' I hounestly cannot tell you the exact reason for my visit, as I was not able to in the past either."

"It's quite clear, dove. This is a church. Ya' feel good and warm and full in here, not like an everyday wanker, which ya' might feel like outside of these walls. We're all the children of the man upstairs and he's always lookin' over us all."

"Apologies, Horris, but religion left my inner most self quite some time ago. Sure, I can debate it on hypothetical level, a logistical level, even a philosophical or metaphysical level. I can weigh it, be open to it, hear various viewpoints on it, though to, in actuality, let it pervade into my beliefs and into my soul, this is simply a difficult thing to do. Whatever one believes, to enwrap oneself to that extent takes a particular kind of person. Perhaps I am not that kind."

"Maybe ya' are, maybe ya' ain't. Maybe all ya' just said ta me is shite and filled with fear. Maybe ya're runnin' and fearin' and it's all because ya' ain't got the guts ta admit ya' wish ya' could do what everyone here is doin'. Ya' can't admit ya've made a cock up in yer thinkin'. But I'm just sayin' maybe, 'hat's all. Come, Kyla, let's here have a seat."

The two sat down in one of the rows closer to the entrance, which was the rear of the church. Kyla stared at Horris for some time, in a sort of awe. She was surprised he had become so forward with her. His comments seemed direct and almost abrasive. Most troubling, she could not figure if she enjoyed this more or less. Horris continued on.

"Ya' see, dovey, I don't mean ta offend. It's all neither here nor there if ya' catch me. No matter what ya' think or feel, ya' are ya'. All these souls here, be 'hat as it may only a few individuals today, they all got somethin', all have found somethin'. Whether it's true or concrete or absolute, does it really matter all 'hat much? Finding peace is beauty in itself, whatever the means. And 'hat is very concrete."

"It would seem that way, Horris," replied Kyla.

"God, whether he is man, woman, black, white, a mouse or a dog, people all see him as the light, and the light we know as inherently good and warm. Ya' see, Kyla? It's not about what ya' think it is."

"Horris, how do you know what I think, what I feel, what I need and don't need? We hardly know one another," replied Kyla.

Chaotic Ocean

"It is easy to tell what any bloke or femme thinks just lookin' at his eyes, his face, his stance. Ya're in need of some clarity, dovey, whether it comes from the man upstairs, me, or a raindrop, is for ya' ta decide. We're all here though, waitin', faithin'. This game ya're playin' has ya' at the controls, no one else."

Kyla was taken back by Horris' comment. She wondered secretly to herself if he knew more about the events in her life than he was letting on.

"Horris, you're here it seems every hour of every day. Have you found something? Or are you still searching for that glimpse into the light?" asked Kyla in a somewhat condescending tone.

"Me? Gawd blimey, I don't matter. It's ya'self 'hat matters, dear. Can't ya' see 'hat by now? Maybe ya' don't. I know what I see, dovey, and I got my light, got my warmth. I'm warm in the bitter arctic cold. I'm here ta make ya' warm, ta make others warm. 'hat's why I'm here. And ya' know, it's truly all-possible through the man upstairs. Ya' should see him sometime. I'm sure he ain't too booked up. Just don't be all bladdered or nothin', don't think he likes 'hat kinda nonsense. Don't get me wrong, he's not a silly wanker. He don't preach about this or 'hat, no one cares for preachin'. He just don't want his time wasted with piss-faced blokes and femmes, ya' know?"

Kyla again was curious as to why Horris kept mentioning her as the one who mattered, the one at the controls. She figured it was perhaps simply her imagination making something little into something entirely grand.

"How does one do it, Horris? How does one, in this day and age, simply sit down, bury his head, and start believing in something so completely improvable?" questioned Kyla.

"Kyla, I told ya' already. These blokes here don't got eons ta live or nothin'. They got the same time as ya' or I, fifty, sixty, seventy, eighty years. They make a decision. 'hat's all it really is, duckey. They make a decision, go with it, and here they are. Ya' think all these fuckers are gonna spend their whole bloomin' life makin' sure each step they take is not inharmonious ta the doors of logic? I know I wouldn't. They make a choice, live with it. Whether it's believin' in something 'hat's real or not don't matter. Think I know for certain all the answers you don't? Nope. These here are good blokes, good fellows. They'll be fine in all they do, and on toppa 'hat, they are incredibly warm. Ya' warm enough, Kyla?"

Kyla seemed moved for a moment.

"I am as cold as a paralysing hail storm that's lost its soul."

Kyla looked into Horris' eyes and gave a look of longing. She yearned in her eyes for comfort, for order. Without a word, Horris looked back, seemingly understanding of Kyla's pain, and gave off a look in his eyes of bleakness, as if Kyla had just entered into an arduous journey of terror. It looked as if he desired to console her, though chose not to, as nothing he could have said would bring back the order that Kyla had been used to.

"It'll be alright," responded Horris.

Chaotic Ocean

Kyla could hear the half-heartedness in the words and understood. Kyla's moment of vulnerability soon faded.

"Horris, this is quite amazing."

Her tone had altered back to that of chirpiness.

"Uhh, what's 'hat, dear?"

"I don't know, I just seem drawn here, perhaps to you. I enter through the doors, you allow me the humble knowledge of religion and its finer possibilities, and there I go again acting as my same old questioning self. And I'm the one who is supposed to do this for a living!"

"Ya're an old, washed up, lonely wanker for a living?" asked Horris in jest.

"No, I am a psychologist at the hospital. Perhaps I failed to mention it in our meetings."

"Well, then I suppose it is pretty ironic! Maybe I oughta start chargin' ya' for my advice, like ya'self would do," joked Horris.

"Ironic indeed. What do you know of weather, Horris?"

"Know 'hat it falls on ya' when ya' least expect it, and 'hat's the most beautiful feelin' known ta man! But maybe ya're lookin' for somethin' else, dovey?"

"There are hills in the rear of my flat that seem to stretch on for hours. They are stunning, like endless pieces of artistic expression. Whatever my troubles are, it seems that I can open the rear doors of my home, stand in the doorway, and just lose myself in the scene. All else fades away like some forgotten nightmare. With the quirky weather of late, with the snow that seems to never end, with the rain that seems to come, as if we were in drought, with random patches of land looking like the Garden of Eden while others seem dead and overlooked, it is difficult to universally explain a concept of weather, of nature, with one being able to completely understand you. I apologise for the longwinded description. The hills that stretch in the rear of my property seem perpetually snow covered. They were once white like cotton. When snow falls, it always appears as if cotton. This is what confuses me. Lately they have been different, brown, ugly, as if laced with a vile and disgusting substance. It's like flavour ice, as if some grand merchant has coated the icy snow with dyed soda pop."

"Well, sounds like yer stools are gettin' confused with yer yard there, dove. Heh. No, 'hat is quite a unique problem. I never heard of one like it before. I mean, sounds like more a question for some sewage technician than for a man like me. The hills do sound quite darlin' though. Maybe I have ta come by sometime when there ain't too many passersby cloggin' up the roads and snap some stills of this land of yers. Ya' know, us simple folk need pictures ta remember these objects of magnificent splendor, just like the church here."

"So you've not experienced anything similar, Horris?" pressed Kyla.

"Nah, can't say I have. All the snow I ever seen is white like the brightest light of a star, white like the pale look on a sickly man's countenance, pardon the negative imagery. The snow is especially this way 'round the exterior of the church. Sometimes those gigantic street sweepers brush snow about ta the sides of roads and seem ta brutalise the beauty, come now, I say the beauty! Ya' look the next day and it's sordid, mixed with dirt and ya' can't help but feel sorry, even shame maybe. But no, no sir, not 'round the church here. Maybe cus it's off a little bit ta the side and the sweepers can't much get close ta it. Just always seems like cotton, as ya' say. But street sweepers makin' 'hat white powder look sordid and the whole of yer backyard turnin' colour are obviously not twins. So, can't say I've experienced anything similar, dove, sorry if I'm of no actual aid."

"It's quite alright, Horris. I merely thought maybe someone else might have come into issue with something similar. It has kind of been on my mind of late, though it seems that apt parties to speak with are of decreasing amount, unfortunately."

"Sorry, dovey, 'hat's too bad. Man needs little in life. He may pretend and create and necessitate his own passions, but he don't need a whole lot. One thing any sane man, woman, or switchy needs, is a friend, many friends, but for sure at least a few close ones ta tell his innermost thoughts, mistakes, and curiosities. 'hat's just how it rolls out. I didn't make the rules. Some don't like 'em much and get plastered, as if prohibition were in effect starting tomorrow! But I'm here, dove. I think ya' know 'hat. And don't forget 'hat the man upstairs is always here, always everywhere. Maybe 'hat's something 'hat ya' didn't remember. Might try usin' him sometime."

"Thank you, Horris. So much runs through the innards of my mind, it is utterly amazing. Certain ideas seem stuck like adhesive, written into the cortex lining of my brain till I submit to them, till I give into their complete forcefulness and contemplate whatever it is they wish of me, be it fear, disgust, or fantasy."

"Ain't ya' got any blue skies or burning sunsets in there, Kyla?"

"Not of late. Unfortunately the bluest skies remain in my past. I still await the return of those skies, of those times," replied Kyla in a troubled voice.

"I'm sure ya' got plenty blue ahead. I can feel it," reassured Horris.

*

"The sewer, that blasted sewer!" replied Kyla.

"Now, I consider myself a fairly okay man up in the head, but eh, pardon? Ya're speakin' like a cheeky sailor now, wait, rather, a cheeky sailor who's repressed his sexuality for fifteen long years and now is takin' out all 'hat anger on his own vocabulary and sentence forming abilities. But eh, ya' get the idea. What in London is it ya're trying ta get across?"

"Horris, please, I am adhering to my own mind's wishes. I feel as if I am unraveling before the world. I become transfixed on various ideas that I cannot purge from thought. The sewer. Pardon the daze of syllables. There, in my humble little flat, there is what I call the sewer of raised deceit. Seems I have said that phrase so many times it has become second nature, a thoughtless nickname that I chant in my dreams and in my waking consciousness. And most troubling of all, I cannot wrap my mind around the reason, around the cause of my angst."

Had Horris been any other person, he may have looked beleaguered from the drawn out description. He was not any other person. Horris seemed as compassionate as he had ever, and listened caringly to the convoluted pieces of Kyla's story. His eyes seemed to encourage Kyla to speak onward.

"There is a door from above with a pull cord in the main hallway area of my flat. It is, how one might say, a storage area, my attic. Each night and day that passes, I am forced to physically pass this area. Each time so doing, with each graze of the pull cord, I am filled with hatred and disgust. These are not emotions or feelings that I am accustomed to, nor are they emotions that I wish to experience. I've come to know this tiny door as a sewer, a sewer of raised deceit."

"Why so much anger, dovey? Why such a harsh nickname? How is it 'hat this door could be deceitful?" questioned Horris.

"That's the thing of it; I've no clue. I cannot even remember when the fear and angst began! Was it a week ago, two? Perhaps years and years have passed in this state. Where is my catharsis? Who holds the key to that door? Why can I not purge this tiny door, this raised sewer out of my mind?"

"I have not all the answers of wise men, dovey. Don't think of it. Ain't it just bad for yer' karma? Let it ease from yer mind. Ya've spoken it, voc'lised it, 'hat's when a dog's a dog where I come from. No need for further troubles, whatever they was to begin with, 'hat's how it goes sometimes."

Kyla seemed half disappointed in Horris' answer. It seemed to her that increasingly his curious wisdom was turning more into everyday rationale in order to simply placate her overworked mind. Perhaps, though, she thought to herself, an overworked mind is not the best judge of such things. Though Kyla knew little of Horris, she harbored a tremendous amount of respect for the odd, little man.

"I suppose, Horris, I truly do wish though that I knew why fear rests inside of my stomach. Why cannot I simply trot home, storm about, pull that cord, and ease my worries? I ask with no hope of reply. It is because the fear is great, and the cause of that is also unknown to me. Shall I be relegated to this kind of trepidation for the rest of my days? I certainly hope not. My once cool demeanor has morphed into a confused and frightened state of being. I know not who I am, and am confused for who I will become. Perhaps there is nothing to be said."

Once again, Horris looked as if he understood Kyla's net of twisted emotions.

"Dove, maybe ya're right, and I can't say nothin' 'hat would make yer mind go 'round about the sun, Earth, moon, stars, and London. But come now, not knowin' yer own identity? 'hats like me sayin' I ain't got a handle on me 'nanner down below. Come on, Kyla, for the man upstairs' sake, ya're viviparous! I say again, ya're viviparous! Ya're tellin' me ya' don't know 'hat? Ya' don't know 'hat a smile can change a stranger's day? Ya' don't know 'hat the sun rises and falls and the moon cools our Mother? Ya' can't remember the pleasure of helpin' people or anythin' of the sort? Ya' know ya'self, dear. I know ya'. Ya're just havin' a bad day. Maybe a bad stretch of days. Ya'll come through just fine when all is said and done."

"Well, maybe sitting here in the church with you will do me some good. After all, I don't feel my mind could be twisted anymore than it already is."

Kyla smiled warmly and Horris reciprocated. She could tell that her comment made him feel worthy.

"Exactly, dove. Good it will do ya'. Ya've chosen well," stated Horris.

"Chosen?" asked Kyla back.

"Ya' know, it's all about 'hat choice, a choice, *the* choice really, good, evil. We all have our minds and opinions, and ya' can choose a road while I take an entirely altered path. But through all the jargon, all the nonsense fed by preachers, whatever is true or not, it's all about a choice. Ya' know? Ain't it pretty simple? Today ya've chosen good, ya're here, ain't ya'? Tomorrow I may not be 'round to guide ya', but I trust ya'd choose correctly then as well, dovey. Good and evil aren't far away concepts 'hat ya' can't grasp like the moon. They're me and ya' and a guy over on the other side of town and a man who no one will ever hear of. They're in stores, in churches, in homes, in streets, and in everyday commun'cation! Good and evil are concrete. Wouldn't ya' say?"

Kyla thought for a moment. She felt Horris had become quite the preacher in recent moments. She appreciated all that he was trying to do for her, to say to her to make her feel comforted, and warm, as he had prior put it. Though, Kyla could not muster the compassion to walk away from a statement that she did not entirely agree with. She then proceeded to speak.

"I don't feel inherently good and wicked individuals exist. They are but figments of the thinking man's imagination. A person's actions, thoughts, and heart are conditioned. One acts, thinks, and feels not from some inherent or innate inner being, but from what is taught and influenced upon the individual. This very idea, these very words are no different. Whether one is told to think for oneself or to question what one knows and accepts, the individual still is never truly himself, for even these ideas are implanted. If such brings this argument to dust, then so be it, for perhaps dust is all any thought or argument can desire to be."

"Suit ya'self, duckey. I know better though, and ya' probably will too one day soon. When the dark and light are pullin' at yer coat, yer fancy words will provide little consolation ta the truth."

Kyla took Horris' comment only half-seriously.

"Well, at least I would have a coat, and then maybe I'd also feel warm, a different kind of warmth perhaps than this church warmth you speak of."

He smiled back as he figured to stay clear from upsetting his friend. Kyla too smiled affectionately once again.

"I quite enjoy our little talks here, duckey. I hope ya' do understand 'hat. I don't get many wankers 'hat actually feel like talkin' bout things of implication any more than petty so-called sins and shite of 'hat kind."

"Oh, the feeling is incredibly mutual, Horris. In recent days, I feel drawn in various directions, and this particular direction yields some degree of goodness."

Horris was silent for a moment or two, and through the disheveled hair that framed his face, looked into Kyla's eyes. He did not respond at first, but instead, turned his body to face the altar and exhaled.

"Ya' know," said Horris, "I really wanna see ya' come out well on this whole thing, this life thing. Ya' might be thinkin' I'm some hypocritical preacher bum who talks about the Lord's flexibility but who himself talks some constrictive, pious game. Who knows? Maybe 'hat'd be dead on bollocks ta assume. But I truly want ya' ta listen, dove."

"Of course," prematurely responded Kyla.

"No, no. Truly. Not for the placation of an old wanker like myself, nor for the fruits of some eye-opening round-about blab of words and nonsense, but for 'hat life thing ya're livin', dove. I ain't really permitted ta say this but sparingly, some rules can't be busted down like brick walls, ya' know."

She did not quite understand him, but nodded anyway.

"Ya' talk lots about yer own bloomin' character and all 'hat about bein' this way or 'hat-a-way, but truly, dove, pull cords or pullin' wankers, it's all the same. Ya' can find somethin' here in this place, in the church. And it ain't just me. Ya' can really find some salv..."

"Horris, I really must be on my way," interrupted Kyla.

She was not in the mood anymore for conversation of this nature and had not the courtesy to let Horris finish his sentence. He could see she would not have been ready to receive it at any rate.

"I must leave for work now, and really, I'm just not sure the church as an institution can offer me anything in my current state" said Kyla.

"Course. It's too bad ta hear a fine thinkin' dove like ya'self say 'hat. Cards fall though, and maybe ya' can't change the order of 'em. Really hope yer snow whitens, dove"

The two exchanged friendly gestures and parted. As Kyla began walking toward the large double-doors, she could faintly hear Horris singing a song. She did not bother to turn around at first.

'*Extra ecclesiam nulla salus*
Ain't what ya' make, all a balance
Extra ecclesiam nulla salus
Walkin' proud wanker, life ain't so callous'

Kyla recalled having heard the same expression earlier in the church and was immediately intrigued with passionate curiosity. She turned quickly to question Horris as to the nature of the meaning. He was

Chaotic Ocean

gone and out of sight. Kyla ran up and down the aisles to search for her friend. She then realised time was passing quickly and thought be off to the hospital. Unappeased, she exited the church and stepped onto the walk.

CHAPTER TWELVE
✝

LA FORZA DEL DESTINO

*

Kyla phoned for a cab to take her to the hospital. She entered the building through the main entrance and stopped at the desk to inquire about Mr. Pem's status. They informed her that he had indeed come in earlier to fill out the required paperwork and had since been working hard on the fourth floor. Kyla seemed pleased that even in the midst of her personal crisis, she was able to have helped a friend. Though having reservations about seeing patients while enwrapped in personal struggles, she felt a certain degree of selfishness and guilt in canceling appointments with troubled youngsters, and thus proceeded onward, attempting to repress her own fears for the duration of the day.

"Ah, my dear, you have finally come."

Surprised, Kyla turned to see Mr. Pem in janitorial dress. She thought to herself that Mr. Pem had been working on the fourth floor, or so she was told, and he must have gone unnoticed when arriving on her floor.

"Oh yes, I've come," responded Kyla. "It's been a long day already, and I've hardly just gotten into it all! Congratulations on your new job."

"Oh, many, many thanks. When the Earth has crumbled into itself, the resulting sands will not forget what you have done for me. I will not forget."

"Most assuredly, my friend, it was nothing at all."

"May turn out to be something more than you think, child," curiously quipped Mr. Pem.

Kyla examined the man for a moment. His janitor's suit was drab in color, some kind of faded grey. He stood curiously proud and seemed to revel unlike normal men in the menial nature of his tasks. Kyla perceived this to have been an indicator of his grounded character. Mr. Pem's goatee was freshly trimmed and his hair was slicked back. The only oddities of his dress that she could notice were the man's shoes. They were a dull scarlet colour, overly ornate for the ensemble.

To herself she thought, as the two casually conversed, "Why the flair of foot-ware? Had I not seen the shoes in our previous discussions? Regardless, it is no business of mine the gaudy colour of foot apparel chosen by a friend."

"Have you taken interest in my slippers, dear?"

Pem perceived the distractedness in Kyla's eyes.

"Oh, surely you do not wish to discuss the wears we choose for our feet," replied Kyla. "I apologise if I was rudely staring."

Chaotic Ocean

"They are scarlet, like the lettre impressed upon adulterers in the old story. I am not a fancy man, nor am I a superficial man. I attempt to make due with what has been given me, or perhaps with what has been taken from me or moreover, made *of* me. Regardless, if you were wondering, to put the irrelevant suspense upon the shelf, as it were, they were a gift from my father from long, long ago. Ever since, scarlet has been the colour I have chosen to adorn myself in whenever an important occasion has arisen. The glory of new work, I thought to be such an occasion."

"It is truly unnecessary to explain. I did not mean to gawk or pry."

"Ah, but what information would we have without prying? So much is lost on the average man for his inability to inquire. The world is old, and much is blurred to even the most learned of creatures."

Kyla looked at her watch, realising it was soon time to meet with her patients. She wished not to stop Mr. Pem in the middle of a conversation though, and also wondered if he had to get back to work himself.

"For instance, Kyla, how soon our race forgets what was just a stone's throw away in the context of time. We are all subdivided in nearly every sense of the word, emotions, opinions, geographical locations, and yet, it was not long ago that Pangea was our truth, our definition, that all was one. As the human race has grown farther apart in distance, so too have they grown remote in their caring for one another. We live in one part of the Earth, and we have a name for those who live in another. And furthermore, we even assume they have no name for us. How distant is that? How subdivided is that? The American's call others Asian, and yet have no clue that the Asian's call other races Occidental. Bah, such is the egocentrism that seems to pervade all that we see or seem."

"Dream within a dream?" quipped Kyla.

"What isn't... what isn't? I know more than you think, Kyla. I trust you consider me a kindly, old man, and perhaps even a friend, but I've more knowledge than you've considered."

Kyla was taken back by the sudden turn in the conversation and was unsure of how to formulate a response. She looked at Mr. Pem's shoes, and they seemed even more pronouncedly scarlet.

"I... am not sure what you..."

"Apologies, child. I simply wish to make certain that you do not feel your time is wasted speaking to a lowly janitor."

"I feel nothing of the kind. What kind of morality would it be for one to make grand assumptions about others based on occupation, let alone an occupation that I aided in?"

"I assure you with the most absoluteness of knowledge that the kind of judgment which you speak is made every single day by most. Regardless though, morality is a quirky term, and it should be used sparingly, I have found. Though, I do appreciate the sentiment."

"How so do you mean?" asked Kyla. "What of my usage?"

"The more I live the less moral I become, child. The moment we assume morality, we pass judgment on every one of our brothers. And that, simply, is too incredible an amount of condescension for one man to bear. Living morally is too heavy a burden, Kyla. No man should be bound by its chains. No man."

"Perhaps. Mr. Pem, I need to get to my patients now," responded Kyla. " I apologise. We will likely speak soon. Good day."

"Good day, my child."

*

Kyla strolled into her office, attempting to clear her head of all the uncertainties that had been surrounding her life. She pushed off all images of Mr. Pem and Horris, both of whom had become integral but confusing parts of her modern existence. She even tried to forget about Sean and his kindhearted gestures. Kyla had not spoken to Zigmund in a little while, but as always, he pervaded deep into her thoughts, and as such, she attempted to forget about him too. Perhaps most pervasive of all though, was the lapis stone that she kept in her flat, which Mr. Pem had originally given her. She could not figure why it had made her feel so entirely vulnerable and weak, yet at the same time, whole and full of satiation. Kyla recalled having been thrust into the air in some inexplicable storm of electricity upon one of her last examinations of the object. Additionally, it disturbed her greatly that the woman murdered in the park seemingly knew her name and, with dying words, mentioned a stone. Kyla was entirely confused and entirely tired of the turbulent turmoil.

"I must think logically, if not for the sake of my own well-being, then for the sake of my patients'," thought Kyla.

Nearly besmirched in comparison to the woman she had been, Kyla trudged onward and sat down at her familiar desk. She looked at a clock on the wall that seemed to mock the pettiness of her existence, as if to say: "Your life is time gone by, wasted, and I am the reminder for every second of every day."

She sat there for a few moments, blankly staring, then suddenly realising her first patient for the day, Laurna Tangly, had been late. It was not like Laurna to miss an appointment. Perhaps something had come up, she rationalised. Kyla's resources were mostly self-supplied at the hospital. She had not a secretary to inform her of any unexpected events or cancellations, and communication was particularly slow in her department. She thought to ring down to the main desk, but then decided the better of it, realising that they would likely have little information to share. Kyla then decided to busy herself with paperwork regarding her primary patients, Laurna, Dorian Knots, and Cecelia Greene. She understood that the opportunity to focus on only three patients afforded her a great gift, and felt the potential for doing much good for the three, retrospective of working as a hospital psychologist.

Time went by, and it became clear that Laurna was not likely to show. The odd thing was that Dorian, who had never missed a chance to banter with his psychologist, was now running late himself. Kyla was visibly rustled and wondered if all was alright with her patients. She wondered if it could have been coincidental that two of her three appointments would be no-shows. When Cecelia did not show, Kyla became enraged with curiosity.

"Cecelia resides in a special ward of this very hospital," said she aloud. "She is forced to see me! Where can she be?"

Kyla decided to ring the ward in which Cecelia resided.

"Excuse me, this is Doctor Demark. I am a psychologist here at the hospital, and I am inquiring as to why one of my patients, who stays in your ward, has not been escorted to my office this evening."

A few muffled scratches were heard, as if the voice on the other end had run his stubbly, non-shaven face across the receiver, like sandpaper over a coarse coal.

"Name?" the voice rudely responded.

"Her name is Miss Cecelia Greene. She is only fifteen years old and certainly stays in your ward. Cecelia is required to meet with me at certain times, and she is late for today's appointment."

The muffled scratches continued again.

"Checkin'," the voice said back.

Kyla thought the man to have been unnecessarily cold.

"Sorry, there is no info available on that patient."

"What on Earth do you mean? Miss Greene is my patient! I treat and meet with her. It makes no sense that there would be no information available. What kind of nonsense is this? Is Cecelia okay? Is anything the matter? Surely you must tell me if it is something of dire nature."

"No info available," said the man. "Also, don't come down here. We've already added your name to the prohibited list. Good day."

Kyla could hear the connection coldly click off. She was befuddled and angered, and now contemplated the whereabouts of her patients, especially that of Cecelia. Kyla even selfishly longed to speak with them, if for nothing else than to get her mind off of her personal crisis, and of course, the lettre she had earlier received which promised death. She desperately hoped all was okay with Laurna, Dorian, and Cecelia. Helplessness overcame her, and, she did not know what to do, or how to waste her unforeseen free hours. Kyla wept like a widow for her patients, for her fears, and for her unanswered questions. She put her head down on the desk.

*

Upon pulling herself together, she realised that she had overlooked the day's newspaper. Not quite certain how it had gotten on her desk, since she had not purchased one for the day, nor had she noticed it when originally entering the room, she assumed it must have been handed out by the hospital. With nothing more to fill her time, she began to page through, as she had done on previous occasions. And once more, Kyla came to various articles that caught her attention, inexplicably, like magnets to metal.

Defecation of Character

Chaotic Ocean

by William Blormy

You've defamed. I've been defamed. You've libeled. Oh isn't it all so darn barmy? All kinds of lawsuits are flung each and every day like an elastor plastor tossed by a child. Defamation of character, bah, ain't it a joke? This suit is predicated upon the indisputable fact that one's character was famed, was good, and was worthy to begin with. Come now, who among us is truly pure of character? I'd bet the royal riches that it be a tiny, nearly microcosmic, microscopic, micro-miniscule percentage. From the days of 'Toss that first stone who among is no bugger, we've known this. We got blokes killing and blokes being killed, maybe for just reasons. We got blokes who witness crimes and do virtually nothing, stand there, like some foggy dear in foggy-bottom front-lights, and we're going to actually discuss the defaming of character? Come on, we all know that no such thing can be real, because character itself is a long forgotten and little practiced art form. Character by nature is malicious, as we all be, hence, as said, no such thing can or does exist. Defecation of character, for sure, that is tried and true. But please, take the other hogwash laundry out of the load, bleach it after the fact, burn it, and stop wasting all of our hounest citisens' time with these cheeky suits of pious, pitiful nature.

Kyla took the column personally. To herself she thought, "Dear, has this been addressed to me? Am I completely mad in thinking thusly? Can it be that I have been targeted for not doing enough for the murdered woman in the park? Zigmund and I rang the ambulance, waited over the woman; what more was there to do? Has my character tarnished like some putrid, soiled snow does? Who is this William Blormy, and why does his name reverberate through my head like a sleeping archetype? I cannot endure much more ambiguity."

Kyla read on, flipping through the pages till reaching another interesting column.

The Bottled Marketplace
by Berg Daye

Oh what an age we live in, oh what an age indeed. Do you think the ancient Aztecs ever conceived of a marketplace that sells us our most abundant resources for prime prices? Wasn't that Smithian idea of supply and demand predicated on the fact that less supply yields more demand? How can it be that surplus supply still leads to demand? Do you think the ancient Romans ever conceived a civilisation in which water, H_2O, yeah you know, the cool refreshing stuff, would ever be bottled and sold for an actual dollar amount? What, the Earth is seventy percent water? It's just fabulous, such a fabulous product. Who would have thought? The products we'll buy, we never cease to amaze ourselves. I for one wish to jumpstart this new and radical economical revolution in which supply has no effect on demand. We've got the *water, but now, why not the air? Bottled oxygen, just think of the glory with slogans like "the freshest air comes in a bottle" and "breathe clean, breathe filtered bottled oxygen." Please credit me with the idea when whomever among you decides to take it to heart. I'm looking forward to the day when I can sit back with a gas mask in some underground shed, kick back in a hammock, sip bottled water, and breathe bottled oxygen, while roasting under an artificial sun lamp. The future – here I come. And just who knows, maybe I'll even enlist the help of some haggardly, overpaid psychologist, of course via the computer. Gotta keep sane.*

Again, Kyla perceived some kind of personal message in the column. She thought it eerie that the closing lines would speak of a psychologist.

"Have my emotions been bottled and sold at cost to any passerby who so desires a clearance? What does it all mean? I am certain that I have read one of Mr. Daye's pieces recently. Why do I feel strange, as with the Blormy article? I have no personal relationship with these men! It is not conceivable that these articles would have any specific meaning for me. But they seem so entirely pervasive, so entirely drawing of my attention, and for what? Have I come to this? To childish paranoia? Are these men writing for my sole attention? What have they to gain?"

She egocentrically considered all the nefarious possibilities and implications. Kyla had convinced herself the columns that she had read over the course of the last few days had been direct, tangible attacks on her nervous and confused mind. She laid her head to rest on the desk in front of her, as if to willingly submit to the chaotic ocean that had engulfed the better part of her days. Her eyes closed tightly, suggesting discomfort and pain. Upon refocusing her thoughts and pupils, she then discovered a piece of paper that had been buried under the newspaper. Kyla shuddered at its sight. Her lips quivered, and she stuttered aloud.

"H...h...how can this be? Another subjectaphor pamphlet? I've not seen any of my patients, and surely the hospital would not distribute such tripe! Would I were inane I'd think nothing. I am not. Would I were impure of mind I'd dismiss the vagary. But I am not. I am of my own person and understanding of the world around me. I am not some raving lunatic. Where from has this pamphlet arrived? I demand an answer. How have Zigmund and his corruption pervaded into the personal space of my office? I demand an answer; I demand reason!"

She sat back as her enraged words echoed through the empty office and with cognisance, perceived the irony in her declaration of sanity. Kyla reflected and began to read the newest subjectaphor.

To All Those Who Wish for Wishing and Whose Wish Has Come True

Turn a shark around, about, and watch out. That's for sure. Those teeth like daggers... those eyes like death... those jaws like the all-encompassing power of mother-nature's provisional and yet destructive

Chaotic Ocean

breast... Well, you can see that seeing makes a beast a beast, and thinking makes a man a man, but turn a shark around, about, and watch out; heed that.

Come now, who are the real sharks? Those prehistoric, highly evolved, preservationalists, swimming deep below all Earthly troubles, or us? Blah blah blah though, it's all pointless anyway, for nothing done or said leads to anything said or done.

Tonic immobility is when a shark is turned upside down and subsequently cannot move. The shark is paralysed. This vicious and precise predator, in all his usual glory, in effect, becomes useless and meek, as if a toddler. We can use this information; trust me.

We are the sharks. We are vicious. Let a tidal wave turn us on our backs and humble our every instinct. Make us immobile and meek. Wish for this if you wish to wish for anything of substantive value. Wish for the superiority of nature. Place your vote for sharks in the next race for the dominant species, actual sharks that is.

Yours truly ill-advised,
-Ziggy Sardoce

"Good Heavens, what is this nonsense," thought Kyla to herself. "The superiority of nature? The meekness of humanity? Sharks? It's as if he merely wished to rave about anything shark related, because he has some personal interest in them and thus attempted to tie them into his vague point.

These subjectaphors are more troubling than before. How widespread is their appeal? How many innocent citisens have been tarnished by their insidious, hazily expressed ideas? Confounded babbling is all it is, and Zigmund has no shame in his abuse of personal power."

Kyla seemed to calm herself despite not knowing the whereabouts of her three patients. She then moved to a comfortable black material chair in the corner of the office and attempted to relax. Suddenly, as if by divine intervention, her mind once again wandered and refocused on the negativity besmirching her life. Kyla thought of the death promise she had received, and could not alleviate her fear of the unknown, or of the possibilities that might manifest. She sobbed in insecurity.

"I do not wish to die," said Kyla aloud.

*

Across the town, Zigmund Sardoce was manically pacing about his posh, aptly enclosed mansion. He could not free his mind of the resolve of which he had decided upon.

"I am resigned of myself. All is clear like that of the glass marble. I am certain of the destiny assigned me. Phantom who has beckoned, who has ordered... are you not present with each firing synapse of contemplation?"

Chaotic Ocean

Zigmund looked about. No response was given. He heard nothing but the sound of nature seeping through the walls and a few passersby shouting obscenities.

"Phantom, apparition, conscience, God, whomever you are, why so now are you silent? Why so now have you left me to myself when it was you who convinced me so verily of my mission?"

He heard nothing once again.

"Regardless, I am resolved in my motive and ambition. I am resolved in my actions and wholeheartedly believe in the promise that has been offered. Kyla must die by my hand, and in exchange, ultimate knowledge will ravage my being, as if some storm of flame engulfing a largely combustible village. Kyla's silence of late, her whereabouts, that strange phone number I rang only to hear her guilty voice in the background... why in Heaven has she done this to me? Why on all of Earth did she order me to bare witness to a wicked park murder, now clearly so, orchestrated by her devious hands? What has become of my old friend? For her sake too, she must be ended."

Zigmund scampered quickly across the rooms of his mansion, as if a mountain lion traversing a vast and harsh terrain. Unbeknownst to him, his foot glanced a shiny, glowing key that had been uncovered from under a piece of fallen paper. The key slid nearly a yard, though in his state, he could think of nothing but the plan by which to execute his old friend. The key lay silent as he continued to pace about.

"The motive, sure, 't is clear. The certainty and willingness, yes, of course, both for have been accounted. But the tact of it, the method, I am not an accomplished villain, nor an experienced man of this nature. How then?"

Zigmund contemplated the procedure for some time. He concocted everything from the blatantly obvious to the obscure and nigh impossible to pull off. Still, he was undecided. He knew that this opportunity of surprise would not represent itself twice. Was he to fail, there would be little likelihood of him being clever enough to outwit any forewarned authorities, not to mention, a precautious Kyla. This was his only true opportunity to execute a well-placed plan, and in turn, receive the glory spoken of for his effort.

He thought aloud, "Shall I place cyanide in her consumables? Shall I violently thrash her with some sharp and tactless object? Shall she be hanged like some criminal, or perhaps, electrocuted in some unexpected combination of elements?"

He then contemplated the repercussions of being discovered in the act. Zigmund considered if guilt was of importance, if being witnessed would tarnish any part of the plan. Rationalising, with supreme knowledge, it seemed neither guilt nor innocence made an ounce of difference. Prison would be no binder to a man possessing of the knowledge how the locks are made. Stigmatisation would be no detriment to a man possessing of the knowledge how to contort and manipulate others' innermost thoughts. Still, he figured conspicuity would be of little aid to him, and thus decided to be as swift and devising as possible.

Chaotic Ocean

"Kyla is no thoughtless dolt. Even if she were to have no expectation of such a plot, she'd not willingly submit herself to some kind of carnage. I am her friend though, and this places me at the greater advantage of trust. Despite her wilde accusations of my part in the creation of some outlandish pieces of publishing, she knows me not for a murderer. Ironically, this is exactly what I've come to discover her as."

Zigmund still was unaware of his marionette role in the subjectaphor pamphlets. He had denied any implication when Kyla first brought it up, and while she did not believe him, he told of an investigation that he would look into. It was now the farthest thing from his mind in his quest for knowledge, and he cared little that Kyla felt he had been lying. He had not been, for lying requires one to manipulate the truth, as one understands it. Zigmund was never given the cognisance to see that he had in fact been at the lifeless heart of the pamphlets. Thus, to his own self, he had not told a lie. He had no clue to the manipulative power of the pond that he had used. He knew that it made him mad with sensation and confused his mind and body. Though, Zigmund knew little of its actual force and possibility. He once thought his ultimate power would be granted by the very pond. Seemingly, this was a forgotten afterthought.

"All that seems worth considering has already been. Who am I, after all, to question the audacity of the spirit, of the phantom? Surely as the sun burns brightly, all I know is objective. There is no room to waver in this, no room to second guess and guess the seconds away. I, after all, am resolved in this act, and certainly have much at stake."

Zigmund little considered the wickedness of his crime to be, and thought nothing of the conversations lost. Murder of any kind might bring forth a contemplative mind, and especially that kind such as the murder of a friend. Kyla had known him for some time, and he truly did value the relationship. No others came to visit with him, and family seemed a dirty word. Zigmund had few social relationships, let alone ones of personal or actual nature. The superficialities that he dabbled in provided little solace to a life lived virtually without happiness. Perhaps the prospect of newfound knowledge was to fill the ever-pervasive hole. The cost: his only friend's life.

"This is nonsense, considering the act even so much as I have done. I shall await Kyla outside of the medical compound where she labours. Surely, she will not expect such a visit, and this is where her naivety creates vulnerability. Cyanide or some other hackneyed plot is all of useless, vile taste. Murder can be passionate, illogical, or sporadic. Though, in this instance, it is of the soundest logic one can imagine. There is no benefit in delay. Upon greeting my friend, I shall slip out a slender, sharpened knife from my frock coat. She will not see some terrifying face of evil upon her last carefree breath. I shall put my arms around her in courtship, and swiftly stab the knife through the centre of her back, piercing smoothly through her heart. It is clean and direct, and in comparison, painless. I shall then await the phantom that has promised me the world. And so then the world I shall truly see for the first time, bathed and cleansed of all forces that shroud the clarity of knowledge."

*

Thus, with his mind made up, and his desire insatiable, Zigmund prepared for his journey. He dressed as if an aristocrat attending a meeting of social deform. His frock coat was elegant and frayed. It hung down in a magnificent display like that of a celebrated ruler. The material was thick and dark purple in colour, and was pleasant to the touch. The coat accommodated for various pockets, and with his slender dagger sharpened, he placed it in the most accessible pouch, the outer hip. On this occasion, he decided to call for an old fashioned coach on which to ride to the compound. The driver arrived inside one third of an hour.

"To Hutchinson Hospital, driver," directed Zigmund as he stepped into the coach.

The wheels were large and wooden, and the canopy of the coach was blood red. To the reins were fastened four obedient horses wearing shoes as loud as clogs. The patterned trampling against the cobblestone street was entirely distinct and reminiscent of time period much simpler. Zigmund had a slightly difficult time entering the vehicle, as it was raised nearly two feet off the ground with an inadequate stepping device. At the control of the reins was a mysterious-looking driver. A tall, black top hat rested atop the man's head, and his face was covered in dark, pointy facial hair. His boots were large and leather and seemed out of place. He was a portly man of unfriendly nature and spoke little.

"Hutchinson?" responded the man. "'ll take about ten."

Zigmund could ascertain that the man was not in the mood to discuss life's vicissitudes. No matter, for Zigmund cared more to contemplate the execution of his well-laid plan.

"Good show, my dear fellow," responded Zigmund with uncharacteristic congeniality.

The two did not converse after that point till they had reached the medical compound. By this time, Zigmund's nerves had taken hold and, he had been attempting various breathing exercises to calm himself. The driver seemingly dismissed the unusual behavior. He courteously stated the required fare in as few words as possible, and Zigmund reached into a pocket.

"Here you are," said Zigmund as he handed over the money. "Good day."

"Good day."

Zigmund carefully stepped out of the coach and watched as it rode off, perceiving his absence to have been the last drop of uncertainty dried up.

"Here I am," he thought.

He checked the chronometer around his wrist to discover his timing was perfect. Kyla would be relieved of her duties soon, and he could thus then greet her. It began to lightly sprinkle snow out as he

Chaotic Ocean

looked up into the vacant sky. Zigmund was pleased in his decision of dress and, for all that was to be, was uncannily carefree in this moment.

"It won't be much longer now," he eagerly anticipated.

In the distance, he could see three young adults walking with a man in lavish adornment. They seemed entrenched in a serious conversation. The man had his arms around them, as if he might have been a father figure. To Zigmund, these four passersby were the only people in sight, and thus stood out greatly.

"Ah, ridiculous Londoners," dismissed Zigmund.

The four soon faded into the distance, allowing for Zigmund's final contemplation of his crime to be. He considered all possible scenarios of how Kyla might act or what she might say in response to his unexpected presence. Nothing seemed to much affect the plan. Zigmund was resolved in his ambition, disallowing any last moment thoughts of doubt to enter his mind.

"It is all worth it. If ever an undeniable fact were ubiquitous as this veracity, it is now; it is thus. End of one, beginning of another. Little to pay, comparatively for the gain."

Zigmund waited for some time in the feathery falling snow. The ground was granted a light dusting like a superficial woman powdering her beak betwixt meals. The slow falling precipitation made the seconds seem as if full days of sunken sunshine gradually losing out to beaming moonlight. Every few minutes he would check his chronometer only to discover his anxiety of the situation worked against his favour.

Motorcars drove slowly over the dusty streets, and Zigmund could hear the soft hum of their collective engine buzzing like a dying fire. The lampposts lining the walks glowed a warm orange colour, illuminating a kind of beauty that Zigmund could not see. The few passersby that happened in and out of sight treaded silently. Still, against the backdrop of warm glowing light and soft falling snow, footsteps crunching the padded ground like some damp and condensed pleasing music could be heard. All who have heard the tune of stepping through the snow invariably understand the static nature of the beautiful melody it brings forth, in addition to nostalgic memories of gaiety and joy. Zigmund was not moved, as perhaps he should have been, in the leveling and stunning nature surrounding his being. Likely, he viewed this natural gift to be of annoyance and inconvenience to his plot.

It was nearing time for Kyla to retire for the day. In her office, she further contemplated the odd nature of her missing patients. She could see through a window that it was snowing outside and thus decided to ring Sean from an outdoor phone. Kyla thought to herself that it would be good to get out into the brisk, refreshing air.

"No matter what occurs, we can always count of sporadic and unexplained precipitation."

And so she was off, exiting her office and stammering down the corridor like a weak and famished bird. Kyla did not raise her eyes from the floor as she passed fellow doctors and clinicians. She did not feel strong enough to have out meaningless conversations while in the midst of growing confusion. All that Kyla could imagine fancying was the comforting sound of Sean's familiar voice, telling her that all would be well. She bothered not to stop at the main desk to tell of her troubles, for she figured likely they would not have had information to offer. Kyla pressed onward and exited through the main entrance.

As she felt the immediacy of the cold run across her body, she shivered in discomfort. The snow had been gaining force and was now dropping at an increased speed and heaviness. It fell quickly on her face and landed mostly on her nose and forehead, cooling her. Kyla began walking to an outdoor phone, neglecting to notice anything around her.

Zigmund was much pleased to finally see Kyla exit the building. His decisiveness did not waver, as may have been feared. He walked quickly over to Kyla, hoping to intercept her before she reached the phone. In a moment of random action, Kyla picked her head up and saw the man walking through the Winterly scene. At first, she thought nothing of it, but then noticed the man was continually walking toward her with increased rapidity. Then, she could see his countenance.

"Zigmund?" she thought.

As he moved closer, Kyla was able to see that it was indeed her friend. His frock coat was nearly turned white from the snow, and his top hat was of the same nature. She was shocked and completely curious why Zigmund was at the medical compound. As he continued to approach, she could see his face. His eyes seemed crazed and menacing.

CHAPTER THIRTEEN
✢

HERMES

*

"Zigmund, is that you?" belted out Kyla.

"It is I, none other."

Zigmund was now only paces away from his friend and grew more anxious still.

"What are you doing here?" inquired Kyla.

Zigmund had now come within reaching distance. He ignored the question and began making the subtle motions of a greeting, signaling to Kyla that he intended to wrap his arms around her in some kind of warm affection.

She began to reciprocate the action, moving inward toward Zigmund's chest, almost in full entanglement now.

"Ah, who is your friend?" said a foreign voice.

It was Mr. Pem. Neither Zigmund nor Kyla had noticed the man sleeking about. Mr. Pem quickly dashed betwixt the two, using his body as a physical divider, at first turning his back to Zigmund.

"I wasn't aware you were still at the compound," said Kyla in a surprised voice.

"Apologies, child, for I meant not to send your senses amuck. Who is your handsome friend here?"

"Zigmund Sardoce," stated Zigmund in an annoyed and angered tone. "Who may I ask are you?"

"Just the lowly writing on the wall," cryptically replied Pem. "Otsih Pem. I work with Kyla. Actually, I have her to thank for employment. She is a wonderful woman, but I trust you know that."

"I know much, perhaps soon more," replied Zigmund.

"Ah, a man who knows something is always of the most dangerous nature. I've learned as much in my existence."

"Thank you for the warning, but it is not necessary."

"Oh, I know. Trust me, I know it well and am certain not to be disappointed," replied Mr. Pem.

Zigmund was confused by the comment.

"I don't mean to be rude or dismissive," interjected Kyla, "but I had planned on ringing for a cab, and while I'd love to converse, it *is* coming down fairly heavy now, and we should all make arrangements to get home safely."

The two half-heartedly agreed. Kyla then thought of Zigmund's seemingly pointless visit. She again decided to question him.

"Zigmund, why is it you've come here?"

Chaotic Ocean

He thought to himself, bewildered, thrown off in the unexpected nature of the present situation.

"Likely a luncheon near the compound," helpfully theorised Mr. Pem.

"Ah... yes, that is precisely it, dear Kyla," responded Zigmund.

He was silently grateful to Mr. Pem and did not know why the man had aided him in deceiving his friend. Kyla dismissed the ambiguity of his response in lieu of the weather.

"Good day, Zigmund, Mr. Pem," said Kyla with a certain degree of closure.

The two responded like machines, and each of the three walked in a separate direction. Mr. Pem treaded on a path that led behind the compound. Kyla thought nothing of it since he had never formally told her where he had taken residence. She and Zigmund had such a mutual distrust of one another that neither cared to continue with any line of questioning. As Kyla was ringing for Sean the cabby, Zigmund walked on a nonsensical path, contemplating his missed opportunity.

"What in all that is holy has happened? The plot was simple and my demeanor calm. How then is it that I've come to failure? Who could have foreseen such a nuisance as that man? Such insolence did he involuntarily provide. I'd have his heart blackened on a platter if I'd the power. Good Heavens, my chance has been nullified, as if a newborn Tasmanian joey failing to reach the nipple upon his mother's breast, and henceforth suffering the cannibalistic death that follows. I must rethink it all. I must travel back to the mansion. There, I shall reformulate a plan that is proof of fools."

Zigmund searched the landscape and eventually found a phone to ring for another coach. Kyla had just hung up with Sean, and he was on his way to the compound. When the two met, Kyla stubbornly forced Sean to bring her back to her home, and refused Sean's offer to stay with him. He did as she wished, for he could not out-argue her.

*

Zigmund, upon reaching his mansion, stepped out into the accumulating snow and paid his fare to the coach master. He began to walk toward the main door when he saw a curious man standing on his property.

"You there, how did you get through the gated entrance?" yapped Zigmund.

The man said nothing.

"This is private property, and your being here is against the law. I demand at once you declare your person!"

The stranger was fitted with a large white coat, lined with grey animal fur. He looked like a native Siberian, prepared to traverse a giant landscape. His pants were black and plastic- looking, possibly indicating a waterproof material. The stranger's boots were large and light orange. He was of medium height and weight, nothing extremely distinct. Zigmund could not see his facial features, as the wind was now blowing the snow around like a cyclone of cotton. Also, the hood of the coat was over the man's head. Zigmund assumed no known relationship to the foreigner, as he had never seen him prior. All that could be made out of the man's face were two confident, glaring eyes.

"My name is not of importance," replied the stranger, after some interval of silence.

"And if not your name, then the reason for your encroachment?"

"I pity you and thus will help you, Zigmund. You may call me anything you wish."

"You are visitor to an unwelcoming host is what you are," sardonically responded Zigmund.

"Then so I may be called Visitor. How I am here or the physics of the situation is of no significance. Time is short now and you are difficult."

"Difficult! You're the blasted..."

"Enough," interrupted the stranger. "All of your fears will be of the most ephemeral nature after you have listened to me. I understand all that you are uncertain about, and can see the frustration in your countenance at the inadequacy of your murderous plot."

Zigmund was now suddenly silent, instantly intrigued at the stranger's knowledge.

"You've been misguided by paranormal paranoia, lead astray by physical pools of history and legend, and now you've nowhere to turn. Think... how far have you gotten, how much knowledge have you truly acquired from that pond that you suspect harbors supernatural ability? How much have you gained from listening to the wind, voices guiding you to murder your closest friend? Could you have possibly thought these were the keys to supreme and infinite knowledge?"

Zigmund was now more humbled than ever. He lowered his head and said, "Let us retire to a more comfortable conversing location inside my mansion, Visitor."

The two walked inside, and Zigmund did not question the mysterious nature of the man again.

"Do not hold yourself entirely guilty friend," said the stranger. "Your quest is admirable, and you've certainly defined your character in your willingness and intent. You will soon be a God, and I will help you attain all that you seek."

Zigmund's eyes lit up like a cigar.

"Please, oh please aid me in this mission, Visitor. I've no clue as to who you are or how you know my deepest dreams, but the very tangibility of your existence proves on some plane that if ever I were, now I am close; now I am alive and inches from the secrets locked from mortal men!"

"Do not assume anything, friend. My being here proves no more of fate than of chance."

Zigmund seemed confused.

"May I have a glass of whisky?" implored the visitor. "Easier to open one's universe and gut it from the inside over a drink."

"Certainly," responded Zigmund.

Chaotic Ocean

The visitor watched as Zigmund scurried about, and found pleasure in Zigmund's entire willingness to do the will of others so long as supreme knowledge was promised in return. He soon returned from a room off the main living area with a silver platter. Atop sat two half-filled glasses of expensive whisky with a cube of ice in each. The visitor could hear the familiar sound of the ice rattling with each step Zigmund took. He could tell that his host aimed to please.

"I hope this to be sufficient," said Zigmund.

"It is," coldly responded the stranger.

The two sat like old acquaintances, sipping their drinks betwixt awkward moments of silence. Zigmund did not wish to offend the man by any measure of accident, and thus kept quiet till the stranger was ready to speak.

"You know," started the visitor, "you're quite sedate for a man who wishes for information in his dreams."

"I... I am merely waiting for your explanation, Visitor. You say you can help me, and yes, likely it'd be in my best interest to question much about you, though this wishing, as you've put it, I've found to yield results abnormal from the general realm of understanding. Thus, I must accept that my ambition will lead me down paths never considered, for if the paths were familiar, I'd likely doubt the trueness of them, since after all, I am searching for the unknown, the supreme. One should not be able to predict the taste of fruit in Heaven when one scarcely knows its location."

The visitor smiled for a moment. His lips curled and then became normal again.

"And let us not forget the consideration of fruit spoiled. This whisky is to my liking, friend."

"I am glad that it has pleased you. Though, my ambition usurps my patience in this instance, and I must implore you. If you know as much as you've let on about every effort I've taken to discover absolute truth on Earth, then please make me linger no longer. No longer hold my eagerness in waiting, for surely you can see its effect upon my person. No longer keep secret all that I desire and have come to need. It is, for me, like air and water, and I fear that I cannot exist much longer without it. I fear that my normality will soon smother my breathing if I do not find the knowledge oft spoken. Visitor, I implore you."

The stranger sat back on the couch on which he had been lounging. Across, he saw a man driven with desire and again took pleasure in his position to the matter. He slowly sipped another ounce or so from the glass. After asking for more whisky, he slowly began to speak.

"You've been quite the opposite of a disappointment, friend. You've made this all very easy on all parties," ambiguously stated the man. "I will tell you all that you wish to know, and be assured that this path will not lead you astray. You will not be guided down another road of dead ends. The time has come for you to know what is necessary. And you shall. And thus, you shall be a God of revelation, knowing all there is to know, all there is to think."

Zigmund nearly salivated listening to his visitor's soothing words. He involuntarily fathomed the transformation into such a being, and was as anxious as kerosene to the flame.

"Make me wait no longer, Visitor."

"You are ready," responded the man. "And it is all in a word. Moksha."

"I do not understand."

"You wish to be Godly and yet, you've not even a clue to the name of that which you desire," responded the stranger. "Now you have it, and it is Moksha."

Zigmund nodded perplexedly.

"Calm your confusion. All will be explained. It is a freedom like none other, like none fathomed by any Earthly man. When one has attained this, then one has tamed the entire world of common men, like harnessing giant bolts of lightning from the sky with one's fists. You will be a God, Zigmund. The freedom is like beauty as liquid, as if a separation from all that is differentiated, from all that is temporal, simply, Zigmund, it shall award you freedom from the mortal world of your ordinary existence."

"Yes, yes Visitor, I must attain what you have spoken of. Now afford me the necessary knowledge to do so!"

"Ironic, no? Knowledge for greater knowledge. You are a fine mammal. We all are."

Zigmund found no humour in the stranger's banter.

"Wet not my palette anymore! I demand of you what you have to tell!"

"Perhaps you've grown to enjoy the anticipation," responded the man.

"That is doubtful. I have not given you my hospitality for empty possibilities of power."

"Ah," began the visitor, "it was for hospitable reasons then that you've offered me a couch on which to sit, a room in which to speak, and a glass from which to sip? Do not allow delusions of benevolence to tarnish your self-serving ambitions. They are much purer and more powerful not veiled behind facades of well-doing."

Zigmund did not respond and was somewhat fed up with the man's stalling. The whisky glasses were now empty and he had no intention of refilling them. The two men's reflections could be seen in the silver platter sitting atop a small serving table. The mansion was quiet when neither man spoke, thus making their voices more prominent when they conversed with one another. Snow steadily fell outside like white glitter in the wind.

"I can see you're more anxious now than ever, Zigmund. And perhaps my welcome has been outlived. That is fine though. The nature of our conversation was never destined for anything more than it has been."

"I implore you one last time, Visitor."

Chaotic Ocean

"I shall be forthcoming. Your wait is over. Moksha will come to you when a combination has been formed, an amalgamation of two very powerful relics. One, you have come to know well, and while your initial actions were inaccurate, your intuition was not. The pond located on this very property is the first half of the combination. You've nothing to do in that regard, for it has already been acquired. The pond from which you experienced much sensation is of much strength and power. The Gods do not create weak relics, though, they do not create simple ones either. Alone, your pond is nothing more than a sensory enhancer."

"Yes, yes."

"You must combine the pond with something known as the lapis stone," stated the stranger.

"The lapis?"

"Precisely. You must acquire the lapis and combine it with the pond. When the two relics touch, whomever has placed them together acquires all there is to know or see: Moksha."

"How then, where then do I find the lapis? I am not an archaeologist dusting off bones and feathers. I do not have the time to travel the world in search of some ancient stone. What good is one half of destiny? All is lost!"

The visitor smiled warmly.

"Oh my friend, it is quite simple. If you wish to have the lapis in your hands, seize it."

"But from where?"

"From your friend, Kyla's grasp. She is its owner. She knows sensations you've never felt."

Zigmund sat back for a moment, bewildered. He could not figure why Kyla would have such an object at her disposal. It did not seem to add up, did not seem to make sense.

"Kyla Demark? Is this some unknown region of her sinister character? Has she somehow used the lapis for evil? If you know so much, surely you know Kyla is responsible for murder. Less than a fortnight ago, she led me into Exmoor Park. A woman was brutally murdered, and I've no other explanation than some sadistic pleasure had by my friend in some nefarious implication to the crime!"

"Ah, but why spoil Earthly questions with answers you will soon be able to know for yourself? Kyla has what you seek. Combine hers with yours and the transformation shall be complete!"

*

Zigmund still seemed confused by it all and had difficulty wrapping his mind about what had been presented him. He looked about and finally exhaled in mental exhaustion. After filling the two men's glasses with more whisky, he again started to question his visitor.

"Why should I take all your words for facts, Visitor?"

"You are a damned fool. Understand them as truthful, because you know nothing to the contrary. Seek out the lapis, for you've no other corner to turn in your quest. Traverse the highway of the mind, for it is what you were born for. This petty questioning is of useless nature. If you discover Kyla has not the object of which I've spoken, then you may conclude what you will. Trust, though, she has it. She keeps it locked away like some abject creature of malicious intent. Kyla knows nothing of its true nature, and she deserves not the fortune it beholds. Her ambition is weak and wavering like some blade of grass blowing in the wind."

Zigmund and his visitor each sipped more whisky from their glasses, a seemingly sedate contradiction to the passionate words barked.

"Suppose I do accept what you've told me," started Zigmund, "how is it then that Kyla came into possession of such a destined object. You say yourself that she is not deserving of its power, and quite the opposite is true of me. How then should I accept that she and I are of the same holding?"

"All forces of nature cannot be controlled by a solitary being, friend. Grains of sand are pulled from each direction, and surely, all directions have motive in mind. Consider yourself fortunate to have stumbled upon what you have, for the forces at cause may have had great difficulty in assuring the reality that you've come to accept as chance or free will. Kyla has what she does for a reason, but it is not for what you're destined."

"Then, where did she acquire the stone, if not by property ownership?" asked Zigmund.

The stranger looked around before answering, his eyes wandering over the high ceilings of the mansion.

"I've not all the answers, friend. You've now the necessary information to act accordingly. You know what must be done."

"Must I be rid of Kyla to take what is mine?" absently inquired Zigmund.

The stranger exhaled in disappointment.

"The thing of being fated is that answers are of little aid. If you can believe in your path to revelation, all these uncertainties matter little, for you will act how you must, by instinct. I cannot tell you the manner or method by which you must perform. I cannot tell you the day or hour by which the task is to be carried out. Even if I were to tell either, they'd matter not."

"Then I must decide for myself," replied Zigmund. "I must act on my own accord. And certainly, I must have the lapis stone that Kyla has clearly kept secret from me."

"Finally you understand, friend. All is clear."

The two continued to sip whisky for the next hour or so, discussing unimportant matters. Finally, the visitor was satisfied with Zigmund's understanding and asked to be walked to the main gated entrance. The two walked casually outside to discover the snow had not ceased in strength and had by now accumulated up past their ankles.

"The weather, just another object being pulled," stated the stranger.

"If you say. Thank you many times, Visitor, for surprising me. I was nearing the end of my sanity."

Chaotic Ocean

"Think nothing of it," replied the man. "If you wish to please or repay me, carry out what I have foretold. Complete what you know to be your truest path. So then, transform yourself and know all that there is to perceive!"

"I shall," responded Zigmund.

The two walked to the gate, snow seeping inside their clothing. Each exchanged a finalising handshake, and Zigmund saw the man off. He walked slowly then, contemplating all he had heard. When inside his mansion, he sat down again, thinking, filling his glass once more. A key glittered on the ground next to the spot in which he sat, though he was entirely oblivious to its existence, still.

CHAPTER FOURTEEN
✟

SETHEUS

*

Kyla lay silently in bed, hoping to find some peace of mind. It did not come. Her eyelids were tired and felt sticky from the stress she had been under, and she desired with the whole of her existence a carefree night of forgettable dreams. Still though, Kyla could not neglect to remember the various events tarnishing her well-being.

"Was I not promised death in a lettre of utmost earnestness?" she thought. "Are not my patients missing? Is not Zigmund involved in the poisoning of young minds with his preposterous pamphlets? Do not I have an object of utter confusion and intangibility residing in a wooden chest? Are not my closest acquaintances a worthless, counterfeit aristocrat, an awkward janitor, a fanatical churchgoer, and a high-charging cabdriver? Woe is the fortnight I seem trapped within."

Kyla could not rest her eyes for long and decided to vacate the bedroom area. It was now late at night, and she desired nothing more than to view the rolling hills behind her property. Opening the back porch glass door, she expected to be whisked into bliss by the brisk scent of fresh snowfall. Instead, a putrid smell, like rotting fruit, greeted her senses.

"Oh, dear Heaven," exclaimed Kyla aloud.

She could see the snow still steadily falling, and yet, when looking upon the snow at the ground, it was browner than ever. It looked like fermented heaps of garbage mixed into a solitary substance of liquid tarnish. Kyla could not figure the reason for the increasingly darkened precipitation. This much distressed her, and she immediately shut the door.

Kyla then paced about, wondering what to think and how to feel. A consideration of an attempt to experiment with the lapis stone crossed her mind, but she figured the better of it, noting the failed attempts and the extreme drain of the one time that had been successful. After some time, she walked into the hallway, accidentally grazing the pull cord leading to the attic door.

"The sewer of raised deceit!" she muttered, almost automatically without any consideration.

Kyla still had much distaste for the tiny door in the ceiling, and could not bring herself to think of it in any kind of rational manner. She really had no clue why it had been a sore spot on her psyche and was never in the mood to confront it. Perhaps this was ironic given her profession, though, more likely it was human. She continued to pace about with a feeling of impermanence in her stomach. Work, which had been so much the staple of Kyla's life, had now suddenly been thrust into the growing pile of things insignificant. She wondered if it would even matter if she showed up the next day. With no patients, Kyla figured, there would be nothing to do, no one to aid.

She then resolved to visit with Horris in the morning. Why seeing him had been her foremost thought was unknown, though, for some reason, Kyla felt it was both necessary and important. Additionally, she generally felt good in his presence, and she longed to feel good in any way possible.

"I will go to see my friend, Horris, in the morning. Surely, he will be residing in the church as he always is. He must be. I need him to be."

She continued to speak aloud for some time.

"I need comfort, answers, from someone. Perhaps Horris is merely an old man obsessed with photographing and observing a place of faith, though, the warmth I feel while at his side is real, actual, and I long for it. I must have sleep, though it seems to reach me so unnaturally these days. I cannot shut down my body when so much has occurred, and when so much is yet a mystery to me. Regardless, I must attempt it."

Kyla again walked into the bedroom area and fell into the mattress like a giant tree having been chopped at the bark. She slept only for short periods, an exhausting process to a body ravaged by an uneasy mind.

*

Dreams and images of clandestine, candle lit meetings invaded her while her eyelids were shut. Members dressed in dark cloaks hustled back-and-forth in some sublevel cave of stone and mortar. Water dripped and echoed throughout the plane, as if magnified through a loud speaker. Members would often mumble an inarticulate phrase to one another in passing, something to the nature of "do not ease your pride."

Kyla could not tell what the members were working on or why they appeared in a rush. There were perhaps hundreds of men in the dark cloaks repeatedly entering and exiting a main dungeon area where a powerful voice could be heard. It was as if the voice had been guiding the men like mechanical beasts of thoughtlessness. The stonewalls were dimly lit by the reflecting candle light, often silhouetting the men's profiles in dark, creeping shadows.

"What are they doing?" thought Kyla while dreaming.

They seemed to be erecting some kind of structure via manual labour in a room directly next to the main dungeon area. The determined workers, who never broke, dragged in parts of metal and wood. The clangs and pings of various hammers striking steel could be heard throughout the cave.

"What can it be?" she thought.

Finally, Kyla was allowed to see inside the mysterious room, as her first person vision panned through the cave. It was some kind of altar with the cloaked men in various specific positions. In the middle stood an empty spot, and suddenly all was silent. All eyes were upon Kyla, who had now physically manifested into the room.

A white flash blinded her for a second, and it was as if all had disappeared and she was now in some kind of parallel area. Kyla was much confused. Instead of a clandestine cave, it was a large hall of sorts. Bright lights beamed, almost blinding her perception of what was before her. Surprised, she again saw fast moving workers, though this time, in light blue cloaks. Again, all the men were moving about extremely quickly, working on something of much importance.

Like in the cave, there appeared a main room from which a loud voice was emanating. Her vision soon panned inside, and she could see a man dressed in normal clothing. He was tall and stocky, and she could figure why his voice boomed as it did. The man looked at Kyla, who now had realised she had physically materialised in this section of the dream as well.

"Hello?" she timidly said, unsure if it would make a difference.

"All is not lost yet, and you've the strength to change it," bellowed the man's voice like a bassoon.

Kyla seemed confused. Was he speaking directly to her?

"Pardon?" said she.

"We must all ease our pride to do what is right. Everything in the world is difficult when our pride is set in stone, when it guides us instead of our truer emotions and thoughts."

She looked at the man, confused.

"Ease your pride to find the strength to do what you know to be right. It is all that simple. All anything is comes to from such easing. Actions are repeated out of habit and second nature even when in our minds our opinions have changed as to the nature of these actions. The actions do not generally change though, for we are proud mammals, and would rather act in our normal ways than adapt our proceedings to our newest definitions of thinking."

She could suddenly see inside the room where the cloaked men had been building, and it was like that of the cave: an odd altar set up with men occupying specific positions. In the middle rested an empty spot, and then all was silent.

Kyla awoke in a sweat and it was morning. She thought little of the dream, as she was relieved to have gotten any sleep at all. After habitually throwing on new clothes and going through the usual morning routine, Kyla set her mind in visiting Horris at the church.

*

"Might as well act somewhat self-sufficient today," she thought to herself while walking out to the heap of metal parked on her property.

Kyla stepped into the automobile and felt alien in so doing, since recently she had depended on the services of her friend, Sean. The ride over to the church was a short and pleasant one, as far as brief rides go. Soon, she found herself standing in front of the tall, well-crafted building, staring at the outer architecture. Kyla was partially nervous, though she

Chaotic Ocean

knew there was truly nothing that should have made her feel this way. She thought it perhaps selfish to occupy so much of Horris' free time, then again, considered, conceivably, Horris enjoyed the company.

The walks were lined with freshly fallen snow. Nearly half a foot had accumulated during the sudden storm of the day prior. Motorcars hummed along the street back-and-forth in the traditional busy fashion. Citisens chatted, walking arm in arm along the walk, some commenting on the weather, others on their children or occupations. Kyla longed to be free of care, as the random citisens appeared.

"Why have I come here?" she thought to herself. "What good does it to miss time from the hospital and spend it in this place? What if my patients have come back today? What if it was all merely some miraculous coincidence that all three had been absent on the same evening?"

She continued to contemplate and rationalise, though, while not wholly understanding of what was occurring. Kyla hoped with all the sincerity of saints that her patients were okay and this had all been some kooky mix up.

"How pitiful is it that I've come to this, to these hallucinations of idiocy? Is there not ignominy in hoping to find comfort in an old haggard? Is there nothing in this city that will bring me comfort?"

The passersby continued on, appearing to have increased in number and frequency. More and more, all seemed upbeat and full of verve. Kyla came to detest this contentedness, and it made her feel cold inside, empty like a drum without oil. She continued to look about the city, procrastinating, delaying her meeting with Horris. The sky was nearly colourless, not blue or warm, nor full of clouds or shine, nor overflowing with potential precipitation of any kind. It was colourless and lifeless, like a limp corpse in coffin. The air was subdued, as if tamed by some powerful force. Autos continued to hum back-and-forth.

Kyla gazed directly into the weakly shining sun, thinking back to numerous parental lectures on the potential dangers of staring into the great star. It all seemed pointless now, as if she had wasted a lifetime, fearful of the sun's glimpse while never wholly recognizing of its majesty. She stared at it for a few moments and it did not trouble her eyes. Kyla thought that she must have seemed like an odd duck, lost and seeking of its mother's care. After all, she had been standing in front of the church for a few minutes now, and had not moved a limb beyond the craning of her neck. Finally, she resolved to walk up to the main entrance of the building – the heavy double doors.

"Perhaps my delay is completely without warrant," she thought to herself. "I cannot feel more awkward than I already do, after all, regardless of what Horris says to me on this occasion. I look forward to my acquaintance."

*

Slowly pushing open the double doors, she peeked inside. It seemed unpopulated. The doors then appeared to open without any extra exertion, as if they had been motorised. This surprised Kyla. There was no room for hesitation anymore, and thus she stepped into the church, scanning the large room for Horris.

A handful of Londoners were present. She perceived their momentary glimpses somewhat menacing in nature, as if the sight of her presence disgusted them in some tangible way. Kyla stepped about slowly and timidly, unsure why the sudden apprehensiveness had taken hold of her being. Most of the aisles were empty, and from the back she could only see a few lowered heads here and there. The gigantic room was utterly silent, providing for the audibility of heavy breathing and low whispering. Some citisens remarked about the craftsmanship of the building and of the various stained glass window carvings. Others prayed for unimportant things like the grades of schoolchildren. After a few moments, Kyla felt it was a mistake to have journeyed to the church.

"After all, why should it have been my blind assumption that Horris would be here to speak with me?" she thought to herself.

"Ay dovey!" she heard, shouted from only a few feet away.

"Now, I's under th'impression ya' felt only the fools and blokes of idiocy resided in this ornery, idolatry laden heck of a bugger beggin' place!"

It was Horris, and naturally Kyla's mind was at peace. She was much pleased to see her friend, and outwardly displayed her affection, grabbing and hugging the dirty man like never before.

"Horris!" she nearly sobbed in excitement.

"Whoa now, deary, ya're in worse a tissy than I suspected. Gawd blimey, maybe a tissy and a half! What's beggin' yer marbles 'bout round and out?"

She stepped back for a moment, wiping her tears away with the sleeve from her coat. After taking the time to recompose herself, she slipped back into her normal demeanor.

"Horris, I know we've only known one another for a short time, and I feel wholly awkward in telling you that it seems as if you're the only person whom I can speak freely with and feel free of all that has been on my mind. It may sound completely absurd to you though, and I understand if such is the case."

He stared at the insecure woman for a few seconds before responding.

"Absurd?? Ya' come inta a church, and ya' think it's absurd ta feel good about spillin' yer guts ta someone ya' don't know extremely well, and ya' ain't sure why ya're feelin' like ya' do, but it's clear ya' wanna keep talkin' and keep feelin' good?"

"Yes," responded Kyla.

"Well I think now maybe ya' can see why all these blokes and femmes alike come here every single day, some just one day a week, others less. Ya' wanna know how buggers can put their faith and beliefs in something they ain't sure of, well, now I think ya' know, because darling, ya're one of 'em. In life we do what makes us feel good, even if we ain't got the exact scientific explanation for it."

Chaotic Ocean

Kyla did not seem to like the comparison drawn by Horris, though, at the same time, could not deny the absolute truth in his words.

"Perhaps, Horris. Still, there just seems so much happening to me and I've never been accustomed to such a course of events. We are supposed to live life and make what we will. We are supposed to *happen* to life, not the opposite!"

"Sometimes it just don't go 'hat way, dovey. Sometimes we're just the innocent bystander, and sometimes 'hat's all fine and well too, so long as 'hat's a role we can embrace."

"Well, Horris," started Kyla, "I cannot exactly embrace threatening lettres, and curious conversations, and wholly ambiguous objects, and people walking straight into my life, all seemingly set forth to drain every drop of sanity I thought I had."

Horris paused for a moment before responding, distracted by a few churchgoers entering the building, instantly creating added noise.

"Don't get yer faculties mixed up inside a blender, Kyla. Everything 'hat happens ta us, no matter what it be, I really believe, presents ya', me, those noisy blokes who just came in, with a choice. Ya' wanna live and move along, or ya' wanna die and stagnate?"

"Horris, it's not that easy or defined," responded Kyla. "Of course I wish to live, but why is it so incredibly difficult to do so?"

"Kyla, dovey, every story has two faces, and ta tell ya' the truth, probably more like eight faces. Ya' wanna birth life, ya' gotta endure the pain. Wanna look great? Gotta do the work. It's all eight sides. 'hat fruity bugger Oscar Wilde said patriotism be the virtue of the vicious. What side is 'hat, the seventh? Ever think if no country ever loved itself or thought itself superior? Ever wonder without 'hat steel bollocks mentality if there'd be as much mass killin' and warin'? Every story has a hundred eyes and faces. So yeah, maybe yer life is difficult now, but maybe ya're only lookin' at it from one face, with one eye."

Kyla stepped back a pace or two to again recompose. She scanned Horris' face. His eyes were wily and seasoned, and too, passionate.

"You're talking in what-ifs and maybes, Horris. I understand what you're trying to get across, but..."

"Do ya'?" interrupted the man.

Kyla continued.

"But I am living a very specific existence of uncertainty, and I've not been presented with a tangible choice of any kind."

"Maybe ya' have and ya' just don't know it. Ya're here, ain't ya'?"

She dismissed the question.

"You act as if I am to be saved," replied Kyla. "As if my being here exonerates my person from all the wickedness of uncertainty."

"Oh no, dovey, for certain there is wickedness which plays yer inner strings, everyone's."

She was confused by Horris' comment.

"Horris, I feel as if I am living with some advanced stage of dementia. The rolling hills I've enjoyed rolling my thoughts off have oddly darkened, as if having been dashed with soot."

"So they didn't whiten any?" he questioned.

"Not at all."

Horris' had a look of concern upon his countenance. He appeared deep in thought before responding. Kyla perceived to sense fear in his eyes.

"Perhaps it means nothing," he starkly replied.

"How can you say that, Horris? For me, yes, it is merely another of the vagaries crippling my sanity, but for you, an observer, how can you, of sound mind, tell me that some unexplainable happening of physical nature is 'perhaps nothing?'"

"I just said perhaps," replied Horris. "'hat is all."

"Well *perhaps* it is something!" she sarcastically quipped back.

He stared at her again for a few moments, seemingly out of pity for the poor woman. She understood what the gaze had meant.

"Perhaps."

"Maybe I was a fool for coming here, for thinking that you of all people could soothe my troubles and fears. Maybe I truly should be at the medical compound, aiding my patients, doing the work that I love."

"And yet, ya' are still here. Kyla, dovey, I feel for ya', I really do. It really seems ya're bein' torn eleven ways from Wednesday. Buggers and blokes and bollocks I say. Come walk with me."

*

The two proceeded to stroll around the large main room of the cathedral. Kyla willingly submitted to the tour, hoping Horris had something miraculous with which to ease her mind. The two walked betwixt the aisles, and he even introduced her to a few of the habitual churchgoers. She shook their hands in obligatory fashion and continued onward. Every so often he would remark on the history of the paintings and statues that furnished the enormous holy place. Horris seemed extremely knowledgeable in areas Kyla had never dreamed of reading up on. He also spoke of the stained glass windows as if the practice had been an art movement. The man's eyes lit up as he described the various items around the cathedral, as if no one had given him the time prior.

Horris brought Kyla to the main altar near the front of the cathedral, and she seemed somewhat uncomfortable.

"It's alright, deary. Ain't gonna jump up and penetrate into yer soul just cus ya're standin' about face it."

There were large, cream coloured candlesticks that measured nearly a foot. The wicks burned steadfastly despite the surges of air from their passing bodies. Kyla counted at least thirty-five candles and wondered what the significance was.

"Impressive, ey?" asked Horris.

She nodded. The two continued to saunter about, each looking in many directions. The various religious statues of popular figures were hand carved and painted with meticulous detail. Even Kyla was taken back.

"I just don't know why I'm..." began Kyla.

"Ah, ah," interrupted Horris. "Don't spoil our go around with megalomania and the like. Let it be about us, or some higher power. We've plenty of words left for what ya' wanna discuss, and believe me, we will discuss it."

Again she nodded in acceptance. He continued to remark on the craftsmanship of the carvings and further elaborated about the holy men involved in the structure's erection. She doubted that holy men played any part in the cathedral's construction. By now, four or five more churchgoers had arrived, and many were walking about, snapping photos of the various paintings. The quiet hush had risen considerably to a volume much more audible. Kyla soon began to wonder if the tour served any purpose, and Horris could perceive this curiosity in the woman's eyes.

After showing her a few more important historical objects, he led her back to the last aisle, which was fully empty. The two sat down and gazed at one another, neither speaking a word at first. Both realised that Kyla's mind was heavy and perhaps conversation would be a little aid. Still, both wished that it would be. Horris put his hand on Kyla's shoulder, and she silently knew that he was reaching out, stretching himself to provide her comfort in any manner he could figure. She greatly appreciated this, and momentarily felt that if religion could lead to such immense acts of benevolence as Horris had displayed, then perhaps there was something to be had in the glorious light of faith. Of course, she did not vocalise the thought, but somehow knew that the man before her understood.

"Thank you," she finally said.

"Darlin', thank you! But there's more ta tell, I'm afraid. And I ain't sure what I've got ta tell is gonna alleviate anything ya' got goin' on up there."

"Oh, come now. I am the creature of apprehension here, not you. Certainly your words to be are of kind nature."

"It is not about nature," replied Horris. "Nor is it about kindness in any possible incarnation. It is about evil and this damned city. It is all about you, Kyla Demark!"

She was shocked to hear the man's sudden change of tone.

"Now I told you, Horris, I am not a woman of the church nor the beliefs implied."

"Gawd blimey woman, shut your trap!" vociferously let out Horris. "Listen while there is time. Listen to the words I speak, and remember every syllable!"

"Now I don't appreciate the rude..." began Kyla, somewhat disappointed in his sudden ranting.

"Appreciate on yer own time. Now ya're on the time of me and all men and all spirits betwixt the Earth, the firmament, and every ill-lit place unknown ta human discovery. Kyla, I say in utmost earnestness, ya' gotta find salvation through the church, and ya' gotta do it now before it's too late for everyone, all buggers alike!"

She stood up dismissingly, signifying her disinterest in the man's tactlessly delivered words.

"I am a woman of logic, Horris. What you're saying just does not seem to make any kind of sense."

"Oh, sure, logic. Ya' got all the tendencies of a schizo, comin' here and whatnot, talkin' of yer sanity, or lack of, and now yer *preachin'* me the book of logic! If 'hat ain't hogwash, I dunno what it is. Listen, dovey, none of this is meant ta put ya' round about, but ya' gotta listen!"

"I simply don't know how some religious diatribe is going to aid my uncertainty, Horris," replied Kyla.

He looked directly into her eyes.

"I'm gonna say this once, duckey, no more is this thing about ya' solitary self. It's about everything ya' know and don't, and if ya' don't listen, sanity, certainty ain't gonna make two dogs bollocks of difference in a world forgotten."

She began to listen as she could see the sincerity of the conviction in Horris' words. Kyla did not know what to expect. She looked around quickly to realise the cathedral had emptied. Before she could gather her thoughts, he began to speak again.

"There's an evil out there," he started in a grave voice. "It's surging through London like a disease in the blood. It's omnipresent: here, outside, flats, places of business, in smiles and frowns, in adults and children, in the air, and on the fallen snow. There's an evil surging about, Kyla, and ya're an important key to it all."

Mostly she had dismissed the man's words till he stated that she was some kind of integral part. This confused her.

"A key?" remarked Kyla. "But, surely you don't..."

"I do," starkly replied Horris. "I expect ya' ta believe my words, ta believe *in* 'em, ta believe in my hounesty and pity an old fool attempting ta fight one last battle. The evil is omnipresent I tell ya'. It cannot be avoided, and perhaps ya've already managed ta get ya' feet stuck inside it?"

Kyla immediately thought of all the curious events surrounding her life, but quickly discredited them as a piece of some old man's hallucination of religion.

"I doubt it," she replied.

"I should hope not," said Horris in a perceptive tone. "Sit down, calm ya'self, dovey. Maybe if ya' let me speak, it will be easier."

"You are free to speak as you wish, Horris."

"Kyla, I'm gonna say it plainly. This evil 'hat's goin' around, well, it ain't a good thing. It can ruin good blokes and femmes, like turning stone into dust. This wickedness, well, it hinges upon the decisions of one Kyla Demark, ya', yer decisions!"

Her eyes intensified.

"I jest not, Kyla. It's a wicked city we live in right now, and ya're the key ta it. Ya' gotta find salvation. No more is it a matter of philosophy

Chaotic Ocean

or intellectualism. It's a matter of finding it for the very sake of existence! Ya're at the epicentre of a harsh brewin' hurricane, and I'm so sorry."

"But why, Horris, even if I were to accept your words as absolute truths, why should it make sense that I am in some way, in some game at the core of the situation?"

"Dovey, I can't tell ya' as much as I can guide ya'. Sometimes things happen for reasons unknown. Sometimes for reasons known but not uncovered. Sometimes the nature of free will is so completely random 'hat it is as if an ancient map of action. Thousands of years pass, and beings live and die awaiting patterns of necessity to formulate. Who knows? I know ya' got a choice though, and I know if ya' want 'em skies to be blue, 'em grounds to be green, then ya' gotta save ya'self, in the name of all 'hat is holy."

She put her head in her hands, wishing for tears, though her ducts seemed dry from over exhaustion. Kyla was nearing the end of a tightly wound rope of consciousness.

"I must go now!" she blurted out

Kyla stood up quickly and ran toward the door.

"Don't go, Kyla!" cried out Horris.

As his voice tailed off behind her, bursting through the main entrance, she could hear him shouting "it all hinges upon you..."

*

The fresh air invigorated her body, and she immediately felt better, though could not shake the warning Horris had given. She did not understand what it all meant. Kyla decided it best to head over to the hospital. While she had no guarantee of her patients being there, she also had nothing more to say to Horris. The drive was brief, as there was no congestion about the city. The walks and streets were still lined with the heavy downpour of snow from the day prior. After only a handful of minutes, she pulled into the medical compound's parking area. It was peaceful out, and the passersby seemed happy and full of excitement.

Kyla stopped into her office to discover it was as she had left it: lifeless. Upon questioning the main desk about her missing patients, the receptionist seemed entirely befuddled, as if there had been no official record of the patients whatsoever. Kyla did not bother to argue with the woman. She plainly asked her if anyone had been in to see her, and the woman responded, noting that no one had come by, patient or otherwise.

"Good day, I suppose," sardonically responded Kyla.

"Mmm," said the woman, pressing her bright red lips together in a forced and artificial smile.

Kyla's

Kyla then stomped off, exiting the building with a helpless feeling. She stood outside for some time, staring at all the random citisens who appeared happier than she. Curiously strolling by, Kyla noticed Mr. Pem. She called to him.

"Mr. Pem! Do you hear me?"

He turned, and his countenance lit up with delight.

"Child," he responded, walking over to where she had been standing.

"I thought that was you," replied Kyla. "How have you been?"

"Ah, I've been well, extremely well. All is as it should be."

"Pardon?" she asked.

"In due time, child. I am glad to see you here. It is, after all, where you belong. You do not belong in the company of others who would potentially mislead you."

She looked into his eyes inquisitively.

"I'm not sure I understand," she replied hesitantly.

Kyla wondered if Mr. Pem could have possibly known about Horris. The paranoia ran through her veins like lightning through a metal conductor.

"All is as it should be, child," ambiguously replied the man. "I am pleased with you."

"Are you not working today, Mr. Pem?"

"I must go now. There is much to be done."

"But what of work?" asked Kyla.

"Have a good day, my child."

"But," she started.

Mr. Pem walked slowly away from the conversation without looking back. Kyla did not know what to think of the man's curious demeanor. She did not know why he would abandon her in mid-conversation. Watching his movement, she could see him meet up with three young-looking people in the far distance. Two seemed women, one a man. From her poor vantage point, Kyla had to squint to make anything out. She could not clearly see their faces. Then, a sudden chill ran through her body.

"Three... three... patients?" she thought to herself. "What has Pem to do with my three patients??"

She again attempted to squint, and while scrunching up her nose like a rat, perceived to make out the face of the man. It appeared to be Dorian, or so she thought.

"Dorian??" she yelled aloud. "Laurna?? Cecelia??"

Kyla started to run toward them, but her legs were of no use. Mr. Pem and his three visitors had disappeared into the distance before she could identify their location or direction.

CHAPTER FIFTEEN
✝
NEITHER HITHER NOR THITHER

*

Kyla stood there, stolid and stone-like, as a cool northerly wind brushed across the flushed cheeks of her countenance. The sky darkened like purple dye having been stirred into a glass of transparent water. She looked around and simply did not know what to think. The possibility of her patients interacting with Mr. Pem distressed her greatly.

"What?" was all she could utter at first.

"Mr. Pem has been nothing but cordial to me. Why on Earth would he connect with my patients? For what purpose has a janitor to seek the company of troubled youths? I simply do not understand Pem's curt demeanor."

She repeated aloud, "Nothing but cordial," as she thought back over her brief history with him. Kyla envisioned the man on their first meeting, a seeming wanderer. It then struck her mind, as if in jerky flashes, Mr. Pem handing over to her the lapis stone as a gift, and so forth the subsequent energised rage that enraptured her body upon examining the stone. This much confused Kyla, and she finally realised that she knew little of the man, and wondered why she had held him so dearly, when in truth, he was nothing more than a curious stranger who happened into her life one quaint and calm day.

She longed for the quaintness that had long flown south. Kyla pressed her face in her hands in an ignominious fashion. Tears neatly streamed down from her eyes with a certain abnormality of control.

"Where am I to go?" she thought to herself. "Neither home nor place of business do I find peace in. Neither sky nor ground fills my breast with comfort. The elements have run amuck, as have my emotions... as has my reality. Is this entire bewilderment not some elaborate plot, an elaborate joke?"

She began to walk slowly to her automobile, as if zombified, unaware of intention or direction, apathetic to both. The commoners seemed different somehow. Various passersby ranted comments of fanatical religious nature. The snow again began to fall, heavy, now padding the preexisting accumulation. A man with glaring blue eyes and a squalid faded coat seemed to mumble to himself as he walked maniacally, arms and legs moving in spastic nature.

"The end is near," he seemed to say. "It's all been blown to dust, to Kingdom Come, to Kingdome Gone. So near."

Kyla bothered not to stop him. She felt his presence was curious, since only moments prior the streets had appeared empty, devoid of human life, and yet, now men and women of unknown nature lined the walks.

A man with a large painted wooden sign that draped across his front and backside paced frantically near where Kyla's motorcar had been parked. He seemed entranced within his own mind and spoke unfamiliar scriptures that sounded of biblical nature. She could not recognise the verses and felt that while they sounded ancient and religious, they were somehow artificial. The man was abnormally tall, nearly six and a half feet, and had a dark complexion. Kyla surmised that he was of African decent.

She then looked to the sign that the man sported across his body. It read, in large burgundy lettres:

All o'er soon
Soon all o'er
Combination of the old
Formation of anew
Hell, Heaven
At last, adieu

Upon reading the man's sign, a chill ran up Kyla's spine. The words seemed plain enough, nonsensical enough, yet they had a profound effect on her involuntary senses. Even the falling snow seemed, as if angry, a quality wholly unnatural to an element of its intrinsic beauty. The clouds appeared to mock Kyla, as if tangibly contorting into giant, cotton faces of frowns and glares.

"Stop your sulking!" angrily barked one passerby.

Kyla took the comment personally and quipped back.

"Rude sir," she exclaimed, "I hounestly don't believe my standing here has any effect upon your well-being or..."

"It is pathetic!" again barked the man, cutting Kyla off.

He was not dissimilar to the other lowly-looking streetwalkers.

"Every man, woman, and dog has his choice. Make yours. Move on. Stop blockin' the bloody streets with your ifsy-antsy person. Pathetic!"

The man continued onward and did not look back to see Kyla's reaction of recognisable dejection. She thought that she had to vacate the premise quickly, so to distance herself from the oddness, from Mr. Pem, from the commoners, and from the falling snow. Kyla walked hurriedly back to the place where her automobile had been parked. Upon stepping in, she tracked large patches of snow and dirt into the vehicle. For moments, she sat there in ignominy, feeling weak and angered in her complete want of sense about her life. The warm hum of the vehicle was somewhat familiar and comforting, though it provided little solace to Kyla's state of mind. She turned the heat knob up to its highest position and warmed her hands on the cool blowing air. The windshield was covered in snow, blinding the front view. Kyla switched on the wipers. They swooped back-and-forth, creating a small semi-circular window of vision against the snowy glass.

Chaotic Ocean

She exhaled in discomfort and could see her breath in the still cool vehicle. Kyla cursed the faltering heat vent, attempting to focus on something tangible.

"Where to?" said Kyla aloud, as if dually taking on the role of chauffeur and client.

She thought of riding homeward and eventually falling deep into the mattress of her bed, perhaps sleeping for days or weeks, bypassing all confusion. She thought of hibernation as a thing of fantastic nature, as if an elixir of life, a pool of vitality even. Kyla conceived it was the ultimate in avoidance of troubles. Time makes all mend, she thought. Though, soon Kyla realised such thinking was nothing more than a grand delusion, but dually accepted the idea that delusion might be a welcome compromise to whatever it was she had been experiencing.

Then it seemed Kyla could think of nothing more than the pull cord hanging from her attic door. The quaintness of her home could not be imagined, nor could the comfort of its familiarity. Images of the door flashed into her mind, as if an artistic montage. Feelings of dread and insecurity accompanied the visions, forcing Kyla to shy away from thinking of her place as an option.

"Has my instinct abandoned me as well?" she thought to herself. "Why these feelings? What gnome has invaded the inner space of my brain, plucking, dancing on and through my synapses, laughing as he plays me like an instrument? What fear of valid nature exists?"

Still, the images continued and persisted enough to fully void the option of traveling homeward.

"Then where, where to?" thought Kyla. "Am I to drive on, seeking out my destiny, traversing the plane till dungeons shine with light and clarity? Am I to search for water in the desert of bulimic feasting?"

Rationally considering her options, she thought only of Horris and the Protestant church. And yet, at the same time, Kyla questioned why she might revisit the man who challenged her word, and who preached the oddly toned gospel. Soon though, she plainly realised that she had nothing else, not the option of home, nor even the option of the curious Mr. Pem, for she knew not where he resided. The hospital had all but closed its doors to her, as if raping her of profession by yanking her patients away. Beyond the ambiguity of a journey without direction, again, she rationalised that there was but one path of current: Horris.

*

Across town, Zigmund paced about as if a timid hyena, alternating betwixt some illogical apprehension of action and spurts of uncontrolled emotion. He thought constantly of his Siberian-seeming visitor. The white coat lined in grey fur stood out in his mind. And then as if a record, "God of revelation" played fluently over the synapses like fingers across a harp. Beethoven's Fifth was lift music compared to the soothing ring of ambition unfolding before his being.

"Truly if ever truth were true, the truest truism would be only this: truth is subjective to the masses, yet objective only to one. I am that one.

Chaotic Ocean

Is it not certain; can it not be proven that the purpose of my existence is now palpable like no known tangibility?"

He now began to march across the floors of his mansion like a militaristic general inspiring his troops. His words were not contained to the space of his mind. Rather, they echoed through the large rooms, booming, like a giant bass drum.

"I and I alone" he began, "have the ability to harness the necessary! For what purpose have I ever paid attention to the opinions of average men? For what reasons have I ever restrained my ideas, letting thoughts float off with fallen pinions? Now, it has all begun to make sense. Mad have I been in the past for granting respect to mortals. I was told assumption be the path leading to destruction. Destruction of what? Truth?"

His hands moved like a dictator's as he preached to the inanimate objects around the mansion. The mansion seemed emptier than ever during the outward ranting.

"A God! Does not the sound of such make the lips quiver? I respond: It does. My lips shake like weakness in anticipation of the power. Is it not so appropriate? Who among men can say in hounest that they've the strength of a God? For certain, men may assume such during bouts of grandeur, but this form of megalomania is by nature false."

He quickly poured himself some whisky into the glass from which he had been prior drinking. Dousing his thirst, he swallowed the alcohol and poured more. For some time, as if breaking, Zigmund looked about the mansion, thinking his life a simple existence compared with what the future foretold of his fortune.

"I dare a man to throw the most wicked of pejoratives at me, for I would surely catch the arrow in my fingers and toss the object back into the dead of his heart. What of plotting though?"

He stood still for some moments, thinking back to the visitor's words of his having been fated.

"Are my thoughts now fated? Is whatever action or inaction I take to be of predestined nature regardless of decision? Is my awareness of destiny part of fate as well? I must have the lapis stone! Kyla is most wicked in her slyness, keeping to herself the facts and fiction. Surely, her nature is of contemptuous kind, but has it always been? Bah, I need not consider, for as my visitor foretold, all will be answered soon. Should not I simply stomp my feet at Kyla's door and demand the object? Should I not physically will the seizure of the lapis? I know its location, for the visitor told of it. Kyla is truly an imbecile, ignorant to all the greatness of time as it rests in some inconsequential chest, housed by an inconsequential woman."

He paced about again, rapidly swallowing more alcohol and repeatedly filling the glass. Zigmund's thought process was no longer linear, for tangents of the most complex kind took hold of his mind. He decided to step outside and survey the weather. His shoes smacked hard against marble floor like the clapping of erasers. For the most part, the mansion was dim and allowed in little external environment. Rooms could never have been considered adequately lit. The eyes would first trouble themselves in adjusting to the irregularity, and so would they when departing back into the normalcy of the outside world.

Upon opening the front door, Zigmund's eyes became wide and then suddenly squinted as the rush of sunlight surprised the ocular rods.

"Blasted natural mother!" cursed Zigmund as he shielded his countenance with his arm.

The sun seemed endless on this day and stayed bright into the stretching hours of the night. It was perhaps half past eight, or whatever arbitrary number one might suppose in order to set one's imaginative mind at ease. Zigmund could see that the snow had quickly amounted on the ground.

"Clouds or snow," he thought, "all obstacles for man."

He sighed as his breath formed in the air.

"Am I to trudge through this? Is this the best that the mischief-makers could send to deter me from my mission? It is nearly laughable. Did they set forth a wall of plastic when hoping to contain Thor? Did they dump sand in the ocean when attempting to slow Poseidon?"

A cool wind blew across Zigmund's flushed cheeks and burned his skin, as if smiting his pomposity. He turned quickly away. His body seemed to yank at him, nagging for his submission to the weather, egging him to turn around and step politely into the mansion. Zigmund stubbornly stood there like a bore, convolutedly assuming some kind of superiority over the elements. The pond could be seen in the distance, covered completely, like a meek child wrapped in lamb's skin.

"So much did I believe in your solitary power," he began to say aloud as he looked to the pond, "and so high were the expectations that you fell from. Regardless, your true genius and purpose will be realised, like all else in this world. Whatever is present is complete, and while you show only fractions of your magnitude, it is obvious that such pieces will form the wittiest of orchestras when wholly composed. You shall have your sister to complement you. You, my Adam, shall soon indeed have your Eve, restriction free, free of orders and rules, and through me shall douse your thirst with any fruit, any form of knowledge you desire. It is nearly too perfect to envision. And yet, I can think of nothing else, can think of nothing more than the end, while the measly means remain to me protocol and necessary motion."

*

He now decided to turn back into the mansion. Satisfied with his dominance over the uncontrollable, he put his back to the light, his back to the falling pieces of flakes and cotton, and stepped again into his home. His glass stood empty in hand, and his mouth felt parched. After licking his lips once or twice, Zigmund again headed for the sitting area where he and the Visitor had conversed. The whisky bottle retained only a small portion of the original liquid, and Zigmund thusly decided to finish it off. He sat in the comfortable couch and kicked his feet onto the table.

Chaotic Ocean

"Why so sedate?" he asked himself. "Perhaps Godliness is nothing more than a purging of all fear and uncertainty. Perhaps such is what I have a glimpse of even now."

His words seemed to make complete sense to him.

"Fate is a wondrous thing, but the plot I must form, for regardless of my action, my destiny is secured. Failure is no longer an option in this. I must move and act without hesitation. I must plan for the unexpected, as I had not before, when that sleeking man intercepted my conversation with Kyla. A God I shall be, and Godlike shall be the planning for which."

Zigmund began to map out his actions and tired endlessly for some time. The exact specifics are not of interest to the reader, for he may already draw his own conclusions about the mental state of our character. Fret not, for we will touch upon Zigmund's plot again.

*

There sat Kyla in her motorcar, resolved in her decision to meet with Horris again. Night had now descended upon London, making it difficult to follow the snowy road. Her headlights illuminated the endlessly falling powder, almost magnifying the precipitation. The cool air from the vent slowly turned warm. Kyla's fingers felt numb and her thoughts were blank for many moments.

"My heart is cold," said she aloud.

The tires sloshed against the road. Kyla could feel the vehicle's control slowly slip as she continued onward, not fully aware of the potential dangers. Streetlights gleamed down in through the windows every so often, creating a kind of intermittency of darkness followed by a greenish-orange glow. She could not figure why she headed for Horris anymore than she could figure the disappearance of her patients. Nor did Kyla attempt to imagine the likelihood of Horris' presence in the church, let alone the odds of it being open at such an hour as was upon her. She drove because she had no direction.

"To whom am I to turn?" she thought to herself. "All that should be static has combusted. The only certainty to which I can point is the complete and utter disorderliness of what has come to be. And now I traverse dimly lit streets, numbing my fingers, in hopes of speaking to a man who raved as if a lunatic upon last visit. What has become of me?"

Still, Kyla's intuition, and a strong feeling in her stomach told her to proceed, regardless of the uncertainties. Strangely, while her limbs became colder and colder, her insides became warm, creating a kind of uncomfortable disparity betwixt the two. Within minutes, the automobile was parked nearside the walk by the church. It looked daunting in the moonlight. Kyla had never been, while in the absence of the sun. The large, stylistically built structure seemed to her a citadel for the weak, and she now admitted that this was in fact where she belonged.

Sauntering slowly up the steps, she took precaution not to slip on the snow. It somehow seemed ironic that in order to attain closeness to the Lord, so Kyla thought, that one must risk his neck, as it were.

"I suppose I am now a member of the rabble," she joked aloud.

Chaotic Ocean

By now her fingers were almost wholly without feeling. Kyla reached timidly for the large wooden doors and pushed forward. They did not budge. Immediately, an aching cry ran through her veins, as if she felt forsaken. Again she attempted to move the doors, but the structures remained stubborn, as if indifferent and immutable to her sorrows. She turned quickly around and walked halfway down the steps, and then stepped into the snow-covered land that the plot rested upon. Her ankles were fully depressed into the white obstacle, but she let this deter her not. Around back, Kyla discovered another entrance, but found that it too was well-secured. This frustrated her much, considering she felt quite uncomfortable, in all truth, going anywhere at this time.

"What have I done to warrant such treatment!" she thought to herself. "Nothing, that is the answer, and yet here I am."

Her spirit had been lessened, though, she was not yet prepared to fail. Again she ventured to the front of the church and began to rap hardly on the doors.

"Horris, if you are inside, please let me in!" she bellowed. Her voice echoed through the desolate London streets. She cared not for the potential disruptions to the nearby commoners. Kyla continued to pound on the wooden structures till the feeling returned to her fingers. It then began to hurt. She would stop for moments to rest her bruised hands and would again rap with might. Suddenly, she thought she heard footsteps. Pressing her ear to the cold doors, Kyla listened as closely as she could manage.

"For certain I hear the steps of a man." She again began to rap, now more controlled than prior. The door began to creak as her eyes widened in anticipation. Indeed, Horris was revealed on the opposite side once the wooden structure had been fully opened. He was uncharacteristically serious, and he welcomed her in with a motion of the arm. She exchanged a brief glance with the man and stepped quickly inside, wasting little time to warm her hands with her breath.

*

The church was dark and emitted a stale stench. The lights were doused save for a few candles here and there. It was obvious to Kyla that Horris was either some vagrant, using the church as clandestine shelter, or was somehow illegally employed there, perhaps as a merciful act by those in charge. She cared not to discuss the specifics of the arrangement, and it too seemed that he understood as much. Silence prevailed over the large building, and it appeared as if Horris had been sleeping. His eyes displayed the half-tired quality of a recent awakening and his breath was sour. He seemed almost vulnerable in present state, a side Kyla had not seen of the curious man.

Large shadows of the two bounced off the walls, as if living their own lives, irrespective of both Horris' and Kyla's movements. Kyla looked into Horris' countenance, and he masticated his lips, as to motion her into dialogue. She too began to masticate upon her fleshy lips, somewhat embarrassed to have woken the man with such a spasmodic fit.

Regardless, she knew it was her move to make, her pawn with which to open.

"I was unsure of where else I had to go," she began.

Horris surveyed the look in her eyes, clearly noting the fear and anxiety that she could not help to disguise.

"I... I just feel drawn to this place, to you, Horris, and while I cannot exactly note the reason, I..."

"The reason is clear," he interrupted. "Be hounest with ya'self! Ain't ya' seen by now 'hat I ain't a madman, ranting upon some high up roof? Can't ya' be fully aware 'hat preachin' is for peace of mind, and what I's doin' ain't nothin' of the sort? Come on, love, for all bollocks' sake, move past ya'self and into some real truth for once. Ya're here because a trouble is about ya', and ya're fearin' and runnin', and here is where ya' thought ta go, because deep down, deep under all 'em fences and walls of intellectual this and 'hat... deep under it all, ya' have no clue why I, of all peeps, would be able ta help ya', but ya' know, ya' believe, ya' have faith, ya' of all peeps have faith, in somethin' ya' can't feel or touch or see."

She thought to herself that this was a most unexpected form of commiseration. Horris could see that Kyla seemed contemplative and understood that perhaps his brazen words may have shocked her.

"Horris, oh, Horris!" exclaimed Kyla as she leapt into the stinking man's arms.

"I know, I know," he repeated.

Kyla proceeded to relay the series of events to the man, admitting her earlier evasion of the topic when Horris had likened her description to a soul whom he had once known. She proceeded to tell of her death promise, her curious interactions with Zigmund, and the baffling disappearance of her patients. She expounded further on Mr. Pem and what possible role he could have had with her patients.

"Mr. Pem" stated Horris. "We have spoken of this man before. I do not feel good about his nature."

Kyla seemed confused by the man's comment.

"I don't understand," she replied.

"Kyla, love, there's plenty not ta understand in this world, but ya' have to be open ta truth, no matter how many preexisting laws are ripped apart in yer assumptive mind. Let us walk ta the altar."

The two slowly stepped to the front of the church where many candles had been lit. A large statue of the Messiah hung artfully, positioned so that all the churchgoers could see. Horris picked up a small, red wax candle encased in a crystal holding cup. He handed it to her and picked up an orange candle for himself.

"Ya' have to believe more than ya' do, Kyla!" ranted Horris.

"Please, I did not come her for a biblical lesson. I only wanted to..."

"It is no longer about what ya' want," interrupted Horris.

His eyes seemed to almost glow, and Kyla noticed that he was clutching the orange candle with much force. For the first time since having met the man, she was somewhat fearful of him. His tone remained the same.

"It ain't important what ya' ascribe ta or what beliefs ya' got goin', Kyla. But it is entirely important 'hat ya' allow me ta get through ta ya' on this day!"

She could see that he was incredibly earnest in his fervor and that there would be no avoiding his rant, as she had done last time. The thought of a quick exit dashed across Kyla's mind, but when reminded of the cold, confusing world outside of Horris' comfort, she opted to stay.

"Whether ya' believe in this or 'hat, it don't change the finite tangibility of this or 'hat. And I'm tellin' ya', this AND 'hat exist, and ya're the conjunction 'hat makes the words connect!"

She bothered not to reply.

"No longer can I remain silent, love. No longer can I abstain from usin' the words just ta go easy on yer sense of pride or whatever it may be. There's an evil about this city. I tried ta convey this last time to ya', but ya' ran out like some ignorant chicken fleeing from the feed. Whether ya' wanna call it a name, or know it only as fear and insecurity, then of course ya' can do either. But ya' can't tell me 'hat outside those gates awaits a pretty palace for ya'. Ya're here because there ain't no palace out there. In fact, ya've told a tale quite the contrary, love. Ya' know 'hat all the wicked uncertainties besmirchin' yer life are connected!"

"Connected," she thought to herself. Kyla's heart beat like a war drum. Beads of sweat rolled down the sides of her face as she listened to Horris' barking words.

"It ain't a dirty word, Kyla: God. Ya' think he's playin' no role in all of this?"

Kyla immediately rejected the sentence.

"Please, Horris, I already told you that I'm not in the mood."

"Not in the mood? The mood is existence, and if ya' plan ta subsist, ya' will listen carefully."

Horris' tone frightened Kyla. The lines of his face seemed more defined as the candlelight reflected off his countenance. The rest of the church seemed pitch-black, as if the two had been spotlighted.

"Do ya' wish ta live?" starkly questioned the man.

"Of course, Horris, but what kind of question is that? What kind of matter hinges upon my belief or disbelief in some higher power? We are not upon the day of judgment or Armageddon."

Horris hesitated for a few moments and masticated his lips.

"We are upon something much worse than an end, Kyla. We are upon a new beginning."

"I don't understand," replied Kyla.

Horris again waited for a few moments to pass. She could see his lips quivering in the candlelight. His eyes were wide. He then began to speak.

"God is dead."

CHAPTER SIXTEEN
✝

THE UBERMENSCHE

*

Kyla was shocked by Horris' statement. While she considered herself a rational person, she found the comment entirely disturbing. A cold chill ran through her body, forming first in the heels and blowing quickly through to the shoulders. Horris' countenance seemed to cringe, as if having spoken the words had been sin in itself. He held the candle close to his face.

"I do not know how ta convey it another way, love. But the words I'm sayin' are as real as the coat on yer shoulders."

The church seemed to reverberate as a loud rumble could be heard outside the building.

"I don't know what to say," she responded. "Religion has always been something I've seen others take part in. Never have I been told that my opinions or beliefs matter."

"They matter more than ya' know. But I assure ya', God is not intangible. And now, he's not invulnerable either, love. He's fallen like beauty stumbles suddenly into old age. God is dead."

All was silent again as Kyla could hear the man's panting breath. The church remained dark and dim. Horris' focus seemed ever-steady. He rarely blinked as he continued to peer into Kyla's eyes, seemingly searching for belief, or compassion, or maybe humanity. Perhaps his hounest and humble approach moved Kyla, or perhaps she was humouring him, allowing him to rant onward.

"I say again," he began, "God is no more! Heaven is weak, Kyla. The gates are as if tattered pieces of cloth. The angels sing not sweet songs of joy, but rather, hum a melancholy tune of loss. Souls are no longer swept into the blissful sea, but instead idle uncomfortably. It is terrible, love. A terrible, terrible existence for sure be up in 'em clouds or wherever."

"Horris, how is it you've come to know this?" inquired Kyla.

He thought for a few seconds and then began to speak.

"I need not question yer methods of psychology, love, because I know 'hat's yer specialty. Well, faith, this, knowledge as ya' say, is what I know best. I feel it deep within the gut, like a tapeworm eating away at my insides. Ya' listen ta yer patients, no? They speak ta ya'. Well, I am spoken ta as well. I cannot define the experience further than I have, for it is an individual sensation, a negotiation if ya' will."

She took the answer to be satisfactory, though perhaps was somewhat skeptical.

Chaotic Ocean

"And for what have I been selected?" she questioned. "Why are you passing this knowledge onto me? Would it not be better suited for a person of the clergy, or perhaps even a frequenter of this establishment?"

Before responding, Horris licked his lips, as if to ready himself for the words that were to follow. He knew well that Kyla was a logical woman and accepted little with lack of proof. Regardless, he knew that he had no choice, and knew that it was his own destiny to reach Kyla as best he could.

"In the absence of God, Kyla, there is but man. Man. Cold, shivering, and alone we remain. The abyss resulting from this absence readies evils of many kinds. I have told ya' 'hat such forces swirl around London while we naively slumber. I say again, in the absence of God, there is but man. Though, man is a dynamic beast himself, Kyla. And the eye does not always catch all there is ta see. Such a form of man exists 'hat goes undefined, unappreciated, and certainly unknown. Such is the super-man, he who can rise above everything, who can cry out with unimaginable power and overcome the forces of evil utilising the power inherent in his soul!"

"I don't..." she began to say.

"Listen, dear," interrupted Horris. "Listen ta my words. In yer heart and soul lies the capability of which I've spoken. Ya're above man, the elevated form."

"I suppose I just cannot fathom the evil you've spoken of, Horris," responded she.

"Is yer life free of cares? Do yer worries dissipate upon slumber? Is yer occupation a form of release? Have yer patients not gone off ta some mythical triangle in the middle of the ocean? Has not the promise of death been stained upon yer person? Are ya' naïve enough ta ignore one and one million pernicious signs?"

Kyla could not muster a response. She desired for the conversation to be over. She longed for Horris' words to be nothing more than a cruel nightmare. Wishing for forgetfulness, Kyla somehow knew that the information relayed was something more than a madman's fanatical raving.

"Kyla, if there is a moment of hesitation, of disbelief, the battle will be lost. Trust in me, love, 'hat there is a battle raging. The man upstairs is out of commission and ya're man's one and only hope. Do not let the whole of humanity down. If ever there were a moment ta put one's faith in, this is 'hat moment! Now is the time ta ease all pride, ta wash away all preconceptions. Save our souls, Kyla. Become the super-man. Understand yer God for the first time and serve him."

She stood there, dumbfounded. Kyla was not a woman of faith, and Horris was not only asking her to believe, but seemed to have been asking more — asking her to act. She wished for nothing more than to ignore Horris' inspired words. But she knew deep down that the shivers running along her spine were not the body's response to some physical sensation — they were intuition and energy, and Kyla understood them perfectly to have been the manifestations of actual belief.

Chaotic Ocean

Perhaps this disturbed her, that Horris was quite able in affecting such beliefs.

"Even if I were to forego hesitation and disbelief," she started, "what am I looking for? What possible role could I have in a battle of any kind? I am not a warrior, Horris, waving some hammer about like a madman. I do not dress in armour, and I have certainly never injured a creature on Earth!"

"I have little else ta tell."

Kyla could not believe the audacity of his response. She was appalled by the unsatisfactory answer.

"Not much else to tell? How on Earth could that be! It is you who are calling for my supposed power. It is you who warns of a Godless existence from which I must free us. Or perhaps I am not to free us, but am to fight endlessly till the closing of time. Perhaps I am immortal now! How can it be that you've little to add?"

Horris could see the anxiety in her countenance. He looked at her free hand and noticed that her fist was tightly clenched. Regardless, the man gathered his thoughts and calmly began to speak again.

"It is simple, dear. I ain't got much more information. I have done my part. Whether ya' decide ta listen is not up ta me anymore. Ya' have the necessary knowledge ta save us, ta save everyone. I know it's confusing, but what ain't? I can only teach ya' so much, because at some point, ya're gonna have ta take on the opposite role. Ya' now know who ya' are. Believe in it and ya'self. Understand yer God for the first time and serve him. Go now and be on yer way."

"But I..."

"Ya' must go now, love. Time is short, and it is imperative 'hat ya' leave. An evil swirls around London like some fog creepin' down from the sky. The fog has been inchin' for some time now. Good-bye."

Horris quickly ushered Kyla to the door. She obeyed his wishes and agreed to exit. Now entirely without direction, she cocked her head back and stared into the bruised sky. Kyla contemplated Horris' words and then regretted the decision of having come to see him, and further regretted the fact that it probably would have come to such a decision regardless, having few friends and fewer avenues of choice.

The night sky seemed as if some dark serpent experimenting with nefarious chemicals. Clouds could be seen, dampening the outline of any visible stars, and partially shading the moon. Kyla then realised that it was still quite frigid out and immediately jammed her hands into her coat pockets. She thought to Horris' mention of Mr. Pem. It was the second time that he had spoken of the man in the direct radius of negativity. It made her wonder.

Unlikely thoughts of Pem and her patients dining on some great feast while laughing ran across her mind. Apart from the flirtation with the improbable, Mr. Pem's last appearance still did bother Kyla to a great extent. He seemed uncharacteristically curt with her, that is, to assume she figured his character in their brief encounters. Kyla questioned the likeliness of his having any kind of connection whatsoever to Dorian,

Chaotic Ocean

Cecelia, and Laurna. It seemed quite silly. Still, the image of him in the distance, standing with three young people stuck in her memory. It indeed made the woman wonder.

Kyla, at this point, knew not what to do or where to go. Was she to believe the words of a man sleeping in the church? Was she to believe the promise of death received earlier in our story?

Kyla somehow knew that there was some inkling of truth in what Horris preached. Whether she believed in destiny or a power greater than man, she did feel a sense of push and pull about the city, about her life even, vibrating like nothing she had felt before. Kyla did in fact now believe in the existence of some kind of battle or struggle.

"Good and evil," she thought, "is there anything *more* outdated?"

She walked over to her motorcar and began brushing off the snow with her hands.

CHAPTER SEVENTEEN
✝

PERDITION AND PAROUSIA, THE FINAL STATE (DEUS EX MACHINA / DENOUEMENT) PART I

*

The spider, in all its wisdom, spins a silky, complex web, biding time in wait for the perfect prey. It is, in every aspect, a calculated stratagem. Innate to its existence is the know-how for this kind of survival. For eons, such creatures have existed in all regions of the cosmos, waiting, like perfect predators employing perfect knowledge. Such webs have been spun an innumerable amount of times, each making the collective strategy that much more resistant to flaw.

What is the inferior fly to do? How is it to avoid this kind of perfection? It would seem wholly impossible. The fly, to take nothing away from its own unique and beautiful existence, is simply of lesser order when compared with the cunning spider. It is not fault. It is nature. The insect is flying about in search of sustenance of some kind, it too attempting to seize advantage of those of lesser order, and unexpectedly gets entangled about some slyly erected web.

At first it slithers and squirms, reacting solely upon instinct. This new and paralysing environment is surely not suitable for a creature normally accusomted to roaming the sky with weightless wings and effort. Though, after many moments, it is obvious, even to the most simple of insects that all is lost. The fly is helpless and is at the mercy of its captor.

To the fly's credit, it does not prolong the process. It does not dream and doubt, nor does it refute with all might the very certainty of the situation. Tears do not stream down from the eyes, and it does not struggle after the obvious has presented itself. The fly knows that the sagacious spider, in all its age, has simply outwitted it. And while it may not have the goodness of heart to commend the animal, it does humbly bow out of the game. For this we must praise the fly. We must praise this form of acceptance and thank it for swallowing pride. The fly understands that personal vendettas were not tied to the events. It simply recognises that it has been outdone.

Chaotic Ocean

Was not the outcome of the entangled fly entirely predictable and inevitable from the start? Had it not been this specific fly, would not it have been some other insignificant, similar insect? The spider, in its magnificent glory, after all, merely needed to erect the web and wait. Its stay may have been hours or even days, a large portion of time out of the creature's short life-span. Clearly though, it knew that sooner or later its silky creation would yield wondrous results. It was unavoidable.

Were all creatures so humble as the fly, stories of escape and triumph would never find imaginative light. Though, it might be of small interest to tell a tale where spider, web, and fluttering fly are all perceptible from the onset. Such would be boring and of little value, for each outcome would end entirely the same.

Here is why creatures of tiny humility make for better tales: while perhaps, as ironic as it may seem, all outcomes fall in the same direction regardless, the audacity of these creatures provides for diverse exploratory possibilities. Flies, in their simplicity, never dare dream of power or pride. They do not waste their lives with fruitless searches for this or that. They are born, live, feed, procreate, and die. This is their pattern and it sustains them. One might ask, is this not the pattern for every beast? The answer is such that it might be, though not all beasts are hounest enough to accept this. They go as far to deny it, and attempt to enrich the pattern, as one can possibly imagine. And finally, in this denial, in this dishounesty with self, all chance at simplicity and contentment is lost.

The spider, in all its wisdom, waits for the perfect victim. The unavoidable fact of the victim's eventual submission is maybe not only set by percentages and strategy, but perhaps also by fate.

*

Zigmund had been pacing about for some length, plotting and conniving his glorious capture of the lapis stone. The hardwood floor of the sitting area in his mansion was now riddled with haphazardly discarded pieces of paper. For hours, he had been attempting to map out some sly, nefarious method with which to seize the stone that he desired. The discarded pieces of parchment had been crumpled into tiny balls of anger, and seemed strewn in some kind of maniacal pattern.

His face had not been shaved in some time, and his hair was not kept. It seemed, as the follicles so often do in the morning, that they had lives and wishes of their own, some bonding with one another, and some independently rushing off on various righteous paths of autonomy. Zigmund had little time to consider his outward appearance when he felt entirely close to becoming a modern God.

Still, through it all, he did consider himself an aristocrat, and felt that he had to do something about the unsightly appearance of his mansion. Having decided to take a short break from formulating, he knelt down to gather the scraps. In the near distance, partially covered by a small, white, failed plan, lay a shining, glittering key. It seemed almost incandescent, and perhaps were the human ears trained enough, they could have heard an impossibly low frequency emanating from the object.

Chaotic Ocean

Zigmund, now on all fours, began collecting the papers into a small, brown trash bin. As he made his way, the key seemed to radiate with increasing strength. He remained oblivious to the object, just as he had been for the length of our novel.

Zigmund thought to himself that it was fairly peculiar that a man of his stature would have had no servants of which to speak. Regardless, he continued to comb the floor, having already collected seven or eight crinkled papers. At this point, only a handful remained scattered. As luck would have it, he did not make his way to the key till all the others had been collected and disposed. Zigmund had even the audacity to break before picking the last piece of trash, as physical labour had not been his strength. He reached for the last like a child might reach for a sweet. Upon lifting it, his eyes immediately locked on the still, glowing key.

"What in the name of," he began to say aloud.

Zigmund reached for the object and grasped it in his hand, tossing it up and down a few times, as if in remembrance. Though, he soon realised that he remembered nothing of this particular object.

"To what does this unlock? Surely it is not to the mansion, for I keep that device in my pocket. Surely it is too large to be the liberator of some desk or cabinet. It is ever-large."

He investigated further, attempting to decipher the notches, as if he would have had the ability to figure the mystery by the simple makeup of the object.

"Damned if I..."

His words were interrupted by a sudden urge to explore. He figured that he would walk about, searching for locked areas about his property. Zigmund rose from his quadruped stance and continued to clasp the key. At first, he paced slowly, uncertain as to where to look. He glided from the sitting area to the marble kitchen, and eventually made his way to the bedroom and all the other many rooms of the mansion. Discovered were a great many areas that he had locked and forgotten about over the years, but Zigmund knew that the key in his possession would free none.

He again returned to the sitting area after fetching a new bottle and poured himself another glass of whisky. Zigmund sat back and began to think, forgetting briefly, but wholly, about his destined plot to seize the lapis. He again erected his body and walked to the front door, opening it, and slowly paced out under the canopy. The sky looked pale grey outside, and he looked to a pocket watch for the time. It was nearly five in the morning, and the sun had only initiated its ascent. It was cold out, and Zigmund grabbed himself to retain heat. He could hear nothing from the nearby street: no voices, no automobiles.

"Hmm," he thought to himself as he surveyed the property. Zigmund made up his mind to venture outside, but knew well that with the accumulated snow upon the ground, it was most wise to fetch a pair of boots. Walking through the snowy property was not dissimilar to walking across a lawn of Fall leaves. Crackling sounds, as if a million embers popping in some fire, rang out from under his feet. He could not figure for

Chaotic Ocean

the life of him why his search had led him in this direction. It seemed to make little sense.

His meticulously kept garden was now dead for some reason or another, and this depressed him somewhat. He contemplated whether or not it would be worth the effort to start over when the season permitted. His treasured rose carvings lay underneath the snow, a fact also at the forefront of his dismay. The large mansion seemed to stretch on for miles as he navigated alongside the front wall (the wall perpendicular to his canopy and front door). He seemed to roam aimlessly, stressing over the nature of the homeless key. Zigmund decided he would survey the westward side of the mansion, which was just around the corner of the north wall. As he turned it, Zigmund was shocked to find a tiny, old-fashioned-looking shed. It was a magnificent sight, sure enough, for he would not have erected anything less, but still the rustic patterned style of the small structure was in direct contrast to his mansion.

"Have my eyes deceived me?"

He did not recognise the building. It seemed entirely alien to him, and this bewildered him greatly. Zigmund thought that he had gone mad, for it was an impossibility to think that this structure could have been built unnoticed in his presence.

"Entirely impossible," he reassured himself.

Still, he could not make familiar the memory of one ounce of wood in the shed's makeup. It stood only about eight feet tall and was likely no more than ten feet by ten. The tiny structure seemed almost straight out of a Bob Ross painting, the humble and televised artist. The roof came together in a point like a triangle, though the edges hung a good foot off the walls. It was all rather brown. Some areas looked darker than others, but this could have been due to different kinds of wood having been used.

Zigmund walked around back in disbelief. The rear was as plain as the front and yielded no more information. He again returned to the area from which he first spotted the shed. It seemed to have had two conjoined wooden doors, as if fashioned after a barn. Zigmund's first intention was to open the small building and shed some degree of light on his current curious situation. He soon realised that a heavy, metallic lock, holding two giant chains stood in his way. Not thinking, he began to yank at the lock, as if to use brute force to gain access. This instantly failed, and Zigmund soon realised that his muscles began to ache.

"Pathetic," he thought to himself.

After a few moments of pacing, he finally remembered that he indeed had a key in his possession, and indeed a keyhole was the original inspiration for his short journey. After some fumbling in his pocket, he gave daylight to the shiny object. Zigmund held it up in the air, as if even this, the smallest of battles, had been some enormous victory.

Sure enough, as he twisted the metal into metal, the chains immediately dropped from the double doors. Zigmund had discovered the key's purpose and was now intrigued to uncover the innards of the shed. His hands oddly trembled with anticipation. The large wooden groove felt smooth on his hand as he reached to pry the doors apart.

Chaotic Ocean

Inside he found a small workshop with some old-looking equipment.

"What matter of treachery is this?" said he aloud.

Still, Zigmund had no memory of the tiny room. Papers lay scattered about the floor as he stepped slowly inside. A single cord hung down that was attached to a simple light bulb. He pulled at it. A large granite desk occupied the majority of the room. It too had scraps of paper about its surface. There was one large machine that stood gallantly next to the desk and hung partially over the surface, as if a neighboring reader sneaking a peak at a friend's leisurely novel. The machine looked old and utilitarian. It was an off-white colour, though this may have been due to the age, or possibly to the gathered dust and dirt. It had large black rollers that looked like oversized typewriter ribbons. The machine was a printing press of some kind and was only capable of minimal functionality.

Zigmund stood there, confounded. He recognised it clearly as a press, though, he could still muster no familiarity with the machine or even the shed itself. It seemed entirely implausible to him, the very fact of its existence and presence, yet he knew that his eyes had not deceived him. A few old paintings lined the walls as décor, and he thought well of them. The floor was cement, and the room emitted a certain smell of staleness. The air seemed dry to Zigmund, and the room's bareness only bewildered him further.

He walked to the beat up desk and thought to investigate the scrap paper. Unfolding one, he noticed it was some kind of draft. The writer had obviously a series of failed attempts, or at least, that is how the situation appeared. With the paper now completely unfolded, he laid it flat on the surface and smoothed it over four or five times with his hand.

Uncommon Sense

When was it that sense was ever truly common? We hear all the time now, declarations and orders for, and admonitions thrown at us for not having this so called common sense, but really, were it all that common, these warnings and verbal beatings would not be all that necessary.

When we think of it, it is really quite humorous, an oxymoron. Sense by the very nature of man is not common, and hence this calling for and praise of the skill is completely inane. Sensibility is a gift, like any other gift endowed through birth.

Unrealistic and deluded are those who yell out: "You must have some common sense, boy!" I yell back: "If what is common is what I long for, then I have no longer to search, for I have all along known my ignorance, my non-sense." I suppose the imperfection of the logic would be exposed if it were called out: "Have some uncommon sense!"

~~~~
~~~~
~~~~

Chaotic Ocean

The message seemed to end prematurely, and there were various lines of scribble under the last complete sentence. Still, though it was unsigned, Zigmund recognised this to be of his own creation.

"My God, this is penned of my hand!"

Fearfully, he smoothed out more sheets of paper, some with his very named signed to them. He did not understand. Instantly then, he winced inside as Kyla's accusation rang in his mind. Zigmund remembered her having accused him of "subjectaphor" pamphlets that he printed and in turn propagated about the community. The unknowing denial he showered her with reverberated through his entire being. He shivered, realising his words had in fact been lies. The large printing press seemed to make sense now, for this was clearly his tool in the ordeal.

Still, Zigmund contemplated, even if he could admit to having done what he had prior denied, how was it that he could not remember writing the words? How was it that he could not remember using the machine or spreading the subjectaphors? It just did not seem to make an ounce of sense to him. Enraged, he quickly exited the small hut and slammed the doors behind him, not bothering to fasten the lock.

*

Nervous and stumbling, Zigmund traversed his property, trudging through the accumulated snow. He longed for answers and knew that he had not the patience to await Godly status.

"What is happening?" called Zigmund into the grey sky. "For what purpose has my memory been tainted with merciless smog?!"

He again began to move about aimlessly, often walking a few nonsensical steps in one direction, and then suddenly turning to pace in the opposite direction, or sometimes, in a zigzag. Zigmund kept this up for many minutes as his rage grew greater.

Instantly his face was in the cold snow, freezing his nose. He had tripped over something quite large. It was the outer stones of the pond. He quickly sat up, looking at the outline covered wholly by the snow.

"You have not brought a speck of joy to my life of yet," he directed at the pond.

Zigmund remembered having been ambiguously guided by the pond, even by a voice inside his head that claimed connection with the water body.

"Have you nothing to say?" he maniacally questioned.

The snow then did something unexpected. It began to glow a deep-blue colour, as if the pond were melting its blanket of outer precipitation. Zigmund inched back a bit on his rear. His brain began to cause him physical pain, as if the glowing were screeching and scraping about his inner synapses. He blacked out for just a second, but it seemed as if an hour to him. When he awoke, the glowing had ceased, but his anger had increased tenfold.

"I am not your play toy! I do not do your bidding..."

He stopped. Could it have been possible, he contemplated, that the pond had some implication in his apparent memory loss?

Chaotic Ocean

"Ah, your game is over!" he continued. "I am not at fault here, am I? I am your vessel no longer, scourge. No longer will I allow this hidden symbiosis to go on without my knowledge. I absolve myself of all duties!"

His eyes were red with rage and his mouth was curved as he continued to shout at the listless pond.

"Host, parasite, we are all dead to one another! Answer me! Phantom, pond, whatever your nature is; do not leave me in questioning. How has the ruse been accomplished?"

The pond lay silent. The water had in fact melted the snow, and was calm and unfrozen in its freed state. Zigmund gave up. He realised what a fool he must have seemed, wasting so much precious time on these tangents of little return. He thought back to his destiny.

"This delaying has caused me much dismay. This plotting has led me astray. I must resolve to seize the lapis, for it is who I am, who I was, and in this limbo I will not stay!"

Zigmund rang for his usual coach, told the man it was urgent, and headed quickly off to Kyla's.

CHAPTER SEVENTEEN
✟

PERDITION AND PAROUSIA, THE FINAL STATE (DEUS EX MACHINA / DENOUEMENT) PART II

*

Let us delve back into our other character for the moment. Kyla had decided to motor about the city, contemplating what exactly Horris had told her. She needed time to herself to truly soak it in. For Kyla, it was difficult to put all her trust in the words of a preacher, though, simultaneously, she understood that going about life in the manner she had, had not brought her any kind of happiness. So it came about that Kyla decided to head home. The sun had crept over the horizon, and by this time was creating significant glare on the front window of her motorcar.

Upon stepping inside, she was overwhelmed with a desire to walk into the narrow hallway that housed the entrance to her attic. Kyla could not recall the last time she had been up in the wretched place.

It looked simple enough, the door. It was something of an eggshell white, though, over the years had faded, like most paintjobs do, into a dingy kind of colourless existence. It stretched about three feet long and was maybe only two feet wide. A black, medium-thin pull cord hung daintily down. The end of the cord was tied into a hoop for easy grabbing.

Kyla stood directly under it now. For the life of her, she could not fathom why it was that she was drawn to this place. Nasty thoughts circumnavigated her head, and for the first time in many years, this confused her. She wondered what grudge she had actually been holding against the inanimate entrance and the like of inanimate objects stored above. It seemed foolish to have harbored such angst. She glowered up at the door in the ceiling, and perhaps inwardly at her own curious behavior, and wondered wholly why her position had become so intransigent over the years.

"For what reason have I been so utterly petty and illogical in this matter?" she castigated.

Kyla decided that it was indeed time to conquer whatever it was that had been restricting her. She yanked hard at the cord, and the door came down, creaking loudly in the process. A light automatically switched on accompanying the action. The steps were made of some cheap wood and folded into the door. They were unfinished and light-yellow in colour. Each step had ridges engraved, possibly for safety's sake. Two angled metal arms stretched down, holding the stairs in place. She pulled the lower half of the steps down and dropped it to the floor. The ladder was now in place, inviting Kyla to ascend.

She slowly inched toward the ladder, hesitatingly placing her foot on the first step, her hands above her head on the upper section. It took little effort, she soon realised, to enter the attic, and within seconds, she had quickly climbed all the way up, now sitting wholly in the storage area with her feet dangling down through the entrance. The room was very quaint and small, and one did not have enough space to stand fully erect. Large wooden planks lay over the floorboards, and she was careful not to injure herself. The light only satisfied the area partially, giving off a certain level of dimness to the room.

Looking around, Kyla could only see a few old scattered boxes. She estimated that there were about six or seven, and one dusty-looking trunk. It was quite barren, overall, and there was not much to see in the attic. Kyla moved toward one of the boxes and began to investigate. It contained some knick-knacks and old college term papers. She quickly reminisced over the memories. After some additional searching, she decided that maybe the trunk contained something of interest. For this investigation, she had to crawl many feet over a plank, as it was lined against the far wall. It was jammed. Upon touching it again, Kyla received a shock. It frightened her and made her shiver up and down. She knew that there was not much chance for electricity to conduct through the wooden boards, and furthermore, through the old trunk. A feeling of unease shot through her stomach, as if the shock had been more than just some random incident. Still, she decided to continue with the dusty investigation. It was plain enough, beat-up-looking, and was mahogany in colour. Clitchkk. The object opened after some toying.

As she pried open the latch, a wave of sour air escaped, like some antique oxygen desperately attempting to flee its long forgotten confine. Kyla's heart began to beat faster, for she knew that the contents had been the cause of her apprehension about the tiny room. At first, she began to slowly finger through. Her hands felt as if they were in an underground bee hole searching for the comb with full knowledge of a hundred angry, protective insects. Beads of sweat started to roll down her forehead and into her eyes.

At first, she came to some familiar items from her past: an old wrist watch, some items left to her from her deceased parents, an outdated novel on cutting edge psychology, and a nonworking trinket. Her fear, she thought to herself, had perhaps been unwarranted. Kyla's confidence grew after sieving through the stagnant objects. Though, soon she came to some curious papers encased in a large plastic folder.

"What's this?" said she aloud.

Chaotic Ocean

It was old file information on her three patients. She could not remember placing this information in the trunk, nor could she figure why she would have done so, as opposed to say, filing the papers in some orderly manner. It did not seem to add up. For each Cecelia, Dorian, and Laurna, there existed an exhaustive workup, including notes, background facts, and detailed case histories. One primary section in each seemed to interest Kyla the most, containing basic statistics from hair colour to contact information. Additionally, though, it contained family information.

She focused first on Cecelia's page.

Name: Greene, Cecelia
Age: 15
Hair: Dyed
Height: 1.57 meters
Weight: 6.43 stones (90 lbs)
Conditions: Bulimia Nervosa, Self-Mutilation, Depression
Comments: Negative Self-Image, Given To Tantrums
Family Unit: Mother (Mary Cecelia), Father (Thomas Cecelia), Siblings (none)
Extended Family: Uncle (Timothy Sleiney)

Kyla dropped the paper, having finished the last line. Her head began to pound, as if some inner cymbal having been thrashed.

"What's happening!" she screamed aloud.

Kyla knew that the last line in Cecelia's chart had brought this on. She struggled to re-read the name "Timothy Sleiney" as again her mind felt as if it were being used as a punching bag. Seemingly random, but specific, thoughts imbued her very being. '...*sands of time with a dismissible spirit and apathy...*' '...*intelligence exams prior to reproducing, in order to determine competence...*' Words flashed in and out of her memory, as if scenes from some classic film. '...*Was it to further our ethics and do what is right for the choice of man? Was it to be moral...*'

"My goodness," suddenly realised Kyla. "I know these words. I know them clearly as I know the sun rises and falls. They are the written words from an article I recently read on the Eugenics Movement."

She hesitated a moment when fully understanding the magnitude of this discovery. Timothy Sleiney was the author of the article, Cecelia's uncle.

"How could I have overlooked this?"

Kyla also recalled having read another of Sleiney's articles, further feeling dumbfounded at this oversight. She decided it best to continue to the other charts.

Name: Knots, Dorian
Age: 22
Hair: Long, Black
Height: 1.75 meters
Weight: 1 cwt, 4.14 stones (170 lbs)

Chaotic Ocean

Conditions: History of Depression
Comments: Tendency Toward Arrogance & Kind
Heartedness
Family Unit: Father (Gregory Knots), Mother (Julia Knots)
Father: Uses "Berg Daye" as Professional Name
Father's Profession: Agent of the Government

Again, Kyla found herself reeling, once again remembering various lines from something she had read, storming in like waves and crashing hard against the shore of her mind.

"It's simply not fathomable. So too with Daye did I read an article! It was called *Chromosapien Man*, or something to the absurd like. In fact, I know I read others as well from this man. How would it be that Dorian would omit his father's business, or even, timeliness and prominence from me? Why would he have done such a thing? Furthermore, in what way has the writing of pish posh to do with government work? It makes no sense! How would a man in such standing drift to writing dribble for the rabble? And dribble it was! What utter confusion this all is."

Having no other choice, she delved into the final chart.

Name: Tangly, Laurna
Age: 20
Hair: Curly
Height: 1.68 meters
Weight: 1 cwt, 1.29 stones (130 lbs)
Conditions: Paranoia, Fear of Being Judged, Fear of
Affection
Comments: Over Emphasis on Ambition & Monetary
Success, Cynical Outlook, Given To Anger, Distrusting
Family Unit: Father (William Tangly), Mother (deceased),
Sister (Allison Tangly)
Extended Family: Aunt (Greda Blormy), Uncle (Phillip
Blormy), Cousin (William Blormy)

By this point, Kyla had almost predicted the third and final strange coincidence. Yet again, she vaguely recalled paging through some eccentric article by none other than a Will Blormy. These could not have been random flukes, she thought. A painful pang rang through her arm, and she thought perhaps her heart had given out. The feeling eventually subsided. Kyla angrily slammed the trunk lid down and began to quickly exit the attic.

Moving clumsily over the floorboards, she stumbled over another dusty trunk, causing her to trip and crash to the floor. She thought she had had enough, and this was no time to investigate all of her belongings. Still, this new crate, which she had not noticed upon first entering the attic, seemed truly curious, and while angry, Kyla thought to explore once more.

Chaotic Ocean

It was black, smaller than the previous, and looked polished. She could discern no known markings on the exterior. It smelled waxy. The thing did not have a lock, and Kyla opened the object with ease. No sour air greeted her this time. Inside the deep compartment was but one item: a book with a layer of dust upon it.

Kyla retrieved it with both hands, and quickly wiped away the residue. In large, olden lettres, it read "Book of the Forgotten, XIV."

"What on Earth is this? I have no recollection whatsoever of having purchased or read such a text."

She was truly baffled. The book had rigid subdivisions and was not quite easy to page through. Kyla turned the cover and came to the first major division. The pages were old and frail, like nothing she had seen prior. She soon fell upon the words, which seemed to call to her.

"And when out of plasma
Men perceived light and dark,
Nature fully understood the folly
Of having bore human beings

Men, of humble mind,
Nature knew to lack the grasp of totality,
And hence came to accept the obtuse idea
Of life and spirit as a kind of dichotomy,
As a series of disparities and divergences

In this acceptance came the realization of necessity

To have shattered an entire image of existence
Would have been to excise all that was human

Those entities in the vast minority of mind
Capable of a truthful acceptance
Would have to be stopped,
So to preserve 'life'

And so were created limitations
On the character of men and gods alike,
Aiming to nullify would-be imposters –
Those seeking tirelessly to disengage the great
Farce

Nature, looking back on its creation,
At the great imperfection of its actions,
Could simply not bare the inelegance
Of erasing an entire experiment

And when Nature avowed its hubris,
So was ensured the modern man, of modern wisdom

Chaotic Ocean

But so too was ensured unrest."

"What manner of poetry is this? Who is the author? In what year was this published? Could it truly be that this is not a work of fiction? It cannot be!"

Kyla sat there on the floor, feeling strange, knowing that this was more monumental than anything she had experienced. She then fell into some kind of trance, capable of feeling the world around her, but somehow much removed at the same time. It was difficult to breathe. As if out of nothingness, an image appeared before her mind's eye – that of a landscape set in some kind of imperceptible blur. The colours were all off, as if having been nature's inverse. The image continued to press onward, despite Kyla's wishes. In the distance, she could make out the outline of a figure. Though, the details were impossible. She could tell that the figure was a human form, or so it appeared, but it was shrouded in a shadow, showing no features, no colour – just blackness.

This struck her with a heightened sense of paralysing fear. While she could not make out the form, nor the area, or really any details about the image, her body physiologically responded by creating a dense feeling of nausea and unease. Kyla silently begged the image to cease, but it would not. Then, as if in forward motion, she could see another figure dashing at the first. It seemed to make little sense. Finally, the vision freed Kyla of its presence.

Physically, she felt decimated. Though, while her nature told her to question, her emotion affirmed that now was not the time to ponder such things. With what strength she had left, she decided to inspect the next subdivision of the book. To her surprise, it contained no writing. Buried deep within the pages was a bright object. Kyla fumbled with the book, and out fell a small, golden sword. It was perhaps only as long as the tome itself, as if a miniature version of a large battle weapon.

"For what possible purpose..." Kyla began.

She turned to the final section, which contained nothing more than a few lines.

"And so with the transmuted
Rescue what must be saved
The path of existence is through the heart."

Kyla could not stand the stale air, nor could she stand the experience a moment longer. With object in hand, she flew quickly down the ladder. Knowing that she needed a fresh breeze, Kyla walked hurriedly to the back porch and slid open the glass door. By this time, the sun had fully captured the land and was bright on Kyla's eyes. To her continued dismay, looking out over the rolling hills, she discovered that the fallen snow in this area had turned putrid black, like boiling tar. The transformation that had brought the precipitation from white to black had now concluded in its present form.

Chaotic Ocean

Kyla seemed to lament the confusion, inwardly sighing, almost expectedly.

"Truly," she began to say aloud, "what harbinger of the macabre has manifested in this place?"

She stopped after the brief thought, knowing all too well that her questions and doubts, like so many in the days prior, would ultimately go unanswered, leaving her empty like a hollowed fruit. She sobbed like a widow might at the end of a lonely and meaningless life. Her tears may have streamed for days, as the emotion and chaos troubled Kyla to no end, though a pounding on her front door interrupted her sorrow.

*

Kyla could not figure who would have had a desire to visit, especially anyone who knew the situation that she was going through. Opening the door, she was very shocked to see her disheveled friend, Zigmund. His eyes were not normal-looking, but rather, were intense like glowing embers. He seemed as if he had not slept in some time. She slipped the golden object into her pocket.

Zigmund knew full well that he had not a plan to show for all his efforts. As Kyla opened the door, he thought perhaps to strike her skull with the nearest blunt object, or perhaps considered drugging her to make it a painless process. Zigmund knew himself to be not a savage, and was not quite sure how any physical rage might manifest, and furthermore, if so, what kind of success such a base strategy might bring forth.

Before he could consider more, Kyla greeted him, attempting to conceal her emotions.

"Zigmund, for certain I had not expected you. I thought perhaps some messenger or delivery person, but you... It was not in my crystal ball, let's say."

He smiled crookedly, clearly forcing the muscles of his face to contort in manners completely beyond his truer instincts.

"Ah, well," concocted Zigmund, "it is not every day that I venture to your abode, but I thought, since you have been so goodly over the years, selflessly traversing this wretched city to reach me, I thought perhaps I'd return the favor."

Kyla was confused and thought back, concluding that Zigmund had not once brought himself to visit with her, and was suspicious. Nonetheless, she invited the man inside, as it was quite chilly out. He was gracious and walked humbly in through the door.

"You know, Zigmund, this may be the first time in all our years of friendship that you've come by. Why the sudden magnanimity?"

The conversation betwixt the two seemed quite stilted, perhaps because both had unique curiosities about each other's nature, and furthermore, because of the mental state each was in.

"Men can change," coldly replied Zigmund.

Kyla ushered him into the small dining area, putting out her arm to signify the gesture: have a seat. After Zigmund had done so, she responded.

"Men can change, yes. But you? I've never been aware of one inkling that you'd any desire *to* change. You, Zigmund, I find it difficult to believe can change. You believe wholeheartedly in your own perfection. I know it well. You need not defend."

His eyes again became red, as these comments seemed to visibly disturb him. After a few moments though, he ordered his emotions to submit, silently thinking that all this small talk – all the unimportant knowledge or exchanges in the world really – would soon be for all but him. Before responding, he looked about the tiny area, scanning the room for the trunk of which he was foretold.

"Do you need something?" questioned Kyla, noticing his jumpy demeanor.

No longer could Zigmund keep his emotions in tow. He rose from the chair.

"Do you need something," repeated Kyla with a look of fear in her eyes.

"I think you fully know what I desire, what I need," cryptically replied the man, his voice and demeanor having altered.

Kyla was taken back.

"I truly do not know. And I do not appreciate the tone you are using with me. I don't think..."

Before she could finish, Zigmund had dashed for an empty wooden knife holder. He grabbed for the item and smashed it into Kyla's head. It was a heavy block and Zigmund had exerted a considerable degree of force in his crude action. Kyla screamed like a fire siren. It seemed to carry out into the yard and up the street. Zigmund was merciless, and Kyla, in her brief moment of conscious thought, was utterly shocked and without answers. The man made sure of his work – he repeatedly bashed his friend in the skull till she lay silent on the floor. Zigmund checked her pulse after the beating to find she was still alive, which was, to him, perhaps an agreeable outcome.

CHAPTER SEVENTEEN
✠

PERDITION AND PAROUSIA, THE FINAL STATE (DEUS EX MACHINA / DENOUEMENT) PART III

*

Her nose was broken, and a stream of thin blood slowly ran from Kyla's left nostril. Her forehead was instantly bruised, and her right eye was very injured. It would likely cause a great deal of swelling. The savage thrashing likely caused a concussion, but it is difficult to say, for in writing, we cannot predict what a medical doctor might diagnose, but rather, can only paint the picture of misfortune.

Zigmund quickly arose and began searching for the trunk containing the lapis stone. He paced about the hallway, entering any areas he could, nonsensically moving the many surroundings of Kyla's home.

"It must be here somewhere. Nay. It IS here somewhere. Locating this glorious artifact is for what I was created!"

Eventually, Zigmund made his way into the tiny back room where the trunk rested. His eyes widened when he saw the wooden sarcophagus.

"No longer must you rest in this nothingness, in this defamed state, uselessly aging and fading away. No more civilisations must build and fall. No more suns and moons must rise and set. I shall be your liberator, and through you, shall liberate myself."

Quickly stepping to the trunk, Zigmund easily pried it open, revealing the glowing lapis. He knew the sight to be one of magnificence and stood there momentarily in awe of the great and storied object. Waiting no longer, he grabbed for it. In his hands it made him feel accomplished. It was oddly warm in temperature, and Zigmund understood this to mean he had in fact succeeded in the procuring of the thing. Pompously, while still on his knees, he kissed the stone, as if in some religious fashion, perhaps as those of Islamic faith might kiss Mecca.

"You shall provide me the greatest knowledge monopoly known to man, nay: for man cannot know what he has not the comprehension to fathom. Such a wealth of information shall be mine to behold, to use, and mine alone to understand!"

Chaotic Ocean

Thunder cracked loudly outside, startling Zigmund. He realised he had spent too much time in the silent room and resolved to depart and head back to the mansion so to complete the artifact's full design. He passed Kyla's limp body, carelessly, and exited through the door. The sky was like nothing he had seen before. It was dark like some stained maroon, though the sun had previously been shining.

"Where has that fiery star departed to?" wondered Zigmund. His coach was nowhere to be seen, and this infuriated him greatly. Again, sounds formed in the off-colour sky. Up and down the street he could hear but the sounds of shutters moving about in the wind. The usual bustle of the morning, those waking and preparing for their daily occupations, was oddly absent. The other dwellings seemed lifeless. Zigmund could not see a single light in the whole area. Clouds no longer appeared white, but rather, a smoky, putrid tone. He thought that he noticed malicious countenances in the billowy formations, but then decided that his imagination had taken the better of him. All seemed strangely listless.

*

This was nothing normal, even Zigmund could conclude. All the polluted chemicals in the universe could not have transformed the atmosphere that he was now witnessing. The puffy, dark clouds moved like noxious poison might distill about an area, stretching and spanning, then contracting in different spiral-like formations. And still, he could not discover a single passerby's faint voice, or even the muddled sound of some automobile engine in the distance, chugging like some dying vulture. He had been used to inaudible evenings, having survived the better part of his days alone in his mansion, though still, this he knew to be out of the ordinary realm.

Soon though, he witnessed a man walking slowly in his direction, calmly.

"Good fellow," Zigmund yelled out, "have you any means of transport? I am somewhat stranded in this neighborhood and long to return to the comfort of my personal dwelling."

The man was a far distance when Zigmund called to him, though, the passer made little haste in responding. He continued to slowly pace the street, heading ever so slowly in Zigmund's general direction.

Zigmund stood there somewhat dumbfounded, for he knew not why the man had delayed an answer. He thought perhaps the man to have been mute or something of the like, or perhaps, Zigmund thought, the man clearly did not understand the situation, or furthermore, the nobility of presence in which he was graced. The person was now within comfortable chatting distance.

Zigmund recognised him as the very man who had originally thwarted his concocted murder at the medical compound. He thought this to have been a curious happenstance. Zigmund was not sure whether to be angered with the being, for his earlier interference, or to forget the ingratitude and look onward to the greater good – the combination of the lapis – since after all, no longer did he care for the failed plot or for the feign promises the outcome would have brought. The man's name, Zigmund recalled, was Mr. Pem. He knew the fellow to have had some kind of relationship with Kyla, and before he thought again to ask for transport, he wondered if Pem had come by this way to visit with her. In his mind, he recounted the brutal thrashing and her listless body lying on the floor just a short distance away. Nevertheless, he had little time to worry for such things, and thought to ask once more.

"Good sir, Mr. Pem is it? Have you means of transport? I recall having run into you briefly at the medical compound. I'd been speaking with" – he paused, unsure if it was wise to mention the name – "Kyla. She is not at home unfortunately."

The man looked into his eyes, seeing the lie for what it was, and before responding, exhaled in some kind of delight.

"Perhaps we should check, to make for certain, if Kyla is about," humoured Mr. Pem with a sinister grin upon his lips.

"I really do not..." began Zigmund.

"Silence!" starkly interrupted Pem. "You have done well, friend, but there is little time to appease egos. I feel as though Kyla might have interest to join us."

"But I've already told you..."

"Ah, ah," responded Mr. Pem, and signaled to the door of Kyla's home.

Zigmund could not believe his own eyes when he saw Kyla stumble out, bruised, beaten, but nevertheless, walking. Perhaps she too was utterly surprised at the strength of her body, and could not account any feasible reason why she should be up and about. Kyla recalled Zigmund beating her skull, and was furious, but such furiousness was usurped by utter confusion when she recognised Mr. Pem.

The three stood face to face, and at first, all were silent. Kyla stared angrily into Zigmund's eyes as he attempted to avoid contact. She then glanced at Mr. Pem, and then the sky. Kyla recognised the atmosphere to have altered and recalled the seizure she experienced when experimenting with the lapis stone. She now knew some pernicious work had been afoot, looking down into Zigmund's hands, seeing that he had robbed her of the artifact.

"Is not this precious?" instigated Mr. Pem. "Is not this how all was meant to conclude?"

"I do not understand," numbly responded Kyla.

"You never have," spoke Pem.

Zigmund could no longer hold his own tongue, or his ambitions.

"Whatever pettiness this is shall no longer matter in the grand scheme of things. You two are foolish to assume whatever you may about me, or my being here. I hold in my hands a glory you could have never imagined, Kyla. It is to be my freedom. It is uncontrollable power incarnate! I have been promised all that I have ever desired, and not a soul on Earth can know the glory in such. Only I hold the key to the design, the foreknowledge to forge the application of Godliness!"

Chaotic Ocean

Kyla jerked back, having seen Zigmund's true character revealed, disgusted by his transparent physiognomy.

"You are an insane aristocrat, coward, robbing others of gifts," quipped Kyla. "What possible goodness can come of that? You have emptied all redemptive qualities from your soul."

Pem stood there silent, as the sky again began to swell, rumbling like the belly of some bloated beast.

"Do not think your insults have an effect on me, dearest Kyla. A wondrous prophet has foretold me of my fortune, though you'd know nothing of the kind. I alone hold the information necessary. You, having been curator of this rock, have not the slightest clue to its truest nature. Though, for certain, I know of *your* nature. Do not think I have fallen for your ruse! Do not think I know not the implications of your involvement in the murder we mutually witnessed in the park. Do you hounestly assume me for a fool? Do you hounestly assume that I know not the collaboration of you and that thug in the park, with his beady eyes and evil demeanor?"

Kyla convulsed, flashing back to the brutal murder, to the limp woman's piercing eyes. The woman had known her name, she frightfully remembered. She also recalled the woman's dreadful last words: "No... Kyla... the stone." Finally, she remembered her last glimpse of the murderer, a man of plain description with a small, pointed black goatee.

She turned to Mr. Pem, her heart beating like a thousand drummers, sinking her eyes into the man's small, pointed, black goatee. In his eyes she witnessed the glare of satisfaction. Kyla again peered into Zigmund's hands, looking over the stone, recalling his brief telling of a prophet, and then instantly thought of the day that Mr. Pem had, without much reason, given her the object as a gift of thanks.

"What have you done?" she uttered to Pem.

"Only what was necessary," coldly responded the man.

"But you... you... how could have you murdered that woman? How could you have come to me and..."

Zigmund was confused.

"Kyla, what on Earth are you rambling about. Have you not heard the words I have spoken?" egotistically questioned Zigmund.

"You damned fool! Have you not the necessary clues to decipher the facts? Can you hounestly still believe in some false prophet? Do you not see the nefarious events unfolding before our very eyes? This man, right here and now, before us, he is one in the same with the man we witnessed in Exmoor Park! Good Heavens, Zigmund!"

Mr. Pem interrupted.

"You'll have to excuse my friend here. He has grandeur on his mind. Is not that correct, friend? Perhaps we shall have to have another glass of whisky to remedy the confusion."

Zigmund was silenced.

Kyla was completely dismayed, and the events unfurling before her were nearly too ghastly to rationally absorb. For a brief moment, her mind flashed over various events from her recent existence – meeting Mr.

Chaotic Ocean

Pem at the medical compound, her utilisation of the stone, the woman in the park...

"The woman in the park. The woman in the park," thought Kyla. "It still fails me. If Pem is indeed the culprit for death, then for what possible reason was the victim chosen? And how was it that I was known?"

She again surveyed the land, and glanced upon Mr. Pem with glaring eyes.

"You do not deny the murder I have assumed of your hand, Pem. And for that, I must assume accuracy. Though, all this, everything, is it not still muddled? Zigmund, for whatever you have promised, is naïve to it all, finding solace in his personal attack of my character so to force all events as true. That woman said my name. MY name. She uttered it upon death, vaguely warning of the stone. Perhaps now I see what she had in mind. Though, how my name was known, and how she had such the ability of precognition, such are mysteries still."

"Let us not delay in our fate," stated Mr. Pem.

Kyla instinctively let her hand fall to her side, feeling the outline of the golden sword in her pocket. She remained silent.

*

The three instantly found themselves on Zigmund's property in front of the pond.

"What manner of witchery..." Zigmund began.

"Ah, but our destiny is not to be spoken of in such denigrating terms," responded Pem.

"I simply do not see what all this is meant for," interjected Kyla.

"Kyla, my dear, the reader has grown weary of your constant questioning. Hold your tongue!"

Mr. Pem turned to Zigmund, motioning for him to step into the pond with the lapis in hand.

"What other choice do you have, Zigmund? Are you not the slightest bit curious to see the outcome of it all?"

Kyla screamed to Zigmund, hoping to reach past his blindness, warning this to be a mistake of gargantuan proportion. She lashed out that his so-called prophet was of malicious and false nature.

Zigmund thought to the fallen victim from the park, and the words which she spoke only to him.

"You will not impede me, Kyla, as I was forewarned."

"What madness are you speaking of, Zigmund?"

"When you departed the victim, she spoke plainly, for one instant, and one instant only, that you would stop me. For what else am I to conclude of your current persuasion? I will not be stopped, will not be seized of the power promised!"

Kyla was taken back by the admission. She could not figure why her friend had kept the information a secret, when perhaps had he been forthright, his sordid impression of her, and the resulting captivation of visitors and voices, could have been alleviated some. All was much.

Chaotic Ocean

"Who are you, Pem!?" demanded Kyla.

"Methinks such a question is ultimately without consequence," replied Mr. Pem.

Perhaps Kyla knew Mr. Pem's statement was accurate. She lugubriously let her eyes fall to the ground, not knowing what to think or what to do. Kyla, sobbing like an infant, had not realised that Horris was now beside her. When she looked up, she knew not whether to seek comfort.

"H...Horris? What in Heaven's name are you doing here?"

"Tying up loose ends, duckey. But certainly not in Heaven's name."

"But you, but we... how did you? What of our conversations? Of your urging?"

"Ah, come now, Gawd blimey, ya', of yer questioning nature, can't hounestly tell me ya' believed all 'hat pish posh! Ain't ya' been listenin'? Figure it out. Pem and I aren't yin and yang. We ain't VP's for respective intangible organisations. Church is just a building. Sorry to say, dove, Pem and I are in this one together, striving for a united goal, and from the looks, seems like it's on the verge of havin' been gotten!"

"But I've been through so entirely much, so many chaotic events in my recent history. It cannot be connected. It simply can't be! I know it can't."

Kyla felt utterly betrayed by Horris, and an overwhelming sensation of sickness carried from her heart to her toes. How was it possible that Horris, who had been so kind to her, so gentle, could be of the same make as Pem, a murderous, deceitful liar? She thought to question his unexpected entrance, but then gave up the idea after recalling having been on the street of her home one instant, and then at Zigmund's the next.

To the surprise of all, a motor hum could be heard in the near distance. The hum grew louder with each passing second. Kyla felt a trembling inside of her, but knew not whether the sensation was agreeable or not. Her eyes brightened some when she witnessed the familiar cab pounce through the gate and into direct view, with its rusted exterior and corrugated lettering.

Sean seemed visibly disturbed by the cast of characters before his eyes, as he walked up to the group. For an instant, Mr. Pem seemed concerned, and it looked as if he or Horris would intercept the man's presence. Ultimately, though, each remained calm.

"Sean!"

Kyla ran into the man's arms, hoping that he too had not been of ulterior make.

"Hey, lady. What's goin' on in this part of town? Some kind of get together?"

"Oh no, Sean. Certainly not. When you sheltered me for fear of death, as much was nothing in comparison to the grander scheme of things. The men I've placed trust in have turned out nothing more than a murderer and an unlikely companion! Please, please, do something!"

Chaotic Ocean

Zigmund smirked to himself, still upholding the superiority of knowledge of Kyla's character. He recalled his brief phone conversation with Sean, and seemed ever-interested in the man's current conversation with Kyla.

"The move is yours, Zigmund," interrupted Mr. Pem.

"NO!" shouted Kyla. "Do not listen to him, Zigmund. It cannot be that you are as obsequious and covetous as you've made yourself to be! I believe otherwise, and regardless of your opinion of me, you must know something is awry."

Zigmund appeared as if the words had no meaning, and became transfixed upon the pond. Kyla somehow knew that something had to be done. She brushed Sean off for a moment and turned again to Mr. Pem.

"I demand to know what must be learned!"

Mr. Pem seemed satisfied.

"At present, you sound not too unlike another in our presence, dear."

"Why did the woman in the park know my name? How was it that she foresaw any of this?"

"A mere hapless detail of the greater *good*, child. You do not understand what is soon to be accomplished, and neither did she. You are unaware of your surroundings, more than we had anticipated, which is a pleasure to Horris and myself. That being you saw murdered was nothing more than a tree obstructing a road. To fundamentally skew what is common is not done with ease, nor is it done in haste. The events laying themselves out here before all of our eyes have been in motion since your very birth, child. And the blueprints have been laid eons ago."

"What are you speaking of, Pem?"

"I suppose it is your privilege, since you have done us well. The woman murdered, if you wish to label her 'woman,' was the third counterpart in our modern trinity. A long time ago, she was of great aid to Horris and myself. She even contributed vastly to the laying of our plot. Yet, some time ago, when you were perhaps only learning to crawl or to speak, she became disenchanted with what we had set forth. She wished to reach you, to tell you of all that had been festering without your knowledge. Though, of course, she was forced to endure lifetimes while your lineage came and died. And finally, as the present is upon us, she resolved to break from the trinity. When you and Zigmund entered the park, she was in wait. I was able to intercept her, and while I did not wish to, was forced to end her existence, or at least the form in which she had manifested."

Kyla looked over to Zigmund, and he seemed to have heard the story, but cared not for the details, as he remained transfixed, poised to unite the lapis with the pond.

"And for what is it that I was brought here, Mr. Pem?" questioned Kyla with indignity. "What ultimate plot is to be revealed?"

"You will know in moments."

Kyla turned to Sean with fright in her eyes. He remained stolid, supportive. But at present, he seemed to have nothing to offer. Kyla finally realised it was she and she alone who had to end this. She knew not what was to be, but understood her role to be direly important. Quickly withdrawing the small, golden sword from her pocket, as if on instinct alone, she held it up.

Mr. Pem seemed unsurprised at the small dagger's existence.

The words from the book uncovered in her attic rang inside of her mind: *And so with the transmuted; Rescue what must be saved; The path of existence is through the heart.*

In a moment of confidence, Kyla stepped over to Mr. Pem.

"The path of existence is through the heart. I know not my reasoning to be a guide in this experience any longer. I must act on what feels to be right."

She raised the object into the air, holding the slender part of the small sword downward. Mr. Pem's eyes showed slight interest in the seeming threat, but did not move. He was not afraid in the slightest.

"I wouldn't do 'hat duckey," quickly chirped Horris. "Ain't ya' got no regard for the man upstairs no longer?"

"Your words are without meaning," snapped Kyla. "You are no religious soul."

"Ah, but I'm more religious than ya' know. Do ya' truly think 'hat killin' Pem is gonna be yer salvation in any kinda way? Maybe it'll secure ya' a place with the man downstairs, but not much more."

"Lies!" screamed Kyla, with tears streaming down. "Lies... are they not?"

Her resoluteness faded to insecurity.

"I don't know no one who thinks killin' is the answer, regardless of religious affiliation or not."

Kyla found herself falling again into the trap of misplacing trust in Horris, even after all that had been admitted. His voice still soothed her. Though, on this occasion, Sean was present to interject, as he witnessed his friend's demeanor.

"Kyla, snap out of it! Now I might not exactly know the ins-and-outs of what's goin' on here, but I well know that if this man is as you've described him, ruinous – partner to some kinda murderer, then for sure you can't still give his words weight."

Sean's statement seemed to have an impact.

"But what am I to do? Are you suggesting that I kill Mr. Pem, and in essence, become murderous myself?"

Mr. Pem interjected.

"The words sound foolish, even you can reconcile, dear. Kill me? For what purpose, to what end? It makes little sense."

Again, Sean spoke.

"I'm tellin' you to do what you think is right, Kyla. Murder ain't no good thing, but maybe it's *right* in a case as this."

Kyla was confused. She had known Horris to be of righteous character, and yet, all seemed now that previous experience was farcical. Mr. Pem she had known to be kind, and made her feel warm inside. And yet, he had been revealed a man of clearly malicious nature. Now the decision was upon her whether or not to put an end to Mr. Pem's life, an action for which she had never once fathomed the possibility.

Horris continued an attempt to sway the girl on the basis of inherent goodness, while Sean's conviction grew more and more.

"Keep the dagger raised, Kyla," furthered Sean. "I believe that you know what is right, and should follow that. Stab Mr. Pem. Stab him now!"

Still, Kyla remained hesitant and pensive. Her emotion grew from her countenance like the grief of one thousand mourning widows.

Kyla thought silently. "The path of existence is through the heart. Pem's heart. Is this what is to become of me? An assassin? All is so incorrigible!"

"Zigmund, again, we are merely waiting on you," cajoled Mr. Pem.

Kyla knew she had but little time to act. With her mind resolved, or at least, with as much resolve possible, she lifted the small sword high in the air, and jetted quickly toward Mr. Pem's heart. The man did not move. He merely stood there, with arms folded behind his back, as if he had been ready to receive the attack.

As Kyla moved to conclude her action, various thoughts plagued her weary mind. She felt suddenly unsure of the decision, and ultimately, dropped the weapon before point of impact, like a beaten soldier.

"Kyla, nooooo!" screamed Sean.

She dropped to her knees, knowing she had not the character required to carry out such an action. Mr. Pem looked down upon the poor woman, arms still secured, as if he had predicted the failure.

In this moment, Zigmund figured that regardless of the uncertainties of the current situation, he had but only one task left to accomplish, and he could not turn his back on the possibility of the transformation into an all-sentient God. With his mind resolved, he walked slowly into the water. Kyla, with an expression of utter fright, attempted to jump toward him, but Mr. Pem grabbed her tightly by the wrist, fully preventing her interference.

The sky again began to change shapes and colours. A certain energy surged about. Zigmund's body was stiff, and he felt strange. The ground too seemed to rumble beneath their feet.

Mr. Pem exhaled and smiled wide.

"It has been done. Dorje."

Kyla slouched, dejected.

"Why so sullen, child? There is no need for that. Surely, you might have known something about the object that you protected for so long? You know it by name: lapis. You know it by touch, by sensation. Do you truly not know the whole of its existence, child?"

Kyla shook her head vehemently, sobbing now.

"My light conquers every light and my virtues are more excellent than all virtues. I beget the light, but the darkness too is my nature. So too, the darkness, is my nature. Such is the lapis. Such is humanity."

Kyla continued to cry, overwhelmed by Pem's words.

Chaotic Ocean

"Tears are not of your character. Have we not thanks to give to our friend, Zigmund? After all, without him, all of this, all of what will come, could not have been possible."

"And what of all this?" asked Kyla.

"You bear witness to the creation of the Dorje," replied Pem.

Zigmund stepped out of the pond as a translucent-blue colour stemmed up from the ground, freezing the lapis stone in place, hovering in the air. The bright blue light seemed to reach in all directions, making it difficult on the eyes. Zigmund receded into the mansion, caring little, as if his body had been taken over by some kind of mechanical automation. His head hung in disappointment. Kyla screamed for him to stay, though his feet kept on moving till she was left alone with Mr. Pem.

"Do you not see, child, that we have unlocked the truest essence of life? All that was, is, or will be, are mere theories. Creation and destruction are only pieces of the greater good, only pieces of the Dorje. What we have done is transcendent of all forces, whether positive or negative. This is beyond such concepts, beyond our definitions of evil, of good. We have forced a new philosophical standard of gold, and you bear witness."

"What have I done in this life?" questioned Kyla, sobbing. "Who haven't I judged? I am no different than Zigmund. I likely deserve all that is forthcoming!"

"Oh, but you *are* different, in fact, quite different," responded Pem.

Kyla, sobbing like an infant looked to Horris for some superficial commiseration.

"This pond has been here for ages, and Mr. Pem, he himself held the lapis before I. The addition makes little sense."

"All ain't dry and cut in this life," responded he. "Powerful, fantastical beings have lively boundaries just as humans do. Pem here, God bless him, or something bless him, but he just don't got it in him ta do for himself what he can make others do *for* him, nor I. And I ain't talkin' about some kind of creeping malaise. Every being is endowed in a specific way, dove."

"I..."

"Ya' been questioning up ta the high skies ever since I met ya'. Ever question if questioning ain't the right way? One little promise of death and ya're like self-doubting, fearin' puddy."

Kyla swallowed her saliva with much difficulty. She was looking at the two men that she had placed the most trust in, and felt betrayed. Though, she knew it was of little use to feel such a way. The sky vibrated as the lapis continued to float above the pond.

"He is correct, child," interjected Mr. Pem. "Though, as the basis of life, events are not immutable. You were chosen, indeed. Would you have confronted your own obtuse and crippling fears, perhaps you would have discovered the vagaries hiding themselves away in your very home long ago. But you did not. Would you have truly looked into your patients' hearts, perhaps you would have noticed a certain absence of

Chaotic Ocean

genuineness. You have been confused, misguided, and easily comforted by these three figments, three disciples of the new epoch. I have little pity for you. Though, just the same, you should not fear me, or what may come.

We have long-awaited this moment – Horris, myself, and that unfortunate soul whom you saw murdered in the park, before her change of heart, at any rate. The two of you are not entirely different, child. Just as her resolve altered, so has yours. As I mentioned, you were chosen. We have searched the globe time and again for a being such as yourself. With each birth comes a truly unique individual. Thousands of years have we waited for one of your make – one who is both wise but also insecure to no end, one who is compassionate, but near-sighted enough to fail in all capacities to view the grander plot, one who is venerable to society, but to herself, a distasteful wretch. And also, one who is of connection to the pond of the ages. Think not that we look poorly upon you or your actions. We have long known that you had the goodness of heart to combat what you may at this moment view as malicious or malevolent. But we have also long known that you do not have the resolve to compliment such character, just as we know the opposite of your friend, who completely lacks this character, but completely embraces covetous resolve."

"And what *of* Zigmund?"

"Zigmund? What of any of us? Zigmund was easily controlled. As you know, the man is a megalomaniac of the greatest kind. He remains now, in his mansion, unfulfilled, not brave enough to even face those who have misled him. The greatest power Zigmund will ever know is his capacity toward greed. Nothing more, child. Likely, he still has little clue as to the grander scope, for he cannot see past his own shadow."

She looked into his eyes and no longer could see the presence of any kind of humanity.

"I do not wish to see the fruits of your malicious labour!" barked Kyla.

"The future is built not on the foundation of the past, but rather on the wings of the present. Embrace newness."

The Dorje continued to buzz, louder and louder, as if approaching a pinnacle. Kyla, frightfully aware, and terrified of the ambiguity having been prognosticated upon, barked back once more.

"Kyla, I am somewhat surprised at your aversion to anything different than you've known," began Mr. Pem. "Cannot you see that the world is merely a place of assumed opposites, when nothing could be farther from reality? Did not you begin your journey a confident and boastful woman, while your friend, you assumed shallow and lacking of reason and capacity? Now look upon the situation. Your mind and spirit have completely tarnished. No longer do I see a confident woman in the slightest. And how is it, seeing what we can now, that you were much apart from Zigmund at the very start?

The two of you are like one in the same, as much to your chagrin as it may be to hear. And what you have all along felt was perhaps a separation, whether wisdom, or intelligence, or knowledge – all are fairly arbitrary. We do not deny the idea that you are more an advanced creature than Zigmund, but we do deny the idea that you had any right to claim such a bargaining chip. You did not work for your gifts, any more than Zigmund worked for his inherited fortune. You have wrought havoc in your friend's life, through various debates which surely you have claimed victorious, and yet, had he even a chance, taking into consideration his own unique genetic makeup?

Intelligence is a farce, just as with most everything else. It is not worked for, and cannot be altered with willpower. Like all other traits, it is merely a gift. Yet, just as you have used your gift to demean and belittle your friend, so too the vast populations of our planet have used such a gift to subjugate, manipulate, and assume superiority over all classes.

Wealth is a farce, surely, for the vast minority are among equals when walking down the street, most never amassing such fortunes as your friend. It is a truly infinitesimal number of workers who gain great wealth through toil alone, and those who do, happen to be blessed by the farce of intelligence. To think all are on equal footing when aiming for fortune, all with equal stake and opportunity is surely naïve. And yet, every single class casts a kind of grin and superiority of being on those less fortunate. All assume that circumstance is the outgrowth of propriety. Hence, those beneath us belong beneath us.

Civilisation is a farce, for there is no man without the dual wish for both barbarism and etiquette. Each night we set up shop at the dining room table to partake in the eating of prepared food with knives and forks. Yet, as we slumber, militaries plunder foreign lands, keeping us well in the knowledge of having fulfilled both ends. We entertain ourselves through thoughtless mediums, numbing our minds, while our battlefields are overflowing with blood.

Sex is a farce, as men and women are of the same damnable make, yet both alike happily cast the label of Other, confining their counterparts to colourless existences. I am man. I am woman. Humanity calls for the names and suffers greatly when anomalies of nature manifest. Humanity cannot accept or fathom the vague, the amorphous, and most harrowing: the equal.

Religion is a farce, as every religion in the world is aimed at creating peace and kindhearted behavior. Yet, the trenches remain open, filled with bodies, wars abounding over pieces of land and territorial ownership, fueled by religious fundamentalism. How can it possibly be that we are so bold to persecute fellow man for the beliefs he holds in his breast? We see the beliefs to be other than our own, and even when in the name of goodness, we cannot accept this, and must douse the threat of opposing thought. We have set up the notion that our religion defines us, and we see that the definitions separate us.

Do you not see the irony? In every single aspect of existence, whether wealth, religion, or personal attributes, man cannot accept a version of existence that is anything but divided. We must assume that classes exist, so to preserve a healthy hierarchical order. We must assume that religion makes us wholly different from our brothers, so to preserve peace of mind. We must assume that our intelligence was toiled for, as it would not suit us to classify ourselves with the less fortunate.

Man has been subdivided from Man since the beginning of time, Kyla. Though, the truth is that, as much is an illusion. None of the distinctions are real. They are all farcical. Man can simply not feel himself equal with another, for his whole existence would fall to ruin. He must, by his very nature, find position and division. This is the modern man, though modernity has been with us since inception.

Nature endowed Man with Mind, ability to see the world in any way so desired. When allowing the plasma to engulf all of nothingness, the formless void, Nature assumed Man to be of reasonable design. This, however, was folly. Man viewed his surroundings, and immediately, unquestionably, and unapologetically stated: "Look yonder – light. Look yonder – dark." Such was the first distinction perceived. The first FALSE distinction, Kyla.

Ever since, humans have been subjected to this ruinous ideal of classification. It is no great secret that man has been in a state of unrest since birth. He has plundered, destroyed, and warred in every recorded epoch. Through and through, he has advanced his own technological innovation, and assumed as much a solution to his own nature. Man believes in God and Eden, the garden of utopia, and deifies technology as his new God. He attempts to restore an idea that which was never a reality.

Though man sits easy in his current existence, he harbors a certain difficulty under his breath. He *knows* that he is safe from all in his prison of distinction, yet knows not why he longs.

It is rather simple. Light and dark are one in the same. The outgrowths of the opposite assumption are innumerable, and plague man in every aspect of his being. Though he finds the ideas of Heaven and Hell pleasurable, Light and Dark, Good and Evil, Wealth and Poverty, Intelligence and Inanity, Civilisation and Barbarism, ALL are of false make, just as you foolishly assumed Horris and I of two creeds. Distinctions of all kinds, Kyla, are ultimately blurred. This is how it was originally intended, and this is what the Dorje shall return us to."

Kyla felt defeated, and knew not how to respond. The words had nearly paralysed her, and she could muster little.

"Go back to the Hellish realm from which you spawned."

Mr. Pem, along with Horris laughed heartily, though Kyla, for once, felt somewhat absolved of confusion. She awaited the response.

Finally, clearing his throat, Mr. Pem spoke one last time.

"There is no Heaven, no Hell... only the Beyond. There is no good, no evil, only perception. Man's final state is a merging. Everyone is sick and wicked, and everyone is beautiful and good. Manicheanism and the like are man-made fantasies. The present is an illusion of existence. Good and evil are wholly without use. Does not Lucifer mean bearer of light? What are we to assume of our externalisations of wickedness? They are entirely lacking and baseless. Man is weak and voluntarily creates his own prison. He knows nothing and deserves to know nothing. He

Chaotic Ocean

competes, cheats, sulks, and assumes superiority in an arena where nothing could be further from the truth. He is a proud mammal. Unfortunately for him, through you, through the Dorje, there will be no more imprisonment, no more walls or veils. We are all equal now. Fear not the future, only man's own insecurity of himself in a world he can no longer control or manipulate to his every sadistic, selfish desire. We are all equal for the rest of time. You played your part expectedly."

From that moment on, nothing was again the same. However, such is a tale for another time.

The End.

Chaotic Ocean

The human spirit is dynamic.

Chaotic Ocean

ACKNOWLEDGMENTS

* Many thanks to those cultivators of thought who have candidly and directly shared their views with thoughtful and open wisdom.
-Scott Cote
-Victor Lee
-Devin Sawyer

* Many thanks to those artists who have emphatically and repeatedly inspired emotionality through eloquent verse.
-Sean Nelson
-Ed Vedder
-John Wozniak

Many thanks to those beautiful souls who have provided the medium upon which this novel was "penned."
-Larisa Perolli
-Devin Sawyer

Many thanks to those who have never judged, but rather, have encouraged, with utter selflessness, to no end.
-Larisa Perolli
-Rina Perolli

Many thanks to the weavers of literary fiction, who have, in part, inspired me to become the writer I am.
-Nikolai Gogol
-George Orwell
-Oscar Wilde

I thank my father for showing me independence and love.
I thank my mother for showing me compassion and kindness.

To my siblings I owe my happiness.
To a friend I owe my earliest feelings of beauty and ache.

Thank you.

And to those unmentioned: vanity is not becoming.

Chaotic Ocean

Made in the USA
Columbia, SC
27 October 2020